A Season to Dance

A Novel

Patricia Beal

Bling!
Romance
Lighthouse Publishing of the Carolinas

A SEASON TO DANCE BY PATRICIA BEAL
Published by Bling! Romance
an imprint of Lighthouse Publishing of the Carolinas
2333 Barton Oaks Dr., Raleigh, NC, 27614

ISBN: 978-1-946016-16-4
Copyright © 2017 by Patricia Beal
Cover design by Elaina Lee
Interior design by Karthick Srinivasan

Available in print from your local bookstore, online, or from the publisher at:
lpcbooks.com

For more information on this book and the author visit: http://www.patriciabeal.com/

Brought to you by the creative team at Lighthouse Publishing of the Carolinas:
Marisa Deshaies, Managing and General Editor
Meghan M. Gorecki, Publishing Assistant to the Managing Editor

Library of Congress Cataloging-in-Publication Data
Beal, Patricia
A Season to Dance / Patricia Beal 1st ed.

Printed in the United States of America

PRAISE FOR *A SEASON TO DANCE*

Readers who believe in second chances and a twist in the Happily Ever After will delight in this tale!

~ **Rachel Hauck**
New York Times bestselling author

For 244 pages I was a world-traveling ballerina. This book was not only a captivating story, but an impacting journey. I am changed. Bravo, Ms. Beal.

~ **Nadine Brandes**
Christy Award finalist and Carol Award winner

Beal's debut captures the drama and lyricism of the ballet - faith, life and love dance across the story, reaching a satisfying and sigh-worthy *dénouement*.

~ **Katherine Reay**
Author of *A Portrait of Emily Price*

Patricia Beal's first novel is a skillfully written tale of a woman's journey to faith and love. *A Season to Dance* will bless every reader.

~ **Lorraine Beatty**
Author of the Home to Dover series

More than a romance, *A Season to Dance* is a layered love story that pulls at the heartstrings while taking you on a trip through dance around the world. I adored it.

~ **Teri Wilson**
Author of *Unleashing Mr. Darcy*
and *His Ballerina Bride*

Patricia Beal has crafted a compelling debut about grace and redemption when life takes unexpected turns.

~ **Kara Isaac**
Author of *Close to You*
and *Can't Help Falling*

Patricia Beal's *A Season to Dance* is gorgeous! Ana's story from emptiness to God's redemption showcases Beal's heart. As a ballet dancer, I loved relating to the tangible portrayal of Ana's dance and performance life. And how fun to taste, see, and smell her experiences in Germany! Thank you for this heart-tugging look into a professional ballerina's world, travels, and God's faithful dedication to us.

~ **Katie Briggs**
Former staff with Ballet Magnificat! and ballerina

A Season to Dance offers readers a beautiful message of redemption and second chances. An elegant and graceful journey across two continents as one woman seeks to fill the God-shaped hole in her heart and finally discovers her own season to dance.

~ **Candee Fick**
Author of *Dance Over Me*
and *Catch of a Lifetime*

Ah, how this brought back my seasons in *The Nutcracker*, dancing Juliet, and years of rigor at the barre. *A Season to Dance* is a story of grace in all forms, ultimate romance and finding spiritual center. Thank you, Patricia Beal!

~ **Tosca Lee**
New York Times bestselling author

A tender romantic tale composed of grace and redemption. Patricia Beal's poignant novel gently touches our deepest emotional cords with a panoply of characters who remind us of our friends, family, and ourselves. As a Christian author with autism who has experienced my own battles decoding relationships and the repeated stings of shattered dreams, I could easily relate to Patricia's voice and Ana's struggles. *A Season to Dance* brims with the light of Christ's healing power to mend wounded relationships and make all things new. Patricia's graceful writing style is a joy to read and I highly recommend her debut novel.

~ **Ron Sandison**
Founder of Spectrum Inclusion and
Author of *A Parent's Guide to Autism:*
Practical Advice. Biblical Wisdom

ACKNOWLEDGMENTS

First of all, nothing happened until Jesus passed by. Thank you, Lord. I don't think there's another activity out there that's as private and yet as others-dependent as the writing and birthing of a book. *A Season to Dance* was often a lonely walk and a personal search, but it crossed the finish line because of the team God blessed me with.

A special thanks to my husband, Mike, and to my children, Logan and Grace. I wrote the first chapter of the story in January 2011, and more than six years of hard work later (and of rejections and rewrites!), they still love me and believe in me. Thank you for not letting me quit, for your love and patience, and for sacrificing all things normal for this dream of mine.

I want to thank my church family. I know what I know today because of Hillcrest Baptist Church. Thanks for supporting me with God's truth and your love and prayers. A special thanks to the Homebuilders 1 Sunday school class and the five ladies who spent more than a year reading revised chapters and cheering me on through a very difficult rewrite. Sofia Green, Nickie Monroe, Savannah Odom, Nicole Rempel, and Ana Risner—I couldn't have done this without you.

Thanks to the Bling! Romance/Lighthouse Publishing of the Carolinas team for making the dream come true, for publishing me so beautifully, and for marketing it so well. Thanks especially to Marisa Deshaies for making the offer and for working so hard to redeem the story for Christian readers. Meghan Gorecki, thanks for working with Marisa to edit the story and for holding my hand every time I panicked during developmental edits. You both were so patient, and the result was so worth it. I think I told you I spent two days crying after we finished because *A Season to Dance* is exactly the kind of book I spent thirty years dreaming I would write one day. Thank you, friends!

I also want to acknowledge my publicist, Jeane Wynn of Wynn-Wynn Media. The day you said yes to *A Season to Dance* was the day I stopped worrying about whether or not the book would be noticed. It will be noticed.

I'm grateful to my agent, Les Stobbe, whose offer of representation first made the dream feel real, and to my mentor, Jeff Gerke, who taught me to write for an (accepting) audience of One. Jeff is also the Lexus of editors and polished the story before I showed it to agents and editors in 2014. His books on writing have shaped who I am as a writer, and we've been working together on my second manuscript already. Thank you, Jeff! Thank you also for introducing me to Nadine Brandes, who proofread the story before agents and editors looked at it. Thanks, Nadine! You made me look much better than I am.

Thanks to the American Christian Fiction Writers family. I love you all! I met my agent and my editor at ACFW 2014 and always learn a ton and meet new friends at every ACFW conference. What a joy to be part of such a wholesome group. Individuals might have an off day—I know I do—but as a group, we shine His light everywhere we go. May God keep us Christ-centered and full of love for each other, for our readers, and for our journeys. A special thanks to those who've been particularly kind to me. Maybe you remember what you did or said, maybe you don't, but I will always remember: Theresa Alt, Amanda Bostic, Kate Breslin, Sara Ella, Penny Nadeau Haavig, Joyce Hart, Linnette Mullin, Tamela Hancock Murray, and Carrie Turansky—thank you.

Thanks also to the whole *Writer's Digest* team. Subscribing to the magazine ten years ago was my first step toward becoming a novelist, and the publication taught me the basics about story, market, and the business. I've also read many WD books (*The First 50 Pages* is my favorite writing book in the world!), listened to several tutorials, and used the 2nd Draft Critique Service twice—once for an editorial review (thanks, Gloria Kempton!) and once for proofreading (thanks, Phyllis Cox!). The day I signed my first publishing contract—for this book—and shared some questions with my agent, he pointed me to a great article for debut authors. The publication? You guessed it—*Writer's Digest*. Thanks for being there every step of the way!

Gloria Kempton later became my first writing coach. Thanks, Gloria! I still think of you when looking for balance between action scenes and sequels and when writing the first paragraph of every chapter. And, yes, there's that quest thing—I wouldn't dare write another questless draft after what you put me through. Thanks for your patience! You're right. You've been right all along.

I want to take a quick moment to acknowledge a few agents and editors who came across my writing before I was ready and whose detailed feedback helped shape me and this debut. Julie Castiglia, Chelsea Gilmore, Erika Imranyi, Anita Mumm, and Katharine Sands—thank you so much. Erika, the in medias res opening fixed so many problems—I love it! Without it, I would have had to change the story. I didn't want to change the story. The story was right. I just needed a frame that worked. You're brilliant!

Kim Stotler was my first critique group leader (Barnes & Noble Writing Workshop of Columbus, Georgia). Thank you for your support and wisdom. I thank the whole group. Kim, you read the first *A Season to Dance* chapter when it was fresh out of my head and out of my printer. You read it out loud, said it could be the beginning of something good, and suggested I look into writers' conferences. See what you started? Thanks!

Closer to home and to publication date—I owe a debt of gratitude to my first readers. Many braved less-than-stellar versions of the manuscript, helped me fix plot holes and character development problems, and still found encouraging things to say about the work. Anett Bearden, Alisha Coffey, Andrea Garber, Michelle Rapp Hall, Rachel Jenkins, Amber Johnson, Cyndi Apple Kvalevog, Carol McDonald, Stephanie McGregor, Miriam Mitchell, Vanessa Montgomery, Mildred Morgan, Esther Mott, and Mary Compton Smith—thank you so much.

A special thanks to Stephanie McGregor for also checking my Huntington's disease research. Stephanie is part of our church family and is a young mom and Army wife. There's a history of Huntington's in her family, and she tested positive the summer of 2016. Your courage and faith inspire me daily. I'm in awe of you. Thanks for your help and for being you.

Thanks also to the amazing "dressing room team"—the team of beta readers who helped polish the final copy: April Root, Anne Prado, J.a. Marx, Jodie Hoklas, Katie Briggs, Kerry Johnson, Mary Compton Smith (round 2!), Paige Howard Newsom, Savannah Odom (round 2!), Theresa Alt, Valeria Hyer, and Voni Harris. I'm in awe of your talent.

Two quick notes on research and I'm done. I've danced in pre-professional companies all over the world but never made it into a paid company. Based on that experience, the life of friends who made it all the way, and research, I think I got the details of company life right. Any mistakes are mine and mine alone.

I will say the same about the German language. I grew up in New Hamburg, Brazil and lived in Germany twice, but my German is not very good. My son said it best a couple of years ago after I ordered three Burger King meals at the drive-thru of our neighborhood store in Idar-Oberstein: "We'll see what we'll get this time." I know a little. I researched a lot. Any mistakes in the German language in *A Season to Dance* are mine.

And thank you, reader, for letting me share this story with you. I hope you get to see the Callaway Gardens' azaleas in person one day—or the Rhine Valley with its vineyards and sunflowers, waters glistening as the sun sets. Maybe we'll go together one day. Book tour!

Love,
Patricia

To God, who didn't give up on me
when I gave up on him during my season of darkness.
And to those who still hunger.

In memory of Sandie Bricker, founder of Bling! Romance.

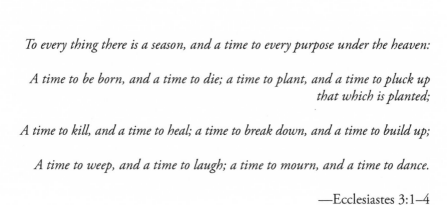

To every thing there is a season, and a time to every purpose under the heaven:

A time to be born, and a time to die; a time to plant, and a time to pluck up that which is planted;

A time to kill, and a time to heal; a time to break down, and a time to build up;

A time to weep, and a time to laugh; a time to mourn, and a time to dance.

—Ecclesiastes 3:1–4

Chapter 1

*T*his is for them. This is for the magic. This is for every little dreamer in the room.
Dozens of little awestruck faces crowded the large studio as I took position
to practice my Sugar Plum Fairy solo. Everyone in the company and the school
had come together for the first full-length rehearsal of *The Nutcracker* season.

I'd been in every one of those shoes: mouse, soldier, angel, every flower, every
food, and every country. Now I was the Sugar Plum Fairy at long last, the one
role that eluded me all those years. Had it been worth the wait?

Images of the first Sugar Plum Fairy rehearsal I'd ever seen flashed before my
eyes—a beloved mental movie my heart flocked to every year around this time.

Could a young dancer ever forget the magic of watching the Sugar Plum
rehearse her solo for the very first time? I hadn't. I peered toward the girls from
beneath the bright studio lights. And they wouldn't.

This moment was going to last forever in their little minds. And I knew that,
within the next three minutes, most of them would be thinking, *That will be me
one day.*

My breathing quickened with the first notes of the music, and I moved to
Tchaikovsky's composition in steps that were delicate, like the heavenly sounds
of the celesta, and precise, like the pizzicato—or pinched—sounds of the string
instruments. The descending bass clarinet punctuated the variation.

Tchaikovsky used the celesta, a keyboard instrument new in his time, to
make the music of the Sugar Plum Fairy sound like "drops of water shooting from
a fountain," the imagery Petipa, the choreographer of the ballet, had requested. I
imagined the fountain: sparkly, flowy, and elegant.

Glittering bell-like sounds inspired the gliding steps that followed, and regal
arm movements came naturally in a variation that suited my strengths.

Sure, twenty-nine was ridiculously late for a professional ballerina to dance
the role of Sugar Plum Fairy for the first time, but I didn't let that bother me.

Piqué, retiré, balance. For a quick moment everything stopped, and my legs
formed a number four, one of the most traditional ballerina poses. *Again: piqué,
retiré, balance. And one more. Sharp. Balance. Good. Catch your breath.*

No, this isn't the Met—it's not New York. That stage couldn't be further from my reality. But look at these girls. Look at their little eyes. I want to remember this forever too.

Mrs. B., the teacher and owner of the company, stood at the front right corner of the studio shepherding the girls to squeeze against the mirrors and walls to free up more space. I would need all the space she could give me because the *manège* at the end of the variation was more like a geyser—thirty-two counts of spinning madness that used up the whole stage.

Last slow steps. Nice arabesque. With my whole body supported on one leg and the other leg extended horizontally backward, I studied the dance space.

The girls were still too close, and I wouldn't be able to go full out. Or would I? No, best not to. That was okay, though. I could still make the end of the solo look pretty for them.

I took position in the front left corner of the studio and squared my shoulders to begin the big circle of turns. My heart beat so hard and so fast that my whole chest vibrated. That second before the manège part of the music is the longest in a ballerina's life.

What was it about pauses that made me nervous? I never felt nervous while in motion. But pausing? Pausing was hard. I would much rather stay in motion.

Here we go. Goodbye droplets. And hello flood.

Piqué turn, turn, turn, turn, chaîné tuuuuuuuurn. I spun as fast as a child's top, and perfect spotting kept me from getting too dizzy. *Piqué turn, turn, turn, turn, chain tuuuuuuuurn.* But unlike a top, as I spun, I drew a perfect circle using the whole dancing space—without stepping on children.

The choreography ended with a diagonal of additional fast turns. *Here we go. Turn, turn, turn, turn, pa, pa, pa, pa. One more set, hit the brakes, step-up, go to fourth, sous-sus.*

Yes!

"Brava!" Mrs. B. clapped enthusiastically.

The studio erupted in excitement and cheers.

Everything spun like a round-up ride. But I stood and I smiled. *Worth the wait.* The studio would stop spinning soon. I curtsied, riding the joy, and made sure to face every direction—even toward the windows, crowded with parents.

If only the rest of my life could stop spinning too.

"That was delightful, Ana." Mrs. B. had seen me rehearse before, but performing in front of a group always brought an extra spark to my dancing. "You're so tiny and perfect. Can you even see your feet beyond your pancake tutu?"

"Sometimes," I panted. I extended my leg and looked at my foot beyond the bell-shaped pink rehearsal tutu. We chuckled together, and I rested my hands on my hips. My chest rose and fell with rapid breaths.

"That was lovely. Well done." Her eyes twinkled like her diamond stud earrings. "In the beginning, when you do your *battus* and *tendus*, really maintain your rotation, hmm?" She showed me the ending position, her slim body and jet-black hair giving her a look of someone much younger than her sixty-plus years.

I did two repetitions. Pointe shoe to ankle, two beats, and stretch leg out. Pointe shoe to ankle, two beats, and stretch leg out.

She tucked a lock of hair behind her ear. "Better."

"Okay." I kneaded my left shoulder and rolled it back twice to ease the tension that had settled there.

"Now, girls"—she looked at the young ballerinas first, then at the teenagers—"I want all of you to try to dance like Ana."

Some dancers smiled timidly while others giggled under their breath.

"I know you can't turn as easily as she does. And maybe getting *en pointe* is still hard for you—if it were easy, every girl in the world would go around on the tips of their toes. But I know that you can smile."

Several heads bobbed in slow harmony as Mrs. B. walked to the speaker dock. "Look like you are excited to be here. Let's try the 'Waltz of the Flowers' again with that spirit. Yes?"

Twelve flowers nodded and scrambled to their starting positions. I found a spot near the piano and stretched, watching the teens waltz—some were more graceful than others, but they were all hardworking girls.

The studio was old—the best always were. The dark marley floor had seen years of pointe work, and the wooden barres looked worn—worn by sweaty hands holding tight to big dreams.

"You are so beautiful," the girl cast as Dew Drop whispered.

"Thank you." I grinned. "Your variation is looking beautiful too."

Her cheeks turned pink, hiding most of her small freckles.

A newer generation was dreaming now, but the ballet studio still was what it should be: a bastion of civility in an everything-goes world.

Mrs. B. crouched next to me and watched Jill dance.

Jill, who was not a strong dancer when I'd first met her, had become a bit of a protégée. In the two months I'd spent working with her, she'd improved significantly.

We'd worked on the position of her shoulders, head, and neck. Her *épaulement* was elegant now, and her arm movements had become smooth and supported. Jill seemed happy and confident, and with that new vigor her leg movements transformed too. They were better defined and more dynamic. She looked like an artist now. She *was* an artist.

"You did a great job with Jill." Mrs. B. rested her hand on my shoulder as she spoke. "I'm glad I let you talk me into giving her a front-row spot in the waltz."

"Thanks." *You go, girl.*

"I want to talk to you before you go." She fiddled with her earring, her eyes on the waltz.

"Okay." *No, I don't want to teach.*

"Much better, girls." She walked to the speaker dock once more and shut down the sound system. "That's it, everybody. I've kept you long enough. Thank you. Now, I need all soloists to go by the sewing room before you leave the studio today. Stahlbaums, I need you to stop by the sewing room too. Everybody else is free to go."

I grabbed my ballet bag and sat by the piano again to remove my pointe shoes.

The younger ballerinas rushed out to their parents and now looked and acted like little girls again. From the large studio window I saw one of them on her tiptoes doing a *bourrée* from my solo. Another sat on her daddy's shoulder. She still wore her ballet slippers, and he held her tiny feet firmly while she lifted her arms to fifth position. He spun around the sidewalk, and she held her pose. I watched their improvised *pas de deux* until they disappeared into the cool autumn day.

"I love these girls too." Mrs. B.'s comment startled me—I didn't know she'd crossed the room. "Having a studio is far more fun than I'd expected."

"Good." I watched the last girl exit the studio. *It's not for me, though.*

She unplugged her iPod and put it in her bag. "Jill is a different dancer now. You have a gift for coaching, you know?"

No, I don't. "Thank you. There's something about her that's special. I like her."

"I don't know what you saw." Mrs. B. removed her ballet slippers and wiggled her long white toes. "She was never good. But somehow you fixed her."

I shrugged. "I can always tell when a girl is holding back. Jill had a confidence problem, not a dancing problem."

She sat on the piano bench. "How did you figure that out?"

I wasn't sure how to explain without making my dad seem like a bad person. He wasn't, but it's amazing the power a parent's words have in the life of a child. Even words they later regret and apologize for. "I had a huge confidence problem myself." I picked a piece of lint from my leotard sleeve.

"Why?" A line appeared between her brows.

4

"My dad once said that if I were destined to be a prima ballerina, we would have known it by the time I was twelve."

"Ouch." She cringed. "Is he a dancer?"

"No." I laughed at the idea of my dad dancing. "He didn't mean anything by it. He says weird stuff sometimes. But yeah, ouch." I imitated the face she'd made.

"That's awful."

"It's okay." I shook my head. "It's old news."

"Well, you're a great dancer and a great example for the girls—always on time, impeccable bun, hard worker, unassuming... Ana, you should teach and help me run the company. Really."

I knew it. "No, I really shouldn't. It's nice that you want me to, though. I appreciate it."

"Why not teach?" She leaned forward.

"I don't know." I puffed out my chest. "I guess I still feel like one of the girls. I'm just not ready to take the leap." I had big dreams too, and teaching wasn't one of them. Maybe my big dreams were dead, but if I were to start teaching now, I would surely become resentful. Wouldn't I? Who was I kidding? I was probably resentful already.

"I'm not saying stop dancing. You shouldn't. But do both—transition and open new doors." She stood and seemed to prepare to dance something. "And just so you know, I feel like one of the girls too." She did little *ballottés* from the ballet *Giselle*, humming one of the first act's solos. "Pa, papa, papa, papa, parararapa... It never changes. It's a blessing and a curse."

We both chuckled.

I shook my head in slow motion. "Not now. I just helped Jill because I know her from church."

She turned to me sharply. "Really? You don't seem like the church type."

"I'm not. I'm not even saved—I don't think." *Why did I say that? Now she'll think I'm weird.* "I just have a lot going on."

"Oh... Well, babies are not easy—or so I hear. I never had any."

She ignored it. Good. "No, they are not..."

"Is that why you didn't want to be in the production last year? The baby was still little?"

"Kind of, but the baby—who's not really a baby anymore—is the easy part, in all reality."

"Is it your husband? He doesn't want you to dance?" Mrs. B. smacked her forehead. "You married a man like your father? I see it all the time."

"Oh, no. It's the other way around. My husband is the one pestering me to dance more." *If I had it my way, I would be by his side all the time.*

"Oh, good. Then I like him already. He should come see a rehearsal one day."

"That's the thing." Did I have to talk about his disease? I swallowed hard. *Try not to cry.*

"What is it?"

"He's sick. He doesn't get around much these days." My eyes burned and hot tears welled up.

"Aw." She handed me a tissue from an old box that'd been on top of the piano since I'd started taking classes there. "I'm sorry he's sick and sorry I upset you. I certainly didn't mean to. When he's better, he can come, huh?"

But he would never get better. He would only get worse. And yet I still had dreams—dreams of a cure and a bright future, dreams of a father playing with his child, and dreams of growing old with my husband. I dabbed my cheeks.

Mrs. B. walked to a nearby shelf. "Here," she said, looking through a long box, "I have something that will cheer you up."

"You do?" I tossed the used tissue in the wastebasket by the piano and pressed my hands to my cheeks. Oh, how I hated feeling sorry for myself.

"Ta-da!" She held the Sugar Plum tiara with both hands.

"Aw…" My heart beat slow, perfectly aware of the unique nature of that small moment. Pink and silver crystals glimmered in a floral pattern that reminded me of my wedding tiara. "It's beautiful."

She put the headpiece on my hair with ease, crowning me queen of the Land of Sweets.

I glanced at the closest mirror—the tiara looked even shinier against my dark hair. *Wow.* "Thank you."

"You're welcome." She took a step back and looked at me with an aura of love and pride that reminded me of the way my mom used to look at me when I was little and she had to help me get ready for performances. "I hope I get to see you dance many ballets and wear many tiaras here."

"Thanks." I rubbed shaky fingertips against my cheekbones. *Still just one of the girls. Good.*

She gave me another tissue and looked in the direction of my ballet bag. "Do you need to get that?"

I cocked my head. What did I need to get?

"I think your phone is vibrating." She pointed at my bag.

"Oh, yes. I have to." I stuck my hand in the old cloth bag, going straight for the phone. *The institute.* "Hello?" I held on to the closest barre while riding a massive wave of dizziness. "Hello?"

"Hi, Ana?"

I recognized Dr. Zimmermann's voice. "Yes. Hi. Is everything okay?"

"Yes, everything's fine now, but your husband took a hard fall during therapy today. We tried to call so you could come get him, but you didn't answer."

"I'm sorry. I was rehearsing. Is he still there?" I bit my lip, trying to fight off worry. *I knew this performance was a bad idea.*

"No. Ed drove him home about an hour ago."

"I'm so sorry. I'll keep the phone handy in case something like this happens again. I feel bad." *I should have monitored the phone.*

"Don't, Ana. You need to take care of yourself too. I just wanted to tell you because he probably won't. Call me if you see him showing signs of pain. I wanted to do an x-ray, but he didn't let me."

I nodded. "I'll do that."

"And have a little extra patience. He had a rough day. He was in a pretty bad mood when he left."

Awesome. "Thanks for the heads up and for having Ed drive him home. I don't know what we would do without you and all the staff there."

"Don't worry. You guys try to have a good weekend, and we'll see you on Monday, okay?"

"Okay. We'll see you then."

When I put the phone away and turned around, Mrs. B.'s eyes met mine.

"I'm sorry." *Sorry indeed.*

"Sorry for what?"

"I don't know." *Sorry for myself. Sorry for my husband. Sorry for our son. Sorry I didn't answer the phone. Sorry I don't understand why we need to live like this...*

"Is everything okay?"

No, everything was not okay, but I chose the polite answer. "Yeah. My husband took a hard fall during therapy. He should be home now. He's okay."

"What does he have? If you don't mind me asking. He *will* get better, right?"

I shook my head and pressed my lips together. "He has Huntington's disease. There's no cure."

Sadness clouded her features. "I've never heard of it."

"He's dying, one brain cell and function at a time. Involuntary movements, thought processes..." I shook my head again. "Everything is a struggle. And there's nothing I can do but watch him suffer and secretly dream of a cure. He's been so angry lately that even my hope makes him mad." I snorted. "We're trying to get him to stop driving now—that's the next big battle. Wish me luck with that one."

"Oh, Ana. I had no idea you were dealing with all this."

"*C'est la vie.*" I shrugged. "About three years ago, we had it all." Images of crowded theaters, travels, and our wedding day reminded me of what happiness looked like—carefree happiness. We were still happy. It was just a different kind of happy.

I had to get home. I dug my clothes out of the bag.

"At least you have your faith." Mrs. B. took a step back.

"I wish I had faith." I stepped into a simple black skirt and put on my old Allen Ballet jacket.

"But you said you know Jill from church. So you guys do go to church, right?"

"Something like that. I've been going on my own, and I've been reading about faith a lot and the Bible a little, but I'm not too sure what to think of it all yet." I placed the rehearsal tutu I'd used at the end of the barre. "But you're right. It helps."

I looked around the room, remembering how it'd been spinning when I'd finished the variation. In ballet, we enhance control and prevent debilitating dizziness with proper spotting. While the body rotates at a relatively constant speed, the head periodically rotates much faster and then stops on a single location, a single spot, again and again.

Spotting worked for life too. My husband was my spot. But while in ballet it's okay to pick a spot that moves, like another dancer, it's not okay to pick a spot that's completely unpredictable.

As my spot became more and more unpredictable, I could only hope that religion would work. I'd run out of other options.

"I need to go." I picked up my bag.

"Let me know if I can help. And I mean it," Mrs. B. said when I reached the door. "I can babysit too, if you need."

"Thanks." That was sweet. "Gabriel is getting his weekly dose of grandma sugars. He's all right." I saw a hint of disappointment in her eyes. Who did she go home to?

"Maybe another time." She wrapped her arms around herself.

I nodded and exited the studio. *Let me find him well, God. Please.*

The blue and beige magnolias of our vintage tablecloth disguised the truth, but the delicate pattern didn't eradicate our reality. My husband got only half his food in his mouth these days.

I looked at what was left of his baked chicken salad still sitting on the kitchen table and mentally ticked off the calorie chart the doctor had given me.

I found him standing by the living room window, his frame still beautiful and strong despite the ravages of Huntington's on his body. "Hi."

He turned around. "Hi, gorgeous."

I think he's actually in a good mood.

"How was rehearsal?"

I kissed him before answering. It was nice to be home. Really nice. "It was awesome. I want to show you something."

"What is it?"

"You have to wait a minute," I said mysteriously. I walked to my bag and found the tiara tangled to a loose thread of the inner seam. One of the little crystals bent as I pulled the tiara out. *Come on.* I tried bending the gem back into place, but it broke off. *Of course...*

"What do you want to show me?" He took a small step forward.

I tossed the broken crystal back into the bag and put the tiara on my head. "What do you think?"

"Wow, look at you!" He nodded with a proud grin. "It suits you."

I enjoyed the heat his approval sent to my cheeks.

His blue eyes came alive, and he smiled and flashed his eyebrows in a rare but welcome moment. "And to think you didn't want to do it."

His voice came out a little slurred.

Please don't get angry...

His smile vanished. He must have heard the slurring.

"I'm glad you talked me into it." *Quick, think of something to say, so he doesn't have to talk...* "Oh, and guess what? Mrs. B. said Jill is looking great—remember the girl from church I told you about?"

No reaction.

Stupid disease.

His hands' involuntary movements became more intense, and he stared at them as if they were foreign objects, found at the end of his arms by chance. The slurred speech must have really upset him—his chorea always worsened when he was stressed or anxious.

I walked to him, the choreography well practiced. I held his unsteady hands in mine, pressed them against my chest, and rested my head on him. His heartbeat was loud and strong, and I watched a quiet and milky sky that helped soothe my unrest. His warmth and traces of his musky cologne—the Burberry I'd given him last Christmas—reminded me we didn't have to be defined by the disease.

He took a small step back and looked at me. His lips parted as if he were going to say something, but no sound came.

His eyes moved to a large portrait my mom had given me when I'd started dancing professionally, a beautiful dressing-room photo of me applying dark shadow to already dark eyes. The makeup was perfect for the midnight blue tutu. Clear rhinestones and silver sequins and beads sparkled in the soft vanity light.

I remembered that recital. I'd already been accepted to the Allen Ballet—not a big company, but a respectable one and a great start of what I'd expected to be a brilliant career.

My old schoolteacher had choreographed Fritz Kreisler's "Praeludium and Allegro" for me to dance at that recital, and it was beautiful. I'd felt so grown up, having a piece choreographed especially for me. I'd thought for sure I was on the path to ballet stardom.

My husband looked at me and then back at the girl in the portrait. Did he still feel like he was holding me back because of the disease? One day, maybe, I would manage to convince him that I loved him more than I loved ballet.

He sat and reached for the Gibson guitar that was on the nearby floor stand. I'd been trying to keep the instrument clean without touching the tuning pegs. He strummed all six strings twice and tried to adjust the tension on the first one, his hands failing to get a strong grasp of the tuning peg with each attempt.

I sat next to him, yearning to be near. Maybe he would let me help somehow. But he scooted away and my heart sank. *Why don't you let me help you, my love?*

His left hand squeezed the guitar's neck, his fingertips pale on the fretboard. His right hand kept hitting the strings too low or too high as he tried to play. But he braved each note and every line, and I recognized the song.

As he sang about a man and a woman who completed each other in the most simple and perfect ways, I did what I always do when I don't want to cry. I counted. I smiled and looked beyond his shoulder, counting the bricks around the fireplace. Seventeen, eighteen…

He finished playing but didn't lift his head.

"I love you so much." *Lift your head and look at me. Let me help.*

"I love you too." He spoke the words without looking up and with no excitement.

That was okay, though. We'd gone through so much over the years. I knew he loved me.

He put his guitar down and stared at it, looking betrayed.

God, help us…

He walked to the coffee table in small, careful steps and grabbed his keys.

Oh, no. Please don't let him drive. Please, please, please. "Honey, do you really think you should—" The door slammed shut. Was he serious? I sat there gripping the arm of the couch with one hand and covering my mouth with the other.

At length, I crossed the room and pushed the curtain aside to scan the driveway. He was gone. I slammed both hands on the cold window. "Why?" Would he ever stop driving? His stubbornness would surely kill him sooner than the disease.

Why?

I put *Don Quixote*, a long and vibrant ballet, in the DVD player, and as I always did when he drove away like this, I tried—with some success—to lose myself in the beauty of the Mariinsky's production, filmed in 2006 in St. Petersburg, Russia.

He was usually back before the gypsy dance, but the third act started without any sign of him. Drizzle now covered the window, and I did my best to focus on Dulcinea's enchanted garden. *God, please keep him safe. If You're still mad at me, hurt me, but don't let anything happen to him. He doesn't deserve to suffer any more than he already has.*

The fourth act started. *Please, God.*

Novikova was finishing her last solo. *Don Quixote* was almost over. I checked my phone. Four fifteen. *Please, God.* My hands were shaking, the palms clammy. I exhaled.

And then I heard it. The doorbell. I pulled in a sharp breath.

No one ever came to our place unannounced. *No, God. No.* Maybe he's hurt. *Spare him.*

I opened the door and saw two police officers. The cold drizzle touched my face, and I heard the distant bark of our dog. But he was next to me. Had he barked? I saw one officer's mouth move, but I couldn't make out the words.

Memories of our wedding day and of our lives together flashed through my mind.

"I cannot lose him again," I whispered.

Chapter 2

They that are whole have no need of the physician, but they that are sick: I came not to call the righteous, but sinners to repentance.
Mark 2:17

Columbus, Georgia
February 2008

Sergei Prokofiev's music filled my heart with adolescent passion as I rehearsed the *Romeo and Juliet* balcony scene with Claus. Each haunting note set me on fire, a slow-burning and all-consuming fire that was as pure as it was intense. I was Juliet, and I was supposed to be in love. It was allowed. On that stage, it was okay to forget how much Claus had hurt me in the past, and it was okay to show love for a man other than my fiancé.

I watched Claus use up the whole stage, impressing me with the perfect combination of charisma and virtuosity, in turns and jumps that were faster and higher in person than on YouTube. *Why are you here?* He touched my cheek. *Why after all these years?*

The spell of the music and the moment slipped away.

"Ana!" The artistic director interrupted the rehearsal and stopped the orchestra. "What are you doing? You're supposed to touch your cheek, where he just touched you. You started so strong. Wake up." He snapped his fingers multiple times. "Let's do it again. Focus. One hundred percent. Here. Now."

"Great. Now I'm getting into trouble because of him," I mumbled as I walked up to the wobbly gray balcony again, thankful my cheeks were already red from the physical exertion.

"Fine. Focus." *What if he told me he was divorced and that he'd come for me? Shh. Stop.* "Here. Now."

I took a deep breath and closed my eyes. *I need to get this right. This is the chance of a lifetime. Next is the Met. I can do this.*

"It's okay. It's allowed," I whispered to myself while taking slow, rhythmic breaths to gain control.

The conductor lifted his baton and the musicians prepared. My hands steadied and my stomach unclenched. The orchestra started. Slowly. Softly. The melody church-like as I, Lady Juliet, paced my balcony dreaming of my Romeo.

A "ta-da" in the music interrupted the melody, startling Juliet and announcing Romeo's arrival in the shadows of the night of old Verona. "Ta-da-da." Between the dry-ice mist and the spotlight, I couldn't see Claus at first, and the staccato of the music reflected Juliet's confusion.

But then—magic. The fog dissipated slowly as if it too wanted to announce Romeo's presence. The music softened, pulsating like a heartbeat. And then I saw him. My Romeo. *What a vision ... breathe.* Claus kept his sand-blond hair a little longer now, wavy and just below the collar of Romeo's puffy cream blouse. His baby face frozen at the sight of Lady Juliet. Who did he see? Just Lady Juliet, or could it be he still had feelings for me? His royal-blue eyes filled with expectation.

It didn't matter. We were on stage. We were Romeo and Juliet. I could love him again. It was allowed.

I ran down to him. The melody became fully established. Luminous. Exalted. Beautiful. We locked eyes. We locked hands. We locked hearts. And then we danced.

I was in the moment, and this time I was able to stay in the moment, wrapped in the red cloak of desire, allowing Romeo to seduce Juliet completely.

Claus held my hands, his grip tight, palms sweaty, and lifted me in the air as if I were an ethereal being. Our connection was tender. He was attentive, and I was receptive. Time and again he begged me to stay. He wanted *me* to stay. He wanted to show his love. Oh, that was everything I'd dreamt of as a young girl.

Romeo kissed Juliet passionately, and lost in the moment, I melted in Claus's arms, aware only of his strong body pressed against my small frame.

I didn't want to stop kissing him, but Juliet had to run up to the balcony. *Oh Juliet, Juliet ... why?* She should have stayed. I rushed back to the balcony, wishing I could remember the words of Shakespeare. What does Juliet say after the kiss? You would think I would know. But the words didn't matter. She should have stayed.

"Bravo!" someone in the crowd of families and dancers shouted amid claps, whistles, and more shouts.

So this is what it feels like.

"Bravo!"

I came down from the balcony, a giant grin stretching my lips. What a treat—to dance the most romantic scene of the most romantic ballet with my first love and lover.

Claus reached for my hand for an improvised curtain call, and I blushed and looked down for a moment. *This is it. This is my time.*

I stepped forward, looked at all the faces, and curtsied. *Next is the Met.*

Brian, our artistic director, walked toward us with a spring in his step. That was all the excitement he was going to show. But that counted. That was our Brian. If he was not yelling, that meant he was happy.

"Ana, I love your little leap at the bottom of the steps but jump in a diagonal. This way when you run, he catches your hand center stage."

"Got it."

"Claus, this stage is not as big as the ones you are used to." Brian chuckled, probably to keep things light. He was talking to one of the best dancers in the world. "You are coming out too far in your initial run. Stay close to the balcony. Work the shadows."

Claus nodded. "Yes."

"That's it for tonight, everybody. We meet here again tomorrow at four for a light class and warm up. We're expecting a full house." Brian raised both eyebrows and lowered his head to look at us over his eyeglasses. "Ana and Claus, feel free to stay and go over anything you may need to. I have a dinner with our sponsors."

I watched him walk toward the dark curtains.

"Do you mind going over my entrance to mark the things Brian mentioned?" Claus used his wrist to wipe sweat off his forehead.

"Let's do it." I stretched my arms and moved my head from side to side. "Wait until people leave?"

"Yeah."

Where is your wife? I should just ask.

Claus was still a principal in the same company in Wiesbaden where he'd started his career, in their native Germany. But there was no mention of her on the company website, not anymore. She'd been the highest ranking dancer there for many years too.

But I couldn't ask. I mean, I could … but I shouldn't. How could I possibly maintain my I-don't-care façade and attitude if I asked? The question would betray me.

Claus went over some of his turns. No, I couldn't ask.

I looked up at the balcony and went over the spacing in my head. Why was it taking so long for the theater to clear?

Suddenly being there felt wrong. I was with Peter now and I was happy. *I'm just working. Nothing to it.*

A hand on my shoulder startled me.

"Didn't mean to scare you." Claus took a small step back. "Sorry. Are you ready?"

"Sure." Why did he have to be so perfect? I touched my shoulder—the spot where his hand had been—and climbed up to the balcony.

"Pa pa." He went through the steps of his entrance without actually doing them, walking and marking the space instead. "Parara, parara, pararara. Pa pa pa…"

"You must have it right because I can't see you at all." I stretched as far as I could to look for him. "You're good."

"Good." He showed up at the bottom of the steps. "Now come on down."

He disappeared again, and I came down looking for him. *Where are you, Romeo?*

Then right where Brian wanted us to meet, I felt Claus's warm hand on mine.

"And that's good." The pitch of his voice was low. *I'm not going to look at him. No way.*

We walked forward. *Right, left, right, left.* I withdrew my hand from his and touched my chest to feel my heartbeat. At that point I was supposed to take his hand and place it over my heart so he could feel it too.

Should I? Did I trust myself around him? *Not today.* I took a step back.

He lowered his gaze.

Did I still love him? I had to be able to answer that question, right? The theater air touched my cheeks and cooled my face. Who was I kidding? I already knew the answer—had always known the answer. So much. There. I loved him so much…

But I loved Peter too. Just as much—maybe more. Definitely more. Didn't I? Claus had to go. "We're done then."

"Do you want to go over anything else with me?"

Like why you're here? "No. I'm good."

He nodded but stayed on the same spot.

"I want to go over a couple of things on my own." *Please leave.* "I'll see you tomorrow."

The orchestra was still practicing bits and pieces of our music. *Enough with the balcony scene already—please.*

"You go to bed early, yes?"

"Yes." I took another step back. "Promise."

I watched him as he walked toward the stage door. His body hadn't changed in a decade—his legs were as perfectly muscular now as they'd been when I'd first seen him. He was compact, like Michelangelo's *David.*

He was walking a little taller and slower than usual.

Oh, I bet he knows I'm looking. I closed my eyes and blushed. Claus needed to stay in the past where he belonged.

I filled my lungs to capacity and exhaled slowly. Peter should have come to the rehearsal. He was the perfect mix of handsome, successful, and easygoing, and the mere sight of him relaxed me and put a smile on my face. He was my future. Everything else was nonsense.

I didn't want to wait another day to see him, but for him to stay away from his Pine Mountain ranch for two nights, he had to plan ahead. Didn't hurt to ask, though. I would call him on my way home. I climbed the narrow steps leading to the balcony, the thin wood moving and squeaking under my Bloch Balance European pointe shoes.

What I'd told Claus about staying back wasn't true. I didn't really need to go over anything. I was just not ready to go home. In the middle of all my heart's turmoil, it would have been easy to overlook the marvelous quality of what was happening to me on that stage, but I didn't want to overlook anything. *This is my moment—my season to dance—the best thing that's ever happened to me in my career.*

Once at the top, I sat on the edge of the balcony, swinging my legs like a little girl—hoping not to freeze in Juliet's silky cream gown.

As I indulged in I-can't-believe-I'm-Juliet thoughts, the structure wobbled and squeaked again. My heart raced and I felt dizzy.

Who could be coming up?

"No way," I whispered, spotting Claus.

He sat by my side and stared at the dark audience, as I did. And like me, he said nothing.

We watched the orchestra pack up and heard the pit grow silent. Soon everything was quiet except for sporadic shouts from one stagehand to another. What was he doing?

His hand inched toward mine, and I closed my eyes. I felt the warmth of his fingertips and welcomed the heat.

And then thin fabric caressed my hand. *Huh?* I looked down and gasped. "You've kept it." The delicate cherries of my small neck scarf had faded, as had the aquamarine chiffon. The tiny white polka dots were barely visible now. I held the scarf up, examining it as though it were a rare jewel.

He'd bought it for me at the Saks Fifth Avenue store in New York and given it to me on our most memorable date.

I'd handed the scarf back to him at the end of every encounter, so he could always have a little bit of me with him.

He'd kept it. All these years, he'd kept it.

I looked at him, my heartbeat loud and strong. He'd kept *me.*

His eyes no longer reflected the exuberance of Romeo's feelings. Instead, they were filled with sorrow. And love, too. It was all so unexpected. I was in dangerous territory, but I didn't stop.

With his fingers under my chin, a Claus signature move I remembered well, he pulled me in and kissed me. I felt his lips part, and as I reciprocated, I resisted the urge to go from gentle to passionate. Gentle was good. Gentle was right.

Things were perfect just the way they were, right there on that balcony ten feet above the stage floor, and I wanted to be there forever.

If only for that moment, the brokenness in me was fixed.

The perpetual ache erased.

If only for a moment.

But he pulled back, nibbling my wet lips with a sigh before a quick kiss in the middle. Then one on the corner.

He faced forward again and held my now sweaty and shaky hand.

Oh, this is amazing. Wow. "Claus…"

He brought my unsteady fingers to his soft, perfect lips.

His kiss was warm. Tender. *Wow…*

But then he let go of my hand.

I wasn't ready. I didn't want it to be over. Again, I didn't want it to be over.

He looked at the scarf on my lap, and his eyes were sad once more.

Why hadn't he stayed with me that first time—ten years ago? Now it was too late. Did he realize that too?

He kissed my forehead and stood.

Hot tears filled my eyes. What could we have done differently? Oh, what I wouldn't have done to avoid the pain of that moment. Hopelessness pooled in my stomach as I watched him leave. *Please look back.*

But he didn't.

I would never—ever—be whole again. We would never be able to make anything right. The balcony was steady again but I wasn't. Would that relationship cloud my entire life?

The stage door opened and closed. Of course that stupid relationship would cloud everything I ever did in the future. Why did he have to show up?

And why had he brought the scarf? I caressed the soft fabric. Was he struggling like I was?

Probably, but he'd brought the scarf back, and he'd left it behind. That could only mean that our story was really over now—the end—for real. He must have needed that closure as much as I'd needed it. That had to be the real end. If for no other reason than because he knew I was engaged.

That's right—I'm engaged. What was I doing? I shook my head hoping to wake up from a nightmare. *I have a man. He's my rock and I love him. When life is out of control, he gives me peace. I love Peter.*

I looked at the workers, busy prepositioning pieces of our set for tomorrow.

Nothing on that stage felt real. The kiss hadn't been real. What we had done could have been part of a ballet, right? Reliving the moment, I set it to music in my mind. My modern piece was complete. It hadn't been real. "Miss! We are closing the stage."

"Thanks. I'm coming down."

As I prepared to leave the theater, the gravity of what had happened hit me. I kept hoping I would wake from a bad dream, still innocent. But the deed was done. The one thing I thought I would never do—betray a man's trust. It *had* been real. I'd let Claus kiss me.

I picked up my bag and turned off the lights. The long hallway between the dressing rooms and the stage door was dark. How could Claus still have such a hold on me? There was only one explanation: I was a moron—a moron and a cheater.

Outside, the cold night air and the city lights lifted me up. With each step the stage retreated farther away, and so did my mistake.

I needed Peter in town. Needed to erase Claus from my thoughts and from my lips. Peter would figure out a way to be here. I called him, unable to resist hearing his voice any longer. *Should I tell him about what happened? I would have to, one day.*

Then I heard a phone ring behind me—the Sugar Plum Fairy solo, the very same song that played whenever I called Peter.

My body went numb. It had to be Peter. Had he seen the whole thing? Had he come from the theater—just now? *Let's not assume. Maybe he saw nothing.*

I turned around and smiled. "Whatever happened to 'I don't want to see it until the opening'?"

His eyes avoided mine and focused on the busy street beyond. His towering frame was still. "I changed my mind." He grabbed my hand and led me quietly toward Broadway. *Uh-oh. He saw something.*

"Did you like it?" I struggled to keep up with his quick pace. What had he seen?

He didn't answer. We had reached the marquee in front of the theater, its electronic sign embedded in the huge cement structure. He picked me up with ease and sat me on top of it, about six feet off the ground.

"We're not engaged anymore." His voice was hoarse, like a wounded animal's, and big tears rolled down his tanned cheeks and disappeared in the light-brown scruff of his face. His beautiful full lips were unsteady, and he made no attempt to hide the disgust in his midnight-blue eyes.

I trembled and all my feelings gathered around one question: *How do I fix this?*

"Peter, no. Don't do this. I made a huge mistake, and I am sorry. So, so sorry. Give me a chance to explain." I had to make things right. I didn't want a life without him.

He started walking away, and my urge to sob turned to anger.

"I don't know what got into me. Stop walking. I love you!" I couldn't believe he was going to leave me there. Should I jump?

No, I couldn't get hurt. I had to dance the next day. The next day would be the most important day of my life in ballet.

"Crap!" I hit the marquee with my heels. "The Allen Ballet presents *Romeo and Juliet* with Claus Gert and Ana Brassfield, and there is stupid Ana on top of the stupid marquee. Why is this happening to me? Why did I have to mess it all up?"

A couple of people spotted me as I ranted, and again I thought about jumping.

Then I saw Peter cross Tenth Street. As he reached the other side, a woman with her hair in a bun patted his back tenderly and started walking with him in the direction of the bars.

Chapter 3

"Hey! How about you guys quit staring and come help me?" The three men who had slowed down near the marquee looked at each other and then came to the grassy area where the structure stood.

"Sure." The tallest approached me with extended arms and a stupid grin while the rest chuckled.

Were they even twenty? They had to be college kids. "Yeah, glad I amuse you." I put my arms out so he could help me. "You're being rude."

"I'm sorry—this is just priceless." He put me on the ground with ease. "I have a blind date, and this is the icebreaker I needed. Too good."

"What? You got a woman off a marquee? I sure hope you've got something better than that."

He crossed his arms, his smile smug. "Nope, I'm afraid that's all I've got."

"Whatever." I beat the dust from my duffle bag and walked away—away from the marquee, away from the theater, and away from the men. All of them.

"Thank you would be nice," my helper called above the Friday-night traffic. "Who's being rude now?"

"I've already said it. Thank you, tall guy in the dark blue shirt." Could the light turn red already? My whole world was falling apart, and I had to listen to college guys call me rude and make fun of me? I considered crossing the street without waiting, but there were too many cars.

"No, you didn't, Ana. And the name is Josh."

I looked back. "Hey! How do you know my name?"

"You said you were 'stupid Ana on the stupid marquee.'"

"Haha." Josh did not have a future in comedy, but he did have a point: maybe I was being rude. It wasn't his fault I'd gotten myself into a bad situation. "Thank you, Josh," I said over my shoulder.

"You're welcome."

The light turned red, and I crossed toward the Chattahoochee River.

I hurried home, one hand clutching the shoulder strap of my ballet bag while the other kept my shrug pressed against my chest.

Who was the woman who'd met Peter across from Tenth Street?

Peter didn't know anyone in the city.

Maybe she was a coworker from the park or a friend from Pine Mountain.

No, probably not. He knew the Allen Ballet always made the dress rehearsal a family-only event. He'd been there for rehearsals before. He wouldn't bring someone I didn't know without talking to me first.

Two beers later at my apartment, I felt courageous enough to call Peter.

At first, he didn't answer. Then my calls went straight to voice mail. I didn't want to leave a message, but I had to do something. A one-minute recorded monologue was my only option.

I tried to figure out what to say and called when I was sure I wouldn't stutter.

Straight to voice mail again: "Hello, you've called Peter Engberg, Director of Landscape Operations at Callaway Gardens. I can't take your call right now. Please leave a message after the tone, and I will return your call as soon as possible."

I considered hanging up, but the Coors Light making its way through my body convinced me that a phone call would be enough for me to earn Peter's forgiveness.

"Peter, I'm so sorry. I love you. Please, call me. Let's sort this out. I made a mistake. I need you, and you know it." My voice became unsteady, and I reached for the kitchen counter. Big tears fell on the hardwood floor and traveled its tiny wooden riverbeds. "I've loved you from that first day, baby." I had to calm down. I counted a row of bricks above the fire stove. "Remember dancing to 'Islands in the Stream' at Aspen's Mountain Grill? I knew it right there on that dance floor—I knew we would end up married. I knew we would be a family. I'd never had that feeling before, not even with Claus." Why did I have to mention his name? "I'm so sorry, Peter. Forgive—"

Beep.

I put the phone on its base, planted my elbows on the counter, and held my head in my hands. Bits and pieces of our first date went through my head. He'd played Big & Rich's "Save a Horse (Ride a Cowboy)" that night, and I was immediately captivated by his country world and his country friends. Everything that was familiar and natural to him was foreign and fascinating to me.

Well, technically, that had been our second date since we'd been together at the park earlier that day.

"I can't do this to myself." The silence in the apartment was maddening. I stood straight, drying my tears, and looked at the phone, quiet on its cradle.

Peter needed time. He would forgive me. He had to. I'd seen good men forgive women for worse infractions.

I had two days to live my prima-ballerina dream in Columbus. That would give him time to cool off. Then I would get him back and start the rest of my life, living in Pine Mountain and possibly dancing in Atlanta, like we'd discussed. With some luck, I would have a chance to perform at the Met in New York at least once in my life. It would all work out.

I'd made a one-time mistake. A big one. But that's all it was—a one-time mistake. It didn't have to cost all my plans and dreams.

My head hurt. I removed the bobby pins and the scrunchie that still held my hair up in a tight bun. *Better.* Peter often took my hair down at the end of the day when we were together and gave me a head massage. I dug my fingers through my hair and tried to do what he would have done, but it wasn't the same. I missed him.

"Oh, God. I'm so sorry." I hadn't prayed or been to church in forever. But I knew better than to act the way I had. I should not have let Claus kiss me. "I'm sorry."

My tan border collie, Barysh, scooted toward me when I opened the balcony doors. "Here, let me help you." Soon I would have to do something about him too. He hadn't stood on his own in weeks and wasn't getting any younger. I picked up his hips and helped him get outside.

"You're still my best dog." He was my only dog. I scratched the aged fur of his head. "Let me get the phone, and we'll hang out and watch the river."

I came outside with both phones and sat with Barysh. The city lights twinkled above a bustling Columbus while the Chattahoochee River gurgled below. Thoughts of Claus and the cherry-printed chiffon scarf drifted through the night breeze. "I'm so stupid."

Peter didn't answer the phone—again. *Seriously?* "Peter, I miss you so much… Don't do this. Answer the phone. I'm so sorry about what I did. Sorry, baby. Call me…" I didn't feel drunk, but my speech was slurred. Could things get any more humiliating? "Remember you lifting me into your truck the first time you picked me up? You said if we kept hanging out, you would have to put steps on it. I'd thought you were joking, but the next weekend, sure enough, the Silverado had steps. We've been—"

Beep.

"We've been glued ever since." I looked at the phone before putting it down.

Eight months later, he'd proposed. That had been the story of us—easy and fun. Until I messed it all up. I dropped my head into my hands. A bag of mulch would have been lighter than the guilt lying in the pit of my stomach.

In the morning, everything seemed like a bad dream. My eyes burned under heavy lids weighted down from my sleepless night and tears.

Furniture, lampshades, and paintings moved past me in slow motion while I searched for my bottle of Advil.

I popped two round pills and checked the coffeemaker. "Too strong," I mumbled as soon as the coffee started brewing. I must have opened the bag of Caffè Verona Mom had bought from Starbucks for me a few months back.

The growing stack of unopened mail was a welcome distraction. My cell phone bill had never looked so good, and I read my water-consumption statement with an eagerness generally reserved for wedding magazines and dance-gear catalogues.

I walked to the balcony with my favorite mug, a large terracotta cup that held twice as much coffee as a regular one. The floor tiles felt warm under my bare feet. I pulled out a wrought-iron chair from the small three-piece bistro set and wished I could go to the theater that very moment. Do my job. Be done with it.

The clap-clap-shhhh of the neighborhood skaters heading to the Riverwalk filled my ears. Where was my iPod? I found it and skipped straight to Peter's playlist.

The Chattahoochee moved to the rhythm of an old Bellamy Brothers ballad—gentle white waters finding their way around glistening flat rocks. It wasn't cold for a change, and the midday sun reminded me of the warm day ten months earlier when I'd first met Peter in person. It'd been early April, and Pine Mountain was in its spring splendor.

I'd met Peter Engberg online that previous February. He had only a couple of pictures in his profile: an older guy, mid-thirties maybe, but good-looking with gorgeous blue eyes—my weakness. His relationship status said "separated," so when he'd contacted me and said I had a beautiful smile, I'd sent him a one-liner asking for clarification on the status. He'd said his divorce would be final sometime in April, and I'd asked him to contact me again then.

His profile said he lived in Pine Mountain and worked at Callaway Gardens. I knew the place since my parents lived there. The gorgeous park, located forty minutes from my home in Columbus, is comprised of thousands of acres of gardens, resort, and preserve in the southernmost foothills of the Appalachian Mountains.

Their famed azaleas usually bloomed in the last week of March but were three weeks late because of the long, cold, wet winter.

When I checked my email at my parents' home on the first day of the azalea season of 2007, I found a message from him:

KITRI1980, I AM NOW A DIVORCED MAN. YOU HAVE A BEAUTIFUL SMILE :) ADAMTOGABRIEL73.

We exchanged several messages that night, but he didn't suggest meeting in person, so in the morning, I took a chance. I made a move.

ADAMTOGABRIEL73, I'M GOING TO THE AZALEA BOWL TODAY. WOULD YOU LIKE TO MEET ME THERE? KITRI1980.

Within milliseconds it'd hit me: of all the dumb ideas I'd had in my life, that was one of the worst. He worked at Callaway Gardens. Why would he want to go to the park on a Saturday?

His reply came just as fast:

ABSOLUTELY. THE ORGANIST STARTS AT 2:00. HOW ABOUT 2:30 ON THE BRIDGE?

I arrived fifteen minutes early, finished my water, and popped a white Tic Tac in my mouth before heading to the trail.

The smell of freshly cut grass lingered in the air. In the nearby chapel, Antonio Vivaldi's "The Four Seasons" sounded loud and clear. What part was the organist playing? Not "Spring." Was it "Winter"?

A little girl ran in my direction ahead of her mom. She was hardly two years old, with little white sandals showing her cute little toes and her spring dress flying behind her as she ran—classic.

I stopped to look at the Gothic-style chapel across Falls Creek Lake. The still water reflected the chapel with its main stained-glass window, the tall pines and oaks, and the flowering bushes and lilies along the water's edge.

I placed my hands together on the warm teak rail.

Is this it, God? Is this the one? I've never met a landscape architect before, and I've never been with someone older than me before. I've wanted to change my life a little—or a lot—and a guy like Peter in a place like Pine Mountain could be just what I need. Mom and Dad don't miss the city. Why would I? If this is right, please help us.

An older couple walked hand in hand ahead of me, and photographers and painters were perched on either side of the trail. The azaleas covered the landscape—by the lake, up the hills, alongside the trails—white, red, pink, lilac, and every shade in between.

Could these artists truly capture the spirit of the place and the quiet reverence of the park's visitors?

And then I spotted Peter. *Wow!* He stood on the bridge looking out at the lake. He was cuter than I'd imagined, and anything resembling quiet reverence departed from me fast. I just wanted to go behind an azalea bush and squeal.

I started walking toward him. He turned to me and smiled. The scruff on his face and his tan made him look surprisingly boyish, and his dark blue eyes were even bluer than in the pictures from his profile.

"Hi." I reached out for the metal rail to steady myself and breathed in his soapy smell. Everything about him was warm and inviting.

He wore a crisp blue-and-white plaid shirt, jeans that fit him perfectly, and work boots that had been around the park a time or two if the broken-in leather and hint of mud along the soles were any indication.

"Wow!" He stood by my side and looked down at me. "I'm sure your height was on your profile, but I wasn't paying attention." He laughed. "Aren't we a pair?"

"I'm used to everybody being bigger than me, so it doesn't really faze me."

"Come here, shorty." He grabbed my hand and walked. "Let's go see some azaleas. I'm sorry about the height thing. I didn't mean anything by it."

"So, you are a gardener?" I asked, trying to get him back.

He smirked but didn't take the bait.

"I'm the Director of Landscape Operations here at Callaway."

"That sounds important. What do you do? Did you design the azalea bowl?"

"No. I design the displays at the horticultural center, the flower beds by the butterfly center, and flower beds everywhere at the park actually."

"That's cool. How did you get into this?"

"I grew up in Cincinnati with my folks. I hate winter, so I always knew I would end up moving south." He kicked a rock out of the dirt path. "I loved helping my mom with our flower beds at home. She always wanted everything to match, but I got her into going for contrasts: purples and oranges or reds, yellows and purples. Drove her crazy at first, but she learned to have fun with colors." He smiled into the distance and brushed something out of his eye. "My dad is the corporate-America type—marketing for Chiquita Brands—and I knew I didn't want to be like him at all. I'm not much of an indoor guy."

"Well, good for you. It's like you've got it all figured out." It must be nice to be so together.

"I wish. Right now, I feel like I don't know a thing." He shook his head as he chuckled. "How about you and dancing?"

"My mom is from Brazil and used to dance. She put me in classes when I was little, and it's what I've always done. I love it, but I'm a little disappointed with how things have turned out," I said, surprised at my frankness. "I'm good, but not as good as I'd hoped."

"What are your hopes now?"

"I don't know," I lied. The last time I told a guy I wanted to dance at the Met, he'd thought I was joking.

"I don't know a thing either." I giggled and then we had both laughed.

Battery Low.

The iPod warning didn't hurt my head—the headache was gone. But my ears hurt. I removed the earphones.

Clap-clap-shhhh.

The coffee was cold and the table was in full shade.

I checked my phone. Two thirty. Just enough time to take a shower and go. "Good." The sooner I could put this weekend behind me, the sooner I could go get my man back.

I was the first one to get to the stage area. I moved the shortest barre to a spot near the curtains and leaned against the end to stretch my calf muscles. A big group of corps girls entered together, chatting and giggling, and as soon as the door slammed behind them, it opened again. Claus. Blue warm-up pants. Pale blue top accenting his eyes.

Could I resist him?

He walked across the stage toward the water cooler.

Absolutely. I looked away and sat to warm up. Holding my feet, I let my upper body rest on my legs, the hamstring stretch painful but gratifying.

Would it be a terrible idea to drive to Pine Mountain after the performance?

Peter hadn't called back and that hurt. He wouldn't be able to ignore me if I showed up at the house, right?

No, that would be terrible. I bent one leg under me and leaned back for a quad stretch. He needed time and space.

I'd made my life complicated enough by crossing a line that shouldn't have been crossed. Untangling the mess would take time. Let's get through the weekend first—the whole weekend. I switched legs.

Professional dancers spend hours breaking in a new pair of pointe shoes, often going through dozens of pairs as we develop our routines. The shoes need to be soft for jumping, strong for balances and turns, and beautiful on the foot.

To achieve that goal, many dancers would cut the sole of the pointe shoe to pull nails out, step on the shoe, hammer the shoe, rub alcohol onto anything they want shaped to their feet fast, and so on. Each dancer has her own technique.

But whether you bend, bind, dam, cut, shave, or strip, breaking in a new shoe is an art that involves destruction.

Maybe that's what Peter and I were going through. A period of destruction in a process meant to make things better.

We'd never been through any kind of fire. If we could get through this, we would be stronger than before.

Brian arrived and walked to the front, indicating our warm-up would begin soon.

I patted the stage floor, then stood. *This is it.*

Claus took a spot opposite mine at the barre, and my stomach was roller-coaster light for a moment. He'd been keeping his distance during classes—just coming near me for rehearsals. It seemed our kiss changed things a bit.

Gallastegui's "Promenade" filled the theater. Exercise music I'd heard a million times before. A simple plié. Dozens of bodies moving in harmony with little to no guidance. Poetry in motion.

My eyes filled with tears, and despite my efforts to keep them from falling, they trickled down my cheeks. Claus moved his hand closer to mine and acknowledged my moment with a gentle touch and a knowing smile.

As the class progressed and movements became bigger, I struggled to get my legs up high with every *développé*. Trying to get the working leg to unfold and extend higher than one-hundred-twenty degrees, I felt my supporting leg shift. *Ugh.*

"Ana, watch your turnout," Brian said as he walked past me. "Higher demi-pointe."

I looked at Lorie Allen, who was on the other side of the stage. The prima ballerina of the Allen Ballet, she epitomized beauty—tall and leggy, blonde and blue-eyed. Everything I was not. Yeah, her mom founded the company and was still around, but Lorie was indeed the best we had—no favoritism.

But none of it mattered. I was Juliet. For a change, I was dancing the lead role. My Romeo was one of the world's best dancers. This was the coronation of twenty years of my effort.

Could I leave the security of the Allen Ballet? Part of me felt old and lacking to audition in Atlanta, but the Atlanta Ballet had danced at the Met a couple of times.

I would be lucky to make the corps, but that would be fine. I didn't have to be a soloist there as long as I got to the Met. Some of my favorite memories of life on stage were not from solos but from group pieces. I just wanted to perform on that storied New York stage where the stars of today and legends like Margot Fonteyn, Rudolf Nureyev, Natalia Makarova, Mikhail Baryshnikov, and hundreds of other fantastic dancers had enchanted generations of ballet enthusiasts.

"Finish stretching on your own." Brian turned away from us and faced the empty audience. "We'll do grand battements in the center."

I hated doing grand battements in the center. At the barre, I could kick my leg really high, but if I tried to do the same in the center, my support leg would slip out from under me, and I would land on my bottom.

Claus removed our barre from the stage and took a spot next to me, where he stayed for the duration of the warm-up—not in one spot, but next to me.

"Beautiful, Ana," Brian said as Claus and I approached the end of an intricate diagonal. "Nice sky-high jumps, and you look like you actually care to be here. Gorgeous."

When I finished the next exercise, Brian stopped the class and asked me to do it again, alone.

"Watch what she's doing. I want to see more of that from everybody." I blushed, knowing all eyes, including Claus's, were on me. "Before the music even starts, her face, her arms, her épaulement was already saying 'look at me.' Isn't this wonderful?"

I'm not sure if Brian was trying to massage my ego before showtime or if he really meant all he said. Either way, it was working beautifully.

"Don't be afraid to perform." He walked back to his notes. "Let's just do a révérence and be done. I don't want you guys to be too tired."

I wasn't afraid of feeling tired, but ending on a high note was a good idea. My brain was turning into mush as the evening approached.

We followed Brian's arm movements, then the men bowed and the women curtsied, to Brian first and then to the pianist.

Once in the dressing room, I put on my fake lashes and dressed in Juliet's soft green and gold gown. The night would be special, but it wasn't going to be complete without Peter in the audience. If only I hadn't kissed Claus.

I was also worried. In theory, my plan was great: be Juliet, get Peter back, dance in Atlanta, and make my dreams come true. But I was not convinced reality would be that simple. I finished the eye shadow and approved the image in the mirror.

"Knock knock." Claus drummed on my door, the accent slight but obviously his.

"Hi." I let him in. *Why am I not surprised? What does he want?* He was dressed for the opening scene, ready to be my Romeo. His thick gray tights and beautiful red and grayish-blue vest did wonders for his fair complexion.

"How are you feeling?" He stood so close that the heat of his body touched mine. His moist lips in front of my eyes and the slight inclination of his head were an invitation—an invitation to bridge the gap, to give in, and to enjoy the moment.

My eye caught a glimpse of my engagement ring, carefully placed on the top shelf of my makeup box. *An invitation to trouble—that's all this is.* I took a step back. "Just because we kissed last night doesn't mean it'll happen again."

"Actually, darling, I can guarantee it will happen again." He looked at his cell phone with a smirk. "In about ten minutes the doors will open and people will start sitting, Lady Juliet. We will kiss. We will kiss many times tonight."

Oh, this accent—this man. A swarm of out-of-control butterflies exploded in my chest. "You know what I mean."

"Yes. I know." He pointed to my dress, which was loose and in obvious need of fastening.

I turned around. "Can you—"

He got to work without a word, his fingers moving from hook to hook slowly.

We will kiss. We will kiss many times tonight. Bad butterflies. Stop.

"Ana, I want to talk to you when all this is over." He continued fastening the long row of hooks on the back of Juliet's gown. "I want you to understand what happened ten years ago."

"Why now?" *It's too late for us.*

"I—"

"Actually, no." I lifted my hand, interrupting his attempt to answer. "Let's just dance. I need to get through this weekend."

"Okay. I can wait."

Good luck with that. The end of our performances together had to be the end of our whole history together—that was the right thing to do. But I didn't want him to perform with a broken heart or disappointed. This was our time to dance.

It was about Romeo and about Juliet. It was also about a faithful audience that deserved a great performance from all of us. And it was about the Met—there were artistic directors from Atlanta in the audience too.

He fastened the last hook and turned me around slowly. "Beautiful," he whispered, touching my cheek with the back of his fingers.

"Thank you." I took a step back.

"I'm supposed to fly back to Germany in two weeks, but I can stay longer." He reached for my hands.

"We'll talk, Claus." But we wouldn't. There was so much I wanted to say to him. The truth about the status of my relationship with Peter, for starters. The trouble I was in. But that was my business, not his. Like the couple we were about to play on stage, we too had our timing all wrong.

The velvety voice of the theater manager came through the announcement system: "The house is now open. The house is now open."

I opened the door for Claus. "See you out there."

"Can't wait, sweet Juliet."

He walked out backward and continued looking at me. "I love you," he mouthed without a sound before turning toward the stage door beyond which our audience awaited.

I love you? My right hand covered my heart—beats uneven, breaths uneven. *We will kiss. We will kiss many times tonight.*

Chapter 4

We had a full house indeed—an electrified and electrifying full house. At the end of every solo filled with jumps and turns, people clapped and shouted with an enthusiasm I'd only seen on YouTube and almost always involved Bolshoi-groomed Ivan Vasiliev.

Twice the applause had been so long and so loud I'd struggled to hear the music that followed. *What a lovely problem to have.*

Should I try a triple pirouette at the end of the masquerade ball solo? The warmth of the audience had already inspired me to take a few risks, and I'd already nailed two triples where I normally did doubles.

This one was different, though. Romeo was watching.

Up to the ballroom scene, he'd been dancing with his friends, and I'd been dancing in my room. Now Juliet was in the arms of the man her parents wanted her to marry—the handsome Paris—but he was about to get distracted, and Romeo was about to seize the opportunity.

Let's go with the triple. Preparation. Turn. Nice.

"Brava!"

Yes!

Now Juliet's life was about to change, in one, two, three ... bam! Claus's hands locked onto my small waist—the lovers' first touch. *Freeze.*

My feet moved in a series of small steps en pointe but nothing else did—arms bent up and still like a porcelain doll's, eyes wide, mouth slightly opened, heart... What was the heart doing? It wasn't frozen.

It'd been zapped, like in medical television shows—that was it. *Charge to two hundred, clear, zap.* Only the shock hadn't been delivered through paddles on the patient's chest, it'd been delivered through my love's hands. *Zap.*

My body traveled to where he directed, upper body still in shock. His grip tightened. *Charge to three sixty, clear, zap.*

And Juliet responds. She turns to Romeo and their eyes meet. *I love you. We will kiss. We will kiss many times tonight.*

Her family responds too, the whole lot of them and Paris. Juliet's cousin Tybalt separates the two before anything can happen. *Sigh.*

I couldn't imagine having my parents decide who I'd marry. What was it like for the young women who had to do it? Some were luckier than others, for sure.

Was it safer? For Juliet it would have been—she'd have lived. But would she have been happy? Would she have truly *lived*?

After all the ballroom flirting, it was finally time for the first kiss—the balcony scene.

We met center stage precisely as we'd practiced. My hand reached for his, and I placed it over my heart. Did defibrillators go higher than three sixty? Claus's hands did. *Zap.*

Both our chests rose and fell with deep breaths. I exhaled hard—it was time to show off a little. More triple turns? Absolutely.

We finished dancing for each other, and Claus buried his face in the hem of my nightgown. It's all too much for Juliet, and she tries to run. Romeo grabs her hand, bringing her back to him.

Claus's lips were six inches from mine. I rolled up onto the tips of my toes, meeting his height. *We will kiss all night...*

He was supposed to close the gap, but he pulled me in instead—his fingers under my chin.

That wasn't Romeo kissing Juliet. That was Claus. That was Claus kissing *me.* What was he doing?

The mixture of excitement and hesitation in my reaction seemed to ignite a fire in him. He was supposed to have his hand behind my back, barely touching me, his arms framing us.

But I felt the pressure of his hands and moaned against my will. His lips parted. Salty sweat, together. Heartbeats, together. Heat, together. Two became one.

By the time he let go, I didn't have to pretend to be dizzy. I pulled away and ran up to the balcony. What had just happened?

Forget about coming back for the final pose. I was supposed to get down on the edge of the balcony and reach for him. But I left him waiting for me to appear one more time and hid behind the curtains instead. I covered my heart with both hands and heard the audience explode in cheers and shouts.

Was he going to do that with every kiss? My heart pounded as I imagined romantic scenes to come.

We will kiss. We will kiss many times tonight.

The wedding kiss was next, and then the bedroom kiss, and then many, many more all the way to the end of the ballet. I would never be able to perform all night if Claus continued to kiss me like that. Had he even planned that wild moment in the garden below the balcony? Or had the kiss just happened? God help me.

Standing in my kitchen the morning after our last show, I enjoyed a cup of my trusty breakfast blend before opening the paper to read the reviews.

I've always believed *Romeo and Juliet* is a ballet best appreciated by dancers. It lacks the bravado and Latin flair of *Don Quixote* and *Paquita*; there are no swans in pancake tutus, no ghosts in long romantic dresses with wings. *Romeo and Juliet* is blood and guts. It's also an hour longer than most ballets, with more purely dramatic scenes than most. People are at the theater for at least four hours. But the intensity of the plot and the depth of the romance make it wonderful to dance.

The response we received from the audience and the critics was especially flattering considering the demand we put on them.

ANA BRASSFIELD AND THE SEASONED CLAUS GERT BROUGHT THE *ROMEO AND JULIET* TRAGEDY TO LIFE ON THE STAGE OF THE RIVERCENTER THIS WEEKEND, WITH BEAUTIFUL DANCING AND FLAWLESS INTERPRETATIONS WITNESSED BY HUNDREDS OF TEARY-EYED SPECTATORS.

THE COUPLE RECEIVED ROOF-RAISING OVATIONS AS THEY LIVED AND DIED WITH THE INTENSITY AND TRUTHFULNESS YOU WOULD EXPECT AT THE SHAKESPEARE'S GLOBE, LEADING ME TO WONDER IF THESE YOUNG DANCERS HAVE ACTUALLY EXPERIENCED THE JOYS AND SORROWS OF LOVE FOUND AND TRAGICALLY LOST, OR IF THEY SHOULD BE PURSUING A CAREER ON BROADWAY.

THIS IS MR. GERT'S SECOND TIME PERFORMING AS A GUEST WITH THE ALLEN BALLET. HE DANCED *PAQUITA* WITH LORIE ALLEN IN 1996, WHEN HE WAS A PRINCIPAL WITH THE ATLANTA BALLET. HE NOW DANCES WITH THE RHINE-MAIN BALLET IN HIS NATIVE GERMANY.

Mission complete.

I grabbed my keys and took Barysh to my neighbor's apartment before driving north to Pine Mountain. It was time for me to go after the heart of the one who'd proved faithful, made me happy, and gave me peace—Peter. I'd had enough with the anxiety and pain I'd lived on stage with Claus.

I'm not taking the scenic route today. I got in my car, found a good melody, and headed for the highway.

Should I go straight to Callaway Gardens or should I go by the house first? *Argh.* My nice melody turned out to be a Christian song. Why did people listen to that stuff? Wasn't Sunday enough?

I looked for my favorite country station. "There. Funny DJ. Miranda Lambert setting stuff on fire. Good." A horn blasted loudly to my right, and I looked up from the radio. I'd almost moved out of my lane. *That was not supposed to happen.* I-185 was busier than usual, packed with cars and trucks driving in a hurry toward Atlanta. Staying alert was not optional.

Why was I queasy? Something wasn't right. My mouth was dry and my chest felt funny, like I'd been holding my breath. But I was breathing just fine. Should I pull over?

No way—I'd waited enough. The radio would help me relax and focus on the drive. I made it louder.

The deejay started talking about Jesus and said something about Scripture. That couldn't be my station. My eyes riveted on the display. It was my radio station. *Might as well turn it off.* I reached for the radio, eyes firm on the white markings on the road this time.

By the time the first Pine Mountain sign emerged on the horizon, I felt better.

I took the STATE ROUTE 18 exit and called Peter. No answer. "To heck with calling." My cell phone hit the back window with a loud thud. *Whatever.*

Five minutes later I was at his house, but Peter was nowhere to be seen.

Callaway Gardens was next.

But was it a good idea to catch Peter in the middle of his workday? It probably wasn't, but I put the car in drive and headed for the park anyway.

How about a stop at Mom's? No, she would worry too much.

If I wasn't going to Mom's and wasn't going to Peter's office, why was I still driving toward the park?

Because I have nowhere else to go. That's why…

The small sign by the entrance had caught my attention before, but today I burst into tears as I came upon it:

REMOVE NOTHING FROM THE GARDENS EXCEPT:
NOURISHMENT FOR THE SOUL,
CONSOLATION FOR THE HEART,
INSPIRATION FOR THE MIND.

I drove around and counted trees in an effort to stop crying. Why was it not working? Hot tears marred my vision all the way to the rustic Gothic-style chapel where we'd planned to get married.

The desert-sand fieldstone quartz and gray mortar of the building blended with the winter woods and dark skies. I got out of the car and dried off my tears, my eyes on the spot across Falls Creek Lake where ten months earlier I'd stopped to pray before meeting Peter. A hawk screamed overhead.

The desire to turn back time and be on the other side of those waters, starting things new, stung my heart, and I ran into the chapel wailing as if chased by a pack of hungry beasts.

Once inside I collapsed by the entrance, my body chilled by the stone floor. That must be what Juliet's family crypt felt like. Cold, hard, empty. Sobs and shrieks echoed throughout the chapel as if they were coming from somebody else, somewhere else, as days of misery erupted.

When screeches became whimpers, I stood, blinking slowly, and breathed deeply.

Finally empty, I walked down the aisle and studied the four stained-glass windows leading to the altar: pines, softwoods, and hardwoods from the four seasons. Each represented a phase of my relationship with Peter: spring, summer, autumn, and now winter.

I curled up on the cold altar floor and touched the rock that held the cross. *Please, God. Help me. Please, please, please. I want to believe in You so badly, but I can't. It doesn't make any sense. People suffer. Good people. And You don't seem to be in control of anything. I have no evidence of You in my life or anybody's.*

Lying flat on my back, I looked up at the small iron cross. *Yet, I can't seem to walk away. Are You even there?*

Behind the cross was the main stained-glass window that colored the chapel with red and pink flowers, orange and green leaves, blue segments, and three trees with many branches. Parts of all seasons seemed to form the art of the altar. All but winter. *Am I imagining this?* I was too spent to go look at the four seasons to compare the parts. *Another day.*

I touched the rock. It was massive for its thin iron legs. I'd never paid too much attention to it. It'd seemed like another big rock in a rock church. But this rock wasn't like the others. This one had gone through fire. It looked like lava rock. Was it?

Standing to look at the top of it, I noticed a simple Bible by the cross. It was open to the beginning of First Corinthians. Closing my eyes, I moved my fingers over the page like I used to as a child. *Let's see what we've got. Verse eighteen.*

But before I could read, someone opened the door.

I scrambled to the first pew. Was that Peter? Not many people had his stature.

Meticulous footsteps approached the altar. *Think of something to say—make it good.* Peter sat across the aisle from me, his eyes on the altar.

"Someone saw your car." He spoke in the same tone he'd used when walking me to the marquee Friday night—controlled and emotionless.

I should have known that someone would spot me and tell him. It's hard to fly under the radar in a 2002 Torch Red Ford Thunderbird. But I had bigger problems—he didn't sound like he was open to listening. Good words wouldn't do—I needed perfect ones.

Think of something—say something. This silence is getting awkward by the second. "I'm sorry about the kiss. It was a stupid mistake." Not exactly profound, but it needed to be said.

He looked at me for the first time since leaving me at the marquee Friday night. "I don't really want to talk about what happened. That's not why I'm here." His face contorted as if he were crying, but no tears ran down his cheeks. "I want the ring, Ana."

"What?" Peter was obviously still upset, but asking for the ring was completely out of character.

"It was my mom's. Otherwise, I wouldn't ask." He looked at the altar again, a fist pressed against his mouth.

Why wasn't the ring on his mom's finger? He'd always avoided talking about his family, and I hadn't thought to question where he'd gotten my delicate rose-cut diamond ring. "The ring *was* your mom's? I assumed your parents were still married."

His eyes riveted on me. "They were—until she died."

"Oh, Peter. I'm so sorry. How come you never told me?" As soon as I took a step in his direction, he broke eye contact again. He wasn't going to make anything easy for me, was he?

"It was a long time ago. And you never asked."

I had asked. I started to speak, but he stopped me.

"The ring, Ana."

"Peter, no." I knelt by him and rested my head on his leg. It couldn't end like this. His woody scent and warmth reminded me of all I had and was now losing. My arms reached for his waist, holding on to what I could while I could. "Don't—"

"Ana, don't make this any harder than it needs to be. How do you think I feel?" He held his hand open in front of my face. "Can I just have my mom's ring back, please?"

His words made me feel dirty, like a whore—undeserving of his mother's ring. I wasn't like that, was I? Did he think that of me? I wanted to touch his hand, every pore and thin hair, and make him feel my heart.

"Ana, please. You're torturing me." His voice broke into sobs, and he brought his hand closer to me.

"Oh, honey…"

"My mom's ring."

What would he do if I tried to hold his hand? Would he withdraw? My fingertips touched his but he pulled away. Why? How could he be so closed to conversation? My behavior was terrible, but why couldn't he give me a second chance or at least hear me out?

He stood, freeing himself from me. His hand still out. "Now, Ana."

I removed the ring and placed it in his palm with unsteady fingers. As he closed his hand around it, a painful lump rose in my throat.

As Peter put the ring in his shirt pocket, out of sight and out of reach, my chest tightened and my throat burned. I brought both hands to my face, hiding my shame and my tears. What could I do? What could I say?

"Why, Ana?" His voice was a little deeper now.

That was my chance. I looked up. His blue eyes were dark like a midnight sky, and the winter stained-glass window framed his strong body. "I was weak." The words came out in short bursts, twisted by emotion. "It was stupid. We were in love ten years ago, and then he disappeared on me. But that's all an old story."

"It didn't look like an old story when I saw you two Friday night." Peter paced the area in front of the pews with a hand behind his neck and the other on his waist, like he often did when trying to sort things out.

"What you saw was one kiss, and it was a mistake. *You* are my life."

"It was more than one kiss, and you know it."

No, I didn't know it. "What are you talking about?"

"The affair, Ana. I know about the affair."

"There's no affair." Where had that come from?

I'd never seen his face turn red like that—never seen that kind of fury. "Stop lying." He spoke the words through clenched teeth.

"I am not lying!" My fist slammed the closest pew. "This is a nightmare."

"We can agree on that one." His voice was louder and echoed. "It is a nightmare."

"How about we also agree that it was a one-time mistake, and then we can talk about what actually happened, not some fantasy relationship you've created for me." My hands squeezed both his arms, and I shook him. "Hmm? How about that?"

"I know the truth! Lorie told me everything!"

"Lorie?"

He pulled away and put some distance between us. "Lorie Allen. She told me."

"Lorie Allen, the dancer? But you don't even know her." The image of the woman meeting him on the street Friday night did match Lorie's. Was it her? But why? How?

"Yes, Lorie Allen, the dancer. She found me online and told me you were having an affair with this famous German guy who'd been your first love—Romeo." He rolled his eyes.

What in the world? "First, there's no affair. Second, how can you believe her and not believe me?"

"I didn't believe her, Ana—I didn't." He folded his arms against his chest. "Why would my fiancée, the sweet, wonderful girl who'd taken me out of a dark pit—a pit of betrayal, lies, and despair—put me right back into it by having an affair with her ballet partner?"

If he didn't believe Lorie then, how come he believed her now? And what dark pit of betrayal was he talking about? "So you didn't believe her, but now you do? What changed, Peter?"

"She told me to come to the dress rehearsal and check it out for myself. And I did." His voice faltered. "And she was right. I saw you with him."

I had to hold him and make things right—take that pain away. But as soon as I moved forward, he moved back. My head pounded. "How did Lorie know there would be a kiss?" I whispered.

"I guess that's what lovers do." His voice was hardened by sarcasm. "They kiss and exchange hankies."

The scarf. Heat filled my cheeks.

"Look at you." Peter pointed briefly at my face. "Guilty."

Wow. Officially judged. "Guilty of a one-time mistake—and I'm so sorry." *Stay calm.* "I don't know what else to say to make you believe me."

"I really do wish that I could believe you—or at least forgive." He sat and seemed less tense. "I'm brokenhearted. I love you…"

He looked like he was going to say something else, but he remained silent.

"I love you, too, Peter." I sniffed hard. "Can we please forget Friday night ever happened and drop the Lorie nonsense?"

He shook his head in slow motion. "Sorry, baby girl, but an affair is a deal breaker for me."

A hot sensation that started in the pit of my stomach spread throughout my body and then exploded. "There's no affair!"

The last word echoed in the empty church, and the cold stones accused me, too, "Affair, affair, affair…"

"Baby, don't lie. This kind of thing happens—believe me. I've seen it before. I'm sure you have your reasons. I just can't be with you like this."

"What you saw was everything. You've got to believe me."

"I can't." His voice was almost a whisper.

When I spoke, mine was too. "So Lorie was the woman you met Friday night after you left me."

"She felt bad for me and has been a good friend."

"She's lying to you. I'll figure out why, and I'll prove it to you." Why was she framing me? And how *did* she know there would be something for Peter to witness that night? Was I that predictable?

"You don't need to do that. It's over, Ana." His lips tightened. "I need to go back to work. Sorry about the ring."

"This is so absurd."

"Bye, Ana." Peter turned to the massive doors and walked out on me. Again.

Watching him go because of what I'd done was doable. Painful, but doable. Now losing him over something I hadn't done? No way.

The chapel doors closed behind him.

For ten years—my entire professional career—I'd watched Lorie Allen dance all my dream roles. I'd tried hard to enjoy my secondary parts, always working to get to her level, thrilled by every new solo and opportunity that came my way.

Now she was trying to spoil my personal life too? Why? What had I ever done to hurt her? Was she jealous because for once I had the lead role?

It couldn't be—she was a Christian. Weren't lying and being jealous on the top ten list of things you were not supposed to do?

There had to be more to the story. I had to find Lorie.

Chapter 5

My hands shook on the steering wheel. *I shouldn't be driving, but I have to get back to Columbus. I have to find Lorie.*

The turn to Peter's house was between Callaway Gardens and the highway home. Should I drive by? Seemed masochistic to do so, but I couldn't shake off the urge. How about a quick peek from the lakeside? That way I could stay on the road instead of going up the long driveway. *I'll do that.*

The skies were still dark. *Please let it not rain.* My life was depressing enough without the heavens crying for me too. I drove a little faster.

How would I go about finding Lorie before class? I bet she wasn't even going to the company since today's class wasn't mandatory. Did she still live at home?

What was going on with her? What Peter claimed she'd done was completely out of character. Could Peter be making the whole thing up? No, why would he? That would make even less sense.

Lorie and I had been good friends when we'd first started dancing at the Allen Ballet more than ten years ago—best friends even.

Time passed and eventually we grew apart.

I'd been hurt when she started getting all the lead roles. I'd thought I would catch up, but two years into our time in the company, it had become clear I would be playing second fiddle for a long time—possibly forever.

That's when I'd started turning to guys.

Lorie's decision to get a college degree while dancing professionally drove us further apart. She studied and danced while I partied and danced. She went to church and I didn't. Her lifestyle seemed boring to me, and she probably didn't appreciate mine. But through it all, we had remained friendly toward each other.

So, what was she doing now?

Would I be able to get to the bottom of it and convince Peter that I was telling the truth? After all, he did see me kiss Claus.

If only I hadn't kissed him.

Turning toward Peter's ranch, I passed the driveway and continued toward the lake. His house appeared in the distance. But that was not all that appeared.

There, next to the house and past the carport, was Lorie's Ford Explorer. *What?*

The Thunderbird's tires screeched as I turned around and headed to the driveway. *What was she doing at his house? And by herself?* The winding wooded path to the house failed to bring the usual peace and awe. It was just long. Too long.

Lorie's car was on the other side of the house, past the carport. I could only have seen it from the lakeside, not from the driveway, where I had pulled in. *Was she here when I came earlier?*

I parked behind her and collapsed, slouching against the steering wheel to wait for a burst of energy that never came.

My eyes riveted on the Ford Explorer. It was time to get some answers—energy or no energy.

With the T-Bird blocking the Explorer, her only way out was a drive into the lake. Or an escape on foot into the woods. *Go explore that.* She wasn't going anywhere without talking to me.

My boots touched the ground gently, and I tiptoed, keeping the sound of gravel to a minimum.

Should I use my keys or ring the bell? Ringing the bell seemed silly, as Peter's house was practically mine, or at least had been for several months. I spent every weekend and holiday there. Vacations too.

Unsure of what I would find, I peeked in through the kitchen window.

Peter's automatic Colt pistol was on top of the fridge, as it was supposed to be. Next to it and closer to the edge, my small-frame Smith & Wesson revolver, also where it belonged.

Lorie sat curled up with a pack of Oreos, looking in the direction of the TV. I moved to a different window to get a better view.

She was watching *Carmen Suite*, possibly the original. It was an old recording, and the camera was on Maya Plisetskaya's fantastic profile—fearlessness defined as she prepared for the "Habanera."

Carmen's passion exploded in grand *jeté en tournants*, and with three of those jumps she had already traveled the length of the stage.

The music was equally strong, and Lorie had the volume set so loud I could hear it through the closed window.

Did Lorie carry that ballet around? It wasn't mine—but the Oreos were.

And she was in Peter's spot, wearing Peter's favorite brown-and-black plaid pajamas. Drinking coffee from Peter's favorite mug.

My fist hit the window hard.

Lorie jumped and hid the cookies under a pillow.

I marched to the kitchen door and busted in to confront her. *I've had enough!* She jumped again. "Oh, Ana! Don't do that! You scared me!" She brushed crumbs off her mouth then stood to face me.

"You're eating my Oreos."

"Sorry—"

I raised my hand. "No." I could picture my heart contracting and pumping blood. Hot. Fast. Loud. *Breathe.*

"I'm embarrassed—"

"Just shut up." *This is a nightmare. I must be imagining all of this.* "What's going on here? How did you get in?"

"How do you think I got in?"

Was that a smile on her face? She was mocking me, wasn't she? "Why are you wearing Peter's pajamas?"

"Do you really want me to say it?"

I probably didn't, but I had to hear it. Maybe then I would believe the impossible was actually happening.

"Ana, you broke the man's heart. I'm just trying to fix it."

"He is my fiancé." My voice came out much louder than I had expected. "What do you think you're doing?"

"Ex-fiancé?" She raised both eyebrows.

I was dizzy again. *Do I want to know?* My mouth was dry. *I need to know.* "Did you sleep with him?"

She nodded without uttering a word. For once, she did look embarrassed.

Tears welled up. I covered my face and sat on Peter's recliner. The manly smell of Peter's cologne enveloped me. When I looked up, Lorie hadn't moved. "Why did you make Peter watch the rehearsal?"

"Ana, I truly believe, and I've believed this for a while now, that this life is just not for you."

"What life? What are you talking about? Listen to yourself!"

"All of this." She raised her long arms and pale hands. "The ranch, the Blake Shelton look-alike man, the small-town life." Her eyes rested on a small picture frame on the corner table between us.

I looked at the picture too. It was the engagement picture Mom insisted we submit to the papers in Pine Mountain and Columbus. *This is not happening. It's got to be a joke, a nightmare, something. It's not real.*

"I'm sorry I had to resort to this, but I did it for you." Her voice was like that of a kindergarten teacher talking to her little students. "This is just not you, Ana. You would be miserable in Pine Mountain, married to Peter."

"Lorie, who are you to know what would and would not make me happy?

You don't know me anymore. Why did you poison him against me?" *Why am I having this conversation?* "This is ridiculous!"

Lorie's body stiffened and so did mine. Had the sudden anger in my voice startled her?

"Now wait just a minute." Her face came within inches of mine as she looked down at me. "I didn't make you kiss Claus."

Could she hear my heartbeat? I could. "Get out of my face. You're done. I'm done with you." She didn't move. My hands turned into fists, and I pushed her backward. "You're sleeping with my man!"

"He's not your man!" She came back into my space. "He's mine now."

I slapped her face hard, and we both drew in a sharp breath.

No one spoke.

I held my shaky, sweaty hand. It ached. I'd never done that before. Her face had the red marks of my fingers. "Don't ever get in my face like that."

"Don't ever hit me like that."

"I don't know what you think you're doing, Lorie, but the truth will come out one day. It always does. I love him, and I *will* get him back. Mark my words. I'll win and you'll lose."

She seemed calm and collected, though her blue eyes were piercing. "I love him too, Ana. I'm tired of you being with all the men I love."

"Excuse me? You saw Peter once, maybe twice, at a party. You can't love him." I put the last two words in air quotes. "What other men are you talking about?"

"Claus." Her eyes filled up with tears.

"What?"

"He was here to dance with me. Why did you have to steal him?" Her screechy voice made my ears hurt.

"Lorie, that was ten years ago, and I didn't steal him from you. We fell in love." Did Lorie have feelings for Claus? That was breaking news. "I never suspected you had an interest in him at all."

"Well, I did." Big fat tears rolled out of her sad blue eyes. "That was my dream, Ana. We were going to dance *Paquita*, fall in love, and be one of those glamorous ballet power couples that grow and create together forever."

Was she for real? "I'm sorry, Lorie. You guys looked beautiful dancing together, but he never showed any romantic interest in you. Besides, look at what a mess that was for me. At least your heart wasn't broken when he ran back to Germany to be with Hanna."

"Maybe if you'd let him fall in love with me instead, he wouldn't have felt the need to run away." Her voice was distorted by sobs. "You gave him all he wanted.

Of course he ran."

I looked in her direction, but my eyes were now on Carmen and Don José, my ears on the unique sounds of the castanets.

"You know it's true." Lorie added yet another nail in her accusation.

"Lorie, come on." I clenched my jaw, working to keep my focus on the present problem. "Talk to Peter. Tell him the truth. Tell him I wasn't having an affair with Claus. He will forgive me if he realizes the kiss was all there was." *Mainly now that he's acted less than honorable too, by sleeping with Lorie. We were more than even.*

"No. I'm with him now."

Like that was going to last. "I feel sorry for you, because whatever you think you've got going on here, it won't last. It's not real. The truth will come out." I looked down and headed for the front door.

"Enough with that already. The truth will not come out, Ana. Life isn't fair, and there isn't a thing we can do about it. Get over it."

That made me stop and turn. My eyes met her sad gaze. "That doesn't sound like you. What about God?"

"God is dead." She froze as if startled by her own declaration.

And I froze too.

Surely I was the worst person to defend God. I didn't have the knowledge or the moral ground. But she was wrong. "What's really going on with you, Lorie? You've always believed in God."

"I don't anymore. I'm tired of seeing people do whatever they feel like doing and getting away with it. I tried to be good, to live a godly life, and it backfired in a major way."

"What happened?"

"I don't want to talk about it. Psalm seventy-three. Look it up. I feel like Asaph. He's able to get his heart right again. But I can't—I can't and I won't." She walked back to the couch and mumbled, "I'm done being good." She sat, got the Oreos, and went back to the beginning of the "Habanera."

I nodded, hoping to find something to say, but I had no idea what she was talking about. "Is that the 'Lord is my shepherd' one?"

"No, numbskull, that's twenty-three." She finished chewing a cookie. "Why do I bother?"

"Numbskull?" We were down to that now? What'd happened to her? I looked outside at skies that seemed less angry. *You are there, aren't you God?* In the distance, I spotted Peter's truck. He was coming home.

He pulled up as I opened the door.

Had Lorie heard the truck over the music? I hoped she hadn't.

My heart leapt at the sight of Peter. *It is not over.* I ran toward him, trying to step lightly to avoid making noise.

But the house door flung open, and Lorie dashed past me, struggling to run barefoot on the gravel. She reached the truck and opened Peter's door. "I thought I was going to die!" She threw herself at him, screaming. "Please don't let her hurt me. I just want to help."

I'd been dead wrong and rotten about her acting abilities. If anyone needed to pursue a career on Broadway or in Hollywood, it was Miss Lorie Allen.

"What is going on here?" His face turned red. "Let me get out of the truck."

Lorie backed away and showed him the red mark where I'd slapped her cheek. The redness was barely visible. "She hit me."

He marched my way. "Are you crazy?"

"As a matter of fact, I am. She's breaking up our engagement on purpose, and she's lying! She said so five minutes ago in the house!" My hands shook and I didn't recognize my voice.

"Lorie?" His teeth were clenched, hands balled into tense fists.

"I don't know what she's talking about. I'm here trying to help, and I'm getting beat up." She touched her cheek. The mark was completely gone.

"Lorie, I'm begging you. Tell him the truth. There is no affair. I made a stupid mistake, and I am terribly sorry." *You are the one having an affair.*

"I've said all I had to say." Lorie stood by the truck with her arms crossed and a less absurd look on her face. "I'm not lying."

"Why are you doing this to me?" I was loud on purpose now. They had to listen to me. "You're crazy, Lorie." I took a step toward her.

She ran behind the truck. "Stop her!"

Peter gripped my arm. "This needs to end."

The madness had to end—not our relationship. "I love you."

"Ana, please leave. We've already said all the things we needed to say. It's best if you leave."

"She's lying to you. There was no affair."

"No, Ana. You're lying. I saw the way you kissed him. Don't try to mess with my head."

"I'm not lying!" I put my finger on his chest. "You're the one having an affair!"

"I don't want to talk about this."

"Well, how convenient." I threw my hands up in the air. "You're accusing me of doing something I didn't do when you are the one doing it." I shook my head. "But you don't want to talk about it."

"Sequence of events, Ana."

"Only the events in your sequence are imaginary. They came out of Lorie's head."

"Ana, stop." Peter raked his fingers through his hair. "I've had enough."

"So have I." It didn't matter what I did, my situation just kept getting worse.

He stared at me with contempt now, like an expert examining a new work by a favorite artist but finding it lacking.

This can't be it. It just can't. "Peter, I know things seem confusing right now, and you probably don't know what to believe. Just take some time. Step back and think. You know me."

"See, that's the thing, Ana. I don't know you." He put both his hands in his pockets and raised his shoulders. "I thought I did."

I shook my head. *Will the truth really come out one day? Or is this really it?* I glanced at Lorie looking all righteous standing by the truck.

"Please leave." Peter took a step toward Lorie.

"Maybe you should try to be alone for one day in your life." *Can't believe he feels it's okay to sleep with Lorie. Sequence of events...* "Time alone will get you thinking right."

He looked at his shoes without uttering a word.

"Some 'help' she's providing you with," I whispered, nodding in Lorie's direction. I wasn't sure if she could hear us.

"Ana, I was alone from the day I found my wife in bed with her news editor, a friend from our time at Auburn, until five months later when the divorce was final."

I am officially a horrible person. I felt small and lifeless, like a sequin that didn't shine. So that's why he'd always been so vague about the divorce. I'd never pressured him for details—half of all marriages end up in divorce anyway—but I wish I'd known. "You never told me..." I said, trailing off when he lifted his hand to stop me.

"And then you asked me out, and I was so happy. I thought what had happened with Catherine had been just bad luck." His face reddened. "And then it happened again." He struggled for control as the words came out through his clenched teeth.

I thought of the pain he must have felt when he saw me with Claus, and the guilt slammed down hard.

"I don't tell anyone. I'm embarrassed by it." He looked down and seemed calmer. "Enough people know about it already."

"Why would you be embarrassed?"

"Well, maybe I am personally insufficient, somehow. She cheated ... and now you. There is a pattern here. It's got to be me. Right?"

"Oh, Peter, you can't be serious."

"Mercy. Stop!" He grabbed his hair with both hands and grunted. "What do I have to do for you to just leave?"

The silence was absolute.

My eyes scanned Peter's perfect property—no longer mine in any way. My hands trembled as I removed his house key from my key chain. "Here."

He took the key. "Thanks." On his face the same agony I'd seen in the morning at the church when he'd asked for his mom's ring. He pressed a fist against unsteady lips.

The lake curled under the cool winter wind. Oh, how I loved that lake. Could it be that I was looking at it for the very last time? Warm tears rolled down my chilled face.

The flowerbeds were being prepared for the upcoming spring. The greenhouse hid Peter's gorgeous ideas and creations. But this year I wouldn't be part of any of it. Spring was going to happen without me.

I looked at the area where we were planning on building a backyard oasis with a swing and a fireplace, and a whimper escaped from my achy throat against my will.

Peter's hand touched mine. He pressed his copy of my apartment key into the palm of my hand. He spoke in the softest and kindest voice I'd heard all day, "I love you, but you must go—you must go *now*. I need this day to end. Can you do that for me?"

I nodded with my eyes closed and my cheeks drenched. *I love you, but...*

As I walked to the car, Peter's black lab, Jäger, dashed toward me from the woods—probably hoping for a ride with the top down.

He was my only ally, and I dried my tears to pat him. "Maybe another day, boy." His soft ears warmed my cold hands. "I will love you always."

I got in the T-Bird and backed out, looking at Peter one more time before turning away from the house and onto the wooded path. *It's over and it's all my fault. My pain and Peter's. I caused it to happen. If only I had stayed away from Claus...*

In my broken heart, a soft melody called me to a better place. In my mind, the piano played and Brian taught: preparation, one, two, three, four—tails in, chin out, port de bras. Delicate and strong. Breathe.

Breathe.

Chapter 6

I got back to Columbus with just enough time to feed Barysh, grab my ballet bag, and get to class.

As expected, only half of the company's dancers showed up. We'd worked hard to make *Romeo and Juliet* happen, and Brian let everyone who wanted to take a week off do so now.

I'd planned to stay in Pine Mountain for a couple of days and then return to the studio, but the fact that my plan hadn't worked out was an understatement, to say the least. *Stupid Lorie—and stupid me.*

She wasn't at the studio, and that was good, of course. But she'd planned to be there, so her absence had to mean that she was still in Pine Mountain with Peter, and that wasn't good at all. Was she going to spend the night? I twisted my mouth and took a deep breath. I had to get my mind out of my misery. *Just don't think about it.*

Claus wasn't in class either. Would I feel better if he were to come? Maybe.

I walked to the rosin box and stepped into it mindlessly with an old pair of pointe shoes I'd decided to pull out for barre. Pointe work was fun for me, and while most ballerinas didn't wear their pointe shoes for the barre portion of class, I usually did. I stepped into the old wooden tray and enjoyed the familiar crushing sound as I applied enough of the amber powder to create good friction between the shoes and floor.

The simple black leotard I wore when everything else was dirty reminded me of growing up dancing. There'd been lots of those. I adjusted the straps and looked in the mirror. My leg warmers needed adjusting too. Walking to the barre, I wrapped on a black skirt that was ancient and entirely too short for my taste—I *had* to do laundry.

Brian started with a simple plié sequence. Ms. Jiménez, the pianist, played the gorgeous but melancholy "Le Lac de Come."

The door opened. Was it him? I looked up. A demi-soloist rushed in and took the first available spot.

A tightness in my chest and in my throat forced me to moan.

The music continued, stabbing me, one note at a time, with its sad beauty.

"Le Lac de Come" is a nocturne, which by definition is a romantic or dreamy piece—"suggestive of the night"—but to me it had always been sad. Why?

Ms. Jiménez smiled and played *forte*.

It was too beautiful. That's what was wrong with it. The piece was about an idyllic lake in Europe and indeed evoked romantic and dreamy thoughts. But my first and only trip to Europe had been a disaster, and my romances and dreams always amounted to nothing.

I was on the verge of tears when the door opened again.

Claus! Thank God.

He took a spot in front of me, and I moved back to give him room.

Seemed like he, too, needed to do some laundry. He was wearing a white T-shirt and black sweat pants, a popular look for guys in the company, but not a Claus signature look.

Still, he was handsome.

The day was unusually warm. Faint sounds of rush hour traffic reached wide open windows, and the late-afternoon sun shone far into the studio through the leafy evergreen trees that lined Broadway.

Ms. Jiménez, who'd had a one-week break, seemed especially inspired this afternoon, playing the music of the most famous ballets, rearranged to suit class combinations.

Brian kept most exercises simple, and, without the mental challenge of more intricate combinations, thoughts of Peter and the ring and of Lorie at his house were always one measure away. I was tempted to let those thoughts reach me—to dwell on them, but I chose not to.

During slow, sustained movements that didn't look pretty for people who didn't have high legs, I was tempted to imagine life with Lorie Allen's extensions, as I often did. But today I didn't.

Instead, stretching to Gallastegui's "Promenade," I found joy in everything that was familiar and beautiful. And I hoped that Claus would want to get together after class. *Might as well hear him out.*

After barre, it was time for a newer pair of pointe shoes. I repeated the rosin routine and picked a spot near the first tall window. The breeze was just right—soft and steady—and the sunshine on my legs and feet made me unusually pliable, casting beautiful long shadows on the marley floor.

Claus picked a spot next to me, and my heart beat a little faster. How could I act like such a silly adolescent? I shook my head in slow motion and got en pointe to let my toes get used to being inside a slightly narrower pair of shoes.

"Here." He stood near, letting me use him for balance. I put my hand on his shoulder and bent my knees, bouncing gently and then stretching my knees again. *Good.*

The smell of his sweet cologne and his sweaty shirt had my attention. I zeroed in on his lips, thinking of salty kisses, and heat flooded my cheeks. *I am so wrong.*

Claus put my leg in arabesque, picking me up with ease and lifting me up high.

"That looks really nice." Brian walked to the front of the room at last and marked the first exercise.

Again we started with simple routines, but ten minutes into the center his excitement picked up with the pace of the combinations.

He stopped us in the middle of a pirouette waltz. "As you all know by now, we are going to dance *Don Quixote* in the upcoming season, and to get ready for it, I want to focus on improving everybody's pirouettes. Ana, do it: preparation, fourth, pirouette."

Doing anything alone in class made me nervous. Doing it in front of Claus was excruciating. But I did it—two solid turns with a bit of a hop in the landing.

"See, what Ana is doing is what everybody is doing: focusing on the landing—on the finish." He stomped his foot and clapped at the same time. "Stay up! Don't worry about the landing. You will land eventually. Gravity will take care of that. I promise you. Worry about staying up there in *relevé*! It's a beautiful place to be." He walked among us, making eye contact with each dancer. "A beautiful place to be, huh? Just stay up."

The class repeated the waltz, and when we finished Brian asked Claus to do the whole combination alone for the rest of us to see.

The spot on the corner of Claus's mouth trembled as he waited for the music to start—the right side. The old nervous tic. One of the best dancers in the world would not be nervous because of a small company class. But a man, best dancer in the world or not, would always be nervous in front of a woman he was trying to impress. *My watching him is getting to him—good.* I looked down and smiled.

He did the combination with pizzazz and finished every pirouette in balance. *Must be nice.*

I might not be able to finish my turns in balance—not en pointe and not every time. *But I can do the pizzazz part. Let's have some fun.*

As Brian marked the first diagonal exercise, all dancers moved to the left back corner. "I want three at a time."

Lorie and I, along with another soloist, Rachel, always got diagonal exercises started, but with both gone I dropped to the back and stayed near Claus.

When it was our turn, no one else joined us.

It was like being on stage all over again—Claus and me, and a grand waltz. I glanced at the mirror when we got to the finishing pose. *We looked good together.*

"I said three, not two." Brian shook his head. "I guess no one wants to get between Romeo and Juliet."

Claus and I did every diagonal together—just us—no one between Romeo and Juliet.

We finished the class with a little bit of partnering. As Claus approached each woman to do the lifts, some blushed. He smiled, trying to put them at ease, but that only made most blush deeper.

We finished with a simple révérence, and all dancers applauded Brian and Ms. Jiménez, thanking them for the class.

I dragged my bag to the sunny spot where I'd done the center to remove my shoes, and Claus practiced some spins as the room slowly emptied.

Alone at last.

"That was fun." He sat across from me and massaged his right knee.

"It was—one of my best ballet classes ever." *I'll remember it forever.* The sun that was shining on me was shining in me too. Who would have thought, after everything that had happened in Pine Mountain? *Just don't think about it.*

I organized my already-organized bag and searched for the keys I knew were in the zipper pocket. It was easier to search in my bag for no reason than to look at him—wondering if he would suggest we get together, wondering if that was even a good idea.

"Can I take you to dinner?" His voice was hardly above a whisper.

I watched the breeze play with his hair. "I need to get home to my dog." I studied his face. His jaw dropped slightly, as did his gaze.

I can't fix my future with Peter, but I can understand my past with Claus... "You can come with me."

"That will be fantastic." He jumped up and reached for my hand, his Duchenne smile full of promise.

When we got to my apartment, we were met by the far-from-homey scent of a dirty dog kennel. "I'm so sorry." I took my fingertips to my nose.

Claus frowned, scanning the room. His eyes stopped on my diapered dog.

"Do you mind waiting on the balcony while I clean him?"

"I don't mind." He opened the sliding glass door and stepped out. "Is it normal for dogs to wear diapers?"

"Some old dogs do. Some don't. Like people." How embarrassing. "It's okay," I whispered to Barysh, bagging the dirty diaper and wipes. "Feel free to close the door—this smell is terrible."

"I'm not going to leave you in there alone with poo." He chuckled. "How old is he?"

"Ten." Claus hadn't lost his sense of humor. Good. I put a large pad under Barysh's derriere and looked into his sweet brown eyes. "I adopted him when he was three. His previous owner was in the Army and had to move to Germany. He didn't want to take him."

Claus approached us and crouched down. "Hi there." Barysh leaned into his hand, enjoying the ear scratch.

"His name is Mikhail Baryshnikov."

"Like the dancer? Your idea?"

"No." I laughed from the kitchen as I pushed the soap pump several times before scrubbing my hands and arms. "The guy's wife used to dance. She was a big fan of Baryshnikov."

"He looks a little bit like Barysh, the dancer." Claus cocked his head and looked at my dog with a smirk. "I think it's the sandy-blond fur."

"No, darling. You look like the dancer." Claus' similarity to Baryshnikov was striking: the thin but well-defined lips, the pointy nose, and the soft blue eyes. The individual parts of both men's faces didn't look particularly appealing, but put together and combined with the virility of their artistic expression—it was enough to make a girl forget to blink and breathe. Oh, and then there was the accent—the sweet little accent—slight, but certainly there.

I shook my head out of dreamland and opened the refrigerator. Good thing I'd stocked up the week before the performance.

The oval wooden platter would do for some Havarti and Jarlsberg cheeses.

"Can I help?" Claus ran his fingers up and down Barysh's chest.

"I'm good." Olives, crackers, and smoked ham along with the cheeses filled the platter, and I set it on the glass coffee table with a matching bowl of sweet green grapes.

Should I use the regular wine glasses? *No, I'm not going to.* I dusted two crystal wine glasses I'd never used instead and took my best bottle of Riesling Spätlese out of the fridge—the Robert Weil Kiedrich Gräfenberg.

"Bring it here. I'll open it." Claus sat on the high pile rug, kicked off his shoes, and grabbed an olive. He examined the label and nodded. "Is it easy to find good German wine here?"

"If you know where to go…"

He opened the bottle with ease, poured a taste, and started inspecting the wine by lifting and tilting the glass.

Claus was a bit of an old soul. Even though he was only two years older than me, he was much more serious, together, and sophisticated. It wasn't a bad thing. I was just surprised I was noticing it for the first time. Or maybe it was more about being European and less about being an old soul. Whatever it was, I liked it.

"This wine is fantastic—well done." He filled both our glasses. "Fantastic place too. Great view of the river."

"Dad heard there's a plan to do something to the river to create rapids right here in downtown."

"In the middle of the city?" He crossed his fingers behind his head and relaxed against the couch.

"I don't understand it either, but I am curious." I scanned my CD shelves. What should we listen to? Claus seemed interested in the architecture, his eyes studying the ceiling and walls. "The building used to be a cotton mill. What you see is a lot of the original architecture: the brick walls, the high ceilings, big windows."

"And your parents?"

"They moved to Pine Mountain two years ago when Dad retired from the clinic." Claus smiled at the mention of Pine Mountain. It was in Pine Mountain where I'd given him my virginity.

I turned to the CD player to hide my hot cheeks. Lorie's insinuation that Claus returned to Germany because I'd given him all he wanted flashed through my mind. *Just don't think about it.* "Anyway, Dad had been going to Callaway Gardens to golf every week, and Mom loves the park too, so they looked at some homes inside the park and fell in love with one." Still Lorie's words rang in my head. *You gave him all he wanted. Of course he ran.*

Norah Jones's debut album had been the soundtrack of my heartache back then, when Claus ran. I found it on my shelf and jumped to the second track before joining him on the rug.

"*Zum Wohl,*" he said, just above a whisper, as he lifted his glass with an alluring smile.

Why *had* he left? "Cheers," I said with a quick lift of my glass. I was surprised by the annoyance in my tone, but I was not about to apologize.

He looked down, his smile altered.

And then I asked, I said it at last, the one word I'd been struggling to utter to him, and the only one that mattered. "Why?"

He took a long sip of wine and a deep breath.

What was he going to say? I covered my mouth and took a deep breath too.

"I love you more than I could ever have loved Hanna."

Had I really heard him use past tense when referring to *her*?

"But she needed me, and we were so young and had so much history. All we ever had growing up was ballet and each other."

"So you just decided—all of a sudden—that you wanted to be with her again?"

"Not like that—"

"She was sleeping around," I interrupted. "That did happen, right? And you guys had been separated for almost a year when we met? Or was that a freaking lie?"

"It wasn't a lie." His voice softened to a whisper. "Please don't swear. It doesn't suit you."

I rolled my eyes but kept silent.

"She called me soon after our relationship had become serious."

Did he mean when we had started sleeping together? I didn't want to ask— he shook as if burning up with fever, obviously struggling to reveal what he was about to say.

"She had been diagnosed with cancer—of the breast."

My hatred for Hanna dissipated like a thin autumn cloud that in one moment is and in the next isn't.

I still didn't like her, though.

"She didn't want anyone in the company to know, so she asked me to go to Wiesbaden to help her fight the cancer and keep her secret—and to dance with her."

"You should have said something."

"I couldn't say goodbye to you, Ana." He finished his wine and poured more for both of us. "If I had told you, you would have talked me out of my decision." He broke eye contact. "But I had it in my mind that going to Hanna was the right thing to do, so I just had to leave."

He lifted his gaze toward the balcony, toward the river, expressionless.

Yes, I would have tried to talk him out of leaving. I searched his silence. Was she okay now? If she had died, he would have said something by now, right?

I reached for a piece of Jarlsberg. "How is she?"

His tender smile was so sad, but his eyes were on me again. "She passed away two years ago."

"Oh, no." I reached for his right hand and held it in both of mine. "No. What happened?" An eight-year battle? I couldn't imagine.

"We fought it. She danced on and off. There was a good stretch of time when the cancer was in remission, and we thought we had beaten it."

His expression turned darker still and reminded me of Peter's—contorted as if crying but with no tears.

"We'd made a baby but she miscarried. She was in bed for weeks after that, and I was beginning to feel there was more to her weakness. A trip to the doctor confirmed my suspicion. The cancer was back. After that, she faded slowly during a very bad year."

"Oh, Claus." I scooted close to him and put my head on his shoulder. "I'm so sorry."

"I'm better now." He put his arm around me and inhaled a deep, steeling breath.

I touched his chest as hot tears welled up in my tired eyes. I'd never told Claus I went to Germany to find him after he'd disappeared. I'd tried to forget him and get over the hurt, but it didn't work, so my mom let me go to Germany to search for answers.

His American company told me he'd gone back to Germany to stay. From there, it was easy to find out he was dancing in Wiesbaden. I arrived in Germany just in time to watch Claus and Hanna perform *Giselle*, the story of a girl who goes mad and dies when she discovers her fiancé, Albrecht, is marrying another woman. Go figure.

Watching *Giselle* in Germany had been heart wrenching on so many levels. Hanna was a much better dancer than me. She had everything: the perfect lines, the perfect body, and the successful career I desperately wanted but suspected wouldn't pan out, as my dad had predicted years earlier. And she had Claus—my Claus.

I'd sat in the hotel room thinking that if it was true that I was not prima ballerina material and also that I couldn't have Claus, I had to come up with something achievable or I would go mad. The dream of performing at the Metropolitan Opera House in New York was born.

That didn't require being the best in a large company. Many companies danced at the Met every year, and the dream wasn't about being the best dancer on that stage but simply being on that stage. I could be in the corps and fulfill my dream.

Sometime during that journey, a new man would come. A good man who I could trust and who would never leave me. I had to believe all those things or my soul would shrivel and die.

"I'm so sorry, Claus." I looked into his sweet blue eyes. "I had no idea."

Giselle must have been as hard for them as it had been for me. At the end of the ballet, Albrecht leaves, knowing he is seeing *Giselle* for the very last time. Claus and Hanna's interpretation had been impeccable. *No wonder.*

We finished eating in silence.

I got us another bottle of wine, an Auslese this time, and then we talked about the trouble he'd caused me with Peter.

"I think we are just unlucky in love," he said with puppy-dog eyes peering at me.

"I just don't understand the deal with Lorie. Do you remember her trying anything with you when you were here for *Paquita*?"

"Not at all. She was young, and talented, and professional—like most girls I meet. That's all. Plus, as soon as I saw you for the first time, I was done. I forgot all about *Paquita*." He put his arm around me again.

Why was I still unsettled in his warm embrace?

Lorie's words still played in the back of my head: *you gave him all he wanted. Of course he ran.* But Claus wasn't that kind of guy. Was he?

"Would it have made a difference if we hadn't slept together?"

"What do you mean?"

"Would you still have left me if we'd waited?" I reached for my glass.

"I guess."

"But you're not sure?"

"I don't think it would have made a difference." He shifted and reached for his glass too. "It would have been a different equation, but the result would probably have been the same. I would still have gone off to do what I felt was my duty."

"Yeah, but maybe I would have been better able to rebuild my life if I hadn't given you so much of me."

"Only God knows what if, Ana," he whispered. "Let's not do this, okay?" He drew me closer and teased my neck with his lips. "I just want you."

His words came out more like a whisper. A soul sound—not a mouth sound. I closed my eyes and focused on his tender kisses and the breeze from the balcony. *Only God knows what if.* I heard his voice in my mind as I took a deep breath. *Let's not do this.* His words echoed within me again as I exhaled, the tension of my miserable day leaving my body like a high fever—suddenly, inexplicably, mercifully.

Claus removed the bobby pins and elastic from my hair and placed me on a large corner pillow on the rug.

He lay down next to me, wrapped his arms gently around me, and kissed my cheek first, then the corner of my mouth, then my lips. *No...*

But being together felt so right. What did I have to lose?

Closing my eyes and kissing him back, I felt like the virgin I once was in those same arms. Ten years of separation dissolved in ten seconds, and I wanted to make love like we used to—before there was so much pain and sorrow in our worlds. But I couldn't.

"Claus, I'm sorry." I pushed gently at his chest and stopped the kiss. "I can't."

"Don't be sorry. I'm in no hurry, Ana."

His face was so beautiful, his eyes hopeful like *Giselle's* Albrecht, but it was too soon.

"No hurry whatsoever." He wrapped me in his arms, and his warm lips brushed my forehead. "You've had a terrible day. You should go to sleep, darling girl."

"You're right about that." I exhaled hard. First the engagement ring, then Lorie, then Peter telling me about his ex-wife, then the key exchange ... I swallowed the lump that had risen in my throat. *Just don't think about it.* "I absolutely should go to sleep."

He got up with ease.

"But please don't leave." I didn't want to be alone. *Please stay.* I hoped with all my heart that he would. *Stay.*

"I'm not going anywhere you don't want me to go." He picked me up and looked toward the bedroom door.

I nodded. "You can sleep on the couch."

"Barysh doesn't snore, does he?"

"No." I shook my head and chuckled. "You'll be okay."

"Good."

He placed me on my bed with the same care he used when putting Lady Juliet on hard stage props. "Covers?"

"Please."

Claus shook open my beige woolen blanket. The soft fabric caressed my cheek before resting on my chest.

"Can I get you some water?"

"No, thank you." Outside my bedroom window, a storm was forming. Bright lightning contrasted with soft rolling thunder. "Take a blanket from that pile." I pointed at a stack by the window.

"I will. Thanks." He scanned the skies beyond the room. "Do you mind if I take a shower and stay up a while?"

"I don't mind, but that's the only shower." I pointed to my bathroom.

"You need to rest. Maybe in the morning, if you don't mind?"

"That's fine. Just don't look this way when you come in if you wake up before me."

"Promise." He cupped my face and kissed my cheek.

He let his cheek rest on mine, and I enjoyed the warmth of his touch.

"Good night, Ana."

"Good night, Claus." I followed him with my eyes as he grabbed the top blanket from the pile, exited my room, and closed the door behind him.

I touched my cheek, where his lips had been. Who would have thought the day would end this way—with Claus on my couch. And Peter with Lorie.

The soft covers caressed my chin, and I tried to get comfortable. Turning to the large window and massaging my left ring finger, I watched as the first raindrops landed on the glass.

Was Peter watching the rain too? Was he with her? My lips quivered, and I cried the quietest tears as I watched the rain become a storm.

Don't. Think. About. It. Peter was gone. Claus was here and still would be in the morning.

What then?

Chapter 7

I woke up to the sound of Claus taking a shower. The rest of the world seemed still and absolutely quiet.

My left arm was uncovered, and my gaze went straight to the ring-less finger that mocked me with its small indentation. *I love you, but...* How long would it take for the engagement ring mark to disappear? A week? A month? It would mock me until then. I had failed miserably.

As I turned to the window, my eyes adjusted slowly to the midmorning sun that streamed in, making my bedroom unusually bright. Outside, wet treetops and rooftops glistened. I covered my head with the blanket and remembered with a sigh the conversation from the previous night.

It would have been a different equation.

Why did I care? I shook my head. Why. Did. I. Care?

You gave him all he wanted. Of course he ran.

I needed coffee, but how could I make myself presentable without going into my bathroom? And I needed a shower too.

He turned off the water.

My breaths came suddenly hard and short. Was having Claus near me a good idea or a bad one? The shower curtain opened, then closed.

Looking at the bathroom door, I pulled the blanket tighter around me. He fumbled with the handle. *Please be dressed.* I kept one eye open, my face scrunched up.

He opened the door slowly, wearing only a towel around his waist. The smell of soap and thick vapor spilled out of the bathroom after him. "Good morning." His right hand went up to the side of his face like a horse's blinder, and he hurried toward the living room.

"Good morning." My hair was flat against my head and felt oily. My skin was dry. Surely I was a sight. *Some beauty sleep.* But he hadn't looked, as promised.

I eased my way out of bed and tiptoed to the door. "I'm going to take a shower." I hid by the door waiting for an answer.

He didn't answer.

"Make yourself at home," I said a little louder. Had he heard me?

"Okay." His voice was upbeat. I remembered him as a morning person—he'd definitely not changed much.

It sounded like he was in the kitchen. Maybe he would make some coffee for us.

I broke into the Crabtree & Evelyn Nantucket Briar soap and lotion set I got at the company's Christmas party last year and breathed in. The soft powdery fragrance was perfect.

After a slow shower, I put on the lotion, combed my hair, and applied light-pink gloss, eyeliner, and mascara.

I dressed in a new sky-blue romper and chose a pair of simple champagne pearl earrings that complemented the look. Checking the mirror before walking out of the bathroom, I felt good. Not too much. Just right.

As I got near the kitchen, I smelled the fresh coffee and saw that Claus had the small kitchen table ready for breakfast.

A bouquet of white lilies my parents had given me after Saturday's performance graced the rustic table. Next to it, Polish pottery dishes intricately patterned with blue butterflies, large yellow flowers, and tiny orange daisies held ham, cheese, big chunks of honeydew mixed with plump blueberries and neatly arranged croissants, butter, and jellies.

But where was he?

I found him by the speaker dock, his iPod queuing to play something. He'd already moved the coffee table off the white shag rug, creating an improvised dance floor. What was he up to?

He pushed the play button before I could tell him I needed to take Barysh out and feed him. Soon the first notes of OneRepublic's "Come Home" filled the space between us. The piano was slow and strong.

"Dance with me, Ana." Claus walked to the middle of the rug and held out his hand.

He wore a snug black tank top and dark jeans. He was barefoot like me. A corner of his mouth lifted, and his blue eyes gleamed. Perfect posture. How could he be so beautiful? I took in the sight of him. Claus Vogel Gert. *The* Claus Vogel Gert. In my apartment.

His thick blond hair was almost dry, and a lock on his forehead invited a caress. He drew one side of his lower lip between his teeth. Oh, how I wanted to kiss and tease those lips.

"Yes? Will you dance with me?" He lifted his hand a little higher.

Looking down to hide the heat in my cheeks, I took a deep breath—no kennel smell, just good smells of coffee, bread, and my soap. Would Barysh make it through the song? *Hang in there, bud—one for the team.*

I walked to Claus, a big smile stretching my lips. The softness of the rug added to the dreamlike quality of the moment. My hand reached out to meet his, and I noticed goosebumps on his forearm. My fingers brushed the skin of his hand to find the perfect fit. *I love you.*

He pulled me near, kissing my fingertips, then my hand, his lips warm and soft. Slow dancing, he looked at me with misty eyes darkened by his black shirt.

My eyes gazed into his. *I love you—I always have.*

I felt his fingers applying gentle pressure on the small of my back, moving our hips closer together until no space remained between us. Resting his cheek against mine, he whispered sweet lyrics in my ear, his breath caressing my skin with every sentence.

What would it be like to have his lips and breath on my body again? My unsteady hands held him tighter, and my heart beat to the rhythm of his words. *Should I be doing this? I gave him... He ran... I can't go through that again. I can't do anything that will make him leave me.*

His lips brushed mine. *I don't know what to do.* I didn't respond.

"Sorry." He put some space between us.

"It's okay. I didn't mean to freeze on you. Don't be sorry." *I don't know how to change—I don't think I can.* Some people were good at guarding their heart, but not me. I teased his lips with mine before kissing him softly. *This is who I am. This is what I do.*

He pulled back and looked at me one more time before losing himself in long, deep kisses.

"*Ich liebe dich,*" he whispered, picking me up in his arms.

"I love you too." I felt like unsettled Jell-O melting through his fingers.

He smiled and rocked me to the music. "Come to Germany with me, Ana." His voice was casual, as if he'd just asked me to follow him to the market or some other place around the corner.

"I can't go to Germany." I chuckled. He couldn't possibly be serious.

"We could live together, dance together, travel." His voice trailed off as he put me down, and, holding my head with both his hands, he searched for an answer in my eyes. "Come home with me."

"Come home?" I echoed in a whisper. "But that's absurd..."

"Why?"

"I don't know. It just is."

He put his arms around me, swaying to the music. "Come home, Ana. We belong together."

Home? I kept my eyes closed and felt Claus's fingertips caress my neck. Being with him was certainly home. Peter didn't understand me like Claus did. Only a dancer could really understand another dancer—the emotions, the soul, the passion for the art form.

"Come with me, Ana."

There wasn't much left for me in Georgia. A ruined relationship and a company at which I'd been too long and where there was little hope of progression now.

If I didn't go with Claus, I could still audition in Atlanta.

But without Peter by my side, the idea seemed dull.

Germany? Move?

"What about my things?" I opened my eyes in a daze.

"Bring them. Leave them. Up to you."

"But my car ... and Barysh?"

"We will ship the car. We will bring Barysh."

I couldn't believe I was even considering this. It was the wrong answer. Peter could still change his mind.

Claus looked into my eyes again. "Didn't you say Barysh was abandoned because his old family didn't want to take him to Germany?"

"Yes..." Where was he going with that?

"Do it for him then. He's a sweet dog, yes? Let him see Germany."

I had to laugh. "Like you care. Look at you being all sly."

"I do care."

"Oh yeah?" I walked toward my old dog and was about to say Claus hadn't thought about him and his needs since waking up when I noticed Barysh had a fresh pad, fresh water, and was sleeping peacefully.

When I looked back at Claus, he was smirking. "He ate and he's clean. I even took him to the balcony to air out."

"Touché," I said teary eyed. "You didn't have to..." I looked out the window and took a deep breath.

A white heron stood on the bank of the rain-swollen river, looking in the direction of the submerged rocks where he normally stood.

Germany, huh? I watched the water flowing—voluminous and fast.

It was an illusion to think I could get Peter back. Much like the heron, I had lost my rock. My life with Peter was over—washed away, out of my control, by waters more powerful than me.

Like the heron, why not look for a new safe place to stand?

Chapter 8

Sitting across from my parents at their tall kitchen table, I waited for them to digest my explanation of the Peter situation before dropping the bomb about Germany.

Mom's new lavender tablecloth bunched near her little ivy pot as I pushed the saltshaker around the table, but she didn't rush to fix it. Didn't even seem to notice.

She must be taking the Peter news hard—it wasn't like her not to try to fix everything within her reach. I put the shaker back on the silver holder, next to the pepper, and smoothed the cloth before picking up my coffee mug.

The Brazilian-style flan she'd made for me remained untouched at the center of the table. Studying her face, I noticed some redness on her nose and upper lip. Was she going to cry?

Outside their cottage window, daylight was fading away as I watched the chickadees and warblers fight for a spot on the old bird feeder.

My parents lived in the Longleaf residential area of Callaway Gardens. Their yard could have been bigger, but I liked the cottage—a three-bedroom modern home with large windows. It had a room for me and a room for my brother, Michael, who was studying pre-med at the University of Alabama and still came home when he ran out of clean clothes.

Dad finally broke the silence. "Honey, let me go talk to Peter." He reached for my hand.

"No, Dad." I smiled at his suggestion. "I appreciate the offer, though."

Just say it. Tell them you have a plan.

"You should have come to us sooner, Ana." Mom blew her nose. "And how about Lorie? At my age, I shouldn't be surprised by the things people do out of envy, but for crying out loud, you guys were best friends." She grabbed another tissue. "And wasn't she seeing someone?"

"She'd been dating a guy from the symphony, a handsome violinist from someplace in Eastern Europe. It seemed serious, but I haven't seen them together lately." I tried to remember who'd told me they were talking about getting married. Brian?

"Maybe something happened there," Dad said.

"Maybe." I shrugged. "Obviously, they're no longer together, as she seems to be with Peter now." I shook my head at the absurdity of that statement. "I think she's lost it—literally. The part about loving my men was pretty ridiculous, but to say that God is dead? Who says stuff like that?"

"God forbid." Mom made the sign of the cross.

"I don't remember the last time I heard you talk about God." Dad looked at me as though he were examining a lab rat, wondering what strange thing it would do next.

"I know, Dad. I just don't understand people who read the Bible all the time, and think it's some magical book with all the answers to life." I folded my napkin and hoped they wouldn't ask me when I had last read from its pages. "It's a book—a very old book with very old ideas." I put the napkin down and looked at my parents. "And I can't understand God either. I don't even know Him. But I can't let go of the notion either."

"The notion?" Dad rested his chin on his hand, still studying me.

"Yeah, the notion. I mean, when something is really important, I do pray."

"To someone you don't understand or know?"

"Well, Dad, when you put it that way, I feel pretty stupid."

"I'm just curious."

I remembered the way I'd felt at the chapel—sad and confused, but not alone. "There is something to it." I looked at my parents. They didn't go to church often, but they did read the Bible sometimes. Mom liked Psalms. "God's there. He loves me. I'm just not ready to explore the idea any further, I guess."

They nodded silently, wearing matching expressions and polo shirts. Did they realize they were matching? It was sweet, on purpose or otherwise. Were they going to drop the God subject now? Maybe it was a good time to bring up the future and Claus's invitation.

Mom spoke before I could insert Germany into the conversation. "And you said Lorie was watching Maya Plisetskaya in *Carmen Suite*?"

"Yep." At least the spotlight was on Lorie again. I picked up a spoon and started eating the flan from the main bowl.

"The Carmen from the Bizet opera?" Dad cocked his head. "Is it a ballet too?"

"It is, but the story of Carmen in the ballet is somewhat different from the story of Carmen in the opera." Mom got up and started a fresh pot of coffee. "In the ballet she is the same free-spirited woman, but the sole focus is the love triangle. The set for the whole thing is a bullring, and you have a judge and spectators representing society's disapproval of her unconventional behavior. In the end, when Don José stabs her to death, she'd been dancing alternatively with him and Escamillo. And with Fate."

"Fate?" Dad scrunched up his face. "Who's Fate? And isn't Escamillo bullfighting when Carmen dies?"

"Well, in the ballet they are all dancing together." Mom sat with us again as the coffeemaker snorted behind her. "Remember the fortune-teller in the opera?"

"Yeah."

"In the ballet the fortune-teller is Fate, Carmen's alter ego, and she shows up as a bull in the closing scene. She dies too."

"Lovely." Dad chuckled. "Doesn't sound like the kind of ballet a sweet Christian girl would be interested in."

"Well, we are not talking about a sweet Christian girl anymore, are we?" Mom started picking at the flan too.

"She said she was done being good." I reached for my purse on the china cabinet to get a mint. What was that psalm she'd told me to look up? Mom would probably know it. It was best not to say anything about a psalm, though, or we would end up discussing religion all over again. "Lorie was probably watching *Carmen Suite* to learn how to be different. I don't know. That girl is a mess right now. Maybe something happened with the violin guy, like Dad said, and it's made her crazy." I stretched my mug toward Mom and hoped she would refill it.

Instead, Mom just studied me.

"Can I have more coffee?" She was still staring. "Please?"

She reached for the mug, her cold hand lingering on mine before she turned to pour the coffee. Dad already had the pot and helped.

"I can't help but wonder if Claus was somehow involved in Lorie's plot." Mom slid the sugar and creamer my way. "How else would she have known something was going to happen between you two on stage that night?"

"Mom, no. Come on." *Of course he wasn't involved.* "Claus loves me. He would never do that." Was she serious? "Lorie and I were best friends when Claus and I met. Maybe she went to him that day and told him I wanted to talk. He would have listened to her. Who knows?"

"Did you ask him?" Dad raised an eyebrow.

"No... Stop, guys. Please."

Mom got up and walked to my purse. "You should ask him." She pulled the scarf out of my purse like a magician, the fabric accusing me, one faded cherry at a time.

Dad groaned. I guess he remembered the aqua chiffon scarf too.

"I'm not asking," I said. "I know the answer. He has nothing to do with Lorie's madness." I took the scarf from Mom's hand and put it back in my purse before zipping the bag. "Having Claus by my side right now is the only thing keeping me from going crazy. Don't ruin this for me, please."

We sat in silence, and Mom's eyes were bright with tears.

This is as good a time as any. "There is something—"

"What are you going to do now?" Dad asked, interrupting me.

I can't say it. It will break their hearts.

He held Mom's hands. "Honey, do tell."

"I'm moving in with Claus." I lowered my head. I couldn't watch them hurt. "I'm going to Germany."

"Are you getting married?" Mom sounded more surprised than heartbroken.

"I don't know. Not now, if that's what you are asking."

"And how is that different from what Peter is doing with Lorie?" Mom's voice had gone from surprised to harsh and accusatory. "Ana, you can't be serious." She slammed both hands on the table and startled me. "You two hardly know each other. And I wasn't going to say anything, but guess what? You should not have kissed him in the first place. I taught you better."

Here we go. "Tell me how you really feel?"

"Don't give me an attitude. You know I'm right."

Sure. You're always right.

Dad looked at her, his eyes sad.

"What is it about this guy?" Mom paced, running her hands through her hair. "He has a gift for ruining your life. This is not happening. Not again. I already watched him break your heart once. I don't want that to happen to you again."

I fought the urge to cry.

"Don't make a decision now." Dad sat next to me at the kitchen table. "You and Peter just broke up. You haven't even had time to process that. How can you possibly make a life-changing decision now?"

"It doesn't have to be a life-changing decision." I imitated his solemn tone. "If it doesn't work out, I'll come back. What I cannot do is go back to the company and look at Lorie every day."

"Weren't you going to audition for some companies in Atlanta?" Mom walked to the window, taking a deep breath.

"I don't want to audition in Atlanta without Peter by my side."

"What does one thing have to do with the other?" Dad tapped his fingers on the table.

"Everything. Dancing in Atlanta was part of my life-with-Peter plan." I put life-with-Peter in air quotes. "Why can't you guys be happy for me? I'm trying to get over this craziness with Peter and Lorie, and you're not helping. A door closed and it hurts—believe me, I get it—but another door has opened, and things just may turn out awesome."

"Take a vacation in Germany, then, instead of moving there." Mom's voice dripped with sarcasm. "How about that for an idea?"

Closing my eyes, I put my lips together in a thin, tight line. There was no arguing with her. She'd made up her mind.

"Sweetie, forgive your mom." Dad held his half-empty coffee mug with both hands and stared at the hot liquid. "But like she said, we don't want to see him break your heart again—we don't think a move overseas right now is what's best. You're a wonderful young woman, but you have this awful habit of wanting things to be black or white, and that's hardly ever the case."

Things were black or white for me, but I nodded to be agreeable. Dad knew how to disarm me.

"Think about a visit instead of a move, like Mom said. We can keep Barysh, and you can go travel, clear your head—enjoy time with Claus even. How about that?"

I looked out the window beyond the bird feeder, beyond the woods.

"Or don't go at all." Mom sat with us. "You were a beautiful Juliet. I bet you'll get more lead roles now."

"Maybe in another ten years." I'd already seen Brian and Lorie working on some *Don Quixote* solos.

"Nonsense."

"Mom, Lorie is already rehearsing *Don Quixote*. She's the lead, as always." My eyes filled up with tears.

Hers did too. She shook her head, and her shoulders dropped.

We struggled to communicate with words sometimes, but ballet we both understood. She knew that with no prospect of moving up in the company, it would be difficult to keep me from moving.

She reached for my hands. "Well, would you dance in Germany?"

"I would audition for the Rhine-Main Ballet and see what happens. Maybe they will let me be stage decoration."

They ignored my sarcasm.

"How soon would you go?" Dad took a deep breath.

"In a couple of weeks."

"A couple of weeks?" Mom asked. "Don't you need a visa? Doesn't that take time?"

"Not right away. With my American passport, I can enter and stay for three months. The company will help me apply for an artist visa once I'm there."

"What if they don't offer you a position?"

"I don't know, Mom. I don't have all the answers." *I guess we would get married.*

"Let's back up a minute." Dad looked at Mom. "Weren't we trying to talk her into staying? Hadn't we agreed that this was all too soon and that the potential for Claus to break her heart again was too great?"

"We're still trying, but did you hear her say that after all her hard work and the Juliet success, Lorie got the lead in *Don Quixote?*"

Dad took my hands from Mom's and searched my eyes. "Stop talking about moving like it's going to happen and promise you'll think about every angle to this, okay?"

"Okay…"

They had my room arranged just the way it was in our old house in Columbus, with my twin bed, ballet posters, vanity … everything the same. I liked knowing I still had a room in their home, and I loved having a place to keep all the things that were still dear to me but didn't really belong in my adult life: my first pair of pointe shoes, my Strawberry Shortcake collection, my Care Bears, music boxes, a series of middle school paintings that were surprisingly good, journals, books, and old photos—lots of old photos.

I flopped down on my old bed after a long bath. I wasn't sure I would be able to sleep. My parents obviously didn't approve of my plan to move to Germany. And I wasn't sure I wanted to go without their support.

After a phone call to Claus, who was in Atlanta visiting old friends, I sat at my childhood desk.

The past few days had been great, but what would we be like in two weeks or two months? How about two years? Mom was right—Claus and I didn't really know that much about each other anymore. We were working overtime trying to be our best selves, but what would happen next? Who would we become as a couple?

Why did I hate to admit that my mom was right sometimes? It wasn't lack of love—I loved her. I just hated when she was right. I always had, and, I was willing to bet, I always would. Was it her attitude? Maybe. She seemed to gloat every time she proved me wrong.

But I wouldn't cross an ocean out of spite. Something was pushing me toward Europe. *Something other than desperation.* I laughed at myself. *Something right.*

I turned on the desktop computer and waited for the old machine to boot up. Tucked away with my First Communion book was my old Bible, looking as new as ever. I reached for it and opened it somewhere in the middle. Isaiah 41. I closed my eyes and put my finger on a verse. Isaiah 41:10: "Fear thou not; for I am with thee: be not dismayed; for I am thy God: I will strengthen thee; yea, I will help thee; yea, I will uphold thee with the right hand of my righteousness."

Okay, that's officially weird.

I closed the book and pushed it away. The urge to read on was palpable but easily squelched.

Noticing the bright colors flashing from the computer screen, I was about to click on my picture folder but decided to surf the web instead. "No use in looking back." I glanced at the Bible one more time before typing "RHINE-MAIN BALLET" in the search box.

Within seconds pictures of the theater, the principals, and the soloists scrolled across my screen. I remembered most from weeks before when I was trying to find Hanna. Then I studied the photos of the corps. Would I be among them one day?

I clicked on the schedule for the upcoming season and started dreaming. Would I be watching or would I be on stage?

The company was dancing primarily at the Hessische Staatstheater Wiesbaden, but there was a trip to Prague coming up in the spring and then a one-evening event in Paris later in the year.

Below all the dates and details, I saw a link for the following year's schedule and clicked on it. It was sketchy—with dates, locations, and some of the programs, but no cast lists. But there it was—a mixed bill at the Met. There were no details about which works would be presented, but that wasn't important. It was *the Met*.

My upper body hit the back of the chair with enough force to make it roll back a foot. "Now that, boys and girls, is fate." I spun the office chair in a thousand happy spins, accompanied by a thousand muffled squeals.

Chapter 9

Fumbling with a keychain that grew lighter every day, I closed my apartment door for the very last time on the day before our Lufthansa flight to Frankfurt. A cold, ordinary Thursday to everyone else—extraordinary to me.

Closed and locked. I exhaled hard. That'd been my first time living by myself. Had it been the last?

Dad would be arriving any minute to take me to Pine Mountain for my last night in America, but I couldn't bring myself to walk away from that closed door.

Resting my forehead against it, memories of two great years flashed before my eyes: parties, friends, and dinners, but quiet nights too—nights watching ballets with Barysh and dreaming of a future I didn't yet have. Then I met Peter.

Peter had visited me in Columbus very little because of the ranch and the nature of his work, so I didn't have very many memories of him at the apartment.

It was the quiet nights with Barysh that I was going to miss the most. Images of the moonlight painting the Chattahoochee River white and silver, and of the lights of Uptown Columbus, filled my mind. Uncontrollable sobs followed.

What if I hated living in Germany? What if nothing worked out? Was I making a terrible mistake? *Argh. Last time closing the door... Last time in my own place... Last time in America... Too many lasts—it's messing with my head.*

"Ma'am, are you okay?" The voice came from a couple of doors down.

"I'm so sorry." I wiped my cheeks with my fingers and looked in the direction of the male voice that'd startled me. A red-haired young man in an Army uniform stood outside a nearby door. I'd never seen him before. "I'm okay. Just being melodramatic—sorry—it runs in the family."

"Happens to the best of us." He looked at the two large suitcases next to me. "Traveling?"

"Moving." I shouldn't have lingered. The guy seemed alright, but I had no desire to make small talk.

"Where to?" He stuffed his hands in his pockets, looking like he planned to stay a while.

"Germany."

"No way. I just came from there." He took a few steps forward without coming all the way to my door and leaned against the wall. "I was stationed in Baumholder."

I'd never heard of it. "I'm going to Wiesbaden." Studying his uniform, I recognized the rank insignia—captain—and the combat infantryman badge. I'd dated an infantryman from neighboring Fort Benning in my early twenties. He'd had one too.

"Wiesbaden is nice and has a large U.S. Army presence. Are you in the army?"

"No." I chuckled. "I'm a ballerina."

"Oh, so you'll be dancing there?"

"That's the idea."

"It can get lonely out there on the economy. I'm not sure you can get on post, but if you want to find the American community, look for a Baptist church outside the main gate. There's always a Baptist church outside the main gate of overseas posts—at least everywhere I've been."

Why would I go all the way to Germany to look for Americans? And what was the economy? Sounded like something I should know. "The economy?"

"Off post."

"Oh…" He was probably picturing me all alone out there. "My boyfriend is German. That's why I'm moving."

"So, you're getting married. Congratulations!"

Him and Mom—what's with the getting married thing? I really had to get going. "My dad is picking me up. I've got to go. It was nice talking to you."

"Do you need help with your bags?"

"Nope. I'm fine." Attaching my carry-on to one of the large suitcases, I prepared to walk away.

"Well, best of luck to you … I didn't catch your name."

I looked back. "Ana."

"I'm John." He waved. "Good luck, Ana."

"Thanks."

Once in the lobby, I walked quickly to the desk. "I need to return my keys."

"Very well, Ms. Ana." The manager at the desk watched me remove the apartment and mailbox keys from the ring. "We have an envelope for you."

"Oh, okay." Probably more paperwork. I gave him the keys, and he gave me the envelope. But it wasn't paperwork. What he'd handed me was a square pink envelope that looked more like a CD sleeve. It had my name handwritten on it—Peter's handwriting. "Thanks." My eyes burned, but no tears came. "Is that everything?" Had he noticed my voice was altered?

"Yes ma'am, that's everything. Come see us if you're ever in town again. Best of luck."

"Thanks." I walked over to my suitcases and opened the envelope with unsteady hands. The envelope smelled of Gucci Gorgeous Gardenia, the perfume he'd chosen for me when we started dating. Inside, a Kenny Rogers CD titled *A Love Song Collection*, and a note that read, "For the road."

"Islands in the Stream" was track thirteen. It'd been our song since the first night we'd danced together. *Peter* ... I touched his words.

Yes, I'd made a bad choice, but we could have moved beyond it. Too bad he didn't see it that way.

In the two weeks since the breakup, I'd come to terms with his position, and in my heart our relationship was no longer defined by that final hour. Memories of lazy afternoons at Callaway Gardens and of planting—lots of planting—filled my head. I would miss him.

Placing the envelope and its contents in my biggest bag, I closed another door and rolled my suitcases outside to wait for Dad.

Bundled up by the cold river, I looked up at my balcony and windows one last time. The future I had dreamed of started now. Life in Germany was going to be good, and I couldn't wait to see Claus at the airport in the morning.

Chapter 10

I think you have an escort." Dad's eyes were fixed on the rearview mirror as he merged onto I-85 on the way to the Hartsfield–Jackson Atlanta International Airport.

I turned back to see what he was staring at. The Silverado. "No way." It was Peter and Jäger. Clenching my chest, I tried to keep my heart from beating like a washing machine with an uneven load. *What is he doing here?*

He pulled up next to the SUV—next to Dad.

If only I could get a better look at his face and study his expression. But his eyes were on the road ahead, and I couldn't see much past Dad and past Jäger.

"What is he doing?" Dad kept one eye on the Silverado and one on the road.

"I have no idea." Was it a coincidence? He sure didn't look like he'd come to stop us. Good thing Mom had said goodbye at home—this would have done her in.

Dad shrugged in the direction of the truck as if asking, "What's going on?"

Stretching toward the windshield, I saw Peter's hand waving us off.

My heart did a free-fall act within my chest. *What in the world?* If he didn't come to stop us, then why was he there?

"What do you want me to do?" Dad covered my hand with his, the steady warmth of his touch contrasting with my chilled fingers.

"Nothing, I guess. Maybe it's a coincidence. How would he have known that we would be on the road on this day at this time?"

Dad turned on the CD player. His Willie Nelson CD was in, and the slow notes of "Stardust" lulled me.

I took a deep breath and exhaled slowly.

"You can play something else." Dad placed the small case he kept in the SUV on my lap.

"This is perfect." I closed my eyes and pictured the Kenny Rogers CD and Peter's note. What would he do when we reached the airport exit? Was he working up the courage to do something?

Closer to Atlanta, Peter switched lanes on us and pulled next to my side of the SUV.

"This is getting ridiculous—you kids are torturing yourselves." Dad shook his head, his voice stern. "If you want me to lose him, let me know, and I will."

Chuckling at the thought of Dad speeding to get away from the Silverado, I offered him a tender smile. "Thanks, Dad."

"I really will lose him, if you ask me to."

"I know. But you don't have to. We're almost there." I didn't have to look at Peter to feel his presence. Twisting my head to the side in slow motion, our eyes met for the first time since the Lorie fiasco and the key exchange at the ranch.

It'd been much easier to maintain my resolve when all I had in front of me was a note and a CD. Facing the man was much harder.

What if I stayed? What if I asked Dad to pull over? The idea was tempting.

But something propelled me to stay the course instead—the new course: Europe, Claus, the Met.

A critical voice inside me screamed "self-serving brat."

But a stronger and serene voice said, "Go—this is a season to go." There was peace in the middle of the heartache when I thought of going. There was no peace when I thought of staying. I had to go. Right?

As we got close to the exit to the airport, Willie was singing "Georgia on My Mind." *Really?* Maybe that's why Dad had suggested a different CD.

The thought of leaving Georgia hurt my heart—I'd never lived in any other state.

I looked at my ex-fiancé again. I was going to miss Peter. No doubt about that. Tears soaked his face now. His lips moved. He repeated my name twice. I swallowed the lump that had formed fast in my throat.

This was it. This was our moment. If I was going to do something, this was the time. I turned to him, both hands on the window.

He looked at me and seemed receptive—expectant even.

A truck passed us. *Beeeep, beep-beep-beep.*

"Whatever," Dad mumbled.

A season to go. A season to fly high. I nodded slowly. *A season to dance.* I planted a kiss on my shaky fingertips and pressed them against the cold window.

Peter hit the steering wheel with his fist, his forehead furrowed, lips pressed together. I looked at his red eyes and covered my mouth, holding back words and emotions that didn't belong.

My head dropped and hot tears fell on my lap. By the time I looked up again, Peter had accelerated, and all I could see was the back of his head, the back of Jäger's head, and the back of the truck.

Traffic was thick, and the blue skies over the busy Atlanta airport were crowded with airplanes arriving and leaving.

Dad got behind Peter to take the airport exit.

This is it. The turn signal sound was like a steady heartbeat. I was doing the right thing, wasn't I? Why was it so hard? Looking at the truck heading north, I screamed into my hands and kept my face there.

When I lifted my head, we were approaching the terminal parking. I turned to the door and held my knees with a whimper.

"Shh." Dad touched my hair. "It'll be okay."

My tears slowed under his touch. "This looks all wrong, and I know I messed it all up, but it feels right at the same time, Dad." I sniffed hard and turned to him. "I'm not making any sense, am I?"

"We're always here for you." He kept a firm hand on my shoulder.

We parked but I didn't move. Dad didn't show any intent to get out of the SUV either. With his less-than-stellar voice, he started to sing with Willie Nelson to "On the Sunny Side of the Street."

"Oh, you sing horribly." I laughed.

"Then you do a better job." He danced with his shoulders, moving them up and down to the happy beat. "Got you laughing."

I shook my head. "Let's get this show on the road."

He cut the engine. "Let us, baby girl."

We met Claus at the terminal.

Between my luggage, Claus's luggage, and the dog, it took us almost one hour to check in, and by the time Barysh had been taken care of, I'd run out of things I cared to say before embarking on my most ambitious adventure ever.

"Dad, I want to be done with the heartbreaking part of the program." I squeezed my eyes shut and opened them back up. "Can we go to the gate?"

"Of course." He held my hand, and we started walking to the security checkpoint. Claus walked a few steps behind us.

Was this really happening? Was I really saying goodbye to everything and everyone? We walked in silence and arrived too soon. I didn't want to let go of his hand now.

Until two years ago, I was still living with Mom and Dad. Then we were almost an hour apart. Now a whole ocean? *This is hard.*

Dad put his strong arms around me. "If you hate it, come back and fast," he whispered, squeezing me.

I squeezed him back and nodded in his embrace. We swayed to the sounds of the busy terminal. "I'm so scared," I whispered.

"Don't be." His voice was gentle but assuring. "Go have an adventure."

I nodded. *An adventure.*

"I love you, baby girl."

"I love you too, Dad."

"Son, good luck to you guys." Dad gave Claus a strong hug and patted his back.

"Thank you, Mr. Brassfield." Claus looked more serious than usual. "I will take good care of her, and you are welcome to visit any time."

Dad's face was turning red, and he bit his lower lip as he nodded with his fist to his mouth. His eyes filled up with tears. "We'll visit."

His voice was brittle, and so was my heart when I heard him. I wished things had been different. Surely that was not how he'd imagined giving me away. And I was going to be so far. Did I trust myself to give him one more hug without both of us falling apart?

Claus helped me with my handbag, the old neck scarf tied to it.

"Let me get the scarf," I said, untying it. I put it around my neck and kissed Dad gently on the cheek.

I reached for Claus's hand with all the confidence I could muster, and we started a slow backward walk.

Quiet tears couldn't stop me from smiling and waving. "Give me a couple of months to get settled, Dad. Then I expect you and Mom to come see us."

"We will, honey." He sounded better, but I could see the distant tears rolling down his aging face.

I waved one more time, and then we turned away. Away from Dad and away from Georgia.

Dad's words still played in my head: *if you hate it, come back and fast.* My eyes rested on Claus's handsome face. His eyes were red, his hand firm on mine. I wasn't going to hate it. I was moving to Europe.

Claus Vogel Gert was holding my hand. *The* Claus Vogel Gert. Would I ever get over how famous he was now?

We were going to take classes together and dance together, and I was going to get my shot at the Met. And could it be that I would be Mrs. Gert one day? *Frau Gert. Wow.*

If Claus could hear the adolescent squeals that filled my head, he would leave me in America. With a smile stretching my lips, I took off my old boots and tossed them in the gray bin at the top of a short stack.

"What are you humming?" Claus placed his tan leather shoes side by side in a different bin.

I hadn't realized I was humming, but as soon as he asked, I knew what it was. " 'On the Sunny Side of the Street.' "

"Frank Sinatra?"

"Yeah, I think he recorded it." But in my mind, I heard Dad and Willie singing it, and I did Dad's shoulder move as I hummed one more verse before it was our turn to go through the metal detector.

That was going to be my song for the road. Not the sad songs of the past or the uncertain songs of the future. Just my father's sunny song, putting a spring in my step as I walked toward the international concourse.

Chapter 11

I was looking at a large picture of Hanna as the White Swan when Claus came into the elegant living room and announced he'd finished bringing up all our belongings.

"I'm sorry about the pictures." He touched the gold knob of a dimmer switch, and one of two intricate chandeliers added a soft yellow light to a space that was too big to be lit by a sun that would soon set. "I had no idea I would be bringing you home." He reached for my hand and leaned against one of three brown leather sofas.

There were five large ballet pictures on a tall burgundy wall that brought warmth to an otherwise pale area. Three were of Hanna alone and two of them together.

The ones of them dancing together were gorgeous, if somewhat expected. The first was a sweet supported arabesque from *Les Sylphides*, a plotless romantic reverie in which a poet dances with beautiful sylphs in a forest. The second was the final pose of a *Le Corsaire* pas de deux. Hanna was an exquisite Medora in a sky-blue pancake tutu, and Claus, in gold and cobalt-blue pants that accented the embroidery work of her bodice, was the servile Ali.

The ones of her alone were altogether unusual. They were all upper-body shots: *Giselle*, the White Swan that had first demanded my attention, and a sylph of some kind. The sylph was possibly from the twisted *La Sylphide* since the arm ruffles and hairpiece were slightly different from their *Les Sylphides* picture. Hanna was probably about my height but even skinnier, with thin lips and a tiny face. In each shot, she looked fragile, withdrawn, and almost scared—haunted even.

Was her fragility alluring to Claus? And if so, then what did he see in me?

Claus broke the silence. "I have some of our *Romeo and Juliet* pictures on my computer, and if you have any others you want to put on the walls, you let me know. I will take care of it this week."

"You don't have to take her pictures down."

"Well, if they don't bother you, I may keep one or two." He kissed my forehead.

"You play?" I asked, pointing at the shiny guitar case next to a large couch.

"A little." He looked down, rubbing the back of his neck. "I need more lessons, though. I'm not very good at it."

"You can't be good at everything, you know." Did he know that Peter played the guitar—and very well, at that? "It's neat that you're learning. I had no idea you played." Claus seemed more like a piano kind of guy, but so far I hadn't seen one.

"There is a lot you don't know." He smiled and dug his necessaire out of his leather bag. "Give me a minute, and then I'll give you the grand tour of the place and get you settled in." He disappeared into what looked like the bedroom.

I glanced at the pictures again. They did bother me, but I didn't feel like it was my place to ask him to take them down. And maybe Hanna's presence would make it okay for me to think about Peter sometimes—not that I was planning to, but I suspected it would happen in the first few months.

What was not okay was to keep hiding that I'd been to Wiesbaden before. My ability to pretend that I was seeing things for the first time had ended. Why was I struggling so much to tell him the truth?

I walked to one of three tall windows and managed to open it after a few tries. Leaning out and breathing in the cool air, I looked at the city beyond the treetops.

Ten years after my first visit to the Hessian state capital, the towering steeples of the brick market church still dominated the cityscape.

Old four-story buildings with beautiful architecture decorated the streets of Wiesbaden. These structures weren't going anywhere anytime soon—if ever. It was safe to say that the steeples of the church would continue to soar high above the historic cityscape for years to come.

I glanced at the pictures of Hanna once more. Would she always be a presence in our lives? Would Peter? Time would tell.

Whatever Claus was doing, he sounded busy. Was he unpacking? He'd said "give me a minute." How long was a German minute?

I turned my attention to the street below. Claus's building was somewhat like the ones I'd been studying before, but in a quieter area—separated from the church, stores, and restaurants by a large park.

He lived on the top floor of a bright-white corner building that was adorned with Roman-style pillars on every level and nestled in lush deep-green vegetation. The elevator was prehistoric, but I was thankful for it. Without it, I would never be able to take Barysh out for a walk by myself.

Downstairs, a narrow stone driveway, edged by clusters of miniature roses, ended at a dark iron gate that led to quiet *Blumenstraße*, two long blocks from the downtown attractions and from the Warmer Damm Park, a large English landscape garden with a lake and a fountain, which bordered the southern façade of the state theater where Claus danced.

"How about we rest for now and then walk downtown for dinner?" Claus popped out of the bedroom and rolled my two suitcases to a room in the opposite direction. "I can't wait to walk past the theater and show you the heart of the city. I love this place. And I know you will too."

Where was he taking my stuff? I followed him into what looked like a guest room. "Claus, we need to talk."

"Uh-oh, that's never good." He put my two suitcases next to the tall double bed and walked toward me. "What is it? Is it the sleeping arrangement? We didn't talk about it, so I didn't know what to do."

"No," I said. "Well, that too, I guess." I'd assumed we were moving in *together*.

"You are welcome in my suite. I just didn't want you to feel like I expect you to…" His face reddened. "You know?"

"I know." We could talk about that later. *If I don't share the suite, I just might be lonely enough to end up at the Baptist church outside the main gate—on the economy.* I laughed as a wave of panic turned my stomach. "That's not it, though."

"What is it then?"

"I've been here before," I said, with my eyes closed.

"What?"

"Ten years ago. After you left, I was confused and heartbroken, and I needed to know what had sent you running." I paused to catch my breath. "So I finished my commitments with the company, and two months later, I was here."

"But you never contacted me…" His voice trailed off.

"I went to the theater to watch *Giselle*, and after seeing you with Hanna, I knew what we had was nothing compared to what you shared with her." Slow tears burned my face.

He put his arms around me. "What we had—and have—is something. It's very special." He waited for me to stop crying. "But I hope you understand now that it was just the circumstances. Timing was against us. I wish you had contacted me, though. Maybe I would have told you about Hanna's diagnosis if I'd seen you in person."

"What do you mean maybe you would have told me?" I took a step back. "It would have been that simple? I spent a decade trying to figure out what I'd done wrong. A decade feeling like I wasn't good enough. And all of it because I didn't want to further humiliate myself by seeking you out in the middle of a foreign city when you were obviously happy with someone else?" I couldn't believe I'd been that close to the truth and hadn't reached out for it.

"I'm just saying, in person, and after a couple of months, it would have been easier to talk." He paced, running his fingers through his hair. "I'm really sorry."

"Whatever." I closed my eyes and shook my head. *Oh my goodness, talk about the missed opportunity of the century—of my lifetime, for sure.*

"I can't believe this. How long did you stay?"

"A week. I stayed a week, but I didn't do anything. I just sat in my hotel room and cried." I still remembered the visceral pain of that first broken heart, that moment in life when I realized for the first time that love didn't conquer all.

"Why didn't you fly back earlier if you weren't going to contact me or do anything?"

"Pride? Whatever was left of it anyway." I leaned on the wood-carved wardrobe and folded my arms tight. "I needed time to figure out what to do and what to tell people. I'd left home hopeful, thinking you would look at me, realize you had made a tragic mistake, throw yourself at my feet, and beg for forgiveness."

Claus listened, silent and unreadable.

"When I realized that wasn't going to happen, I had to reinvent myself." *That's when I decided I wanted to dance at the Met. But now was not the time to discuss that dream.* "By the time I got home, I'd recovered some. I'd had some closure. And I had a new dream, so the trip served a purpose."

"I still can't believe you were here and that you were at the theater and watched me dance." He shook his head. "Wow." He raised both eyebrows and sat on the edge of the bed.

"I know." I massaged my forehead to relieve the tension that had accumulated there. "And I still can't believe that I came all the way here to find the truth, that the truth was available to me, and that I ended up going home with nothing because I was too intimidated by Hanna, by her beauty and by the love you shared, to try to talk to you."

"You should have told me all this before, though." His expression hardened. "I feel like a fool now. I went on and on about Wiesbaden, and you already knew about it."

"Sorry." He was right. I should have said something sooner.

"Are there other things you haven't told me?" His mouth was set in a hard line now.

Really? What kind of question was that? "No."

He sighed. "Let me take this in. We'll rest and then go out." He stopped at the door and looked at me and at my stuff. Maybe now we would talk about sleeping arrangements.

"We won't walk past the theater since you've already seen it." His tone was now dripping with sarcasm. He tapped on the doorpost as if not finished with me but then walked away.

I guess I'm staying in the guest room. Wow. Not exactly a good start. But I had to tell him about that trip—now it's done. Ought to be uphill from here.

After organizing my things, I grabbed a jacket and went to sit outside with Barysh.

Opening the double glass doors, I found him on the best corner of the large terrace and sat with him to enjoy the view through the classic wrought-iron railing.

A sudden breeze ruffled the treetops and brought the alluring fragrance of jasmine to our noses. Barysh lifted his head and closed his eyes. His state of bliss brought a smile to my face and tears to my eyes. I lifted my head and closed my eyes too.

Would Claus really have told me the truth if I'd contacted him? That would have made a huge difference in my life. I kept my eyes closed as the sounds of a thousand dancing leaves filled my ears in a crescendo. As a young woman with Claus, I'd felt like the worthiest person in the planet because of his love. And then for years and years, I'd kept looking for that first-love magic. Forever looking—from bed to bed—but never finding it.

I opened my eyes and reached for the railing.

You know what? You want me in the guest room? That's fine. Why not?

The smell of jasmine lingered, but there was no jasmine bush in sight. Looking around the terrace, I had a couple of ideas on how to make it greener and add dimension to a space that had potential.

Peter would have reacted differently if he'd realized something he did or didn't do had upset me to the point I'd crossed an ocean to fix it.

But Peter didn't want to be with me. Peter was on the other side of the Atlantic.

Claus is here. I checked the quality of the dirt in a nearby pot, pulled up a small vine that had dried up beyond recognition, and tossed it aside. *And if I were to give him my heart again—who knows? He just might mend it.*

"And if it doesn't work out?" I whispered, putting my arm around Barysh.

He looked at me as if waiting for an answer, and I lowered my nose to his. "If it doesn't work out, I will still be dancing." I looked at the horizon. The sky over Wiesbaden was turning pink and orange with the impending sunset. "At the Met—because this will be my season to dance. Come what may."

Chapter 12

I let Claus' shopping basket fall to the elevator floor and pushed the top button. My face and chest were hot, despite the slow start of the German spring season. My hands and arms ached from the weight of carrying the basket the four blocks between the store and Claus's apartment but I couldn't be happier.

I'd gone to Aldi all by myself and returned with everything we needed for our first picnic on the Rhine. On the agenda—discussing the company's schedule and his upcoming return to regular classes and rehearsals. He hadn't said anything about my potential in the company. Maybe this would be the day we would talk about it.

He was hanging pictures when I pushed my way in. The only one of Hanna that remained was the White Swan. Next to it was a full-body shot of me at seventeen in a red-and-white short tutu, a simple B-plus leg position—the position dancers take before starting most combinations—and arms up framing my I-will-conquer-the-world expression.

"What do you think?" Claus worked on the bottom row with an extra nail clenched between his lips, as though it were a miniature cigarette.

His antique gold frames with beige linen made my friend-of-Paquita picture look especially glamorous. Gorgeous even.

Lorie had been Paquita, of course. Back then, I'd thought that watching her shine while playing one of her best friends on stage was going to be a temporary thing, and I'd made the best of it.

Ten years later I was still at it—and still trying to make the best of it, but through the years that took more and more effort. Friend of Paquita, friend of Kitri, friend of Swanilda, friend of Giselle … but then came *Romeo and Juliet* and everything changed. I was the lead—she was the friend.

Was that why she did what she did?

Nope, I wasn't going to think about her anymore. Or about Peter.

My thoughts turned back to the photo in front of me. My body was the same, but the face was so much younger in the picture—the brain was much younger too. Something in me just wanted to smack that girl on the side of the head—her and her prima-ballerina dreams—along with perfect-love dreams too.

He put the last picture in place and stepped back.

"Don't you like it?"

"I do." He was trying—I needed to make an effort too. "I like it. I just hadn't seen that *Paquita* picture in a long time."

"How about the others? Too unusual?"

The other three pictures were the same size and had the same frames as the portraits above them. "Unusual? Yes." I stepped closer. "But perfect." They were side-by-side masquerade ball shots of our *Romeo and Juliet.*

He was obviously more interested in the emotion of his ballet pictures than in arches and extensions, as I had already suspected from the photos of Hanna that I'd seen.

In the first picture, a masqueraded Romeo shows off to Juliet, who plays the mandolin. She's infatuated with him, and when he stops in front of her, she cannot meet his gaze. She looks at the mandolin instead. Click.

The second shot shows the moment Juliet's life changes. The guy she's supposed to marry and her dad lose interest in her dancing, and she starts dancing for Romeo, who surprises her center stage. He is touching her for the very first time, and her upper body freezes. Click.

The third picture is of Romeo and Juliet's time alone at the ball. He has just ripped off his mask, which remains in midair in the photo. *Great shot.* His arms are open, and Juliet runs to him. She still doesn't know he's a Montague.

All three moments are innocent, pure, and hopeful. Is that how he viewed me? I liked that.

I wrapped my arms around Claus and squeezed him tight, hoping his soul would feel embraced too. "They're perfect. Thank you."

"You're welcome."

He followed me to the kitchen as I opened the small fridge and put away the extra cheese, the cherry tomatoes, and the basil I'd bought for a salad.

"Look at you." He poked around the basket.

"Next time, I'll brave the market." I raised both eyebrows and widened my eyes in pretend terror.

"It's easy. All you need to do is point and say '*Ein Stück das, bitte.*'"

"Um, can I get *ein Stück das?*" My lips teased his. "*Bitte.*"

"Yes ma'am," he whispered before his strong arms made me his willing prisoner. With one hand behind my head and the other firm on my back, his lips touched mine, and playful kisses grew deep and hungry with the speed and intensity of a small dust devil that forms when hot and cool air clash and conditions are just right. And conditions *were* right.

This separate-rooms thing is making me crazy. Would I be able to stand when he let me go?

"See, I told you it works for just about anything." He held me with one arm and pulled a chair out with his free hand.

"Yeah, you did." I eased myself onto the chair.

I shook my head and organized the items we were taking on our picnic: cold cuts, fruit, chocolate, a little *kuchen* that looked like Grandma's crumb cake, and a sweet-tasting bread I'd learned to love in the two weeks I'd been there. Then I put aside pantry foods we weren't taking before folding an extra bag I ended up not needing on my trip to the store. "Something's in it," I whispered, pulling it out.

Claus looked over his shoulder as he washed our grapes and physalis. "It's a paper—church, I think. Somebody handed it to me at the market last year, just before my trip to America. I'd just shoved it in the bag. I guess I never pulled it out. What does it say?"

"Calvary Baptist Church," I read. The soft brochure in shades of green was elegant and simple. On the front, YOU'RE INVITED..." and on the back a bunch of Bible verses. I didn't open it. Everything was in English and German.

"I should have known. I've seen them in the market before."

"Calvary Baptist—original."

"Baptists are Christians, so I don't think Mount Olympus Baptist Church would have worked out for them."

"Ha-ha. Everybody's got jokes."

"They were at the market last weekend too." Claus dried and bagged the fruit.

"I didn't see anything at the market."

"A couple was talking to a young guy about the church. I overheard the conversation. It was your first market. You stopped at every stand." He kissed my head. "I overheard a lot of conversations."

"In German?"

"Yes. All in German."

"I think this is an American church, though."

"I think so too. The church is probably near an American *Kaserne*. But they probably get Germans in there too."

"*Kaserne?*"

"Barracks, I think you say."

"Oh." *Probably by the main gate.* I smiled, remembering the guy I'd talked with at my apartment building the day I'd left Columbus. "Do you know for sure that Jesus Christ is your personal Savior?" I read. "I hate the way they word their pitch like they are privy to some secret source of divine information. Mom has people knock on her door sometimes. Same talk. 'Do you know for sure you are going to heaven?'"

"What's wrong with it?"

"I feel against the wall. It doesn't seem like a friendly approach. It makes me not want to talk to that person."

"Maybe it's your American sensibility." He winked and reached for my hand.

"Then maybe you should go visit Calvary Baptist Church." I chuckled. "Here." I pinned the church pamphlet to his corkboard before grabbing Barysh's bag.

"Maybe I will," he said with a shrug and a smile. "Get the food. I'll take Barysh to the car."

We followed the Rhine River for thirty minutes to Rüdesheim. I'd seen the river from Wiesbaden and couldn't figure out what the fuss was all about. It was bigger than the Chattahoochee outside my old apartment—maybe more like the Ohio—but it was just another pretty body of water, with Wiesbaden on one side and Mainz—also a state capital—on the other side.

Beyond the busyness of the capitals, I understood the uniqueness of the Rhine Valley. Steep hills were covered with old vines that showed new green shoots. The road became narrow. And the river, filled with tourist boats and barges, slowly became the romantic Rhine of magazines and travel shows.

"So this is Rüdesheim." Claus stopped at a red light. "One day we can take a boat to Koblenz. It's about sixty kilometers from here. There are more than forty castles and fortresses from the Middle Ages on the way and many wine villages."

"We should do that." I squeezed his hand and studied the long row of beautiful double-decker white boats—or were they called triple-deckers because of the third open-air deck?

Crawling from red light to red light through the quaint little town, I didn't know where to fix my attention next. Most restaurants and hotels by the water had the charming half-timbered architecture generally associated with Germany. Lush vegetation and vibrant flowers shaded outdoor tables, and window boxes overflowed with bright geraniums, petunias, and begonias.

At a restaurant with a large courtyard and a fountain, a group of women— three generations for sure—danced the polka, accompanied by a live accordion, and a teenage boy who was watching them from the sidewalk picked up his girlfriend and spun her around to her giggles and protests.

Everybody looked happy and relaxed, and I noticed that even though we were surrounded by vineyards, most people were drinking beer—*vom Fass.*

"See that statue?" Claus pointed to a huge figure high above the city and on the edge of a forest. "That's Germania."

"Who's Germania?" Was it a woman? The shape of the body was feminine, but even from a distance, I could tell that Germania was powerful—maybe a conqueror or a warrior. One hand held a sword and the other lifted something—a crown?—high up in the air.

"Hmm. How do I say this in English? She's a personification? Yes, the personification of the German nation."

"You mean like Uncle Sam for us?"

"I suppose." He chuckled. "She represents all Germans. The monument was built to celebrate the reestablishment of the German Empire—after the German–French War."

"Nice." *Germania* is *a woman. Cool.*

Claus turned onto a quiet brick road that soon became an uphill dirt path through the cultivated area. "See the cable cars going over the vineyards?"

I nodded as metal cable cars traveled up the mountainside, at times no more than ten feet above the vineyards, before disappearing into the forest close to the mountaintop.

"Takes you all the way up to the monument."

"We should go one day."

"We will."

Ahead of us, an older couple—each holding a wooden stick—walked uphill between the vines. Maybe they didn't like cable cars.

Claus drove onto a grassy area and soon brought the Mercedes to a full stop, turning off the engine. "This is my favorite spot."

It was a small quiet patch of tiny green plants amid the vines, about halfway up the mountainside.

"These will soon be the tallest sunflowers you've ever seen." Claus spread our blanket on the grass next to the patch with ease. "Well over two meters."

"Nice." I walked Barysh to the blanket with the help of a towel placed under his belly. "Come on, bud. Use what you've got."

"I can do that. He's heavy." Claus approached us.

"I'm … good," I gasped.

"Okay. I'll get the food then."

Barysh had to keep trying or his back legs would end up completely lame. I'd just supported more than half his weight on that towel. My hands ached, and I massaged them until they felt normal again. Claus could help Barysh when it was time to go home.

I watched Claus finish unloading the car. *He's so beautiful.* The soft breeze of the Rhine Valley played with his sandy-blond hair. He looked fantastic in a white button-up shirt and light designer jeans. His tan leather belt matched his leather shoes.

Was I underdressed wearing my old boots, beat up jeans, and avocado-green hoodie? Probably. I chuckled looking at Barysh. *We're not in Kansas anymore, Toto.*

Claus sat next to me and used a simple, classic waiter's corkscrew to open a bottle of Riesling Spätlese with ease. He unpacked two wine glasses and handed me a taste before filling both cups and proposing a toast. "To buried and forgotten passions. May they grow back strong this season like the nature around us."

"To buried and forgotten passions." I raised my glass. Was he talking about us, dance, or both? "Thank you for bringing me here, Claus. This is perfect."

He caressed my hair. "You're welcome."

"I love this wine," I said, breathing him in and enjoying everything about the moment.

"Isn't it perfect?" His lips grazed mine.

His sweet-wine breath invited me to taste his lips. "It is … perfect," I said before kissing him—the best and sweetest kissing of my life. His lips were cool, like the Riesling we were sharing, and our kiss ripe like the late-harvest grapes of the wine.

"Good." He touched my cheek with soft fingertips.

"Hmm?" I muttered.

"The wine," he said before turning his attention to the picnic basket. "I'm glad you like it."

His smirk let me know that he knew the effect he had on me. "I do—I like it." I touched my warm cheeks and watched him unwrap our sandwiches.

"Here." He offered me the first one.

"Thank you." *Life doesn't get any better than this. I love this man, and I love this country. Good decision.*

He got a sandwich for himself, and we ate enjoying the quiet peace that surrounded us.

Claus finished first and broke the silence.

"Next week I go back to the studio." He grabbed a small bowl of fresh physalis.

I nodded and took two of the little orange fruits he offered me.

"We have a performance in Prague coming up next month," he said. "And I start classes and rehearsals again on Monday."

"Okay." I nodded again. "I was wondering what your schedule was going to look like."

"It will look very busy." He raised his eyebrows.

I made a sad puppy face.

"I want you to be there with me." He got very close and put his arm around my shoulder. "I hope you'll want to do that, yes?"

"Yes, I want to be there with you." I watched him. What kind of plan did he have in mind?

"Good." He refilled our glasses and handed me mine. "So tell me what you're thinking."

"I'm thinking about joining the company," I said matter-of-factly. "Do you think I have a chance?"

He looked puzzled. "I don't see why not, but that's a big change, from wanting to quit to wanting to audition for a prominent European company."

"Who said anything about quitting? I wasn't going to quit anything."

"But I heard—"

I leaned toward him and covered his mouth. "I was going to move to Pine Mountain and audition in Atlanta. I want to dance at the Metropolitan Opera House in New York."

He stared at me and looked confused, as though he were watching a familiar ballet with the wrong characters in it—the curtains opened to a *Giselle* set, but *Don Quixote's* Kitri took the stage.

"Stop dancing? I would sooner stop breathing."

"This makes no sense." Claus blanched.

"What did you think I was going to do here? Sit in the apartment all day?" *Why do I have a feeling Lorie has something to do with this?*

"No, not at all. I expected that you would want to continue dancing once you moved here with me."

"In the spirit of all's well that ends well, we don't have a problem—we both believe I should dance here." I shook my head. "But who told you I was quitting? Let me guess—Lorie?"

Claus grew paler still. His eyes were intent on the horizon—on the other side of the river gorge.

"Was it Lorie?"

He nodded without looking at me as if he too needed to think hard to make sense of reality—reality according to Lorie Allen.

"What is up with that girl?" I slammed the blanket with both hands. "First Peter and now you? What's her problem?"

He shook his head and his jaw went slack.

My eyes riveted on the Rhine River below, glittering in the midday sun. Ten minutes earlier, that would have been lovely, but now I had a sudden headache.

My arms reached for Barysh, who was scooting my way. Claus had helped me bathe him and brush him the night before, so Barysh smelled fresh and looked especially handsome. My fingers caressed his soft copper fur and rested on his chest, his steady heartbeat lulling me.

Was Claus feeling any better? His expression hadn't changed. What was going through his mind? What had Lorie said and what had he done?

I remembered Mom and the nonsense she'd said in her kitchen before my move. Was it nonsense or was she right? *Did Claus know Peter was in the audience when he kissed me?*

He caught me staring and I looked away.

"Why do you want to dance at the Met?" The corners of his eyes crinkled. "Sorry—it just sounds a little random."

"Why do you think it's random?" I was afraid he was connecting the dots and would soon suspect I had agreed to move in with him because of his company's schedule. No, I did not like that question.

He shrugged. "I don't know. People dream of being in certain companies or of working with certain choreographers—not dancing at this theater or that theater."

I shouldn't have mentioned the Met. "It's not random."

"What is it then?"

"Claus, you are so talented." *Take your time and explain—he will understand.* "The people you dance with here, and the ballerinas you've partnered with since becoming the world sensation that you are, are all amazing." I swallowed the lump that had risen in my throat. "My talent..." I lay down on the warm blanket. "My talent is limited."

"Nonsense." He reached for my hand.

"Hear me out." I looked straight ahead at a milky spring sky.

He nodded and laid down next to me.

A mild breeze brought to us the lovely perfume of the only rose bush in sight. I breathed it in twice before continuing. "I'll never be a prima ballerina in a large company. I'll probably never even be a soloist in a large company."

"You don't know that—"

"Shh. Please."

"Sorry."

"I decided that dancing at the Met would be an attainable goal—something I could pursue instead." I shrugged. "Everyone needs a holy grail, right?"

"You have talent, Ana."

"Just not enough." I pressed my lips together and shook my head. "It hurts to realize that you can't do what you've always dreamed of doing. You don't understand. I will never be Giselle, or Kitri, or Odette, or anyone else—not anywhere important and not with the best partners of this generation."

"You can't say that for sure." His voice was soft.

He knew I was right. "It hurts."

"You were Juliet with an okay partner." He brought my hand to his lips and smiled.

"Well, yes. That I was. I was Juliet, and my Romeo was this amazing guy who can jump and spin like no other I've ever met—he's all over YouTube."

"And that doesn't make you happy?"

"It does, but sharing the stage with you in a lead role, that's the exception to the rule of my dancing life. It will probably never happen again. If I get into the Rhine-Main Ballet, I'm sure I'll be in the corps forever. And I want to be happy with that." *Or I will go nuts.* "My way of coming to terms with eternity in a lower position is to shoot also for something else—something that's exciting and that I can reasonably accomplish."

"The Met?"

"Yes. Without that goal, I feel bitter and ungrateful about everything, and I hate that. I know I have some semblance of a gift and a handful of things going for me. I should be thankful." I looked at him. "Am I making any sense?"

"You're right about the gift part. You do have a beautiful gift. Your technique is good enough to keep you afloat in the professional world. Your gift is your stage presence. You could be in the corps—last row—and I would still have eyes for only you."

Good enough to stay afloat? I had to laugh.

"Did you mind that I was honest?" He cringed. "I'm sorry." He put the palm of his hand on my chest as if to touch my heart.

"I don't mind. You're right on target." I chuckled. "I'd never thought about it that way. Your wording is perfect—I'm good enough to stay afloat."

"Well, did you hear the 'I only have eyes for you' part?"

"Yes." I nodded. "Thank you for your unbiased opinion." I shot a smirk his way.

"Let me continue to the best part. Your stage presence is a rare gift. Dancers either have it or they don't. Of those who have it, some have a little, others have more, and then there are very lucky people, like you, who overflow with it."

"Thank you?" I said sheepishly. *I wanted more. I wanted all the way. I don't feel very lucky.*

I turned my head toward the rose bush and dried a tear. Its cream blossoms, about a dozen, had reached the end of their bloom cycle.

"You do know that success is overrated, right? Everyone's always looking for the next thing—the next holy grail, like you put it."

He was right. But that didn't make me feel any better.

"I enjoy my success, but I don't consider myself satisfied," he said. "And I don't think I will ever be. I go around looking for different projects and most end up in disaster—according to the critics anyway. People want to see me in the big classical roles again, and again, and again. So the experimental pieces that I enjoy and that challenge me and take me someplace new in terms of movement and interpretation are not at all well received. It is very disappointing."

"Oh, poor little rich boy." We both laughed. "Nice try, but every company in the world wants you, so hush. I'm sure you will figure it out."

"I'm just saying that I understand you more than you realize."

"You're killing me. People love you—hard-to-please people."

"People love you in Columbus."

"It's not the same thing."

"Why not?"

"Having the most educated audiences judge your work and love you must feel amazing. Surely you read a good review and feel justified."

"You got fantastic reviews for your Juliet—by good critics who came all the way from Atlanta. Didn't you feel justified?"

"No. Columbus is small, and the Allen Ballet is small. And the Atlanta people came for you."

"But they loved you too." He sat up. "Come on, Ana. How justified is justified enough?"

"The Met," I said. "Then I will be happy."

"No, you won't."

"I will." *I had to be.*

"Why the Met?"

"Do you have a problem with the Met?"

"No—I love the Met. I'm just curious, is all. Why not Le Palais Garnier?"

"Because I'm American. If I were French, or at least European, I would probably have picked Le Palais Garnier to be my Holy Grail. I don't know." I shrugged. "The Met is pretty, and I grew up watching it on TV. And everybody who's anybody has danced there."

"I still think it's a little random."

"Don't take it away from me. It's not random. It's what I want. You're my boyfriend. You're supposed to be supportive or something."

"Okay." His eyes widened.

"Good." I finished my wine. "Then stop looking puzzled. If you have something else to ask me, ask me already." *Let's get it over with.*

"Since we are in the business of being sincere…"

Here it comes.

"We are dancing at the Met next spring." He cocked his head and looked at me as if searching for a reaction.

"I know."

"Is that why you came to Germany?"

"No." *I'm not taking advantage of you.* "I saw the company calendar the night I told my parents I was moving in with you."

"So the decision had been made?"

"Yes." *Pretty much.*

He nodded in slow motion, and I reached for his hand. He was looking at the horizon again.

He held my hand and brought it to his lips, turning his full attention to me. The kiss was warm—his expression not as much. "Sorry. I just want to make sure you are here for the right reason. 'Poor little rich boys' feel funny about girls' motivations sometimes."

Ouch. "I loved you before you were famous, remember?"

"That is true." He grabbed the wine bottle and divided what was left between our glasses. "Remember the dinner at *Di Gregorio* tonight?"

"Yes, with the artistic director."

"Jakob Arnheim, yes." Claus's brows knitted. "I'll go on my own."

"Okay?" What was his idea?

"I thought you could take classes with us, watch rehearsals, and kind of—how do you say? Go with the flow. But if you want to perform with the company and be part of the next season, we will need a plan."

"Sure." *That makes sense. The dinner is no longer a social event. It's business. And it's best that they talk without me there, so Claus can get a real feel for what I can expect moving forward. That's good. I'll meet him soon enough.*

My eyes focused on the mountaintop—on Germania. Could I be strong like her? I would have to try. We did have one thing in common for sure. We liked crowns. It was a crown that she was lifting up for all to see.

We finished our wine in silence and traveled back in silence too.

Close to Wiesbaden, dozens of giant wind turbines stood absolutely still on a field, like a ready army waiting for the big battle. Then a few started moving in slow motion. Others followed. Soon all moved at a good pace. By the time we drove past them, they were spinning so fast that they looked dangerous and seemed unstoppable.

Was my life like that? Was stopping an option now, or was it all bigger than me and in motion and unstoppable?

Leaning against the window, I looked up at the massive white structures, each taller than the water tower in front of my old building.

"They look much bigger up close, don't they?" Claus looked up too.

"Yes, they do." *So much bigger.*

Chapter 13

Walking to the theater for my first class with the company, I moved in spurts, like a little girl going to a new school. One moment, excitement propelled me forward, and the next, fear brought me to near paralysis.

I'd put my hair up while it was still wet, and the perfect bun helped me stand tall. The little teardrop earrings Mom had given me as a departure gift added to that feeling, and I was certain my day would be fabulous.

But now that we were on our way, my confidence was shaky at best.

Jakob had told Claus I could start as a guest and be an understudy during rehearsals until fall auditions—my chance to join the company for real.

"What if they don't like me, Claus?" I stopped and covered my eyes. "They probably worshipped Hanna and will hate me when they figure out we are together."

"Nonsense. Don't worry about them." He put his arm around me and gave me a quick kiss on the temple while pulling me along. "Plus, no one worshipped Hanna. She was very private and came across pretty standoffish."

"Ugh. I'm so nervous." I walked faster.

"Just go out there and have fun like we did in Georgia."

"I have a hard time enjoying myself around girls who are better than me." I chuckled realizing just how wrong I was. "That sounded petty—crap—sorry."

"You're competitive. Nothing wrong with that." He looked at me and hesitated before adding, "Now the cursing, that doesn't suit you."

"Oh, Claus, you've said that before." I rolled my eyes. Was *crap* really a curse word? "Who cares what I say and don't say? Cut me some slack. This is a big day." I palmed my fingers against my sweaty hands.

"I'll try." He grabbed my hand as we reached the end of the tree-lined streets of his neighborhood. "But it really doesn't suit you."

We waited for traffic to stop and crossed *Bierstadter Straße,* leaving behind silence, shade, and the fragrance of jasmine.

Downtown was architecturally pleasing and greener than most, but it was still a city center busy with buses, cars, shoppers, workers, and students.

At the Warmer Damm Park, even the ducklings seemed to be in a hurry as they swam after the mother duck who appeared to be after three ladies walking their dogs.

What if I don't understand the class? What if I'm too crazed to memorize the combinations?

Men in suits walked mostly in groups and engaged in what looked like animated conversations. Only the tall magnolia trees and the swamp cypresses were still and at peace. Could I borrow their stillness? My eyes looked heavenward. *Please let this work, God.*

A woman's voice singing an aria from Verdi's *La Traviata* turned my attention to the huge Neo-Baroque-style theater.

"Violetta." Claus pointed to a row of windows from where the music came. "'Addio, del Passato.'"

"Is that what she sings when she's dying?" Dad was the opera buff of the family, but I had seen that one.

"That's what she sings when all the lies that had separated her and Alfredo are clearing up—but she knows that it's too late now and that she's dying."

"That's right." They get to see each other, and he apologizes for not believing her. Then she dies—in peace. I let Claus lead me closer to the entrance. Only the Friedrich Schiller Monument stood between me and the opulent state theater now. I'd come this far. A dead poet and his odd-looking muse were not going to stop me.

Claus walked me to the door of a ladies dressing room, kissed my cheek, and winked. "I'll see you in the studio."

I nodded—my throat was too dry for words. *Let's do this.*

"Hi." My voice came out faint, but the beautiful young blonde who saw me walk into the dressing room had heard me.

"Hi." She smiled, her big brown eyes offering a gentle welcome, as three women nearby looked up.

I got a wave and two eyebrow nods from the group—all with smiles. And then they returned to their original conversation in what sounded like Russian. *Not too bad.*

The dark-brown velvet of my favorite three-quarter-sleeve leotard caressed my arms as I finished getting ready. Looking at the blonde from the corner of my eye, I was convinced she was one of the principals whose pictures I'd seen on the website.

More people arrived, but they didn't seem to notice me in the small dressing room that got crowded fast. I put on my warm-up pants and organized my ballet shoes for class to the music of at least three more languages: German, English, and Spanish.

Then a woman in street clothes came to the door and said something in German. Everyone stopped talking and started moving toward the door with big bags, water bottles, and extra warm-up gear. Following at least forty girls, I wished I'd already started my German lessons with our downstairs neighbor.

I walked into the studio and picked a spot far from the front and far from the pianist and hoped people wouldn't wonder how I'd ended up in their class.

Claus walked in with a tall dancer whose olive-tinted complexion, deep brown eyes, and dark hair hinted at a Spanish heritage. Light stubble on his square face and a perfect cleft chin added to his handsomeness.

Next, Claus talked to the pianist, an elegant man in his fifties, and handed him what looked like sheet music.

I'd expected him to go to whatever his favorite spot was, but after putting his bag down near the piano, he came straight to me.

There goes the flying-under-the-radar idea. Dozens of eyes were on us.

Stretching his calf muscles, he winked as the corners of his mouth turned up. "The ballet mistress is not here today, so Jakob will teach. Still nervous?"

"I wasn't." *No pressure.* "I shouldn't have taken such a long break. This will be a disaster. What was I thinking?"

"I feel nervous when the director comes," the girl behind me whispered with an accent I couldn't figure out.

We were both chuckling when Jakob walked in. He didn't seem to notice me or our soft girlish giggles, and if he did, he didn't look like he cared.

"I am Luciana Pilar," the girl behind me muttered. "Luci. From Chile."

"Ana—United States," I said before turning my attention to the director.

Jakob showed us a simple foot and ankle warm-up, going through it quickly and without music. I had it memorized fast. We faced the barre to start, and the pianist played the first notes of Josu Gallastegui's "Promenade"—the same music that had touched my heart during our opening night warm-up in Columbus. *Is that what Claus gave the pianist? That was sweet.* Looking at him from the corner of my eye, I mouthed a silent, "Thank you."

He offered me an encouraging grin, and my cheeks warmed up. Now, to focus on the rest of the body.

As expected of a prominent ballet company, the room was crowded, the combinations elaborate, and everything was fast-paced.

"*Preparación*, let's go, and the one, and the two, and the three, and the four…"

Sometimes I heard three languages in one sentence come out of Jakob's mouth, but the fact that the names of the steps remained in French everywhere in the world helped me get through the exercises.

Jakob kept his verbal corrections to a minimum, often simply touching or pointing to a shoulder, upper back, or whatever part of the dancer was out of place.

For the second part of the class, the center, I was in group two with Luci. All three principal dancers were in group one along with other women who were probably the soloists. Claus was in group three with all the other men.

Being in group two was good because I had extra time to memorize the combinations, but it also meant that the best dancers—and Claus—would be watching me.

Each group took turns working on the first slow exercises—exercises designed to help us transition from having the support of the barre to working without anything to hold on to. We now had to find our own balance as we got our whole bodies dancing.

In a way, each ballet class took us through a baby's whole cycle of learning to walk. The barre was equivalent to the cruising stage.

Then in the center we did small, slow steps first, like a toddler taking two steps between two pieces of furniture. Still in the center, the movements became bigger and more ambitious—the toddler's longer and more controlled distances.

After that came the diagonals which were often combinations so beautiful they were fit for the stage. That would be equivalent to the toddler becoming a confident walker—and runner.

But ballet positions are so unnatural, and balancing a whole body on the tips of one's toes so difficult, that every day dancers have to start at the cruising stage again to position the body—reminding it of what it takes to go from mere body to an instrument of magic.

It was time for group two to do the first more ambitious exercise of the center, and Claus and all of group one were casually looking either in my direction or in the direction of my reflection in the mirror.

I'd done that a million times when someone new showed up in class. There were no evil feelings toward the new arrival, but there was always a palpable curiosity—a need to categorize her. There were only two categories: competition and not competition.

I cannot mess this up. They will forever judge me for what I do in the next sixty seconds. Even if I end up in everyone's not-competition category, I want to at least look pretty.

Waiting to start, my breathing was even, heart rate normal. Claus had said that my stage presence was a rare gift. I had to use that. It would be silly to smile a big smile in class, but I could be serene and ethereal and make sure my arms and head positioning were impeccable.

Claus was looking at my reflection in the mirror. His forehead furrowed. *Relax.*

Jakob walked to the front of the room. "*Preparación*, and…" As soon as he said "and" the piano started.

Ethereal.

The combination involved pirouettes and big *fondu développés.* I bent the supporting leg slowly, melting, while placing my working foot pointing on the ankle. *Big and light now.* As I straightened the supporting leg, the working leg unfolded and extended high in the air. *Good.* After repeating that step in different directions and switching legs, it was time for pirouettes.

I remembered what Brian had said about not rushing and staying up, letting gravity bring me down when it was time. *Triples? No … clean doubles. Stay serene.*

Letting the soft music flow through my body, I plied and prepared and spun. Clean double. *Deep breath.* Repeat once, twice. Change direction. Repeat. *Breathe. Good. Smooth ending. Arms. Ethereal. Exhale. Yay.*

Jakob lifted his hand like a maestro. "Third group."

Claus passed me as I walked toward the barres, and his mouth curved into a smile.

I'd survived the judgment minute. *Phew.*

The flow and direction of the diagonal jump combinations that followed were beautiful and smart, helping the body transition from one step to the next. During an exercise that ended in a series of *pas de chats*, I landed gracefully after flying as high as the piano. *Oh, how fun—this is certainly the life I'm supposed to live.*

It was the guys' turn to do the same combination. There were fourteen of them. Eight were really strong dancers. The others were good, but they didn't have the same effortless ability to dance that Claus and the rest did.

Not as good—is that what people are thinking about me right now? I'd succeeded at not embarrassing myself and had managed to follow the class so far. But was it enough?

My eyes glanced at the simple wall clock. We had five minutes left.

The men jumped as the pianist played *fortissimo*, and Jakob pushed them hard. "*Der Sprung*—schtep, schtep, *sprung, und sprung, und sprung—gut.*"

Was I good enough?

"Révérence." Jakob stood in front of us, and the pianist played another Gallastegui composition. We followed his arm movements and breathed together, then he said something in German and everyone started exiting the studio.

I walked to him to introduce myself. *The moment of truth.*

"That was a lovely class, Ana." He made notes on a big binder without looking at me. "You will be Luci's understudy. You just shadow her all day, yes?"

"Yes." *I guess that's good.* "Thanks."

The company was rehearsing Balanchine's *Theme and Variations* first, a twenty-minute ballet that's a challenge to anyone's technique and physical endurance, and I looked forward to learning it. Luci was an understudy.

Claus partnered Ekaterina for *Theme*, the gorgeous Russian girl from the dressing room who was also the best of the three principal dancers. Ekaterina's technique was flawless, and I looked forward to seeing her in rehearsal.

"Let's do everything that requires Claus and Ekaterina to be here first." Jakob had two people standing with him now, a man and a woman, but I had no idea who they were or what their jobs were. He turned to Claus. "That way you and Ekaterina can move to one of the smaller studios and go over 'Paquita.'"

Don't be jealous.

For the first two minutes of the ballet, we stood like statues while Claus and Ekaterina executed a few simple steps. I watched them through five rows of dancers. Her arms came into view. *Elegant, regal, and effortless. How beautiful.*

The corps accompanied Claus once. After that, every time I tried to learn something, Jakob cut to the next part that had the lead couple in it. *It's all right— look at him.* Claus's first solo was an explosion of talent and stamina.

"*Sehr gut.*" Jakob took a step forward. "Corps can step out. I want to see the pas de deux now."

What if I don't want to see it? Why can't it be me up there? I walked to a corner barre and rested my leg on it to watch them. *I hate feeling sorry for myself. Hate it. But oh, how I wish…*

As soon as they looked at each other, a strong heat that originated in my chest traveled up my throat and settled on my cheeks. They had a familiarity with each other that takes years to build—they must have been partnering forever. *Wow … they even breathe as one.*

She looked at Claus as if he were the only person in the room. How could I not be jealous?

It's just work—better get used to it. There'll be lots of prima ballerinas in his life.

They finished their part, and he waved at me from the door.

I raised my hand with a small smile to acknowledge his gesture. Good. I couldn't take it anymore. Ekaterina … even her name was pretty.

Now I could get to work. Luci and I and the whole corps continued rehearsing *Theme*, dancing until we had nothing left to give.

By the time we were done, I had big chunks of the choreography memorized. I would find *Theme* online at home to get the missing parts memorized.

The rehearsal had made me want to be in the company even more. Would they let me do an individual audition, or would I really have to wait for the general audition? It would be hard to watch performances without being a part of the show.

Luci approached me. "I have a one-hour break. That means you do too. Do you want to go get something to eat?"

I'd brought some energy bars and fruit, but a break from feeling like I was a zoo attraction with eyes constantly on me sounded pretty good. "Sure."

At a little café by the theater, we sat outside and ordered cheese omelets and juice. The midday sun brought a more peaceful pace to the park. Dozens of people read and sunbathed on the grass, small children played soccer, and a group of bikers stopped under a big tree.

They spoke in American English, and I couldn't help but feel a little homesick. *Nope, not homesick enough to endure Calvary Baptist.* I shook my head. What was a Baptist anyway?

Luci pulled out a pack of Jin Ling cigarettes and offered me one.

"No, thank you." I took my orange juice from the waiter and placed it on the bare circle table between us.

"I forget people in America don't smoke anymore." She drank half of her juice before putting her glass down.

"So, how long have you been with the company?" I asked, watching her light her cigarette.

"Four years in the school, two years in the company."

"Did you make it in your first audition?"

"No." She laughed. "Four times. Then I passed."

Oh my goodness—bless her heart. The waiter came back with the food, and the pause gave me time to find something nice to say. "That's good that you didn't give up."

"Yes. It is very good." She smiled.

She ate fast, and I followed her lead.

When we finished, she lit another cigarette and asked for two coffees and the check. I was thankful to be there with another dancer and someone who knew how to order, what to order, and when to go back to the theater. Did she do this every day? Should I?

Three girls and one guy from the company sat at a table twenty feet from us, and when I looked at them, one of the girls waved our way. I waved back.

"So Claus is taking care of you?"

I laughed and everyone looked our way. "I'm sorry." I covered my mouth. "I wasn't expecting—"

"It's okay." The corners of her eyes crinkled as her lips stretched.

"He *is* taking care of me." Was I prepared to answer questions about my relationship with Claus? I wasn't sure.

"Good. That's very good." She put out her Jin Ling and leaned back on her chair, relaxed and looking happy to be there. "You know him a long time, yes?"

"Ten years."

Her eyes widened. "Very long time."

"Long time indeed." Was she fishing for information or just trying to make pleasant conversation? I couldn't tell.

The waiter arrived and Luci gave him some money. "Give him nine euros," she told me, looking at our check.

We walked back fast and in lively conversation. She told me she was happy dancing in the corps and had no ambition of being a soloist.

"You will see the energy here is good." She snubbed out another cigarette before entering the building. "Small companies—people still want to arrive somewhere. Here, people are happy. They have arrived."

I knew exactly what she meant and wanted that feeling more than anything. I was approaching my thirties and the peak of my technique. I wanted to be stable someplace to enjoy that technical maturity while growing more and more artistically. *Oh, God, I don't want to audition four times. Please make all my dreams come true now. I've never been so close. Or so tired...*

Did God hear prayers? Did He hear *my* prayers? Probably not. Why would He? I only talked to Him when I needed something—big somethings. *Please, I don't want to audition four times.*

I heard Claus's voice and told Luci I would catch up.

"Be quick." She continued walking. "Corps starts *Paquita* in twenty minutes. I dance this one." She turned around and looked at me with a wide smile. "If I break something, you have to dance."

"Okay. It'll be just a minute."

She shook her head and chuckled as she approached the dressing room.

I liked her—my new friend. *I'll just say hello to Claus, and then I can join her again for some* Paquita *action.*

Claus's voice was coming from the office area. Maybe I should go straight to the dressing room. Then I heard Jakob's voice too. Could they be talking about me? I was dying to know what people were thinking about my dancing. Maybe I could listen in for a minute.

But even if they were talking about me, they would be speaking German, and that would do me no good.

Checking the hallways for dancers or staff, I took a step closer to the voices. *English? That's odd.*

"I'm sorry, Ekaterina, but I cannot let you take any time off," I heard Jakob say. "You will have to figure out a way of working together."

Ekaterina? I could hear my heartbeat, but nothing from the room.

I heard Jakob's voice again. "Claus, this would be a good time for you to say something. You started it, yes?"

"Where are my zings?" I heard her cry.

Zings? Things? What in the world?

"I will bring them tomorrow," Claus said.

Claus has Ekaterina's things?

I heard what sounded like someone getting slapped and rushed to the nearby bathroom. Squeezing behind the door, I held my breath.

Peeking over a rusty hinge, I saw Ekaterina walk toward the studios as she covered her mouth and squeezed her brown eyes shut. How could he not tell me he was in a relationship?

Jakob came out of the office too. Claus followed, and Jakob talked. "Make Katya happy. I am not going to lose her because of an average American girl."

The smell of the thick glossy paint mixed with the embarrassment from Jakob's words sickened me. *Average?* I slid down the wall and hugged my knees.

Do I even have a future here?

"I looked for you everywhere." Claus found me on the terrace at home, pulling the last dead plants out of his large Victorian planters. "What happened?"

"I finished rehearsing." I got a large root ball and put it in a cardboard box I'd found in the laundry room. "We did *Paquita* and a new modern piece Luci is learning."

"You had a pretty good first day." Claus sat on one of two iron chairs and picked up the bottle of Kirner I'd put on the circle table. "You know you are supposed to pour this in a cup." He lifted the bottle and looked through it.

Looking at him for the first time since he'd been home, I picked up the pilsner glass I'd been using.

"Sorry, I didn't know you had a glass." He took a deep breath. "The glass is not really important. Why are you upset? Did someone say something that hurt you?"

"Someone said something that hurt me, all right." I put the glass down close to my chair, got the box of dead plants, and dumped the contents on the floor by his fancy leather boots before handing him the box.

"What is this for? What happened?"

"I didn't see her 'zings' in the guest bedroom, so they must be in your room, but I wouldn't know—I haven't been invited there yet."

"You are welcome in my room anytime, and as for Ekaterina, it was nothing serious. We were just … I'm really sorry, Ana."

"Looks like it was serious to her." I cleared the table and walked inside.

Claus followed me in. "I didn't think she wanted a committed relationship, Ana."

No, he didn't think—he was right about that part. "Are you committed to me?" I opened the fridge and got another beer.

"I love you, Ana." He took the bottle from my hands and opened it for me. "I've loved you for more than ten years now, and I've thought about you every single day of this whole time."

"Then take her stuff back to her and be done with it."

He nodded and watched me drink. "No glass?"

"Nope. This average American girl is gonna drink beer the average American way tonight. Cheers." I lifted the bottle in his direction and walked back outside.

He followed me again. "Remember, German beer is a lot stronger than what you're used to."

"Good." I went back to the flowerpots, working the soil with my bare hands.

"I'm really sorry about putting you through this," he said before disappearing with the box.

By the time I got in, he was gone, and I had three missed calls. All from Mom. Was something wrong? I tried not to panic as I waited for her to answer her phone.

"Is everything okay. Mom?"

"Hi, Ana." She sounded cheerful enough—if something was wrong, it wasn't anything big. "Was today your first day? How did it go?"

"Yeah, today was my first day. It went well, but I'm really exhausted. Can I call you tomorrow? I just saw the three missed calls and thought something was wrong."

"Well, I saw Peter at the park today and something seemed odd." There was a moment of silence. "Do you know if he's sick? Do you guys talk?"

"We don't talk, Mom." What was she trying to get to? "What do you mean by odd?"

"I can't quite figure it out—just different."

"Are you making this up to find out if we're talking?" My hands were filthy from gardening with no gloves. I had to wash them before doing anything else.

"I wouldn't do that."

She wouldn't—I believed her. But it was one of the weirdest conversations we'd ever had. I said goodnight and hung up, only mildly concerned.

During my first days in Germany, I had thought about Peter a lot and often felt as if I was just going through the motions of my new life. But with time, that had improved.

Lifting my eyes to the kitchen clock, I did the math. Two-fifteen in Pine Mountain. He was probably at work. I went back to the terrace and sat with Barysh.

Was he still with Lorie—playing the guitar, singing, planting, and building with her? I'd had enough to drink, but the lump in my throat needed another beer.

While in the kitchen, I checked the time again. Almost three in Pine Mountain. Before I could talk myself out of it, my cold fingers dialed Peter's number.

"This is Peter."

The pain came in waves as I replayed his voice inside my head—*This is Peter.*

"Hello?" His voice was casual. He had no idea who was on the other end of that line. If he'd known, he would either be mad or happy—not casual.

I'm gonna be sick.

I heard a quick click after what sounded like him dropping something. And then nothing. Just silence.

Slow tears rolled down my cheeks, and I walked an uneven line to the bathroom, my pace faster as I approached it. My shoulder hit the doorframe hard, but I was in.

I didn't make it to the toilet, though.

"Classy," I mumbled, looking at the vomit on the floor. I was thankful Claus wasn't home.

"Ana? You okay?" Claus was at the bathroom door.

Really? "I didn't know you were back."

"I just walked through the door. I didn't mean to startle you. I'm sorry." He looked at the floor.

Could life get any more embarrassing?

"Can I help?"

"No!" I walked to the door and stood between him and my mess. "You can help me find *Theme and Variations* on YouTube," I said before locking myself in the bathroom and turning on the shower.

I shouldn't have had so much to drink. Claus had warned me that the beer was strong. It was nice of him to not say, "I told you so." I would have deserved it.

Shouldn't have called Peter either. What was I thinking?

Chapter 14

Separating from my favorite *Blumenhaus* and from our unfinished terrace garden in mid-May was unfair and unfortunate, but the reward was majestic Prague.

The company was rehearsing for three days and then performing for four nights at the National Theatre.

The drive had been a strong selling point. Claus had promised 540 kilometers—335 miles—of lush vegetation in every shade of green, interrupted only by fields of bright yellow *Rapsfelder*, a flower cultivated for its oil-rich seed.

Halfway there, the scenery hadn't disappointed, but I was still unsettled.

"How about my *Spargel* man?" I asked, staring out the giant window of our orange tour bus when I spotted a white asparagus vendor after our Nuremberg stop. "Will he still be there when we get back?"

"His stand will be on the same corner." Claus opened one eye with a smirk. "In a week, he might even have a 'strawberry man' next to him. You can smell German strawberries from our terrace. The ones we are buying now are from France, not as good."

"White asparagus with melted butter, roasted potatoes, and a side of fragrant strawberries," I dreamed out loud. "That sounds so good."

"German strawberries," Claus mumbled, half-asleep.

I tickled his ear when we entered Autobahn 6 but got no reaction. "Asleep again."

From our front-seat spot, all I could see was the driver and the road ahead of us—the road to the Czech Republic—the road to a big decision. We were sharing a room at the hotel in Prague since it would look strange not to. But we were still in separate rooms at home. *Would we sleep together? Should we?*

Our celibacy had started quite by accident just before a strong southern storm, when I had stopped his advance—a rare move for me, reserved usually for creeps and drunks. It had continued because of pride, when he'd left me in the guest room, and I'd decided not to work my way into the suite. And then it had come to define our relationship.

When other couples went home to act married, we lingered at the park and fed ducks and pigeons. We couldn't tell the pigeons apart and were not sure which were residents and which were visitors, but we knew the two mommy ducks and the two daddy ducks by name. They'd just had sixteen babies—eight per couple—and we hoped to name them too.

We cooked often. Often badly. The rabbit *cabidela* had been especially dreadful, for the blood never turned grayish-brown as the recipe had promised. That night we ate *spaghetti aglio olio* at Di Gregorio instead.

"Ah, bad recipe again, Signorina Ana?" the skinny waiter had asked as he led us to our favorite patio table before tidying my coral linen napkin and explaining the day's specials.

But how long should we wait? That was the nagging question. Was it time to take the next step? Luci was right—this wasn't normal. She was the only one who knew what was really happening, and not happening, on quiet *Blumenstraße*.

Once in the Czech Republic, we made a stop at the Pilsner Urquell brewery in Plzeň before continuing the journey to the capital. Claus was only mildly interested in the production process, and once he started talking to Jakob, I found Luci.

"How are you?" Luci put her arm around my shoulder and led me outside.

"He's cute," I said of the dancer she'd been talking to before I showed up. He was very young and had just started.

"Cute and not into girls, I'm afraid." She lifted her flimsy tasting-room cup in a mock toast. "My luck."

"German?"

"*Ja.*" She lit up a Jin Ling. "And you, friend, have Claus." She put her cheap animal-print lighter in her jeans pocket and blew the smoke out fast. "Gorgeous and straight, but you won't sleep with him."

"Maybe we will here," I said, just above a whisper, heat flooding my cheeks as I waited for her reaction.

"You should." She rubbed her naked arms and motioned to the bus with her head. "He is straight, right?"

"Of course he is straight." I laughed it off. "You should have brought a jacket. You look frozen."

"I know." She flicked her cigarette butt. "How do you know that he is not gay?"

"Ten years ago, remember?"

"Ah ... ten years ago." Her voice trailed off as she walked up the steps. "People change, friend," I heard her say as she disappeared toward the middle of the bus.

A thud on the front window caught my attention. Jack, the only other

American dancer in the company, was lifting Claus, who pretended to be splattered on the window. I covered my eyes and shook my head. When I looked again, Claus was already inside, flopping down next to me and giving me a kiss.

Curling up on the seat, I turned toward him. Pilsner Urquell flavored our kiss as the driver started the engine.

"Get a room," I heard Jack say, walking past us.

"Working on it." Claus covered our heads with his leather jacket as I giggled.

By the time we got our keys to the hotel room, we had twenty-three minutes to drop off our bags and take quick showers. The whole company was meeting a local guide at the lobby at four o'clock for a walking tour and sunset dinner cruise.

We were staying next to the famous Old Town Square, surrounded by historic buildings, houses, and palaces of various architectural styles and colorful history.

One landmark soon commanded my attention: the Church of Our Lady before Týn. Its soaring Gothic steeples excelled at directing the eyes to the heavens, and multiple small spires made the building the most unique and aesthetically pleasing sight on the square.

A plain school building hid the base of the church, but while many might say the Týn School distracted the eye, to me it added visual interest. It was like seeing a bouquet of twenty-four red roses emerge impossibly from a bud vase.

"Look at the two spires." Our guide pointed to the steeples. "They look like they are the same, but they are not identical."

I turned to Claus and drew his attention to the spires. "I hadn't noticed that the spire on the right was slightly thicker."

He glanced upward before kissing my forehead.

"The two spires represent the masculine and the feminine sides of the world." The guide shaded his dark eyes as he looked toward us and the afternoon sun. "This is a characteristic of Gothic architecture of the time."

I walked away, intrigued by the concept. *Masculine and feminine ... two sides.* What was going to happen to our two sides tonight? Our room had one bed. Would Claus sleep on the small couch?

On our way to the river, we walked past the Jewish Quarter, where a few synagogues, the old cemetery, and the Old Jewish Town Hall had been left standing by the Nazis.

"The Nazis collected Jewish artifacts from all over central Europe and planned to display them here in an exotic museum of the extinct race." The guide stopped before a gorgeous triangular city block. "The race is not extinct, so you see no exotic museum in front of you. Just Europe's oldest active synagogue, the Jewish Town Hall clocks, and exotic Judah walking you through beautiful Prague." He motioned for us to cross the street after him.

Three city blocks later we were at the river and boarded the *Natal*, the boat the company rented for our dinner cruise. We set sail as the Vltava River changed from charcoal blue to glowing orange with the setting sun.

After a simple but elegant full-course dinner that tasted as beautiful as it looked, I walked outside to enjoy the fresh air and see the city by night. Historic buildings bathed in soft yellow lights spread warmth and welcome along the river despite the cold evening breeze as I climbed to the upper deck.

Watching the Czech flag fluttering at the stern, I could still hear the musicians in the dining room as they played a tender Bohemian folk song, the two violins more prominent than the wind instruments from the outside.

The beautiful National Theatre with its rectangular golden dome reminded me of my grandmother's massive music box with its amber crystals adorning the filigree along the sides. As a child, I'd spent hours dreaming in front of that music box, watching its delicate ballerina spin to the sounds of a *Doctor Zhivago* medley, and dreaming of ballet, of Russia, and of the wonderful man I would meet one day.

Prague wasn't Russia, but it was close. The *Natal* passed the theater now. The illuminated windows looked exactly like the amber crystals of the music box. Would a vintage ballerina with gold leotard and eternally disheveled tutu pop up to the sound of "Lara's Theme" if I were to open the lid? My lips stretched with the thought.

My eyes traveled to the other side of the river, and as I looked in awe at the sumptuous Prague Castle complex and its famous St. Vitus Cathedral, Claus joined me on the deck and handed me a glass of the late-harvest Czech Chardonnay we'd been sharing during the meal. Out here, as he embraced me, it tasted sweeter.

We drank slowly amid soft kisses, and he held me close. My heart reveled in his nearness. It was natural, like breathing. And I knew I would never forget the wonder of that moment and the beauty of that old city.

The smell of his cologne had me in a daze. Was it new? Woody undertones. Flower overtones. Violet?

We finished the wine and set the glasses on the long wooden table behind us. The kisses deepened. My hands slid around his waist and felt the warmth of the soft cashmere. His touch became more passionate, urgent. I was overwhelmed by a sensation that was both familiar and exotic.

Claus stepped out of my arms with a soft sigh and interlocked his fingers firmly with mine. His eyes—enthralled like Prince Albrecht's eyes in *Giselle*—were on mine. That was my home, his arms, his scent, his kisses ... we'd come home.

"Sweet Ana." He kissed my forehead.

I rested my head on his chest and was surprised to see the upper deck full. Luci was in a large group and lifted her glass in my direction in a silent toast when our eyes met.

When the boat docked, Claus and I were the first ones out, and we walked to the hotel ahead of everyone.

He is *interested in women.* I squeezed his hand.

He brought my hand to his lips and kissed it without slowing down the pace.

I wish Luci hadn't said anything. This is going to bug me now.

Inside the traditional burgundy-and-gold room, Claus found Dvořák on the old radio. "This is perfect." He put his arms around me, warm and sweet. "I love being in Prague. I love this music. And I love you, Ana."

"I love you too." My skin tingled to the powerful sounds of *New World Symphony.* "Be with me, Claus," I said, my breathing uneven. "I'm done waiting."

"I am with you."

"All the way. Be with me."

"Are you sure?" he whispered, his cheeks a lighter shade of the bedding behind him.

I nodded and buried my face against his chest.

With his fingers under my chin, he pulled me in and kissed me.

Kissing him back, I felt his hands sliding to my hips. *Claus Vogel Gert. Mine again. At last.*

As one movement ended and a new one started, I realized I'd been wrong. The composer was Dvořák, but the work was not the *New World Symphony.*

The new movement was a lento. A simple melody. A pulsating accompaniment. I'd danced that before. The second movement of the *String Quartet No. 12*—the *"American" Quartet.*

Is this a mistake? Is this, too, more of the same? A dance I've already danced? We can still stop.

His kiss was so warm. His touch so perfect. His accent. The city...

No. I can't stop.

We didn't sleep. Instead, we watched the sunrise from the Charles Bridge, and his tender kisses were as precious to me as the pedestrian-only stone bridge in the soft light of the morning sun's rays.

Next to us, a father and son fed the hungry morning pigeons, and painters captured the structure's splendor.

Tourists trickled onto the bridge as the sun played hide-and-go-seek over Old Town in a sky filled with long, thin clouds. First, a young couple showed up, then a family. A group of ladies photographed the towers that protected the bridge and the thirty religious statues mounted to the balustrade.

"Claus, look." I pointed at the young couple. They'd stopped, and the guy was on one knee holding up a ring. "I hope she says yes."

Claus squeezed me tighter, and the other couple hugged too. "I think she said yes." He kissed my temple, the scent of last night's perfume still on his soft skin. Would he propose like that one day?

Next to us, an old violinist put his open case on the ground. Would he play Dvořák for us?

"Do you mind waiting here?" Claus's eyes gleamed. "I want to buy something," he said, pointing at a nearby souvenir kiosk on the bridge.

"I don't mind. He'll keep me company." I tilted my head toward the violinist, who was now looking at us and seemed ready to play.

"I'll be right back."

The violin fooled me at first with an elaborate melody that could have been Dvořák, but then it bridged to a familiar melody. Images of Maya Plisetskaya as the sultry Carmen, and of Lorie watching her, flashed before my eyes as the old man's violin cried a gypsy version of Bizet's *Carmen*—the "Habanera." *Was I like Carmen? Self-centered and overly sensual? I didn't want to be. I wanted to be like Giselle—passionate but pure. Virtuous, not sultry.*

Claus returned and handed me not a ring, but a pair of small garnet earrings. "Do you like them?"

"Thank you." I forced a smile. *How very noncommittal.* "They're beautiful." *But they are earrings—not a ring. Sleeping with Claus now was a mistake, wasn't it? I did it again—what Lorie said. I gave him all he wanted. Now what?*

"Is everything okay?"

"Um-hm." A crisp breeze played with my hair, and my tight chest labored to fill up with some of that clean morning air.

My eyes spotted the *Natal* as it sailed under the bridge, away from the city and toward quieter waters—the place where we'd stood now empty. Could I go back to that spot—to the night before on the boat and make a different choice?

No, of course I couldn't. *Can't go back… What's done is done.*

There were no do-overs in life. I held up the deep blood-red earrings. Once you made a mistake, it was yours to carry forever.

Jakob only wanted understudies for a quick run-through of a small portion of the program, so the next day my rehearsal was short.

As I walked to the hotel, a light drizzle became a soft and steady rain shower. I couldn't be alone in a small room, in a foreign place, watching the rain. No way. My life, which in Germany had been as close to enchanted as it'd ever been, had lost its spark overnight.

Getting in an old cab, I shook the water off my small German umbrella, wondering how I would explain my desired destination to the driver. What was the name of the church with the statue of the Infant Jesus of Prague? Was it even a church? He had to be in Prague somewhere.

"Infant Jesus?" I asked.

The round man behind the wheel looked at me and raised his graying eyebrows.

"Infant Jesus?" I asked again, biting my lower lip.

He looked annoyed, like Grandpa when interrupted during a World Cup soccer match.

Ooh, I have an idea. Opening my wallet, I showed him the card Mom had given me ages ago and that I'd carried with me my whole life.

"Yes," he said slowly with a nod.

He started driving, and within two minutes there wasn't a tourist in sight. *Is this even safe? Where's he taking me?* "Is it far?"

He shrugged but said nothing. Instead, he pushed a button on the radio and soon lively music filled the cab. Was that a polka?

Loosening the death grip I had on the Infant Jesus image, I turned it around and tried to read the words. It was a prayer in Portuguese.

My mom had always been a huge fan of the Infant Jesus of Prague, and every time we went to her hometown of Porto Alegre in Brazil, we visited her *Igreja Santa Teresinha* and saw the statue of the Infant Jesus that's there.

That church had never meant anything to me, but watching Mom arrive there was always neat—she was at home and in peace.

Was it Saint Therese of the Child Jesus that made her feel at home? I was never able to understand who exactly that saint was. It wasn't the woman from Avila—that much I knew.

Maybe the serenity that overtook Mom came from the Infant Jesus image … or from God Himself. But wasn't God everywhere? Why did she need a building to feel good?

Could it be that it was the return to a place of peace, beginnings, and innocence that made her happy there? And could I get that same feeling by visiting the church here? *Let's hope so—that is if he is indeed taking me to the church. Should have gone to the one by the hotel.*

The driver parked by what looked like a church. *Phew.* I paid for the ride, and he gave me an image he'd removed from a stack he'd pulled from his glove compartment. He showed me the back of the card. It was the same prayer in Czech, I assumed.

Was I supposed to keep it?

He then showed me several images from a second stack. He turned each around, and I recognized German, Italian, Spanish, and French. But there were other languages too.

"Portuguese. Brazil." I said and let him add mine to his foreign collection before putting the Czech image in my wallet.

He thanked me and I said bye—happy to be part of the Infant Jesus in-group.

The rain had diminished, but heavy clouds swirled across dark skies. Inside, I dipped my hand into the holy water and blessed myself with the sign of the cross: *In the name of the Father, and the Son, and of the Holy Spirit. Amen.* I genuflected, bowing my head before entering the main aisle, and then started looking for the Holy Child.

To my surprise, the image was to the side of the pews. I had expected it to be near the front somewhere since He was so famous worldwide. It was also smaller than I had anticipated. The shrine was grandiose in elaborate gold, but the image itself was two feet tall, if that.

Mom needed to see this. I grabbed a brochure from a pew rack and sat.

The wax-wooden statue in the guise of a king came from Spain, I read. The right hand is raised in blessing. The left holds a sphere—our universe—in his hands.

The legend tells that the Infant Jesus appeared to a monk, who modeled the statue based on the appearance. According to another legend, the statue belonged to Saint Teresa of Avila, the founder of the Discalced Carmelites, a Catholic religious order that placed special emphasis on prayer.

Lifting my eyes to the Infant Jesus, I realized I'd been looking at various depictions of Him all day—statues that told the story of His life in reverse. At the bridge this morning I'd seen the silhouette of the lamentation first, when the sunshine was only a hint. Soon after, I saw Calvary. Then Jesus as an adult, also on the bridge. Here, the Child. *Life in reverse.* The image from the Jewish Quarter of the Hebrew clock that went backward came to mind.

Why couldn't I go backward too? And why was it so hard to admit I wish I hadn't slept with Claus? And above all, why did I feel that way? It'd been great.

Was it because I wanted our relationship to be more than physical? Of course I wanted that, but nothing had really changed and nothing was going to change—Claus would continue to love me the same and as much. There was nothing wrong with what we'd done. It was the natural development of a relationship in our day and age.

Yet something *was* wrong.

My head—that's what's wrong. I skipped to the end of the brochure. There was a museum dedicated to the Infant Jesus and a gift shop. *Let's check it out.*

After walking past every painting and every statue, I finally found the museum behind a door next to the main altar, at the top of a spiral staircase. *They sure like to hide the goods around here.*

Some of His little clothes and one of His crowns were on display. He had about a hundred outfits, and a video showed the Carmelite sisters changing the clothes of the statue.

Searching for a book for Mom, I came across a history book written in English with a picture of the original image on the cover. As I flipped through the pages, I came across a famous passage associated with the image, one that Mom had read to me before: "The more you honor me, the more I will bless you. Occupy yourself with My interests, and I'll occupy Myself with yours."

Would He really? Was any of it real, or was Lorie right?

"Well, what a small world," a lady in her late fifties said, touching my shoulder. "I'm from Georgia too."

How did she know I was from Georgia? She must have sensed my confusion because she pointed at my chest.

"Oh, yes." I smiled and realized I was wearing an old company hoodie.

"I live north of Atlanta, but my son is a preacher in Pine Mountain. I make it all the way to Columbus sometimes."

"Wow, my parents live in Pine Mountain," I said, a bit louder than I'd meant to and drawing the attention of two other groups in the little museum.

"Well, here let me give you a tract…" She trailed off, searching her purse for whatever a tract was. "Here you go."

She handed me a church brochure. For Calvary Baptist Church. *Seriously?* I didn't want to be rude, but half a chuckle escaped before I could act grown-up again.

"That's my son." She pointed to the handsome man with his gorgeous wife and three little girls in matching pastel dresses.

"Beautiful family."

"You should go check it out one day."

"I don't live there anymore, but maybe one day when I go visit my folks." I maintained my most polite smile and stuck the brochure inside the book I was about to purchase. "Thank you."

She nodded and looked like she was going to say something more, but she didn't. "Have a blessed day."

"Thanks." I watched her as she moved toward the spiral staircase. What was the mom of a Baptist preacher from Georgia doing at a Catholic Church in Prague? She looked back before going down, and we exchanged a smile and a nod. I could swear I saw her shake her head on the way down.

When I reached the Infant Jesus area again, she was there. Not praying, just looking around, and so I sat next to her. "I'm Ana." I offered my right hand.

Her cool hand met mine. "Jackie." She cocked her head.

"I didn't mean to laugh upstairs. I hope you weren't upset. It's just that I live in Germany, and I got a brochure for a Calvary Baptist Church there. The coincidence made me laugh."

"Why would I be upset?"

"Nothing." I shrugged. "I saw you shake your head on the way down."

"Oh, no." She laughed a delicate laugh like a little girl playing with her little girlfriends. "Just puzzled, that's all."

"Puzzled?"

"I had no intention of coming here—today or ever. I was supposed to be spending the day in Karlovy Vary. Yesterday at lunch, I was going through my copy of Rick Steves' *Prague and the Czech Republic* travel book, and the waiter pointed to the paragraph about this place, saying I should visit. I told him I had only one day left in my trip and already had a plan."

A man photographing the statue brought a quick index finger to his lips as he walked past our pew.

Jackie nodded an apology before whispering closer to my ear, "In the afternoon, the tour company that was taking me to Karlovy Vary called saying they were overbooked and offered an earlier tour with a sister company. I accepted. This morning, the alarm didn't go off, and I missed the tour."

"I'm so sorry."

"It's okay. I should know better than to fight the Holy Spirit of God." She raised her right hand to the heavens. "Praise the Lord, I always lose."

She was completely at ease talking about these things, and I was jealous.

"But you are right, I did shake my head. I expected something big to happen here today. Maybe to tell someone about the Romans Road to salvation and lead someone in the sinner's prayer. Instead, all I did was hand out a tract—something I do all the time anyway. But that's okay too. Sometimes a tract is all it takes. The Lord knows best."

What was she talking about? What was the Romans Road?

"I figured I would just sit here a while." She looked around the church with a sigh. "Maybe someone else needs a tract."

No, it's me. I need the tract. I got up to squelch the thought that came against my will. "Well, thanks again. I'm sorry you missed your trip."

"Maybe next time, dear." Sadness clouded her features.

I moved to a pew in the back and opened the kneeler.

Thank you, Jesus, for not giving up on me and always bringing me back to Your house. Thank you for Claus and for dancing. Sorry if I can't do better. Help me so I never hurt anyone again like I hurt Peter. Help me let go of the past and enjoy the future. Please hold my heart in Your hands. Amen. And I really wish You'd let Ms. Jackie go to Karlovy Vary, but like she said, I suppose You know best. Amen—again.

Lifting my head, I peeked over my folded hands. She was gone. I crossed myself and sat. Next to me, a tract marked a page within a New Testament from Calvary Baptist Church. I read the words in red:

My Grace Is Sufficient For Thee: For My Strength Is Made Perfect In Weakness (2 Corinthians 12).

That's right. I'd showed up feeling weak and now felt better. I'd prayed, was thankful, said sorry, was sincere... Now I could carry on, right?

Outside the Church of Our Lady of Victory, a timid sun tried to shine through the thinning clouds. I unfolded a map I'd found in our hotel room, crossed Karmelitská Street in the Lesser Town of Prague, and walked in the direction of the river.

Chapter 15

We picked up Barysh from boarding as soon as we arrived back in Wiesbaden and were told he hadn't eaten in two days.

The Hundehotel Jürgen veterinarian had checked him but hadn't found anything wrong—other than old age—so they didn't call us.

We took him to our regular vet, and she said his vitals were weaker than normal. "Maybe it is time to let go, yes?"

I'd heard that so many times that the words didn't really have an impact on me anymore. But this was the first time I was hearing it from a professional. My lungs emptied. Was that the end of denial? Were our days together numbered?

Claus squeezed the edge of my shoulders, the gentle pressure keeping me together.

"We could help." Dr. Joel's voice was kind but matter-of-fact.

My words stuck around the lump in my throat. "We'll just take him home." Looking at Barysh, helpless on the exam table, I forced a smile. His slim and bony hips didn't match the strong torso or the intensity of the get-me-away-from-the-vet expression. Nothing new there—he'd never liked vets. But one thing was new: a hint of affliction in his eyes.

Back at the apartment, I couldn't get Barysh to eat anything either.

"Are you sure you want me to go?" Claus asked after getting us settled in the apartment.

"I'm sure." While in Prague, I'd received an e-mail saying the Thunderbird had arrived. We'd planned to travel the ten hours to the North Sea port of Bremerhaven together to pick it up, but with Barysh not well, that was no longer a viable idea. Claus had arranged for a special power of attorney so he could handle the car situation for me.

"I'll be home by dinnertime tomorrow," he said before taking Barysh's head into his hands and giving him little Eskimo kisses. "When I get back, we will take you on a picnic by the river—your favorite, yes?" He hugged his head and petted him.

My heart squeezed at the sight. *Please don't die while Claus is gone.*

Two days later, we finished moving my things to the suite and took Barysh to our Rüdesheim spot, as promised.

The ride and being back in the Thunderbird and by the river must have opened his appetite at last. He ate grilled chicken breast and fresh cheese from our salad and tried a fine German Riesling from the palm of my hand before scooting to the sunflower patch for a nap.

Summer was officially starting in three days, and the sunflowers were a foot taller than me and ready to bloom.

"I want to take some seeds home to plant at Mom's." My fingertips brushed against the brown center of the tallest sunflower.

"We will wait for the right season, and I'll teach you to harvest." Claus sat on our blanket and closed his eyes.

Joining him, I rested my head on his lap and watched a procession of milk-white clouds roll by to the rhythm of the lazy warm breeze as we reminisced about the trip to the Czech Republic.

When Barysh woke up, we had an improvised photo shoot. We took pictures of him among the sunflowers, of him with the Rhine, and of him in the middle of the vineyard as he sniffed tiny grapes that were still deep green and hard to the touch.

Claus grabbed the camera and motioned for me to get in the shot. He walked up the hill past us so he could frame the river and the sunflower patch in the photo too.

I rode home holding on to Barysh while enjoying the wind by his side. As I scratched his ears, he barked at the wind before looking at me. *Is that a thank you?* I smiled at my friend. *Of course it is.*

At night, Claus put Barysh on the bed with us to watch a movie. I had already framed the sunflower patch picture and placed it on the side table.

We started watching *Last Holiday*, and as Queen Latifah turned the Czech spa city of Karlovy Vary upside down, enjoying what she thought were the last days of her life, I remembered poor Ms. Jackie who didn't get to go there.

My eyes abandoned the TV and rested on the New Testament she'd left for me and that now shared the table with the new picture frame. *My grace is sufficient for thee,* I'd read, not really sure what grace was—His or anybody's. It was more than feeling at peace at a church, wasn't it?

Whatever it was, I wanted it. Nothing had ever been sufficient for me in my life. Ballet achievements were never sufficient. Great boyfriends were not sufficient. Living in Europe was cool but not really sufficient. How could God's grace be sufficient? That was a promise I had to look into.

I wanted something sufficient. And I had a feeling I'd need something sufficient to get me through saying goodbye to Barysh. He snuggled against my feet. *Don't die. Not yet.* I tightened my lips, fighting back tears, and watched him drift off to sleep before turning my attention back to the movie and to Claus.

In the morning, Barysh didn't wake up. He was warm in bed, looking as comfortable as ever, but nothing moved. I tried to pick up his head, but the limpness made me stop in dismay. That limpness came to define death to me who had known no death. It was like lifting a heavy comforter. There was nothing there.

He was gone.

Barysh was gone.

Claus woke up, his lips parting at the sight of us.

Tears were streaming down my face, but no words came out of my mouth. I lay next to Barysh, and ran my fingers through his thick fur, missing the feel of his rhythmic breathing. My hand touched his face and caressed his forehead as I longed for one more look into his sweet brown eyes.

Claus was busy around us. Was he asking me something? What was he saying? He knelt by the bed, his tears steady and quiet like mine. He held my hand and touched Barysh's head to form a circle. And there we stayed for probably close to an hour, until I was able to say something and do something.

At first, I thought of arranging to cremate him so we could spread some of the ashes in Germany and some back home, but as soon as the thought crossed my mind, I knew it wasn't right for us.

A burial in Germany didn't make sense, but it felt right. Barysh would have liked a spot by the vines and the river, so Claus started making calls.

He found a small animal cemetery near Sankt Goar, an hour from Rüdesheim. The owners swore it would be there for years to come. Many of the little graves had been there for almost two hundred years.

We wrapped Barysh in a blanket like a baby, put him on the backseat of the Mercedes, and headed to the river again.

I stepped out of the car and went straight to the burial grounds. The place was well kept and the view beautiful, similar to the one from our picnic spot. I stood there clutching a small bag with some of Barysh's things and remembered our many adventures.

My favorite ones of all were from our first months together. I smiled as I remembered when I started taking him to doggie daycare. His old family had just moved to Germany, and he was being destructive when I wasn't home, so I wanted to find a way for him to let loose some of his energy.

The daycare had several shallow pools for the dogs to cool off, but Barysh didn't care for the water. Any other dog would just have stayed away, but not my dog. He went to the muddy puddles his friends created when water splashed out of the pools, backed into it, and kicked mud on all the other dogs.

My favorite memory was from obedience training—or rather, disobedience training. We didn't learn anything, couldn't do anything, and were finally asked to drop out of the class. So what if he didn't get the point of heeling? Quite frankly, I didn't either.

Then there was the time he wouldn't let me get out the door. He'd planted himself between me and the door and growled at me for the first and only time ever. Later that night, a police officer came by the building asking residents if we'd seen anything suspicious—two neighbors had reported a strange man roaming the hallways. Brave Barysh. Smart dog.

And now Germany. He'd been with me through so much. How could I ever get on without him?

Claus' hand on my shoulder startled me. I turned around and noticed he'd been crying too. It was time. We walked toward Barysh's tiny grave.

Barysh's body looked fragile in Claus' arms, and I touched the soft fur of his face one more time before placing a copy of our photo by his head and covering his face. My shoulders shook and my heart hurt, but he was so much better off now.

Claus eased the wrapped body into the grave, and I put his favorite yellow rubber football by his side before touching his body one last time.

The owners of the cemetery were helping with the burial. The wife handed Claus a giant sunflower—possibly the first to blossom on the Rhine that year. Claus placed it on Barysh and then grabbed the shovel.

Turning to look at the Rhine River below us, I smiled through my tears imagining his little soul chasing his yellow football like old times—freed from an old body that had quit suiting his active spirit a long time ago.

I looked at my copy of the picture. Barysh and I both had our noses toward bunches of tiny grapes with the sun shining on our faces. Beyond us, you could see the Thunderbird next to the sunflower patch with the Rhine glistening in the background.

Claus had finished and had his hand on my shoulder again. I looked at the grave and held his hand before walking to the car.

As we walked away, I whispered a little farewell wish, knowing the gentle afternoon breeze would carry it to my friend's ears. "Run, Mikhail Baryshnikov. Run and dance and drink all the wine, my friend. I love you."

My grace is sufficient for thee. What was it and why was it sufficient? I hadn't forgotten the verse—I was going to read the book.

That night, I got on social media for the first time since I'd left the US.

My newsfeed was filled with ballet photos, ballet videos, magazine covers, and plants—lots and lots of plants—mostly from Mom. She knew I'd been planting both at Claus' apartment and at my German teacher's apartment, so she'd been all ideas.

At Claus', I had planted eight trays of pink and white geraniums that contrasted with the dark iron of the terrace's railing, and I'd used smaller pots to plant columbines, foxgloves, and hawthorns. Now I had a beautiful picture of Barysh surrounded by pots and flowers on the day we started the garden. *Oh, Barysh.* My eyes hurt as if they were going to implode or pop. *Plants—focus on the plants.*

In our garden, delicate white flowers I'd never seen before brightened the pinks and purples, and little evergreen trees and bushes brought a soft contrast to the space. I had planted the same for Frau Jöllenbeck, my teacher, but in a different color scheme: reds and yellows. The right vine, maybe a wisteria, would add height and dimension to my terrace—and hers—one day, but I hadn't found the right plant yet. Mom had posted a couple of things that had potential. *I'll look it up later.*

Barysh had loved the scent of the garden and lifted his head every time a strong breeze ruffled the plants, surrounding us with a warm perfume. My throat hurt too now. *Focus.*

I should call my parents to tell them about Barysh's passing, but I didn't have any energy left in me. I didn't want to talk to anyone—not tonight. But they needed to know. Everyone needed to know that a devastating loss happened here in Germany today. My lips trembled and I wept as my fingers typed R.I.P. Barysh.

There. Then I turned off the computer and the phone, losing myself in my many memories—all I had left—of beloved Barysh.

Chapter 16

When I turned on the phone in the morning, I had two missed calls—one from my parents and one from Peter.

I talked to Mom, and I talked to Dad. They were heartbroken for me but relieved for Barysh.

Should I return Peter's call? *Nah ... he must have called on impulse. He only tried once and didn't leave a message. If he really wanted to talk, he would try again.*

Mom had never asked about him again. Had she seen him since the time he'd acted weird?

After walking into the bedroom, I reached into a bottom drawer filled with out-of-season clothes. Under it all was the pink envelope with the Kenny Rogers CD and Peter's note.

"For the road," I whispered. *A Love Song Collection.* Should I listen to it? My hand traced my name on the front of the envelope. I shouldn't...

Should I throw it away? I couldn't...

I returned the envelope and its contents to the bottom of the drawer.

Last Christmas I'd told Peter that I knew it was time to let Barysh go. Every time anyone said anything about my dog's health and the need to put him down, I fought it, but Peter knew that I agreed with all of them. My heart simply didn't have the courage to ask a vet to do it.

Peter had never pressured me to make a decision for Barysh and insisted that if it were really his time, I *would* have the courage to make the call.

But we'd hoped together that I would never have to get to that point—we'd hoped that death would visit gentle and comforting, like a warm moonlit night bringing quiet peace.

It had, and I wanted to tell Peter that. I smiled through tears, my eyes on the spot where Barysh had closed his eyes for the very last time. I petted his corner of the empty bed.

But it was best not to talk to Peter. I dried my tears. If I had answered the phone when Peter called, he would have expressed the same feelings my parents had expressed, I was sure. It would have been a compassionate but polite conversation about dogs, ending amid awkward silences and adding significant volume to my well of tears.

A well that right now needed a lid, as there was a full day of class and rehearsals ahead for me.

Life went on.

After the last rehearsal I checked my phone. No missed calls.

"Ana, are you in there?" I heard Claus ask from outside the dressing room.

"I'm almost ready."

"Jovana wants to talk to you." He peeked in with an eyebrow flash.

Jovana, our ballet mistress, had danced with legends like Fernando Bujones, Alicia Alonso, and Cynthia Gregory, to name a few. She rehearsed the corps de ballet often and taught the company classes most of the time. In the studio, she was very strict, severe even, but she was a sweet lady when there was no marley flooring in sight.

I walked into her office with Claus. The place was simple and tidy. Efficient. My eyes stopped on a *Swan Lake* photo of her and Bujones.

"I need just Ana," she said without looking away from her laptop.

He looked surprised but left, closing the door behind him.

"Ana." She came around her small desk with her arms crossed in front of her and stood next to me.

"Yes, ma'am." Was I in trouble?

She pushed her glasses into place and ran her fingers through her short black hair. "I can't wait to see you on stage. There is something about you—an artistic potential I haven't seen materialize yet but that I know is in you."

"I can't wait to be on stage." I beamed, wondering where she was going with this conversation. *Is she about to tell me that I don't have to audition in the fall? That we can start working on something right away? That I'm in the company?*

"There is a problem, though." She looked down.

Of course, there is a problem. This is my life we are talking about. There is always a problem. I braced for the worst, unable to read the twist of her mouth.

"Did you meet the new girl from Berlin today?" Jovana asked, as if she hadn't just broken my heart. "She sent a tape last month, showed up, and is now a soloist."

"I saw her, but I haven't met her," I said, relieved that I sounded composed.

"It's the nature of the business, and you know it. Some people are born with the ideal body type and dance well naturally. Others work hard and become very good but can't ever compete at the same level. It makes me sad because I like you." She picked up my hands and spoke as she looked in my eyes. "But you have Claus, and in him, a chance."

"Claus?" What was she talking about?

"We think he will be a great choreographer one day—we see an incredible potential. But he doesn't seem to be in a hurry to show us anything."

I nodded in slow motion. Claus was working on choreography, but how did everything connect? I wasn't understanding it.

"We want you to audition in the fall and perform a ballet, choreographed by Claus, immediately after." She sat behind the desk again. "You blow us away with his choreography, and you're in."

I nodded again, once more in slow motion. Did he already know about this?

"And we place it in the New York program," she said, as if she'd just said there was tuna salad in the kitchen.

Claus and me dancing at the Met? Together? I covered my mouth to muffle my childish squeals. "Sorry," I said, as soon as I was able to speak.

"Go." Jovana laughed, a confident tilt to her jaw. "And don't disappoint me. I'll be rooting for you."

"Yes, ma'am."

I found Claus outside with Jack, who waved and walked away when I came out of the theater.

"What happened?" Claus asked, his face scrunched up.

"I'm not sure." I started laughing and tearing up at the same time. "I'm really not sure if I should be happy or sad."

"I can see that. But what did she say?"

So he didn't know about the ultimatum. "Shhh," I said to quiet Claus and to calm myself. "Let's sit a minute." Grabbing his hand, I led him in silence past the statue of Schiller and the muse to a park bench by a large magnolia tree.

I sat, looking at the gorgeous opera house. The evening breeze ruffled the fragrant summer blossoms by the lake. It also ruffled the water and sent a cooling mist from the center fountain over our tired, sweaty bodies.

The lake was crowded with pigeons, and the baby ducks were almost grown now. We never did name them, I realized, with tears in my eyes again. We didn't linger at the park anymore. We had become like everybody else. I missed the way we were before Prague.

"Ana, what?" Claus asked, startling me.

"Well, she said there is no way I can pass an audition."

"What?"

"But that I can go ahead and audition, and then dance an original work choreographed by you. If I blow them away with your choreography, then they will let me in the company and put the work on stage in New York at the Met." I let my jaw drop on purpose to emphasize the insanity of it all. "No pressure on either of us, huh?"

"Wow." He looked whiter than usual. This was news to him, too, wasn't it?

"Wow indeed."

Claus moved closer and put his arm around my shoulders.

"I know you've been working on something." Hopefully, he would volunteer some information.

He didn't.

"What is it?" I asked. "Is it for me? Is it ready? Is it narrative?"

"It's for us. It's almost ready. It is narrative."

Okay. That's good. And that it's a narrative piece is good. If I'm to impress them, I need to tell a story.

"Here's what I suggest." He turned to me and held my hands. "I finish the work in the next couple of weeks, and then we go to Mallorca to get away from everyone—and away from the pressure. I will teach it to you there. When we return, we are ready to rehearse."

"Mallorca?" I put my legs on his lap and my arms around him.

"It's an island in the Mediterranean off the coast of Spain."

"I know, but why go to Mallorca?"

"Because I'm German, and that's what we do." He laughed. "I've been wanting to go for a while now. I was going to look at a couple of different resort options before running it by you."

"Okay."

"Good idea?"

"Great idea." I kissed his shoulder and hugged him tighter. "So what's the ballet about? What's the music? Can Luci be my understudy?"

"Let me finish it first." He caressed my legs over the pink tights. "Are you sure about Luci, though?"

"Yeah. She dances mostly classics, but she always says she's not much of a tutu girl. She would love to do something more contemporary."

"That's taking a big risk. I don't remember her dancing anything modern."

"Well, give her a chance."

"What am I? The patron saint of lost causes?"

"No." Swinging my legs down and shoving myself off his lap, I watched one of the ducks stick her derriere in the air as she searched for food at the bottom of the lake. "That would be Saint Jude. You're just a royal jerk."

"Ana, I didn't mean it that way. Sorry."

I walked away fast, but Claus caught up with me. "Listen, I am really nervous about this whole thing. I know I can dance, but I'm not sure I can choreograph."

"But you said you wanted to." My feet kept moving toward home fast.

"There is a big difference between wanting to do it and actually doing it—and doing it under this kind of pressure."

"Then don't do it, Claus."

"This is coming out all wrong." He punched the air. "I'm not able to express what I'm feeling."

"The understatement of the year," I said, without slowing my pace.

"Ana." He grabbed my wrist and forced me to stop.

"Can I please just go home? I need to go through Barysh's things and figure out what to do." Sudden tears flooded my eyes and spilled over.

"Come here."

I shook my head before stalking away, drying my face with the palms of my hands.

He didn't attempt to speak again until we'd reached the building. "It's called *Praha* because I loved our time there and how our relationship changed during that time." His voice was much calmer, his steady hands opening the elevator for us.

Of course he loved our time in Prague.

"We'll be dancing to Dvořák's *New World Symphony*."

And then he kissed me, the tenderness of his touch melting my anger and my sorrow.

"The *largo*," he said amid slow kisses. "*Molto largo*."

His lips stretched against mine, and I smiled too. *Praha*.

"I really didn't mean the lost cause comment the way it sounded." His voice was throaty now. "I'm sorry."

Walking around him to get to the elevator panel, I closed the flimsy metal door before pushing our button. "I know."

Once inside the apartment, Claus went straight into the kitchen, and I heard him pop open a bottle of champagne.

Champagne?

He came back with two flutes, and I immediately spotted a marquise-cut diamond ring in the one he handed to me.

"Can't say I saw this one coming." Why right now? "Is this a pity proposal for calling me a lost cause?"

"Ana, come on. Yeah, I keep a diamond ring around the house just in case I stick my foot in my mouth."

"Do you?"

"No. I got it before Prague."

"And then what?"

"And then I was looking for the right occasion. I was going to give it to you in Mallorca."

"But decided to use it now, so I can stop thinking about the previous conversation?"

"Decided to use it now because I want you to know how much I love you, and that I love you no matter what, and that I want to be your partner no matter what. Forever."

Wow. Is this really happening? All of it?

"Ana, will you marry me?" He got down on one knee and held my hand.

Of course I wanted to. Images of our lives together flashed before my mind. The beginning, his return, *Romeo and Juliet*, him at my old apartment asking me to move in with him, the trips, the loss of Barysh, the dancing ... our life.

"Ana?"

Now we would start a new phase. My eyes met his. Surely, he knew I would say yes, right?

"If you need time to think—"

"On one condition," I interrupted. My eyes riveted on the *Paquita* picture.

"Condition?" His eyes followed the direction of mine.

"This *Paquita* picture has to go."

He filled up his lungs, then exhaled fast. "Okay." Grinning, he took down the picture of me at seventeen. Claus fished the ring from the champagne and put it on my finger before enveloping me in an embrace.

I listened to his uneven heartbeat and exhaled, enjoying the warmth of his protection. *It is really happening—all of it.*

And for once in my life, what I had was sufficient.

My parents were thrilled with the engagement and planned to spend Christmas in Germany. Once Mom settled down and stopped crying, her tone changed.

Why did I have a feeling she was going to say something about Peter?

"At least one of you is moving on." *Knew it.* "I was at the horticultural center the other day to buy a birthday gift for my friend, Janet, and, if you know anything about plants, you just know the designer was not well—false agaves, bleeding hearts, black pearls..." *He's had my number all this time.* "Don't get me wrong. It was beautiful, but so incredibly sad...." *He chose not to use it.*

Chapter 17

Seventeen minutes after takeoff, Claus was asleep.

I reached for the thin white envelope in my purse and held it against the bright blue skies outside the small window. Peter's handwriting, straightforward and masculine just like him, called to me to open the letter. It had been a little over an hour since we'd left Wiesbaden for the small Hahn airport, and soon we would arrive at Cala Romantica in Mallorca.

"*Was möchten Sie trinken?*" the flight attendant asked as I ripped open the envelope.

Heat flooded my cheeks. *Trinken* was drink—I knew that much. "*Mineralwasser, bitte.*"

I wished I hadn't checked the mail. The letter would have been perfectly fine sitting in the mailbox for one week.

The attendant stretched over Claus and handed me a napkin and a plastic cup with ice and lemon. She reached over him one more time and handed me a small bottle of water with tiny bubbles floating to the top.

I tried to remember how to ask for regular water instead, but the possibility of what was in the letter kept all German phrases from coming to me—all fifty of them. "*Danke Schön.*"

"*Bitte Schön,*" she said, already turning to the elderly couple across the aisle from us.

I looked around. Claus was fast asleep. It was just me, alone in my little corner of Ryanair flight 9832 to Palma de Mallorca.

This is wrong.

I squelched the pesky voice inside my head and pulled the one-page letter out of its envelope to unfold it with unsteady hands.

It had been four months, and what he wanted to say fit on one side of the yellow paper from the old legal pad that he had kept on the kitchen table—the one with the lower corners of every remaining page forever curled and slightly smudged by the breeze that came in from the lake. Whatever happened to the five-page love letters he used to write?

The sudden knot in my throat told me I shouldn't read. This was a simple condolence note, wasn't it?

I looked out the window. Green fields and forests stretched as far as the eye could see. Was that France? The plane was steady again, and I took a deep breath, turning my attention to the yellow paper on my lap.

Heart turbulence kept me from reading, and I filled my lungs to capacity. *Calm down ... breathe.* Did someone near me order coffee? My eyes examined the trays of the passengers closest to me. Nope. Bringing the letter to my nose, I realized it was the letter. Coffee and biscuits. I tried to laugh it off, but it was too late. In my mind and in my heart, I was in Peter's kitchen, ready to listen.

> ANA,
>
> I'M SO SORRY ABOUT BARYSH. HE WAS A GOOD DOG. I HOPE YOU ARE FINDING COMFORT IN THE KNOWLEDGE THAT HIS SUFFERING HAS ENDED.
>
> I'VE BEEN TRYING TO MOVE ON. SOME DAYS ARE GOOD. SOME DAYS ARE NOT SO GOOD. I BLAME MY COUNTRY-MUSIC HABIT FOR THE BAD DAYS. DO YOU STILL LISTEN TO COUNTRY?
>
> OKAY. I'M JUST GOING TO SAY IT. I CAN'T BELIEVE YOU JUST UP AND LEFT, ANA, GONE TO GERMANY WITH SOMEONE ELSE. I KNOW YOU WELL ENOUGH TO KNOW THAT'S JUST YOU BEING YOU—NOT DWELLING ON SUFFERING, BLAH, BLAH, BLAH—BUT HOW DO YOU DO THAT? THAT'S JUST NOT HUMAN.
>
> YOU MUST REALLY LIKE THIS CLAUS FELLOW. THAT'S THE ONLY ANSWER. AND THAT LEAVES ME IN A REALLY BAD PLACE. IT REALLY DOES.
>
> I HOPE HE'S GOOD TO YOU.
>
> AS FOR YOUR FRIEND LORIE, SHE'S A CHARACTER ALL RIGHT. AS I WATCHED HER BATTLE GOD, I WAS REMINDED THAT NO ONE HAS EVER WON THAT FIGHT.
>
> AND WHILE I WOULD NEVER—EVER—GO BACK TO CHURCH, I DID START READING THE BIBLE AGAIN—LORIE'S BIBLE. SHE ABANDONED IT AT MY HOUSE WHEN SHE LEFT THE RANCH FOR THE LAST TIME.
>
> YOU SHOULD READ IT. I READ ROMANS LAST NIGHT AND THOUGHT OF YOU A LOT.
>
> HOW DID THIS HAPPEN TO US? UNBELIEVABLE.
>
> I WILL LOVE YOU ALWAYS, ANA. I WISH YOU WERE HERE, SO WE COULD TRY TO BE TOGETHER, GO ON A DATE ... SEE WHAT HAPPENS ... BUT YOU ARE SO FAR AWAY FROM ME—FROM US.
>
> JÄGER SAYS "HELLO"—WOOF.
>
> YOURS ALWAYS,
>
> PETER

Lowering the letter to my lap, I felt sick to my stomach, and the carbonated water became a good idea fast. I placed the lemon on my napkin before pouring the water over the melting ice.

I'd spent a decade looking for love and struggling. Suddenly, I had two wonderful men who loved me. Precious men. I should have been happy, but I wasn't. There was no way we could all be happy. Someone would hurt. I put the letter in the envelope, folded it once, and rolled it tight.

Looking at Claus peacefully asleep, I squeezed the roll into the empty water bottle and handed it to the flight attendant. "*Danke.*"

"*Bitte.*"

Being at the resort in Mallorca was just like being at a resort in the Caribbean. Only the geography of the shoreline differentiated the two regions. In Mallorca, giant mountain ranges and cliffs gave way to unexpected corridors that took the water inland to little white sandy beaches—dramatic and beautiful, like a small artery carrying blood to the most distal part of a faraway limb.

We worked in the mornings under an oversized thatched gazebo nobody seemed to use until sunset and enjoyed the beach in the warm afternoons and breezy evenings.

When we were not swimming, Claus was reading Barbara Milberg Fisher's biography, *In Balanchine's Company: A Dancer's Memoir*, and I thumbed through the only book in English Claus owned, *William Wordsworth—The Major Works*.

Halfway into our stay in Mallorca, and with the work almost finished, I couldn't sleep.

Peter's letter was gone, but his words were etched in my brain and rang unwanted in my ears every time I let my guard down. *She left the ranch for the last time… I would never—ever—go back to church… Romans… I wish you were here…*

I looked for the little green book I'd packed with Barysh's last photo. *I didn't know Peter was ever in church. Watch him be Baptist too.* I shook my head and grabbed Ms. Jackie's New Testament to look for the book of Romans.

The tract she'd given me flew to the ground as I thumbed through the pages. I picked it up and looked at the picture of her son with his perfect little family as if I were studying aliens from Pluto. Who were these people, and what were their lives like?

There was something wrong with the posture of the youngest girl. I brought the tract close to the yellow lamp that sat on the old desk. How did I not notice this before? Was she being supported by her mom? Looking for more pictures of the family in the tract, I found some verses from Romans—just what I was looking for.

But the tract had only five verses. I wanted the whole thing, and so I grabbed the New Testament.

"Everything but Romans," I mumbled, searching through it and noticing some verses were underlined. I looked at the book cover: "A Marked Edition— See Page 216." *Why not?* "For all have sinned, and come short of the glory of God." I realized the verse was in Romans. *Of course. Peter read it and remembered me. Awesome.*

An arrow at the bottom of the page preceded a note asking me to go to page 219. "Sure, entertain me." I skipped forward. "For the wages of sin is death; but the gift of God is eternal life through Jesus Christ our Lord." Romans. I came short of rolling my eyes and instead plowed forward to continue the treasure hunt from arrow to arrow, page to page, in what could end up being an abbreviated tour of the New Testament.

One set of underlined verses made me stop the journey: *saved by grace and not of works?* The verses read like a foreign language. *You've got to do something to earn it. Come on.* "I need to stick to Romans," I whispered, shaking my head and trying to find it again. "Enough with arrows and underlines."

I found Romans, opening it to chapter seven. Too confusing … the law and sin, marriage, Christ… *I'm not following this.* I skipped some verses looking for something I could understand. "…the law is spiritual … but I am carnal…" *I think I get it—it's like me wanting to be like Giselle but acting like Carmen. Hmm.*

Chapter eight was even better and filled with soothing words about children, heirs, liberty, hope. "Wait a minute."

"What are you doing?" Claus asked, half asleep.

"Did you ever hear that when you want something with all your heart, the universe conspires to help you achieve it?"

"What?" He sat up beneath the beige sheet. "Are you reading that New Testament you got in Prague?"

I nodded. "Mom says the universe conspires to help you when you fight the good fight. I didn't know it was an idea from the Bible."

"The good fight?"

"Something you really want."

"God makes all things work together for the good of those who love Him. That's in Romans." He reached for his water. "The good fight is in Timothy somewhere. Sorry, it's been a while—the good fight of faith."

"Am I the only person who doesn't know the Bible?"

"You're Catholic, huh?"

"What's wrong with being Catholic?" I stood and crossed my arms over my chest. "I know the same stories about Jesus that you know."

"Nothing wrong." He put his head down on the pillow and patted the spot next to him.

"What are you?"

"I grew up Lutheran."

"Okay." What was a Lutheran? I put the book down and turned off the lights, wondering in the darkness if Mom knew that her "universe conspiracy" theory was fresh out of the Bible. She'd studied in Catholic schools when she was little, so she probably was familiar with the verse. She should have told me it was from the Bible. Showed me. I would have liked to read it in context and learned more.

But I would *learn.*

After a remarkable seafood dinner by the natural harbor of Porto Cristo on our last night, we purchased a bottle of local red wine and went back to our beach to celebrate the completion of the work and to wrap up our vacation.

"Today's dancers are so athletic." Claus held my hand as we waded in the cool water of the Mediterranean Sea. "Seems like overnight women went from double pirouettes to triples and more, with *fouettés* being a crazy display of balance and control. Doubles and triples with every rotation ending in what? Quintuples?

"Men are doing one million perfect pirouettes, finishing in balance, jumping higher than ever…" He trailed off, lost in his thoughts for a moment. "I think it's all incredible, but I want to challenge that somehow. I want to showcase artistry and lyrical quality."

"You are so good at ballet acrobatics, though." My hand caressed his. "You should just embrace it. I hate that I can't do it."

"You probably hate me for complaining, but the technical expectation gets so high for me that there are nights I walk away without any sense of artistic fulfillment. And that's just not right. Technical accomplishment is cool—don't get me wrong—I am very thankful for it. But I'm an artist first, and something is just missing. Do you understand?"

"I do." We'd reached the end of the beach and turned around. "I do understand what you're saying, but I still want what you have, though. The things I would do with a better ballet body. I feel so limited—it's depressing."

Jovana had said it best—some people are born with the ideal body type and dance well naturally, others work really hard and get very good, but can't ever compete at the same level.

"I'm sorry." He ran his fingers through my hair. "It isn't fair, is it?"

"No. It isn't." Did he really walk out of performances feeling empty as an artist? That was depressing too. "Will you be jealous if I tell you something?"

"I don't know." He stopped. "What are you going to tell me?"

"Do you know how often I get a sense of artistic fulfillment?" I watched his eyes narrow.

"Most of the time?"

"During and after every single performance." I lifted the bottle. "Here's a toast to low expectations—there are perks—when people expect nothing from you technically, you're free to be an artist."

He cocked his head. "There are plenty of expectations placed on you too, and you know it. But I am jealous."

"Where is the trading-places genie when you need him, huh?" I laughed and had a sip of the warm wine.

"Listen, I want you to have what I have." Claus hugged me. "I want to make this happen for you." He took the bottle and finished the wine. "We need to explore your talent—the things you do well."

"That is so *Center Stage*." I watched him plant the bottle on the sand. In the movie *Center Stage*, a dozen teens begin their American Ballet Academy training hoping for a spot in the company. Jody Sawyer has talent but, like me, has a body that doesn't help her much, with feet that lacked high arches and legs that didn't turn outward as much as the other girls' did. In the end, a star dancer, Cooper Nielson, starts a company and invites her to be a principal, vowing to explore her strengths.

"Are you mocking me, Jody Sawyer?" Claus held his chest as if heartbroken.

"Shut up, Cooper."

The sound of our conspiring laughter rolled through the night air like the gentle waves that rolled into our Cala Romantica beach, rhythmic and unassuming.

"Can I speak seriously now?" His brows drew together.

"If you must."

Claus held my hands and looked into my eyes.

He did look serious. I hadn't seen him that serious since the day we left Georgia.

"I want to create ballets that will inspire people to dance with heart, like *Praha*. That's my dream."

Squeezing my hands, he gave me soft angel kisses mixed with the salty sea breeze. *Nice.* I looked at him when he stopped—still serious.

"You are perfect for my vision." He met my lips again.

"Really?"

He brought a finger to his lips. "Shh… Frederick Ashton choreographed for Margot Fonteyn and explored her charm. Kenneth Macmillan enjoyed exploring Lynn Seymour's dramatic talent. And I have you. You are my canvas. We are going to mature—as artists—together."

"Wow." That was a fantastic list of people. Sweet, sweet words.

His arms wrapped around my body. "How does that sound?"

His heart beat fast against mine. "Sounds fantastic." We swayed to the sweet sounds of the sea, and staring at the stars in the moonless sky of that beautiful Mediterranean night, I felt everything was right with the world.

I was his woman, and I would be his ballerina—his inspiration—and we would experiment together. He would create new rides through movement and expression, and I would be the willing passenger. Terrifying? Yes. But absolutely fantastic.

"You know what else?" Claus asked looking relaxed and content.

"What else?" What else could there be?

"We should make a baby." His voice was dreamy, his beautiful accent thrilling.

Wow. That sounded wonderful, but was that the right time? "But how about all the stuff we just talked about—*Praha* and the Met and your future as a choreographer?" I asked, hoping with all my heart that he had this all figured out.

"We get married on Christmas when your parents are here and then start trying. But you should get off the pill sometime soon. It takes forever for that stuff to get out of your system. It took Hanna almost a year to get pregnant when we tried." He faked a smile, either regretting mentioning her name or concealing his feelings about the baby they'd lost.

I kept my expression pleasant on purpose but maintained my silence. How many more dreams would he shoot at me in one night? And how serious was he about each?

"We can use protection until Christmas if you want. I just don't want to run into an over-planning issue again." He shook his head, as if waking from a bad dream. "Everything will work out just fine. Even if you get pregnant on our wedding night, you wouldn't be showing in New York." He looked down amid deep-throated chuckles.

"What?" I asked.

"It's silly."

"What?"

"I know the choreographer." He kissed my hand and kept his gaze down. "I will make sure he plans some loose clothing for *Praha*—just in case."

"Letting it get to your head already, Mr. Choreographer?" We laughed together once more.

I looked into his blue eyes, made darker by the midnight. My heart raced and my body quivered as I embraced his idea. "We should."

"We should what?"

"We should make a baby."

Chapter 18

I wrecked the Thunderbird," I blurted when Claus answered his cell phone after what seemed like twenty rings. "Can you come get me?"

"Are you okay? Where are you?"

"I'm two blocks from the nursery." I struggled to sound calm. "I was buying mums." *Stupid mums.* "I'm okay. Nothing happened to me. I'll probably be sore come tomorrow, but I'm fine."

"Oh, thank goodness." He exhaled hard. "You're sure?"

"Positive." I touched my neck where I could feel some stiffness, but I wasn't in pain. It was just a little tight. "Can you come get me? I'm at a bakery."

"Do you know the name?"

"I'm not sure, but look for leftover dirt and trampled mums baking on the road." I dried a tear and took a deep breath. "I'm inside hiding behind the *Financial Times*." I picked up the oversized pink newspaper from an abandoned pile on a small table next to mine.

"I'm on my way."

"Thanks." My chin quivered against my will. Opening the paper, I pretended to read the latest UK news, but my mind drifted to the job I'd planned on finishing that afternoon and now couldn't.

A young couple, newlyweds from the ground floor, had asked Jutta, my German teacher and neighbor, about her flowers, and she'd mentioned my name. They'd offered me five hundred euro, in addition to the cost of the plants.

I took a sip from my creamy cappuccino. I'd finished most of the work and was just waiting for mum season to wrap up the project. Now my mums were in pieces, half all over the road and half with the tow driver who'd tried hard to clean up my mess.

When Claus arrived, I showed him two business cards. One for the shop where the Thunderbird was, and one for the person whose car I'd hit.

The guy from the garage said he'd looked at my car and couldn't fix it, so Claus arranged to have it towed to our building.

"I will go by one of the Army kasernes tomorrow." Claus put away both cards. "I think they have a garage and mechanics at the Mainz-Kastel Kaserne or maybe at the airfield."

Not knowing when or how the Thunderbird would be fixed made me feel worse. It was just a car. I shouldn't be so bummed about it, but I was—that car was special to me and was my last connection to the U.S. Everything else was going so well. We were one month into the *Praha* rehearsals, and the piece was looking beautiful. Classes were going great too.

But now this. "I could never have everything be just right. Something always has to be wrong in my life."

"It'll be okay. We'll get it fixed." Claus kissed my forehead gently. "I'm so glad you're not hurt."

Me too. Thankfully, no one was hurt. The accident could have been much worse. I'd thought I had the right of way. Good thing I wasn't driving fast. Priority to the right is such a ridiculous right-of-way system that most intersections in Germany are controlled with priority signs—or traffic lights—so people are not constantly stopping to give way to cars approaching an intersection from that direction.

But I'd failed to notice that the intersection where I crashed didn't have a priority sign—obviously. I assumed I could keep going since my road was bigger, but then the Thunderbird hit a Mercedes that came from a smaller and almost deserted road—but who cares? The August Diehl lookalike I hit approached from the right.

"Do you want to go back to the nursery?" Claus opened the bakery door for me. "We can get a plastic bin for the plants. I don't mind."

I shook my head. "Not today. I just want to go home."

It was the first week of September when my mom called, her ragged breathing evident despite the distance between us. "Ana … Ana, your dad is fine, but—" I placed my hand over my heart as I listened to her take a breath. "Sweetheart, he had a heart attack."

"No, Mom…"

"He's okay now, but it was bad, honey." Her voice faded, and I waited for her to continue. "He had to have an angioplasty, and we will be in the hospital for a few more days before I can take him home."

"Mom, I'll go see him." I wrote down 'angioplasty,' so I could look it up later. "I'll call you when I have flight numbers and dates. Is Mike there?"

"Yes, your brother arrived this morning." Her voice was calmer now. "Are you sure you can come?"

"Yes." There was no way I *wasn't* coming. "I'll call back soon, Mom. Hang in there, okay?" I wouldn't leave Mom and Dad to deal with this without the whole family there. No way.

Two days later, Claus and I were on a flight to Atlanta to stay a week and then fly back five days before the audition.

As we waited for the plane to leave the gate, I pulled a tin box with a few sunflower seeds out of my purse.

They were seeds of the sunflowers we'd watched germinate and grow. Our graceful giants had followed the sun across the horizon, turning back and facing east every morning. They had climaxed fast, and then the heads had slowly bowed.

It was still too early to harvest them, but Claus went to the field shortly after my mom had called and found a dozen plump seeds for me to take home.

As Lufthansa 444 taxied to the runway, Claus caressed my cheek with his fingertips and watched me as I touched the seeds in the small tin box one more time.

"I could swear you were wearing your scarf." He cocked his head, his hand gentle on my bare neck.

"I was going to." I held his hand as the plane gained speed on the runway. "I draped it around Barysh's picture. I didn't want to leave him alone. I'm silly, I know. I hope you don't mind."

"I don't mind." He kissed my hand before closing his eyes. "I just wanted to make sure it wasn't lost."

"Nope, it's not lost," I said as the nose of the plane tilted skyward, and the chaos of tires speeding against hard cement became peaceful blue skies that matched the strange stillness of my heart. Dad's situation was still critical, but the doctors were happy with the results of the surgery, and I was happy to be Georgia bound. I was where I needed to be—taking care of family with my ballet bag in the suitcase and with Claus by my side. Everything would be okay.

Chapter 19

I want to go to Columbus for classes." I looked at the chickadees and warblers outside Mom's kitchen window and remembered the pain of the last time I'd sat at that table.

What I really wanted was for Lorie to see us, together and happy. And engaged. She had to know that her efforts to ruin my life had amounted to nothing. But Claus did not need to hear that.

Dad was home from the hospital. He was upset about not being able to golf and complained about the diet the doctor had prescribed, but otherwise he was okay. What could have been fatal wasn't.

"We should go to Atlanta for classes. You need to be challenged. Falling back into your old routine in Columbus will accomplish nothing."

"What I need is to hang out with people I know." But Claus was being as stubborn about Atlanta as I was being stubborn about Columbus.

"What you need is to keep your eye on the ball. Isn't that how you say it in America?" He raised an eyebrow. "You have a major audition for a major company, and you've made major progress. Don't slow down now. Let's go to Atlanta and take classes where you won't lose any momentum."

"But I want to go to Columbus and see everyone. That's my studio. My people."

Claus shook his head. "Isn't there a school here?"

"Oh, and a school in Pine Mountain would challenge me more than a company class in Columbus? You're not making any sense."

He walked quietly to Mom's kitchen window. What was the big deal? I thought he liked Columbus. "There may be a fairies and princesses class down at the Y." I tried to stay serious, but the idea of showing up at a school where the average age was six had me smirking behind his back.

"Would I be the fairy or the princess?" We both burst into laughter at that.

It was good to hear him laugh. He'd had me concerned for a moment. "How about this: two classes in Columbus and two in Atlanta. And then we will be on our way back to Germany."

He looked worried again. "Fine, Ana. But it's a mistake, huh?"

The Allen Ballet had danced *Don Quixote* the previous month. Next was a mixed bill in late-October. They were doing *Les Sylphides*, the *Sylvia* pas de deux, Benjamin Millepied's *Closer*, and Nacho Duato's *Arcangelo*. Brian had wanted to add a fifth piece but hadn't found the right thing.

"You guys should stick around and do your balcony scene," he said.

"I wish we could, and I wish I could dance *Archangelo* too," I said. "I love that ballet. I'm officially jealous."

Maybe after class I would mention the audition. For now, I just wanted to get changed and do a little stretching. And see Lorie.

I peeked into the bright dressing room.

She was in the same area she'd claimed a decade ago when we'd started dancing at the Allen Ballet—the last locker on the right, by the showers.

I glanced at my old locker, opposite hers. It didn't look like anyone had taken it yet. The door was open like I'd left it. A small image of the Met entrance, seen from Lincoln Center Plaza, still decorated the inside of the tall metal door. I'd printed it for that purpose, soon after my first trip to Germany. The five concrete arches and tall glass façade were lit up by the famous sputnik chandeliers in the grand lobby. It was beautiful.

I'd left the image behind, hoping it would inspire someone new to dream big. I was already on my way there. I didn't need it anymore.

But the image didn't seem to be inspiring anyone at the moment. It looked sad and lonely—abandoned.

The thought of taking it down crossed my mind, but maybe one day it would still mean something for someone at the Allen Ballet. It should stay.

Lorie was putting her long blonde hair up into a bun and was surrounded by the youngest girls in the corps—teenagers all. They were chatting about last week's performances.

"Did you read our wonderful *Don Quixote* reviews?" Lorie's exaggerated Southern drawl couldn't be more annoying.

"I sure did," the thinnest of them all volunteered. "They love you, Lorie. If I remember correctly, the word 'perfection' was used to describe the wedding pas."

"Oh, it's easy to look good with the perfect partner." Lorie sure had changed. "Daniel is the best partner I've ever had—better than Claus Gert and way more gorgeous."

Oh, whatever. Sure he is. Daniel was a good dancer and a sweet guy, bless him. But his technique was nowhere near Claus's. And he looked like a mouse—a skinny mouse, with skinny facial features and skinny little legs.

I'd heard enough. Where were all the normal people? I backed out of the dressing room and changed in the hallway bathroom.

Claus had been right. The idea of taking classes in Columbus had been a mistake.

By the time Claus came in, I had a spot behind Lorie at the barre and was stretching. He shook his head when he saw me.

What? My heart pounded so hard, I felt the beats in my head. I'd never plotted revenge of any kind before, but I'd never been intentionally hurt before either. There had to be consequences for what Lorie did to me and to Peter.

Claus walked over to Daniel, the mouse, who was at one of the center barres. They chatted for a while, and Claus ended up staying there when Brian started the class.

He was too far from me. But now wasn't the time for a display of discontentment.

After doing our first warm-up exercise to the right, it was time to turn around and repeat the combination to the other side. My left hand was now free to dance, and Lorie was free to watch it.

The first wave of jealous energy came with the very first port de bras.

Mission complete.

When our work at the barre was over, I stretched with Claus.

"Why did you have to be so far away?" I adjusted my shoes.

"You wanted to be with your people." He touched my cheek and then wiped off the sweat from under my eyes. "I was giving you space."

"I don't need space. I just wanted to be here."

Brian marked a simple *tendu*, thus continuing the class.

"I should have sent you to Germany a long time ago." He walked past me during the pirouette part of the combination. "You look amazing."

The class was turning out to be one of the best I'd ever had at the Allen Ballet. I really had improved a lot. More turns, bigger jumps, sharper movements. More confidence—at long last. Germany had indeed been a great idea.

After class, I talked to Brian about my upcoming audition in Wiesbaden and about the new choreography. We promised to come back the following day, bring the music, and show *Praha* to him.

But I wasn't sure I really wanted to. Showing off to Lorie had brought less joy than I'd expected, and I couldn't help but feel small and infantile. My peace and happiness had been shaken, and it had been my fault.

I squeezed Claus's hand on the way to the elevators and was happy that home was far away from the Allen Ballet. "Do you want to dance in Atlanta tomorrow?"

"Yes." He dropped his head hard, like a tired soldier declared victorious at last, after a long and exhausting battle.

"I'll call Brian later and explain."

As we left the company building, I was surprised to see Lorie standing outside next to a parking meter.

"Ana, I just want to say I'm sorry for all the things that happened earlier this year." A corner of her mouth lifted.

Since when did people apologize with a smile on their face?

"Let's just go." Claus grabbed my hand and led me away.

"I saw the ring," she said above the street noise. "Congratulations. I'm glad you were able to forgive Claus."

Turning around, I saw her mischievous grin and icy blue eyes confirming she had one-upped me—again.

Claus was staring at the sidewalk. That couldn't be good. Why would I need to forgive him? He'd said he didn't know Peter was at the theater when he kissed me after the *Romeo and Juliet* dress rehearsal.

Was he going to say something? It had to be something else. Something less grave. Something unrelated to that painful chapter of my life—the one I thought I'd just closed forever. It *had* to be something else.

A car alarm went off. A woman helped a man cross the street. A little girl ran ahead of her father. "Don't you let go of my hand," he said, crouching down to her level when he caught up with her—stubborn little fingers still squirming under his massive hand. The alarm stopped. The little girl let her father hold her hand.

Claus was still staring at the sidewalk.

It couldn't be. Mom's suspicions came to mind, distant now, but still very clear. *I wonder if Claus was somehow involved in Lorie's plot. How else would she have known something was going to happen between you two on that stage that night?*

He would never do that. It couldn't be. "I'm waiting. Y'all better start talking."

"I thought you were making a big mistake in moving to Pine Mountain," Lorie said. "I already told you that—the day you beat me up."

"I didn't beat you up."

"You beat her up?" Claus looked up at last.

"What do you think?" Surely we'd successfully established Lorie can't be trusted.

"I knew you would end up quitting the company." Lorie raised her chin. "I wanted you to stay, so I told Claus you were blind in love, and that Peter was forcing you to stop dancing to move to the ranch." She giggled and shook her head. "And Claus came to your rescue. He knew Peter was in the audience when he kissed you. He wanted your engagement to be over. He wanted you for himself, and he didn't care what he had to do to make it happen."

Claus marched toward Lorie and held her by both arms. I'd never seen that kind of intensity in his walk or in his eyes, but she didn't flinch.

People walking past started to stare. A man about my dad's age wearing a nice gray suit slowed down.

Lorie's eyes were wide, but she was still grinning—leaning into him—provoking him.

The man who'd slowed down walked away.

How could Claus have lied to me like that? I covered my mouth with shaky fingers. And for all those months? My heart raced, and I was dizzy.

No one talked. The three of us were paused in time while all around us life went on. Cars passed. People passed. A cool breeze caressed late-summer leaves, large and deep green, baked by months of Georgia heat. By this time next month, they would be dried up. With the right wind or storm, they could be gone.

When Claus let go of Lorie's arms, red impressions from each of his fingers had stayed on the pale skin. She didn't move.

Claus grabbed my hand and led me away, but the distance didn't stop her words. I could still hear her voice, muffled and dreamlike. "He knew everything, Ana, everything."

I shook my head, realizing we'd already crossed the street, leaving behind the company building, and had reached the theater where we'd danced *Romeo and Juliet*.

How had we walked so fast? I looked for Lorie on the other side of Tenth Street, but she was gone.

We reached the same marquee where I'd sat seven months earlier ashamed, scared, and lost. So humiliated. It all played back through my mind. Peter's tears, my desperation, my fear, my uncertainty...

And it was all Claus's fault. *Everything—he knew everything.* It had to be a mistake. There had to be a different explanation. He loved me. He couldn't—wouldn't—do that to me.

"It's not true, is it, Claus?" I asked, stopping. "Please tell me it isn't true." I shook his hand up and down, setting his whole arm in motion.

He nodded and embraced me, stopping me from shaking him.

"It is true?"

He nodded again.

Like a volcano that had been dormant too long and was now ready to inflict damage, I erupted. I pushed him hard against the marquee. "Why?" I hit his chest with both my fists.

He grabbed both my wrists. "You're going to beat me up too?"

"Answer my question." My voice came out distorted.

He held my hands over his heart against my will. "I'd been thinking about looking for you. I called my friends in Atlanta and scheduled a visit to talk about dancing in the States again."

His eyes searched mine. I didn't like his intensity any more than I liked his actions and his lies.

He took a deep breath, keeping my hands over his heart. I stopped fighting his intent, but I was as angry as before. My anger had simply taken on a different form. Its lava flow now ran slowly through the hollow scars and wrinkles of our relationship, covering the entire landscape with deadly heat.

When he finally spoke again, his eyes were gentle. "I'd contacted the Allen Ballet, and Brian asked if I wanted to dance *Romeo and Juliet* with you."

I shook my head. *What a disaster.* Why did that have to happen? Why did he have to call, and why did Brian have to offer me up like that?

Claus smiled and shrugged. "I thought that was a sign—a sign that I'd done my time—that I'd suffered enough and that it was time to be happy again."

I didn't realize I was crying until I tasted a salty tear that had found its way to my lips. I used the sleeve of my hoodie to dry my face.

Claus lifted my chin. "I was heartbroken when I realized you were engaged." He looked at me as if trying to read my response. "I asked Lorie about your fiancé. I remembered you and Lorie were friends, so I figured she would know about it."

"She was my friend when I was seventeen." I sat on the edge of an oversized cement planter and held my head in both hands.

"I know now that talking to her was a mistake, but at the time it seemed smart." He sat next to me. "She told me you really loved the guy, but that he didn't want you to dance and that you were going to quit. That made me mad, Ana. No one should tell a dancer when to quit."

"Claus, in what world does it seem possible for some guy to tell me what to do and what not to do?" I lifted my head and looked at him sharply. "Don't be ridiculous."

"I hadn't seen you in a decade. People change. They become more accommodating." His cheeks, his lips, and even his eyes seemed to droop. His shoulders dropped, and when he continued, his voice was hardly above a whisper. "You are a lot sweeter than you give yourself credit for."

"I don't have a single accommodating bone in my body," I said with my eyes closed. "Or a sweet one for that matter. Just continue. Lorie told you about

Peter—lies—and then what happened?"

"Lorie came up with the plot." He fidgeted and his cheeks flushed. "I thought it was a bit much for her to tell him that we'd been sleeping together, but she said that, knowing you two, it was necessary."

"And then you proceeded to frame me?"

"It was a mistake, Ana. That first day we went to Rüdesheim, I realized Lorie had lied to me. I really thought Peter was going to make you quit."

That was so ridiculous. I shook my head hard. Could I just wake up from this nightmare?

Claus stood and looked like he was going to say something, but he didn't. He crouched down in front of me instead and caressed my hands, his hands warm.

I was so cold and so lonely.

Again.

He touched my engagement ring, his smile tender. "I carried this ring around for months. I almost proposed at the park one day. Then at Di Gregorio. Then I almost proposed on the Natal in Prague. Then at the Charles Bridge."

"Why didn't you?" I asked, remembering the other couple on the bridge and remembering how cheap I'd felt listening to the "Habanera" and being presented with garnet earrings instead of a diamond ring. I'd wanted a proposal so much.

"I didn't feel that I had the right. What I did here weighed heavy on my heart, Ana. Still does." He rested his cheek on my hands. "I am so sorry. I'm sorry about everything. I should never have done it."

My head bobbed in slow motion, and we were silent. Staying with Claus was not an option. I couldn't forgive him. He'd ruined everything. Sure, I'd been happy for the past seven months. Sure, I'd built new dreams—a new path to the stage of the Met. But it was all a lie. He'd lied. He'd framed me. How could that be?

"We can't build a life together on a lie." My breaths quickened. "We can't build a life on hurt."

"Just understand that I did it in good faith, out of love. Can you do that, Ana?"

"Just understand?" I couldn't 'just understand.'

"Please, Ana."

I have to do this—there's no other way. "I hope you can 'just understand' this, Claus." I removed my engagement ring.

"Ana, no," he mouthed without a sound.

"I'm sorry about everything too." I put the ring on the palm of his hand and closed his fingers over it. Part of me pitied him. Lorie had had him good—she'd played each and every one of us. But I couldn't continue with Claus after all he'd done.

"I'm sorry Lorie lied to you, and I'm really sorry that you believed her. But no matter the reasons she gave you, it was wrong to do what you did. I can't be with you, no matter how much I love you. I'm sorry I didn't listen to my mom. And I'm sorry I moved to Germany..." *And I'm sorry I slept with you—again. Please God, let me not be pregnant.*

He closed his eyes—easing the tension of the lids just long enough to free his shapeless tears.

Traffic grew louder as rush hour started. "We need to get going." I inhaled hard and started walking, knowing he would follow.

We reached Dad's SUV, and I got into the driver's side, bringing the seat closer to the pedals and adjusting the rearview mirror.

"Where are we going?" Claus asked in a monotone.

"To Peter's house." I turned on the radio and looked for my old country station. "You'll tell him the truth. And then you'll go home." I couldn't find the station, so I switched to CD.

Willie Nelson started singing "Stardust." I shook my head. No music would be best. I turned the player off and pulled out of the parking lot in silence.

We crawled past a dozen traffic lights and were finally on our way out of town.

Claus broke the silence. "How about the audition and *Praha?*" he asked, looking out his window. "The Met?"

"You can dance *Praha* with Luci. It would make her day. Or Ekaterina. Would make her day too. She should be back from her stint in Berlin in time for *The Nutcracker*, right? Everything goes back to normal. Jakob can have his beloved prima ballerina back, and she can have you back. And forget about the Met." It had been a ridiculous dream—like my whole ridiculous life. I hit the steering wheel with my fist and merged onto the highway.

I looked at the horizon, and melancholy replaced anger much faster than I could fight it.

In addition to the truth about Claus's involvement in the events surrounding the *Romeo and Juliet* dress rehearsal, another truth broke my heart so badly that it felt like rosin dust—a few scraps and chunks remained, but it was mostly all dust.

If I can't pass an audition in Wiesbaden without Claus's help, I won't be able to pass an audition in Atlanta on my own merit either.

I nodded in silence. *No more.*

"No more." I shook my head. "I'll be busy getting a real life."

Claus looked at me. "No more what? What do you mean? You have a real life."

"I don't want to dance anymore," I heard myself say—only mildly surprised at the words rolling out of my mouth. "This is just too exhausting."

His lips parted and his expression dulled.

As I focused on the road ahead, a single teardrop trickled down my left cheek, a teardrop that was years in the making, slow and steady, like the door that was closing in my heart. "I'm done. Done dancing, done with you, done with everything."

No more. I remembered the Met picture from the locker room, Lorie boasting… I shook my head. *No more.*

Should have taken the picture down. Should have ripped it, burned it, whatever. Should have gotten rid of it. Stupid dream.

Time to close those heavy curtains. No more.

Chapter 20

The small road leading to Peter's house was curvy, the woods thick. I raised my hand to protect my eyes from the late-day sun that insisted on shining over the treetops.

We reached the clearing and the house, but he wasn't home.

"We're going to wait." I parked on the grass and got out of the SUV.

Claus nodded and got out too.

Jäger came running from behind the house.

"Come here, boy." I stopped to pat him. "What's up with all the white hair?" I was stunned by his salt-and-pepper snout. *I haven't been gone that long. Maybe the white hairs were there before, and I'd just failed to notice them somehow.*

Once he moved his attention to Claus, I started walking to the lake.

Cool air filtered through an unsteady breeze, and a riot of sweet scents hit me in waves as I followed the lulling sound of ruffled leaves.

As soon as I got around the porch, I saw Peter's greenhouse. *Is it new?* I'd always called his greenhouse an eyesore because of the plain white panels. I'd offered to plant some vines, but he'd said no.

Getting near it, I realized it was the same greenhouse. He'd replaced the front and side panels with clear ones, and yellow climbing roses covered a third of the structure already, their warm fragrance inviting me to get even closer.

I peeked inside and noticed that the blue-flame heater was now mounted to the wall and that he had installed the solar panel and the carbon dioxide generator he'd wanted for some time.

Two three-level display benches and a back shelf filled with unusually large, multicolor blossoms proved the upgrades had been successful.

Turning my attention to the lake, I realized the greenhouse was only a small part of the transformation that had taken place at 676 Water Well Lane.

Natural flagstone pathways, edged by gerbera daisies and zinnias, connected the back porch to three different spaces on an acre of land that used to have nothing but Bermuda grass. The area where the tree line met the lake had become a charming outdoor kitchen, complete with a built-in grill and a rugged dining set that blended with the woods. A large stacked-stone fireplace sloped down, becoming a short wall. Next to it, foxgloves, delphiniums, geraniums, and roses grew in tiers, forming a colorful enclosure.

The second path led to a simple arbor of red roses over a rustic country garden swing, and the third led to the dock and Peter's quaint red rowboat. Two large lounge chairs, the same color as the boat, were added to the far side of the dock.

I walked down the third path and got in the boat with ease. *There's enough daylight to be on the water for at least an hour.* I slipped the dock line eye off the rusty cleat and pushed off to look at the creation from where we'd planned it.

Jäger stood at the edge of the back porch and watched me run the oars through the oar locks.

No sign of Peter. Or of Claus.

I placed the blades in the water behind me and pulled hard before lifting them, gliding away from the house.

From twin barrel planters on the water's edge, showy hollyhocks accused me from the top of their leaning spikes and dimmed everything good inside of me until all I could see was fault and all I felt was shame.

A roguish wind gust thrust the boat from the dock area faster than I expected. I shook my head and reached toward the stern.

A good breath of untainted Pine Mountain air prepared me for the work ahead. I put the blades in the water again, leaned back toward the bow, and lifted. Soon I had established a strong rhythm.

I thought of stopping to watch a golden eagle in what looked like a high-soar-and-glide attack, but I chose to continue rowing, keeping my momentum.

Comfort came on the wings of my decision to stop dancing and was nurtured by the cadence of my labor.

I'd killed a piece of my dream the first time I was in Germany. It'd hurt, but I'd done it.

"Time to kill the rest of that stupid dream," I mumbled, despite the eagle that emerged from the woods and defied aerodynamics with its oversized prey. *What had Claus called it? Silly and random?*

I worked, watching her disappear toward the horizon. *Yep. That's me. Silly and random.*

Stern, bow, lift. Stern, bow, lift.

But that's enough. I'm gonna get a real life now.

With a jolt of energy, I peeked over my shoulder and figured I just needed a dozen good strokes to arrive where I needed to be.

The sun was resting behind the trees, but its light still painted orange the thin clouds that hung around to usher in twilight, and I rowed surrounded by an equally orange lake.

Reaching the small bay, I lowered my eyes.

Help me, dear God. I'm so tired.

I traced the oar handles, worn where Peter's hands had been so many times, and brought my fingertips to my face, conjuring the memory of his touch back to life.

And as I looked at our romantic cottage garden from the best fishing spot on Red Tree Lake, a feeling of coming home overwhelmed me.

I welcomed the evening breeze that caressed every leaf and looked skyward, letting the remaining daylight soothe me. When I looked across the lake again, Claus was walking toward the dock.

Or is it Peter? I compared the man's frame to Jäger's. That was Peter and his dog. I knew what the two looked like side by side.

Gasping and turning the boat around, I rowed as fast as my arms would let me, certain that I looked like an idiot but not caring one bit. Why couldn't this boat have an engine?

After rowing to the middle of the lake, I looked over my shoulder. Could I read his face? *Nope. Too far away.* He stood at the end of the pier, firm and still, as if planted, with his hands in his dark-jeans pockets and his black button-up shirt untucked.

Once closer, I looked again. Strands of soft brown hair framed the expression I couldn't yet decipher.

Docking with a hard bang, I turned to him. *Please let me come home.*

He reached for my hand and helped me out of the rowboat. His hand lingered on mine, and my head bowed.

I shivered because I was cold—and afraid. But above all, I shivered because being next to Peter was still absolutely exhilarating.

"Girl, you're a mess."

Looking up, my eyes saw what they'd hoped to see all along—there it was—the boyish smile that had thrilled me on our first date and every date since. "I am." I nodded. "I am a mess, Peter." I got closer to him, hesitantly.

He didn't back away.

"I'm a mess without you." Letting my cheek touch his chest, I breathed in his cologne. "Oh, Peter. I missed you so much." The palms of my hands rested on his chest, too, the soft fabric of his shirt cool to the touch. Was I forgiven at last?

He put his arms around me. "I missed you too."

"I wasn't having an affair," I said, feeling warm and protected in his embrace.

"I know."

He did? "Claus is going to tell you all about it."

"He already did." Peter's voice had the same tranquility of the lazy afternoon breeze. How could it be? "I already sent your boyfriend packing. He told me all I needed to hear."

Where was Claus now? A piece of my heart stung. "How did he leave? We drove here together."

"Walking."

"Walking to where?"

"How would I know, and why would you care?"

My body shuddered. Why did I care? There would be a time to grieve that relationship, but this wasn't it, was it? "Did he tell you that—"

"He did." Peter held my face with both his hands.

"But you don't even know what I was going to ask."

"It doesn't matter. I just want to be with you." His eyes were tender, his smile warm. "Can we do that?"

My head bobbed in agreement. But why was he making this reconciliation so easy on me?

"Did you eat?"

"Huh?" Did I eat? I'd been gone for seven months, had left under the worst of circumstances, and now that we were face to face at last, all he wanted to know was if I'd eaten?

"I have some steaks in the fridge. Let's grill."

"You don't want to know anything or ask anything?"

Peter jammed his hands in his front pockets, and a faint line formed between his brows. "Ana, this nightmare has consumed me for the past several months. No, I don't want to know anything or ask anything. I just want to start a fire for you and grill some steaks, if that's okay."

"That's okay." He would want to know more one day. But maybe it was best to start slowly.

"Good." Wrapping my hand in his, he led me to the fireplace area.

"Zeon zoysia?" I asked, surprised I hadn't noticed the Bermuda grass was gone.

"Yep." He crouched and picked two pieces of fine-bladed zoysia grass. "I've always wanted it." He handed the soft green blades to me.

Bringing the delicate grass to my nose, I remembered the first time we'd met, the date at Callaway, at the azalea bowl. The grass had just been cut, and the air smelled of new beginnings and of fresh starts. Today it did again.

I stopped to pat the ground, the turf known as the perfect stage for family fun. Catching up with Peter, I sat to watch him arrange the pine and the cover of the Sunday paper in the fireplace.

Mom did say he was different. I couldn't figure out what it was, but something about him was indeed different.

What was it? An aloofness that hadn't been there before? It was as if part of him was all there and engaging, but part wasn't—there was a missing set of emotions, a missing dimension. No … the only missing dimension was probably in my brain. I remembered my reaction to Jäger's white hair. It was probably nothing. Just the passage of time. Or maybe it's the hurt I caused. Maybe he's being a bit guarded.

"How do you like it?" He raised his arms like a conductor as he walked to his cord of walnut firewood beyond what was now the kitchen.

"I love it—everything is perfect." I watched him walk back with four logs. "It's like a Thomas Kinkade painting. Remember we went to a gallery at the mall in Atlanta one time? Remember dimming the lights by each painting and watching it change?"

"Of course I remember." He looked as if he were going to say something else, but he didn't.

"It's everything I'd hoped it would be." Watching him light the fire, a hint of melancholy tried to surface. Thoughts of my life in Germany appeared before my eyes, dull and lifeless, like an old photograph that had lost its color. But it had been so bright. How could it all have ended like this? Was I right back to the feeling that nothing was ever sufficient for me? Seemed that way.

My head hung low with the weight of the day, and images of Lorie's face came to mind uninvited. I had to stop the madness. All of it. Stopping dancing was a beginning, but could I really do it? I had to … Columbus was not an option, and Atlanta wasn't either.

The sounds from the flames demanded my attention. Peter rested his hands on my shoulders, and we watched the fire together. If he only knew the comfort and courage that he gave me by simply standing next to me.

We cooked together and enjoyed the cool night as we talked about his work and about my landscaping adventures.

"So this German couple paid you to landscape their terrace?" Peter asked, cocking his head.

"Yep." I picked the reddest tomato out of the produce basket to cut for our salad. "And there was the teacher's terrace too." I decided not to mention Claus's garden. Or the Thunderbird.

"I never knew you cared about planting beyond showing support for me." He shook his head and pulled a head of lettuce and a Samuel Adams from a small fridge under the kitchen counter.

The vibration signaling a new text message startled me, but I decided not to look. I grabbed the open bottle Peter offered me and drank, wondering why he'd switched to a full-bodied brew.

"You can sit," he said. "I can finish."

"Okay." I chose the chair closest to the fire and filled my lungs with the steak smell that surrounded me. Should I check the text? Where had Claus gone? Did he make it back to my parents'? The text was probably *from* my parents—they were probably wondering what in the world I was doing. Would they be okay with my behavior and my decisions? Or would Dad give me his "life is not black or white" speech? His voice played in my head. *You have this awful habit of wanting things to be black or white, and that's hardly ever the case.* Why not?

Peter put a Tracy Lawrence CD in the player he'd brought from the house and finished preparing the salad. I remembered that CD. It ended with "Paint Me a Birmingham." How perfect would it be if he asked me to dance? Would we dance all night like we used to?

I checked the text, just in case, and saw it was from Claus.

IF YOU ARE SERIOUS ABOUT QUITTING, LET'S DO A FAREWELL—*PRAHA* IN COLUMBUS. BRIAN SAID HE WANTED A FIFTH PIECE FOR THE MIXED BILL.

"No," I said to myself, putting the phone away. Famous ballerinas danced farewells. I wasn't famous. And I would never, ever, dance *Praha* now. Ever.

Peter turned around, looking at me from the kitchen. "What did you say?"

"Nothing." At least if Claus was texting about ballet, he must have made it safely to somewhere. No other texts or missed calls, so if he was at my parents, they must not have freaked out.

As we ate, we talked about Europe. He asked me about my travels, and I told him about Prague, Mallorca, a quick trip to London to see a ballet, as well as an even quicker sightseeing trip to Paris. I avoided talking about Germany, and I hadn't mentioned the audition or the Met. I'd blushed at the mention of Prague.

Another text message came in.

"I'm getting another beer." Peter stood up. "You?" he asked while collecting the two empty bottles.

"Sure." I checked the text. It was from Claus again.

IF YOU DON'T WANT TO DANCE *PRAHA*, WE CAN DANCE SOMETHING ELSE.

Even if it were something else, the right answer was still no.

"Paint Me a Birmingham" started. Peter would certainly hate the idea of Claus and I dancing together a final time too. *I need peace, not more complication and turmoil… No more.*

Peter placed two just-opened bottles side by side on the table, drops of condensation forming fast. "Wanna dance?" He reached for my hand.

How could he be so kind to me? "Yes, I absolutely do." Before entering the church, on the day he'd asked me to return his mother's ring, I'd looked at the bridge on the other side of Falls Creek Lake, wishing I could be there, starting over. *This right here, right now, is that wish come true. We* would *start over.*

I took his hand and accepted his gentle embrace as we slow danced by the fire. The smell of wood smoke mixed with his musky scent invited me even closer. My legs were tired from the morning class, my arms tired from rowing, hands aching, heart aching … but here I was with a man who didn't need me to do anything to earn a spot in his life, with whom I could just be. *This is life. This was the way things ought to be*—forever. "Do you think you can give me another chance?"

"I'll sure have to try. I was miserable without you." His lips touched my neck, his face tickling me with his scruff. "I missed your salty ballet taste."

"I missed everything about you." I ran my fingers through his hair and pulled him closer. He moaned, making me melt completely, and I kissed him as if we'd never been apart. My hand slid to his chest. His hand met mine, and he spread my fingers. I felt his heartbeat on the palm of my hand as we swayed to the music.

When the CD ended we stayed together, listening to the fire and rocking to his heartbeat.

Peter's fingertips caressed my cheek. "I'm sorry I didn't believe you."

"I would have felt the same way if the roles had been reversed. I'm sorry."

"It'll pass." He inhaled before continuing, "When you were with Claus, you never called me back. You didn't write me back either. You didn't look for me until you ended your relationship with him, and that means something to me. It means I can trust you won't do things behind my back and break my heart, just like you didn't do anything behind Claus's back. He broke his own heart."

"I wanted to contact you, but I knew it wasn't right." The cool night air prickled my skin. "If there's anything I've learned through this whole mess, it is to be way more cautious and understanding when it comes to people's feelings and perceptions."

"I believe you." His hands rubbed my arms. "You're freezing."

"A little." A duck quacked in the darkness, the sound familiar. *Warmer Damm Park.* The times Claus and I had spent at the park had been so precious, more precious than the intimacy we'd shared.

"Let's get you inside."

Maybe my arms were cold, but my cheeks weren't. What if I didn't want to go inside? He'd said something about reading the Bible in his letter. Was he of a religion that read the Bible a lot, and wasn't there something in the book against people sleeping together without being married? Maybe that could be an out.

"I'm cold." Picking me up in his arms with ease, he started walking toward the house.

"What are you?" I asked.

"What am I?" He laughed. "I don't know. You tell me."

I laughed too. "I mean what religion? You wrote you would 'never ever' go back to church."

"Oh." He laughed again. "Baptist."

Of course. "Calvary Baptist Church?"

"No. Grace. Why?"

"Nothing." We were within feet from the back porch now. "Weren't you reading the Bible again? Isn't there something in there against, you know, people being together like this?"

"I *was* reading it there for a while … oh—" He stopped walking and his expression dulled. "We don't have to, if you don't want to…" His lips stretched but his eyes drooped.

Was I breaking his heart again? That was not my intention. And what if he changed his mind about letting me back in his life if I didn't allow for everything to go back to normal—our normal?

"It's up to you." His smile looked forced.

A tight feeling in my chest warned me. I couldn't handle his rejection—that was too big a risk. "I want to."

"Good."

A hint of melancholy that I didn't understand but very much felt squeezed my heart, and I nestled my head on his chest as he opened the back door. *I need to get back on the pill.*

Chapter 21

M om called me in the morning and said Claus was still at her house and wanted to talk to me and to Peter.

"I'm not sure about that, Mom." I stopped cleaning the kitchen and sat by the window. "Is it about dancing? Do you know?"

"Yes, he said he wants to talk about the audition and about an opportunity to dance in Columbus. But he also wants to talk to Peter. I'm assuming that means you and Peter are back together? What happened, Ana? I'm so lost."

"Ask Claus—he'll tell you all about it." *Saves me from having to admit to Mom that she was right about Claus's involvement in the Romeo and Juliet thing.*

"Well, obviously you still love Peter, and he still loves you, or I wouldn't have a German dancer moping on my couch."

"You've got that right, Mom." Might as well make her day. "I'm staying in Georgia—the engagement is back on."

"Wow! That's a lot of change."

"It is..." She was going to put two and two together fast and gloat about being right.

"Well, then let Claus talk to Peter. Claus deserves some closure, don't you think? He's in bad shape. Don't you think talking would be good? And how about this dancing opportunity? Do you want to do it? Are Claus and Peter on good terms?"

"I don't know, Mom. My head's still spinning with everything that's going on. Dancing is the last thing on my mind." If she did put two and two together, she didn't mention anything. That was unusual. Did she know I was planning to stop dancing? Had Claus told her anything at all about what'd happened?

"Try to figure out what you want, then talk to Peter and let him decide. This way he can't complain later, and you'll know for sure if he can handle it."

"That doesn't sound right either." I traced the white cherry blossoms of the vinyl tablecloth with my fingertips. "Should I put this burden on him?" And should I put him in a position to have to handle more stress after all we'd been through?

"Of course you should. What's the point of sharing your life with someone if you cannot share your burdens?"

Let him decide?

"Talk to him and then call me, okay?"

I nodded, getting up. "Okay."

"Good luck, Ana. I love you."

"Thanks, Mom. He went to a meeting but should be here soon."

I finished cleaning our four-cheese omelet dishes and our coffee mugs.

Let him decide, huh?

I put on Peter's blue-and-orange flannel jacket and opened the back porch door to a gorgeous Pine Mountain September morning—sunny, fragrant, and bright.

But I couldn't step out.

Jäger, who'd rushed out ahead of me, cocked his head, as if asking, "What's the holdup?"

Wondering the same thing myself, I wished I had my New Testament from Prague, but it was at Mom's house.

Is Lorie's Bible still here? I closed the door and walked to the living room bookshelf. "Lorie Ashley Allen" was engraved on the bottom-right corner of a pink and purple Bible. I touched the fading silver letters on the worn cover as Jäger scratched the door in protest, wanting to come in too.

Peter hated when he did that.

"Let's go, boy."

We walked straight to the water's edge, and I sat at the end of the pier with Lorie's Bible on one side and Jäger on the other. I buttoned up Peter's jacket almost to my neck and enjoyed the lingering masculine scent, anxious for him to get home.

Better decide what I want to do before wishing him back. I picked up the Bible and folded my hands over it.

Dear God, I don't know what to do.

Of course, I want to dance. Always. It's like breathing for me, and You know it.

If You are there, You made me, and if You made me, You know it. I have to dance.

But I can't do it anymore, Lord. It feels wrong. Everything feels wrong. I don't even know what to pray for.

I can't decide. I make bad decisions. I'm never happy.

I almost was—twice. And twice everything fell apart.

Just tell me what to do. This is your shot. I can't fix my life. You do it.

Please...

I looked up at the bright blue sky and resisted the urge to ask if He were really there, if He cared, and if He was listening. A tiny puddle pooled on Lorie's Bible, and I swiped it away. I tried to pat dry the spot with Peter's sleeve and hoped the stain would disappear with time.

I opened the book with a deep breath and a quiet hope. *First Kings? Okay.* Chapter three. Blinking slowly to clear my eyes of the tears, I zeroed in on the word LORD in verse seven. *And now, O LORD my God, thou hast made thy servant king instead of David my father: and I am but a little child: I know not how to go out or come in.*

"Amen to that." *Who said it?* I looked for context. "Ah, Solomon." I went back to read the chapter from the beginning.

Halfway through it, I rested the open book on my lap and dropped my chin to my chest, unable to keep it up any longer beneath the weight dragging down my heart.

God, in a dream, had asked Solomon what he wanted. Much like a genie, He was granting a wish. Solomon, who'd just become king, didn't ask for riches, for a long life, or for military victories. He thought of the people, the chosen people of God, and he felt inept to be their ruler. So he asked God for an understanding heart to judge the people.

God gave Solomon the wisdom he asked for, and He was so pleased with the character of Solomon's wish that He also gave him the riches and honor he hadn't asked for.

Selflessness. I nodded slowly and raised my eyes to the sky. *I'm praying for selflessness, Lord.*

The bright blue sky didn't seem so empty anymore.

Teach me, Father.

I opened to another random page—Matthew, in the New Testament.

"And Zorobabel begat Abiud; and Abiud begat Eliakim; and Eliakim begat Azor; And Azor begat Sadoc; and Sadoc begat Achim; and Achim begat Eliud..."

Okay, let's just stick with what we've got—selflessness. I patted Jäger, who looked at me with eager brown eyes.

Let him decide?

Yes.

Peter arrived at lunchtime and found me asleep on the swing—in the perfect shade of hundreds of red roses. I woke up with him teasing my nose with a rose and sat up, happy to have him back.

"Nice pillow." He picked up Lorie's Bible and sat next to me. "When did you become so interested in religion?"

"I don't know." I shrugged, my cheeks warm.

He handed the book to me. "That's cool. I didn't know. That's all."

I put the Bible on my lap, with Lorie's name facing down.

"Claus came to see me today." Peter's eyes searched mine.

"He did?" Maybe I shouldn't have been surprised, but I was. What had he said? "Mom called earlier saying he wants to dance…" Peter couldn't help me decide if he didn't look at the whole picture. "Did he tell you I'm quitting?"

"He did, but I don't buy it. I'm sure that's what you told him, and maybe that's even what you think you'll do, but I know you better than that." Peter relaxed on the swing, with his elbow on the back of the seat and his head on his hand.

The man knew me too well. Balanchine once said, "I don't want people who want to dance, I want people who have to dance." I was definitely the kind who had to, and in my mind, I was on the stage of the RiverCenter rehearsing already. But I could change, right? I'd prayed, and selflessness was the word that had come up, so I had to be selfless. *Let him decide.*

"What do you want to do? Do you want to dance in this mixed bill?" His eyes widened and his eyebrows rose.

"It would be weird to dance with Claus, after all that we've been through." Could I do it and handle it professionally? Absolutely. Should I put Peter through it? No way. *Let him decide.* "I don't have to do it, baby."

"Why are you talking about quitting dancing?"

"It's not working out." A hurtful lump formed in my throat. "I'm just not good enough."

"Nonsense."

"Yes-sense," I said, the urge to cry miraculously gone. "In Wiesbaden I had a chance because of Claus. Without him, I'm ordinary at best."

"The ballet people in Columbus would beg to differ, and so would I."

"Well, I'm not in Columbus anymore."

"How about Atlanta?" Peter ran his hand through my hair. "The old plan?"

"The company there is big, like Wiesbaden."

"You were in the company in Wiesbaden."

"Not really. Not officially. I was going to audition late this month."

"You would have made it."

"Not exactly." I shook my head, not sure how to approach the choreography and the Met part of my German life.

"What do you mean?"

If I were to have a future with Peter, I would have to be honest with him. No more secrets, or hiding, or framing. I had to tell him about my life in Germany, even if meant talking about Claus and unfulfilled dreams. "They pulled me aside in the summer, saying I wouldn't make it, but that there was a chance under certain conditions."

"Conditions?"

"Claus had been talking about choreographing, but he didn't seem motivated to start anything." I looked down and brushed my palms together. "So they told me I would have a chance if Claus created a piece for us to perform immediately after the audition."

"Wow. What did Claus do?"

I made him mad. He made me mad. Then he proposed. "He choreographed. I guess, with the prize in mind, he just did it."

"The prize?"

"The Met."

"The Met?"

"His company is dancing at the Met in the spring. They were going to put the choreography in the Met program if they liked it. It would have been the perfect plug to sell a few extra tickets during a recession, I guess. Top dancer choreographing for his American wife."

"No way." He leaned closer. "You? At the Met?"

"Lots of 'ifs,' but we were hopeful."

"Wait. Wife?"

"We were going to get married this Christmas."

"Ana, wow." He stood up, running his fingers through his hair, his hands stopping interlocked behind his neck. "Are you gonna be okay with not doing that?"

"Not doing what? The Met or marrying Claus?"

"Both."

"I'm okay about Claus—I ache over what he must be going through, but you said it best, he broke his own heart. I'm not okay yet about letting go of the Met, but I will be."

Peter looked at me, his smile quiet and fitting.

"I'll be fine." I tucked my hair behind my ear and tightened my lips.

"Oh, Ana, you will wonder forever."

"True, but see, it was all just a possibility. If I had already auditioned, passed, and rehearsed, then it would be harder."

"Then I would tell you just to do it."

"Oh, you would tell me?"

"Yes," he said, his cheeks flushed. "I would tell you."

Let him decide? I tried to ignore the new feelings the mighty man in front of me had just ignited.

"Ana, are you okay?"

"Uh-huh." I centered myself on the swing and pushed back before hugging my knees. "You know, to wonder forever doesn't have to be a bad thing." I shrugged, looking at the still lake. "I couldn't have handled it if they told me it was still not good enough. Could you imagine? Traveling to New York to watch him dance with someone else what he had choreographed for me?"

"You would have made it, though."

"Only God knows what if." That's what Claus always said.

"I'm sorry, Ana." He sat back down and patted his lap.

"Me too." I rested my head on his thigh and curled up on the swing. "Me too."

A gentle breeze made delicate ripples on the lake's surface and stirred up the roses just enough to make their sweet smell suddenly stronger.

"Do you love him?" Peter played with my hair, his voice tender.

This is the perfect time for a white lie. But the lying part of the program is over. Big time over. "I do. I love you both so much. So much, Peter."

He nodded, quiet and composed. "Are you sure you want to be with me?"

"Positive."

"How can you be so sure?"

"I don't know how I know—I just do. I love you. Life with you is laid back and fun. We're complete opposites, and that's exciting to me." How could I explain to him what I myself couldn't quite understand? His eyes were still on me. "See, when I'm not with you, I get intense and crazy and too busy. I'm never still, nothing is sufficient." That was it right there. With Peter next to me, being was sufficient. *I* was sufficient. Our love wasn't performance based—it was absolutely unconditional. With Claus I felt like I had to always be doing something to feel good about myself—not because of anything he'd ever said or done. It was just the way I was around him. "I'm absolutely sure that I am exactly where I need to be."

"Need to be?"

Cautious, hmm? "Want to be." I looked up at him. Couldn't blame him for being cautious, could I? "Don't lose any sleep over this. I'm one hundred percent sure I want to be with you. I was with you until the day you told me to go away. When you welcomed me back last night, I stayed. I'm here to stay forever. I *do* love you."

"I love you too." Peter organized my hair, securing loose strands behind my ear to keep them off my eyes. "And are you sure you don't want to go back to the Allen Ballet?"

"Positive. There are many things I don't know, but that's another thing I know with absolute certainty. I'm done with the cycle of hope and disappointment and the pretense that I am happy being second best. I'm done with Columbus."

Peter nodded.

"Maybe someday I can find another small company, a small place with good ideas. But not now and not with the lofty dreams I've been dreaming. I can't take that kind of intensity anymore. If I dance again, it will have to be for the fun of it—not as a professional."

"Would you teach one day?"

"One day." I shrugged, unsure.

"Well, it does sound as if you need a farewell of sorts then."

He caressed my face, his gentle cool fingers on my warm cheek.

"Let Claus do it." He rested his hand on my chest. "He told me he talked to Brian last night, and Brian said he would put it in the October program. Sales are rough, and he thinks you and Claus will draw a crowd."

"That would be nice." I looked at the sky beyond the roses. "I haven't been on stage since *Romeo and Juliet*, and that was all so tumultuous. I do want to be in this performance." I brought his hand to my lips and kissed it. "Thank you."

"I think this will be good for all of us," Peter said. "Does that make sense?"

Had the *Romeo and Juliet* dress rehearsal been his last experience at the theater? I nodded yes without asking questions.

At Peter's request, Claus joined us for dinner.

"I'll grill while you guys come up with the farewell plan," Peter said after awkward hellos.

I pulled a chair out for Claus and sat opposite him. His eyes were fixed on Peter, who was busy arranging hickory chunks on only one side of the grill for a two-zone approach to grilling he'd learned from the men in my mom's family. The hot side would create the crust and get the kosher salt to stick. The other side would cook the inside to perfection: tender, juicy, and pink.

Think of something to say … the food, the weather … anything?

Watching Peter light the fire, I wondered if the farewell was a good idea after all. It was certainly good in theory, but could we deliver? We couldn't even talk.

Peter turned around and chuckled. "Are you guys just going to stare at me?

I know this is all really odd. It's odd for me too. But talking about dancing has got to be better than watching me grill all night."

He cleaned his hands with a kitchen rag and approached the table. "You seem like an okay guy, Claus. And I have no desire to beat a man who's already down. But for the sake of being productive here tonight, wrap your mind around this idea—game over, my friend. I got the girl.

"Treat this ballet as a consolation prize that I'm only letting you have because I love Ana and believe she should have something better than the *Romeo and Juliet* mess, which you and Lorie created, to hang her pointe shoes on. If that's too much for you to handle, maybe the company can squeeze her into something that's already on the program."

"Sorry," Claus said, his voice throaty. His jaw tightened and his face dulled.

I nodded, lowering my head.

Peter went back to the grill, and the smell of hickory slowly dominated the air.

"So what are we dancing?" Claus cleared his throat. "Do you want to dance *Praha*? It's ready, so it would be the easiest."

"Dancing *Praha* anywhere, other than the Met, would be depressing." *And that's a ballet about beginnings and two people in love.* "Absolutely not."

"Balcony scene?" Claus's eyes narrowed.

From the corner of my eye, I saw Peter's head snap in our direction. "No." I cocked my head. Was he serious?

"That leaves us two choices." Claus made a steeple of his fingers. "Pick any grand pas de deux or come up with something new. We have a little over a month, so that's enough time to do either."

I faced the strong fire in the fireplace and put my legs up on the chair next to me. "How about that Gallastegui music you've been listening to?"

His mouth twisted. "An intermezzo?"

"Ta, dada dada dada dada dada dada dada, pa. Ta, dada dada dada dada dada dada dada, pa." I hummed the melody with precision, my hand making a circle with each "dada" and ending with an accent, like an old amusement park rotor ride.

He nodded and hummed along. "I've been obsessed with it, but it's short—and it's class music."

"I don't need a big splash. It doesn't even need to be the closing act. I'm a soloist, not a principal."

"We can run it by Brian. He may have a spot where people are rushing to change, so we can go in, have some fun, and buy them some time."

"I'm perfectly fine with that. Quality, not quantity, right? We'll make it special."

Claus nodded and closed his eyes. His right hand moved much like mine had when I was describing the music.

My eyes rested on Peter as he prepared the steaks. He caught me looking and smiled with a wink.

"How about a music box?" Claus cocked his head. "The magnetic ballerina kind with the lit-up circle, a gold puffy tutu, a mirror. Your breathtaking *bourrées*, finger turns, promenades of all kinds. Good idea? Bad idea?"

"Ooh. Good idea." *Like my grandmother's...*

"Let me run with it a little and talk to Brian."

I nodded with a grin. "I like that idea."

"Good." Claus smiled for the first time since he'd arrived.

As if he'd been waiting for his cue, Peter brought over a party tub with a selection of American beers on ice.

We each chose one and lifted our bottles in a silent toast. So the farewell *was* a good idea, and yes, we could deliver. Perfect. From my grandma's music box to the onstage music box, everything dance would come full circle after this final piece. I would be free to start the rest of my life.

"The house is now open. The house is now open."

The theater announcement elicited the usual butterflies and ignited a fight-or-flight response I'd learned to manage.

I looked like the music box ballerina of years gone by in my gorgeous tutu with its dark gold bodice of rich velvet and undulated white skirt layered in large-holed mesh. Red lipstick and a glamorous bun enhanced the look, and glancing at the mirror, I placed one hand on my shoulder and extended my opposite arm up, just like my grandma's music box ballerina.

For five weeks, Claus and I had rehearsed daily in Atlanta and finished early each day so I could be home when Peter got off work. Evenings with my fiancé were filled with music, laughter, and wedding planning. Our relationship felt incredibly right—like I knew it would—like it once had been. We were back on track.

We'd decided to keep our original wedding date, November fifth, but we had dropped the idea of having it at the Callaway Gardens chapel and planned a home wedding instead.

For once in my life, I had it all.

I'd enjoyed it cautiously, though, knowing that my ballet glory had an expiration date. I hoped my last time on stage wouldn't be defined by managing difficult emotions. But as tonight's performance had approached, managing my emotions became harder and harder.

The class we'd had on stage in the afternoon had been easy on the body but hard on the mind. I'd started thinking things like, "How many pliés before I retire from professional dancing? Am I really within hours of my last grand battements? Last pirouette preparation?" Staying calm became a challenge, and I'd had to resort to counting—twenty seats in the center portion of the first row; nineteen on the second; fourteen lights hung from the mezzanine; seventy line sets in the theater; forty-four dancers on stage.

That had been my theater experience, until that moment, on my last day at the RiverCenter for the Performing Arts.

And then there was a knock on the door.

"Ms. Ana?"

I recognized the voice of the wardrobe mistress and opened the door. "Perfect timing." I turned around to let her close my tutu and immediately felt her quick fingers on my back. "Thank you."

"Are you coming to the stage area?" Her voice cracked, and I held both her hands.

What a sweet lady. "I will soon." The intermezzo would be the second piece after the interval, but I didn't want to spend the whole first half of the program in the dressing room. But I didn't want to talk to people either, so I would have to find a happy medium. I put on my headpiece, a delicate gold tiara, and bundled up to keep my muscles warm.

I particularly didn't want to be around Lorie, not when she had the opportunity to talk. When the Allen Ballet moved classes and rehearsals to the theater a week prior to the performance, Claus and I moved our operation there too. Peter showed up often, and Lorie avoided all three of us the whole time. But I didn't want to give her a single opportunity to spoil my day.

The first notes of *Les Sylphides* came through the dressing room speakers. *Time to go to the stage area.* I wanted to watch a young dancer make her professional debut alongside Lorie. I'd noticed her in class. She was fifteen, had impeccable technique, a perfect ballet body, and the presence to go with it. How would her in-class elegance translate to the stage? That's what I wanted to see. With a powerful stage presence, she would be a prima fast.

As I reached for the doorknob, I noticed a small envelope under the door. It contained a simple note.

You've always been my favorite ballerina. Good luck tonight.
– J.

"Oh, that's sweet." The wardrobe mistress, whose long name was difficult to pronounce, went by J. But what was her actual name? My mind was blank of anything except dance.

"It's a full house," a man I'd never seen before told me as soon as I got to the stage area.

"Good," I whispered.

I didn't expect to see Claus watching from the wings, but there he was.

The new girl was the first to catch my attention as I stood next to him.

Claus noticed my presence and pointed at the girl. "She's fantastic. Look at her lines."

"And graceful," I placed my hands on my hips. "Great stage presence—she's Lorie and me put together, stuffed into one tiny young body."

"I think you're right." The corners of his mouth turned up.

She needs to watch her shoulder blades. There's a little bit of tension, and it's transferring to her arms. "Give her a couple of years, and she'll be a prima here."

"Right again."

We watched the entire first half—the classical half—from the obscurity of the wings and spent the interval on stage, getting warm again and practicing along with two *Arcangelo* couples.

Soon, Lorie and her partner showed up ready for *Closer*, and they practiced a lift by the piano that had just been placed on the stage for their piece, set to composer Philip Glass's haunting "Mad Rush." She looked beautiful in a short white gown that emphasized her long legs and perfect lines, and with every *passé*, her lower body looked like a perfect number four.

"Just so you know"—Claus held both my hands—"I'm scared."

I tightened my lips, bobbing my head. "Me too."

He wasn't talking about the performance. Performances excited him and made him nervous, at best. Now life—life was scary, and we both knew it.

Claus was going home with broken dreams to an empty apartment. I was going home with broken dreams of my own but to a completely different life. How would I ever empty myself from the brokenness, and what dreams would take their place? I had no idea.

As I watched Claus pacing in slow motion in the wings, I wished things had ended differently for us. *I hope something good happens for him. I hope he can find someone nice.* He caught me staring at him, and I turned my attention to the dark stage.

Tonight was a turning point. Nothing would ever be the same. This was our last goodbye and last révérence. The heavy curtains opened and the second half of the program started.

Lorie and her partner moved as one in *Closer*, with intertwined legs and braided arms that rarely ever broke skin-to-skin contact in a twenty-minute romantic piece in which their blent shadows were a third character, with a story of its own, and in which movement and music alternated seamlessly from quiet to severe without ever lacking flow, like a Virginia Woolf sentence that started casually and was too beautiful to end.

They received an enthusiastic and well-deserved ovation. And then the stage was dark. The crew set up the music box floor and mirror, and Claus and I followed them to the stage to take our positions.

"I guess this is it," Claus whispered in my ear as he squeezed my cold hands. *Yep, this is it, and we'll make it beautiful—one last time.*

When the amber and red circle under our feet lit up, my pose was that of the vintage music box ballerina: legs in passé, one hand on my shoulder, and the other arm up. Claus held the hand that was up in the air as butterflies flew in formation in my tummy—I was ready to start a dizzying series of finger turns and fast promenades.

Over the next fifteen minutes, I would be spun, supported, lifted, and carried with movements that were delicate and beautiful, transporting the audience into the purity of the relationship between the ballerina and her cavalier.

The circularity of Gallastegui's "Intermezzo" would evoke the music box mood—for the ladies, the ballerina dream, and for the gentlemen, the love of ballerinas.

After the initial turns, we used the full length of the stage to paint a picture of the elegance and chivalry of the ballet world. Oh, how I was going to miss that world with all its customs and civilities—niceties now so lost beyond the doors of the theater and of the studio.

Balanchine's words were in my head again. *People who want to dance ... people who have to dance.* How was I going to stop?

The orchestra played faster as the end of the piece approached, and we finished back where we'd started, in the circle, repeating the opening series of finger turns and fast promenades. Were they my last ever?

The music ended gradually, amber lights dimmed slowly, and the stage darkened completely.

My intermezzo ... Lord, please bless what comes next.

"Bravo!"

Claus led me toward the audience, and I was overwhelmed by a shower of flowers and multiple shouts of "bravo" from the standing crowd. My heart beat loud and fast as I curtsied in these last moments of my career.

The warmth of the public, of the orchestra, and of my fellow dancers in the wings filled my heart with gratitude and emotion, and I planted a kiss on my hands and shared it with everyone.

Brian met us on stage with more flowers as Claus caught a bouquet midair, reviving the fervor of the audience. He presented it to me and then held my hand for a final bow.

That's when I realized we were probably holding hands for the very last time, and a painful lump formed in my throat. In front of me, my mom and dad cried as they clapped from their front-row seats across from the orchestra pit. Peter sat next to them, proud and handsome and beaming.

In two weeks I would be his wife.

And I couldn't wait.

The heavy red curtains closed, and the crew moved in a frenzy to remove all the flowers and set up *Arcangelo*, with its uneven ground, hidden lights, dark curtains, and lustrous banner. The piece would wrap up the evening with soul-piercing baroque music.

Smiling at Claus, I squeezed his hand, then let it go.

"I still love you," he mouthed without a sound before turning to the wings.

Walking in the opposite direction, I tried to enjoy the interest of the well-wishers with grace. Once everyone's attention had moved to the new attraction, I sat.

Across the stage—in his own darkness—Claus sat too.

On the stage between us, eight couples entered and exited layers of darkness seamlessly and bathed in warm shades of yellow and gold. Their bodies, in minimalist dark unitards, tangled gracefully in intimate duets, filled with flexed feet, deep pliés, and bird-like arched arms that were beautifully contemporary yet impossibly classical.

It will be okay.

Alessandro Scarlatti's "L'innocenza Paccando Perdeste" announced the end of *Arcangelo* and the end of the evening. The voice of God, in countertenor magnificence, promised a redeemer with a message of love and forgiveness that touched me—not because I understood the message, but because I believed in the promise. In that moment, I was at peace with everything that was going on. Hellos and goodbyes. The old and the new. The friends and the foes. *Yes, it will be okay.*

And as one couple was lifted into heaven by a silk drape while three others lay motionless on the dark stage floor, I noticed Claus was gone.

Chapter 22

"If I didn't know better, I'd think that you're having second thoughts about tomorrow." I approached Peter, who was on the back porch watching three workers set up our wedding altar and arch by the lake.

His frown became a genuine smile fast. "But you know better."

Placing my arms around him, I felt the rest of his tension dissipate.

He kissed the top of my head. "If anything, I wish we were married already."

We chuckled together. "Well, good." His eyes were warm but held a hint of a shadow. What was bothering him?

"I want to play something for you, Ana." Reaching toward his Gibson guitar, he somehow missed its neck, grabbing it on his second attempt.

My eyes stayed on his hand as I took a step back to give him space. There was a slight movement to his fingers that wasn't normal. "What's wrong with your hand?"

"Nothing. Must be nerves." The corners of his lips turned up as he placed his long fingers on the fretboard and prepared to play, his hands now steady.

It must have been nerves, like he'd said. *Big day tomorrow.*

His eyes closed, and he started playing slowly.

There was a difference in his approach to playing, a reverence that I'd never seen before. I melted against the dark porch railings as I recognized the last movement of Bach's Cantata 147.

This time tomorrow I will be getting ready for my wedding. Closing my eyes, I focused on the music—the music I'd selected to walk down the aisle to start the rest of my life. The better part of it, I hoped. *No more competition. No more moving. No more chasing men. Just peace. And happiness. With Peter by my side, I could do anything.*

When he finished, he rested the palm of his hand on the chords, stopping the vibration.

"Thank you." It was perfect.

"You're welcome." He sat on one of two rocking chairs and put the guitar down. "I'm surprised you didn't pick 'Here Comes the Bride' to walk down the aisle."

I sat next to him and held his hand. "Wagner's "Bridal Chorus" would be too much for a small backyard wedding. Don't you think?"

He lifted his shoulders. "Maybe. I just don't want you to miss out on anything. I thought every little girl rehearsed their wedding day to Wagner."

I chuckled. "True. But the music needs to feel right." *Once a dancer, always a dancer—can't take big steps to the wrong music.*

He nodded. "If you say so…"

"I say so." *Of course the "Bridal Chorus" is wonderful, but it screams big church wedding. Which we would have had, if I hadn't had the bright idea of moving to Germany.* I breathed in the crisp autumn air. A gentle breeze brought the fragrance of English roses and peonies our way. *Things are perfect just the way they are.*

Peter brought my hand to his lips again.

"I can't believe you learned Bach's cantata so fast," I said, breaking the silence.

"I've known it for a while." His smile was small and tender. "It's a hymn— 'Jesu, Joy of Man's Desiring' is the common English title. My mom used to sing it at church."

"But it's a wedding song. I've heard it a million times."

"It became a wedding song, but it was not meant to be one."

"What does it say? Do you know the lyrics?"

He shook his head with his lips pressed together. "Something about souls going toward light and people looking for truth. I don't know. God giving them joy?" He shook his head again. "It's been a while."

My eyes filled up with tears. Had God planted the music in my head so I would choose it for my wedding?

"This God thing's still bugging you, isn't it?"

"I don't know that 'bugging' is the right word." I shrugged. "But there's something there, and I have a feeling I can't avoid it forever."

Peter nodded.

"I feel like God's after me, you know?" *I don't think he knows.* "Like this wedding song—I didn't mean to walk down the aisle to a Jesus song, but it kind of just happened." *It's probably all in my head.* "It's probably just a bunch of coincidences."

"I thought you knew it was a hymn."

"Nope." I shook my head. "Anyway,"—I did not want to discuss the subject any further—"hymn or wedding song, the music is beautiful and perfect. I'm happy." I stood to look at the workers, who were almost finished building the arch. "It's really coming together down there."

Peter didn't answer, and when I turned to look at him, he seemed distant.

"You're doing it again," I said. "You look tense."

"Sorry."

"What is it, sweetie? Is it about your family?"

He shrugged and squinted at the sun glittering off the ripples in the water beyond the deck. He had told me his mom had died of heart failure in her forties and that he hadn't talked to his father in more than ten years. But getting him to share anything else was impossible. I couldn't understand the distance and the secrecy. I really couldn't.

"You should call your dad." My eyes studied his.

"Ana, there's something I want to tell you." He stood and raked his fingers through his hair.

"What is it?" My feet walked to him slowly. "I can handle it." *Right?*

He didn't say anything; his gaze was on the water.

"Is he in jail?"

"No. Not that."

"Runs a meth lab?"

"No," he said, his voice rising.

"Sorry." *Why did I have to try to be funny?*

"Never mind." He shook his head. "Why don't we go in and pack? That's what we need to be thinking about, huh? Honeymoon?"

"Come on, tell me." *I should have kept my mouth shut.* I rested my hand on his arm.

"No, I don't want to spoil things."

"Peter, you're not going to spoil anything. You drive me crazy sometimes, you know?"

"Sometimes?" He kissed my neck and squeezed me. "You drive me crazy all the time."

"You know what—"

An awful horn-honking cacophony approached the house, and we looked at each other, puzzled, before walking around to the front.

"Whoa," I said, when I saw Dad in a brand-new red midsize truck.

He hopped off and looked at Mom, who'd parked the SUV and was almost to us.

"For me?" I beamed, looking at the keys he held in my direction.

"Honey, you've got to drive something, and I'm not sure it's worth fixing the Thunderbird and shipping it back." He shoved his hands in his pockets. "So here's your new ride."

"I love it, Dad. Thank you."

Dad put his arm on my shoulder and showed the truck to me. "It has room for you to carry flowers, dirt, groceries, and whatever else you may want to."

"Even kids." I laughed and poked Dad's chest as I checked out the roomy backseat.

"Yes." Dad blushed and then mumbled, "Even kids, of course."

"No kids yet." Peter scratched the back of his neck. "We are not ready."

Where did that come from?

"Well, thank you, Dad." I wrapped my arms around him. "It's perfect." I looked into his eyes before reaching out to hug Mom.

Glad I got back on the pill fast.

The next day, I stood on the edge of the porch for a moment to enjoy the sight of my wedding before becoming part of it.

No, we weren't at a church. But there was a refined elegance to our romantic wedding. Farm tables with vintage china and linen napkins created a rustic charm. Light orange hyacinth, blush peonies, and cream English roses decorated every table, the wide aisle, the altar, and the arch.

We each had about fifteen guests. No wedding party. I didn't have close friends, and Peter didn't have parents present. Our guests were seated in short rows of cross-back style chairs decorated with blush and cream tulle sashes. Most people knew each other well and were engaged in lively conversation.

The string quartet, four elegant ladies in blush dresses who sat to the left of the altar, ended the prelude and began playing the last movement of Bach's Cantata 147.

Dad walked my way, all talk ended, and all heads turned. My family and our guests stood.

Everyone looked at me in my sweetheart tea-length wedding dress, and dozens of smiles warmed me and encouraged me. I'd put on three pounds since I'd quit dancing, but I didn't feel guilty. I felt beautiful and womanly. I'd wanted a new life—a different one. *Well, here it is. New life, here I come.*

As I came down the back porch steps, the full, ivory skirt of my satin gown danced to the perfumed cool breeze, and looking at Peter, my heart danced too.

The physical distance between us reminded me of the day I'd come back to the ranch—the day I'd spotted him from the boat and wondered if it was really him. *Thank you for letting me come back. Thank you for letting me stay.*

Dad reached for my hand. "You look so beautiful."

"Thank you, Dad."

"Shall we?" He offered his arm.

As we walked, I could almost hear the piercing voice of the Celtic Woman ladies I'd seen on YouTube before going to sleep. I'd wanted to know what "Jesu, Joy of Man's Desiring" was all about before walking down the aisle to it.

The lyrics of the English version are beautiful, but I'd struggled to identify a unifying theme. A close-to-literal translation of the original German poem didn't correspond to the common English version, but even though the text was choppy, the theme was clear and touched my heart: a close friendship with Jesus. A friendship that was simple, constant, and familiar.

Fifty feet of fine-bladed zoysia grass was all that separated me from Peter and my happily-ever-after. *Jesus, I want what that poet had—has—or however it works. I know it's not a bunch of coincidences. I know it's not just in my mind. Once things slow down, we'll find a church.*

I acknowledged Mom with a warm smile and a nod before taking the final steps toward Peter.

Help us, Jesus. Bless our marriage.

Peter stood, displaying the usual boyish grin, but there was a peculiar satisfaction in his face and a security to his stance. He looked stable—almost as if planted on the ground, like a centennial tree.

He'd looked somber the night before, and I'd worried, but his wedding-day quiet happiness assured me and made me happy too. Whatever it was that had bothered him in the hours leading up to the wedding seemed to be behind us.

"Who gives this woman to be married to this man?"

"Her mother and I do." Dad kissed my cheek and sat next to Mom.

I took Peter's hand. He looked fantastic in a three-piece beige suit, ivory shirt, and beige tie. The lighter ensemble softened his midnight blue eyes to a lighter shade. His wavy brown hair was combed back, and he wore a citrus fragrance that was also light and lovely.

"Hi," he whispered when he stood by my side.

"Hi," I whispered back, resting my hand on his strong arm. *I am the luckiest girl in the world. In just a few more minutes, I will be Mrs. Peter Engberg. Mrs. Engberg. Ana Engberg. Oh, how I love the sound of it. Engberg. Engberg. Engberg. The search is over. The hurt is over. This is it. This is the best day of my life.*

"Do you, Ana, take this man, Peter, to be your husband, according to God's holy decree; do you promise to be to him a loving and loyal wife, to cherish and keep him in sickness and in health; and, forsaking all others, to be faithful only to him as long as you both shall live?"

"I do."

Twenty-four hours later we were bundled in a rowboat, floating on San Francisco's Stow Lake.

"I've never seen so many ducks in one place before." I tossed my last bread crumbs in the sparkly green water. "Look at those right there," I said, pointing at a group of red-eyed ducks with shiny green and purple feathers that were separated by white stripes. "What are they?"

Peter, who'd been looking intently at the greenery on the shore, scanned the water. "Wood ducks. They're probably passersby, flying south for the winter."

"Maybe these will follow us to Georgia." My heart warmed to the idea.

"Probably not." He reached out to touch my cheek. "We're in the Pacific Flyway here, and in Georgia we are in the Atlantic Flyway."

"What? They have highways for birds?"

"Kind of. It's what they do." He shrugged. "They stick to a pattern."

"Can't they pick a back road and end up in Georgia? Just for the fun of it?"

He shook his head and chuckled. "I'm no bird expert, but I don't think so."

"Let me guess—that's the female version?" I pointed at two gray-brown ducks with white teardrop shaped patches surrounding their dark eyes.

Peter nodded. "Soon they'll pair up. You can see them at Callaway sometimes. Then in the spring, they return home paired and ready to breed, which may be why the wood duck is the only North American duck that produces two broods every year." He shrugged. "Bird trivia."

"It's cool." Frankly, all the talk about pairing and mating and breeding had me thinking about what Peter had told my dad when I'd gotten my new truck.

"I won't bore you with any more of it."

"You're not boring me, I promise." I reached out and touched his hand. "But I am curious about why you told my dad we're not ready for kids."

He laughed and clapped his hands together. "How did you go from ducks to babies?"

"You were talking about breeding grounds and broods."

"Alright, mama duck." Peter chuckled and nodded. He patted the spot next to his, and he held my hand as I moved carefully to sit by his side.

"Can you give me a year or two?" He drew circles on the palm of my hand.

"Sure…" Resting my head on his chest, I breathed him in. "But why wait?"

"I just don't want to rush into it. I feel like a bit of a kid myself."

This is probably not a good time to mention that he's in his thirties and has been in his thirties for a while. "But you do want kids?"

"Yes." His lips touched the top of my head as he played with a long strand of my brown hair. "Just not right now."

Nothing wrong with waiting, I guess.

My eyes turned to three turtles sunning on a log, and I remembered the ones from the little lake in Germany. So much about Stow Lake reminded me of the Warmer Damm Park in front of the Hessisches Staatstheater in Wiesbaden.

"What should we do tonight?" Peter's voice got me back to the present and to the boat.

"Fisherman's Wharf? Dinner at Alioto's?"

"Let's do it." He put his arms around me. "We can ride the cable car there."

"Hanging off the running boards, Doris Day-style?" I planted a tiny kiss on the corner of his mouth.

"Why not?" We both chuckled. "Come here and give me a proper kiss." The corners of his eyes crinkled as he tapped his lips.

A proper kiss? I sat on his lap carefully and put my arms around him, my lips teasing his until he groaned and gathered me against him. Losing myself in his masculine scent and protective warmth, I was transported to a place in my heart I hadn't been to in a while, the place where dreams take shape and grow. I could do this forever. I had a new dream. He tightened his embrace as autumn leaves danced to the music of a steady breeze. I moaned against his lips, holding on to him with fisted hands. *I want to love you like I do right now forever.*

When we walked out of the boathouse, Peter shrugged.

"What?" Had my kiss not been proper or the time on the lake not fun?

He looked at me, puzzled.

"You shrugged."

"No, I didn't."

"Did too."

He shook his head and held my hand as we walked in the direction of the hotel.

After almost two weeks in northern California, we returned to the ranch with great memories of Fisherman's Wharf and Stow Lake, a love for Sausalito, and ten small sequoias from a nursery near Muir Woods. Peter insisted we could get coastal redwoods to thrive in the South, so we brought them home and planted nine near the existing tree line at our lake and one at the azalea bowl at Callaway.

Married life suited me well, and as fall turned into winter, I hardly ever thought about Claus, Germany, the Met, or any other aspect of a life I didn't have. I was perfectly content with the one I had.

Peter spent his days working at the park, and I visited often. I'd also found a surprisingly good ballet school in LaGrange and went there three times a week—mostly just for fun, but also in hopes of dropping a couple of the pounds I'd gained since coming home.

In November, I helped Mom clear the dying spring and summer blossoms from her garden, and we planted some hardy bushes to serve as background for the flowers she would plant in future seasons.

She chose yellow delight pansies and crown scarlet viola pansies, both of which added beautiful color and life to her gray house.

Neighbors who saw us working asked for advice, and I offered to help. By Christmas, I had landscaped fourteen houses in Mom's neighborhood, and everyone was asking me to help in the spring months too.

We didn't need the money, but I enjoyed the work, so I spent the second part of the winter researching gardening magazines and looking through Peter's school books to get ideas for the warm months.

On a Friday night in late February, Peter and I were home watching *Nights in Rodanthe* when my breasts felt suddenly and uniquely heavy. *This is a first…* As I crossed my arms in front of me, I remembered two missed pills in late December.

It can't be. I only missed two. It could take six months or more for a woman to get pregnant after being on the pill for a long time like I had been. I'd only taken a two-month break toward the end of my time in Germany. I should be okay.

But what if?

I looked at Peter. He'd brought home the movie, fresh red roses, and a crisp North Georgia wine he was able to get from the executive chef of the main restaurant at the park. *He loves me. Certainly, he would be happy if I turned up pregnant, right? An unplanned pregnancy, too soon for him, but still a happy event, right?* More than once, I'd caught him teary-eyed as he watched dads and children playing at Callaway. *I know he likes kids.*

And then I panicked. *Claus. No, it can't be his.* I went back on the pill soon after Peter and I got back together. *When was the last time I was with Claus? Early September? No. Mid-September.* I did the math. *Mid-October, mid-November, mid-December, mid-January, mid-February. Impossible. I would be five months along.*

I'd gained almost seven pounds and had to buy new pants, but the weight gain was probably from dancing very little, cooking rich foods every night, and eating lunch at Mom's almost every day. *I can't be five months pregnant. I haven't even missed a period—not one.*

I looked at Peter. *I'm not five months pregnant.* He caught my glance and winked, his expression gentle. *It's Peter's and it's recent.*

If it's anything at all.

It has to be Peter's.

The next day the discomfort was gone, but by the end of February, I'd gained another pound and missed a period.

"Enough with the wondering," I mumbled on the morning I flipped the calendar to March.

When Peter went to work, I went to the store and got a test.

Back at the house, I fumbled with the packaging and read the instructions. *Can't be that complicated. Let's do this already.* Even though telling Peter would be hard, I hoped the result would be positive. He would probably be mad at first but then warm up to the idea. *That's if I'm pregnant.*

Before I had a chance to put the test on the cold counter, the result was already obvious. The two pink lines that would change our lives materialized right in front of my eyes, in my hands, as I put the cover back on the tip of the test. Maybe if I waited the prescribed three minutes the result would change. I put the test on the vanity and waited. *I don't think it can change.*

Three minutes went by. No change.

This is it. It's positive. "Wow," I whispered. "I'm going to be a mommy. Wow." A smile grew on my lips, and I spun from room to room, humming "The Sleeping Beauty Waltz."

"Pa-ra-ra-rarararara-rara-rara. Pa—"

"So that's what you do when I'm not around," Peter said, smiling by the front door.

I stopped and giggled. "What are you doing at home?"

"Just picking up a tray from the greenhouse." He placed the mail and his keys on the china cabinet and approached me.

Might as well tell him. "I have some big news," I said, fidgeting. "Wanna know?"

"Hmm ... I don't know."

I cocked my head.

He chuckled. "Of course I want to know. What is it?"

"It's not exactly how we'd planned it—I know—but it just happened..."

"What just happened?"

"You're going to be a daddy."

"Oh, no. Please ... no." He groaned and ran out the back door.

What in the world? I opened the door and ran after him.

He stopped by the swing.

I caught up and placed a hesitant hand on his shoulder.

"Please don't touch me right now."

"Okay." I moved back.

"What happened, Ana?" His eyes riveted on the lake. "I thought you were on the pill."

"I am. I started soon after we got back together."

"Then what happened?" He faced me this time. "How can you be pregnant?"

"I don't know. I got back on the pill two or three days after we got back together, so there were those first few days, but I would have to be really far along, and I doubt I am." *Please don't ask about Claus.* "My bet is New Year's—I missed a couple of pills around New Year's." I cringed. "I'm sorry."

"Ana, how come you didn't tell me? We could have used protection."

"I'm sorry." *Why is this such a big deal? I don't get it.* "We were getting married, and then we were married. I know we'd agreed to wait, but it just happened. I didn't plan to get pregnant. Promise."

He shook his head. "We talked about this. I told you I wasn't ready." He had his eyes fixed on the lake again.

"I didn't do it on purpose..." *He's not telling me the whole truth. No way. There's got to be more to this story.* "I'm sorry, Peter. I really am."

Then his head snapped in my direction.

"Wait a minute. How about Claus? Were you not sleeping with him?"

And here we go. I lowered my gaze and exhaled hard. "Claus and I were trying to have a baby."

"You've got to be kidding me."

I shook my head. "Not kidding."

"So this could be Claus's baby?"

"It's not." *It can't be.* "Do I look like I'm five months pregnant?" He'd never mentioned my weight gain, but I'm pretty sure he'd noticed.

Peter shrugged. "I don't know."

Safe answer. "What's really going on here? Is there more to it than wanting to wait? Do you not want kids?"

"I want kids."

"Doesn't seem like it."

"I want kids!" He hit the swing structure with his right fist.

I took a step back and put the palm of my right hand on my belly.

"I'm sorry." He shook his head as if trying to wake up from a bad dream. "It's my fault."

"What?" I spread out my arms. "What's going on here? I'm completely lost."

He looked away again.

"Talk to me, Peter. I love you. Whatever it is, we will figure it out." I approached him and placed my hand tentatively on his arm. He didn't complain.

"It's Huntington's, Ana," he muttered, covering my hand with his. "I have Huntington's disease." He looked into my eyes.

"What's Huntington's?"

"It's a genetic disease." He took a step back and raked his fingers through his hair. "It's an ugly disease, with no cure. With time, you lose control of movements, forget things, can't make decisions, can't control emotions, can't control anything. You become incapacitated and then you die."

"What?" *This can't be.* "Why do you think you have that?"

"It runs in my family. I got tested in my twenties, but the results were inconclusive." He was looking away from me now.

Inconclusive. He probably doesn't have it, and we're stressing for no good reason. "You said it runs in your family. Is that why your mom died young?"

He nodded. "She had it."

"Does that have something to do with your relationship with your dad?"

He nodded again. "He wouldn't let me get tested when Mom was diagnosed. I was nine. He had to authorize testing and refused." He pressed both eyes with the palms of his massive hands and turned to me. "I'm sorry I didn't tell you earlier, Ana. I tried the day before the wedding, but—"

"Don't be sorry." I covered his mouth and remembered his pre-wedding tension. *Everything makes sense now. He did try to tell me that day.* "Listen, I promised to love you for better or for worse, sickness and health. I meant it. We will just deal with it if we have to." *But we won't have to. Surely he doesn't have this Huntington's.*

But what if he did? I touched my belly again. *Could the baby have it? What's the likelihood? It's best if I don't ask right now...*

"Ana, we are going to get the fetus tested."

"We can do that?"

"Yep." He nodded, then opened his mouth as if to add something, but stayed silent.

I wasn't sure I wanted to know ahead of time if our kid was going to develop something bad as an adult, but the topic didn't seem up for debate.

Peter fidgeted. "And we can make sure the baby is mine while we're at it."

My heart sank, but I nodded sheepishly. "Does it help to know ahead of time if a baby has Huntington's? Or do you just want our child to know, instead of growing up wondering about it like you?"

He looked at me with empty eyes that scared me.

"What?" *What now?*

"Ana, if the baby has Huntington's, we are not having it."

"Peter, don't be ridiculous."

"I'm not the one who decided to get pregnant."

"I didn't. Decide. To get pregnant. I already told you." I took a deep breath and sat on the swing. "How could I have known any of this?"

"I already said I'm sorry."

"So have I."

Peter crossed his arms and leaned against the swing frame.

"You should have told me about the Huntington's." I massaged my temple. "And you should have told me about not wanting kids."

"I want kids."

"Then why are you talking about aborting this one? You're making no sense."

"I thought we were going to plan the pregnancy, at which point I was going to tell you about my possible HD."

"And?" I shrugged. "What difference would that have made?"

"We would do in vitro fertilization, test the embryos, and implant one without the disease."

"Well, that's a lot of engineering, isn't it?"

"It's the responsible way." He sounded matter-of-fact, like a doctor.

"Responsible or convenient?"

"Responsible. I happen to find the whole ordeal very inconvenient."

"The embryos that didn't get selected would probably agree with you on the 'inconvenient' part." I crossed my arms too and wished I had a jacket. "Or do you have a responsible plan for them too?"

Peter took off his jacket and put it over my shoulders. "The other embryos?"

"Yes, the other embryos. What would you do with them in your great reproduction plan?"

He shrugged. "Keep the healthy ones for future pregnancies."

"How about the others?"

"I don't know." He threw his hands up.

"Don't kid yourself, Peter." I pointed at my belly. "You would have them killed—some responsible plan."

He shook his head. "I can't have a Huntington's baby. Please don't be unreasonable about it."

I'm not the one being unreasonable. "Let's not test." I felt a spark of optimism amid that gloomy discussion. "Let's just go with it."

"And hope for the best?"

"Why not?"

"I can't. You don't understand."

"You're right on that one. I don't understand. This is all brand new to me, and it breaks my heart that you've dealt with it since you were nine, and that you've lost your mom because of it. I don't know what that's like. But one thing I know." I stood next to him. "I love you, so much. And I'm glad your parents didn't get rid of you."

"You don't understand, Ana."

I shrugged. "Sorry you're not happy." I fought the urge to cry. "But I'm still happy that we're having a baby."

"We *might* be having a baby."

I tightened my lips, unwilling to engage any further and knowing the baby would be born, no matter what. *I am having this baby.*

Peter tightened his lips too. Then he walked down to the dock, got in our little red boat, and rowed away in long strokes, gliding easily over the flat water.

I heard two groans before going back into the house, shaking my head.

From the cold beige counter of the bathroom vanity, the pregnancy test mocked me. *I always come up short, no matter how hard I try.*

"Ugh!" I tossed the test on the floor with violence. "What else is new?" I looked at the broken pieces of my First Response scattered all over the tiled bathroom floor reminding me of how quickly dreams can be given and taken away.

Chapter 23

Peter had been gone for an hour, and for most of that hour, I'd sat by the large living room window and looked at the still lake, waiting.

Waiting for an apology that I knew would come.

Waiting for wisdom.

Waiting to react.

Jäger followed me into the kitchen. I knelt to scratch his thick black fur and realized I hadn't thought about Barysh in a long time.

This hurt, too, will pass.

"Bud, you need a bath." I washed my hands to remove the dusty feeling and the farm-dog smell. "But that can wait, I suppose. I will at least brush you tomorrow, huh?"

I fixed myself a turkey and cheese sandwich and grabbed a little bag of baby carrots from the fridge. The beer shelf had my attention, but I got a bottle of water from the pantry instead.

I took my lunch into the formal dining room and placed it by my laptop, which I'd neglected for weeks. I was about to sit when I heard Peter start the truck.

By the time I opened the door, he was far from the house.

Seriously?

Looking at the blue sky, I shook my head.

"You really don't like me, do you, God? What do you want from me?" I looked at the bright day one more time before slamming the door shut. "Thanks for nothing. What good are you?"

I powered up the computer and sat. "Me and myself. What else is new? Here I am with my dreams falling apart again, and who's gonna help me? A whole lot of nobody. Just me." My head hurt. "I should be reading *What to Expect When You Are Expecting*, not researching Huntington's."

My stomach was unsettled, but I forced myself to eat and resisted the urge to apologize to God for the outburst.

Not apologizing. I'm sick and tired of watching everyone do whatever they want and end up happy. I'm trying my best here, and what do I get? This isn't fair.

"Do you hear me? Not fair."

I took what was left of my sandwich to the kitchen and washed my hands to get rid of the buttery smell that suddenly bothered me. *Sick of it.*

On my way back to the table, I spotted a book I'd never noticed before, a collection of flower paintings. I recognized the cover: *Roses and Sunflowers* by Vincent van Gogh, a selection of white flowers dominated by half a dozen white roses and four sunflowers. I'd seen the original in Germany with Claus at the Kunsthalle Mannheim, and we'd decided those were going to be our wedding flowers.

"Um…" I touched the cover and swallowed hard. "No. No, God. No signs. No coincidences." I placed the book under Grant Reid's *Landscape Graphics.* "No feeling sorry for myself either."

I opened the browser and started with the basics on the heartbreaking disease that could take both my husband and my baby. I skimmed over the symptoms and studied the advances toward a cure.

Scientists seemed optimistic about finding ways to slow or stop the progression of Huntington's in the near future, but the research on curing the disease and rebuilding a damaged brain seemed sketchy to me.

Do I want to read and watch testimonies? I need to. I need to see real people talking about their reality.

One lady's testimony, in particular, helped me understand Peter's anguish.

My husband is transitioning from the intermediate stage to a more advanced stage of Huntington's. He struggles so much to speak, and it's so hard for me to understand what he's saying that he often doesn't bother trying anymore. He can still dress himself with help. His ability to walk is deteriorating fast, and he is ready to start using a wheelchair to cover long distances.

He falls daily. Sometimes he doesn't get to the bathroom in time. He agreed to wear incontinence pads, but they don't really do anything. I just hope it's a step toward wearing something bigger. He doesn't want to bathe, but once he is in the shower, he enjoys it.

Feeding is getting harder, as he struggles to swallow the 6,000 calories he wastes on involuntary movement that's equivalent to running a daily marathon. He lost thirty pounds this year, and the feeding tube I used to dread might actually be a blessing. When we discovered he had HD twelve years ago, I made him promise he would let me care for him at home to the

END. I'M NOT SURE IF HE FORGOT THE AGREEMENT OR IF HE'S PRETENDING TO HAVE FORGOTTEN FOR MY SAKE.

WE NEED HELP. THIS WEEK HE IS MOVING TO A NURSING HOME. HE CHOSE THE SAME ONE WHERE HIS MOTHER SPENT HER LAST TWO YEARS. I WILL BE THERE MOST OF THE TIME AND STILL DO MOST OF THE WORK. THERE IS A BEAUTIFUL GARDEN THERE WITH A LARGE POND AND A FOUNTAIN. WE'VE ALWAYS LIKED GARDENS. JOHN HAS SAID I CAN WHEEL HIM TO THE GARDEN EVERY DAY, AND THAT'S GOING TO BE OUR SPECIAL TIME—A TIME TO LOOK AWAY FROM THE BUILDING, AWAY FROM THE DISEASE, AND INTO THE LIFE AND LOVE WE CAN STILL SHARE IN THESE FINAL YEARS.

If Peter does carry the gene, how much time would we have?

No, I couldn't think that way. I had to stay positive. *We don't know if he has it, and there are lots of smart people working on a cure.*

Peter showed up at dinner time, and Jäger led him to me.

I was still in the dining room, red-eyed but okay. I didn't feel alone anymore—there were other people out there dealing with Huntington's. There was a community of support in place. We would handle it. I knew we would.

"I'm sorry." He got on his knees and wrapped his arms around me while resting his head on my lap.

"I know."

"I'm sorry about my reaction, Ana. Sorry I didn't tell you about it sooner, and sorry I plucked you out of a perfectly good life with Claus to give you this mess."

"I am where I want to be. Just don't run from me ever again. I'm strong. All I need from you is a little bit of optimism."

He nodded in silence and touched my belly with both hands before kissing it.

Our little family. Oh, this must be Peter's baby. Please...

"Now, I'm not trying to be pessimistic," he said, just above a whisper, "but you do realize, if the baby tests positive, that means I'm positive too, right?"

I nodded slowly. *We've always liked gardens,* the lady's words echoed in my head as tears rolled down against my will.

"Shh. You're right. We'll figure this out. We just have some hard choices to make."

"I want our baby, Peter. I don't care what he has. There has to be a cure in his lifetime."

"Like there is a cure for cancer?"

"Not for cancer, but today people live with AIDS. Remember how it used to be a death sentence? Scientists seem really optimistic about stopping the progression of HD in the near future. I read a lot about it."

"Successful scientists are optimistic by nature. They are good at getting funds, and you get funds by being positive." He sat on his heels. "More power to them. But the reality is that a cure or any useful medication is still a dream, Ana. They need a breakthrough that's yet to happen." He kissed my hands and looked at me. "I know your heart is in the right place, but it's too big a gamble."

"Don't you think your life is worth living—even if you do develop HD one day?"

"Yeah. But the idea of dying, after years of falling apart physically and mentally, kind of puts a damper on everything. You want a baby; I will give you a baby. Just not an HD baby. I don't like the idea of abortion any more than you do, but it happens a thousand times a day and for no good reason. We have a good reason."

No, we don't. I closed my eyes with a deep breath. "Can we stop talking about HD? Let's do the test and go from there."

"Yes. We can. I don't want to argue either. Just, please, have realistic expectations."

"I'm hungry, and I didn't cook anything. I want to eat out. Can you take me to Aspen's Mountain Grill? Or is that an unrealistic expectation?"

He stood. "That's a fair expectation." He pulled me up and into his arms. "I love you, Ana."

"I love you too."

I didn't know if HD would ever be a reality for us. But right now, it didn't matter. Right here, right now, my perfect little family of three was all I needed.

Three days later we went to Atlanta for the chorionic villus sampling that would determine our fate. An ultrasound would guide a catheter that would collect a sample of cells from my developing placenta.

"Can you tell when the baby was conceived?" Peter asked the doctor.

I blushed.

The doctor applied warm gel to my skin. "Absolutely. That's the first thing we're going to do."

I closed my eyes and breathed deeply, aware of Peter standing next to me.

The doctor moved the transducer back and forth, and then he stopped. "Ten weeks and four days. That's where we want to be."

Yes, that's where we want to be. I opened my eyes, happy to squelch the small and nagging voice that had explored a far-fetched possibility.

"New Year's at Callaway." Peter looked at me.

I nodded, remembering how especially handsome Peter had looked that night in his dark Jack Victor suit. "Aw, look," I said, seeing the baby's complete silhouette appear on the screen. From the corner of my eye, I spotted Peter's first proud-papa smile. "Is it too early to know if it's a boy or a girl?"

"A bit," the doctor said. "But based on where your placenta is located, I have a very strong suspicion."

"How strong of a suspicion?" Peter squinted at the screen.

"Ninety-seven percent strong."

Peter looked at me, and I nodded.

"What do you think it is?" Peter's upbeat tone matched the hidden sparkle in his eyes attempting to come forward.

"A boy."

We exchanged grins and then heard what sounded like an accelerating train.

"This is the heart." The doctor pointed at a white moving object on the screen. "Healthy at one hundred sixty-seven beats per minute."

Peter squeezed my hand, and I returned the gesture.

We are safe. He is not going to insist on stopping a heart he's seen and heard—the heart of his baby boy.

The genetic counselor called five days later, saying the results of the biopsy were in and that we could still choose not to receive the information. "If you decide you don't want to know, don't come," she'd said. "You don't even need to call."

"Can they make this thing any more dramatic?" I said, ending the call. "The results are in. The lady said we don't have to go get it."

"Let's go." Peter grabbed his keys.

We got in his truck and drove the seventy-seven miles to the clinic in less than an hour.

I had avoided thinking about the disease, but knowing a result was available put me in a state of absolute agony the whole drive, an agony that only got worse in the waiting room.

We were called in after eight minutes that felt like eight hours.

I looked for concern or happiness in the genetic counselor's expression but couldn't read her at all.

She sat and opened our file.

"The CAG repeat size was found to be in the normal range." Her eyes lingered on the paper for another moment.

"Yes!" Peter punched the air as if he'd just scored a goal.

"So that's good?" I asked. "That's what we want?"

She smiled at me and nodded. "That means your baby does not carry the genetic mutation for Huntington's disease and is not at risk for developing the disorder."

I covered my face and exhaled. *Thank God!*

"See?" Peter put his hands on my shoulders. "Everything will be all right now."

My head bobbed as I laughed and cried, covering my mouth like a child trying to be quiet but finding it impossible.

"This is wonderful news, indeed." The counselor looked at the file again and then at Peter. "And I don't mean to spoil the moment, but it is my job to ask. You said you got tested back in the nineties and had an uninformative test result? Would you like to retest?"

"No," Peter said, without thinking. "I couldn't deal with the stress of another test, only to get a meaningless result again."

"You are thirty-nine now." She looked at his information. "Have you tried undergoing a neurological exam to—"

Peter lifted his hand. "I spent the first half of my life wanting to know. Now I don't want to know anymore. I appreciate your concern, though."

"I understand, Mr. Engberg." She looked at Peter's hands, and I followed her gaze.

Had she seen something unusual?

"Congratulations to both of you on the baby, and remember we're here to help if you decide to have more children."

"Thank you." He shook her hand.

She looked at me briefly as she shook my hand but seemed more interested in watching Peter, her gaze on his shoulders.

Once out the door, we embraced in silent relief.

On the drive back to Pine Mountain we agreed to stop at my parents' home.

They still knew nothing about the pregnancy.

"I'll be holding the ultrasound picture when she opens the door." I beamed as Peter acknowledged my excitement.

"What do you think about Gabriel?"

"Who's Gabriel?"

"As a name for the baby. Gabriel." Peter raised his eyebrows.

"Oh. I like it. What does it mean?"

"I'm not sure. Just seems like a good, strong name."

"Okay." As long as it didn't mean anything weird.

"You don't sound convinced." Peter twisted his lips.

"I just don't know what it means."

"It's the name of an angel."

"Okay." I tried to sound more convincing this time. Gabriel, Michael, Mary … I didn't really care. We were having a baby, and we were finally both happy about it. The name was not that important.

He squeezed my hand as I touched my belly. *Hi, Gabriel.*

"I have a little gift for you." Peter's eyebrows rose. "It's in the glove compartment, under the truck manual," he said, as I looked for something that didn't belong.

I unwrapped Clint Black's *Greatest Hits II*. I didn't know much about Clint Black, but I liked most country artists. "Thank you."

"Put it in." He gave me his pocket knife. "Go to fourteen."

"Little Pearl and Lily's Lullaby," I read from the back cover as a mellow melody and baby giggles filled the Silverado.

Peter upped the volume and sang an impromptu duet with Clint Black, a duet about all things baby and about preparing for a new life.

When he finished, he touched my cheek and brushed away a tear. And his smile filled my heart with lovely warmth and the promise of a new beginning.

Chapter 24

"Well, the baby is breech now," the doctor said, touching my belly during our thirty-eight-week appointment.

"What does that mean?" Was the baby safe? The doctor continued to touch different parts of my belly with both hands, putting slight pressure near my ribs. *Speak already.*

"His head was down, but now he flipped." His hands moved to my lower belly again. "This right here is his bottom. His head is up by your heart."

Peter rubbed his forehead. "Is that bad?"

"Not bad, but we might have to deliver him via C-section."

"What about my birth plan and my doula? I have everything packed for labor."

"Plans change." The doctor patted my hand, his voice soothing.

My head turned away from the room and to the large window that faced the woods.

"We can try to rotate him manually, using pressure on the abdomen, but there are no guarantees."

"Is it safe?" Peter's voice was calm too, and I tried to let their tranquility wash over me.

"It's not comfortable, but it's safe. I would monitor the baby while attempting the external version, and if something were to go wrong, we would take Ana to surgery and deliver the baby that way." He crossed his ankles in front of him. "Don't worry. One way or another, you'll have your baby in your arms soon."

Don't worry? Could I snap my fingers and have the baby in my arms right now? The external version did seem worth a shot... "Does manual rotation usually work?"

"Two out of three attempts are successful."

"Wanna try?" My eyes turned to Peter.

"I don't know." His weight shifted and a deep line formed between his brows.

I wanted to ask him to stop tapping his fingers on my arm but decided against it. He'd been tapping his fingers a lot lately—on the steering wheel, on the dinner table, on the pillow, and now on my arm. What had him so tense lately? He didn't like it when I asked, so I didn't.

"Let me give you guys some time to talk." The doctor walked out the door and left us alone.

As his footsteps faded away, Peter's gaze turned to the beach picture on the wall in front of him. Was he not comfortable with the—what was it called? External version?

"Ana, what do you think about keeping this simple and scheduling a C-section?"

"Simple?" Did Peter have a clue as to what a C-section entailed?

"Sorry. You know what I mean."

No, I wasn't sure. "But the manual rotation sounds safe—and simple. Why not try it?"

"I don't know."

"Come on, Peter. Let's give it a shot. Hmm?"

He stopped tapping on my arm and folded his hands, elbows on his knees, head down. But then he started tapping his feet.

"Please stop tapping."

He nodded without looking at me, and I suspected he would be in one of his moods for the rest of the day, regardless of what we decided to do for the baby.

Early in the summer he'd started having noticeable mood swings. I used to tease him saying, "It must be that time of the month again." But after a while, those comments made him even sourer, so I learned to ignore the behavior. *God, please help us make a good decision—a wise one, like I read a while back. Was it Solomon? I know I haven't prayed or read much lately, and I still think things that happen to me are not fair sometimes, but I need You. Please help us.*

Did I even know anyone who'd had a C-section? I knew they were common, but how about my birth plan? Surgery wasn't part of it.

Plans change. Yep, the doctor was right.

"Fine, let's try." Peter rose to his feet and squared his shoulders.

"Oh, good!" *Yes! Thank you, God.* I reached for Peter's hands, and his lips touched my forehead as the doctor walked in.

We scheduled the external cephalic version for the following Monday, three days away, and we went home to enjoy what could be our last weekend without a baby in arms.

After a quiet dinner, I stood by the nursery window and followed a red-tailed hawk as it flip-flip-flip-glided near the wood line. Our sequoias had been growing well for almost a year and were taller than Peter now.

"Sorry I've been a bit of a grump." He walked into the nursery.

"I've been grumpy too. I'm sorry."

"You're almost nine months pregnant, and you've been carrying a big baby inside of you all summer. You're supposed to be grumpy." He pulled the string of the mobile, sending its four silver angels flying in circles over the empty crib. "Let's dance."

My hand reached for his, and as we swayed to the tune of "When You Wish Upon a Star," my eyes turned heavenward to the first stars of the pre-dusk sky over the lake. Everything would be all right. Gabriel was almost here.

I spent the weekend trying to imagine myself as a mom and reading the C-section chapters of the two birth books we owned, just in case. Would I be a good mom? *Will I, Gabriel?* Wrapping my arms around my belly, I realized that he was in the right position to be held already—head up and by my heart.

Peter was quieter than usual and went out on long walks both Saturday and Sunday, but by Monday he seemed nervous and fidgety again. When we got to our appointment, his agitation became worse.

A nurse showed up with an ultrasound machine, and the doctor walked in right behind her. "We'll take a quick look inside and make sure there've been no changes since Friday, and then we'll get you upstairs for the external version."

Peter held my hand as the doctor applied warm gel to my belly and studied its contents. He added more gel. "Hmm."

"Is everything okay?" Peter squeezed my hand.

"Yes, but we'll not be able to proceed as planned." He stopped the exam. "On Friday your amniotic fluid was fine, but today it isn't."

"What do we do now?" My heart was beating so loud I wondered if they could hear the sound through my chest. My mouth dried up and I was suddenly dizzy.

"We go to labor and delivery and prep you for a C-section."

"Today? Now?" Couldn't we wait for me to reach forty weeks later in the month?

"Right now—we need to deliver this baby. Your fluid is dangerously low. We caught the problem just in time. If you hadn't had this appointment today, there's no telling what could have happened." He turned to Peter. "Are you ready to be a daddy?"

He beamed and my eyes filled up with hot tears. *I'm going to be a mom. Today.* Wasn't I supposed to be afraid? I was about to go into what's considered a major surgery. *I'm going to be a mom. Today.*

Four hours later Gabriel was born with big brown eyes and a head full of honey-colored hair.

Gabriel was exactly six weeks old when I took him to Columbus to visit the company.

Of course I wanted people to meet him, but that was not the only reason we went. There was something I needed to do.

Amid the oohs and aahs from the group that surrounded us when we walked in, I saw Lorie walk past us. I had to find a way of talking to her in private.

"We have a second principal now," Brian said. "Young girl. She's only sixteen."

"I met her, right? Soloist in *Les Sylphides*?"

"Yeah. That's right. Last year's fall program. We're staging *Giselle* for her next spring. Lorie will be Myrtha."

I giggled but felt sad for Lorie at the same time. Myrtha is a great role. She's the queen of the betrayed spirits who rise from their graves at night to seek revenge upon men. But once you are Giselle, you want to be Giselle always. Had Lorie's career already peaked?

"We didn't have a chance to talk much after your farewell." Brian tickled Gabriel. "That was a great piece that you and Claus put together. If you ever feel like choreographing, let me know. We can see what you can come up with on your own."

"Thanks, Brian, but I've got my hands full in Pine Mountain." I took a deep breath and looked around the place that had been my second home. "I'm doing well with my new life, and I even found a school in LaGrange. I've been dancing on and off, mostly off, since the summer. But I'll be going back in a couple of weeks."

"Well, I'm glad everything is working out for you. Just remember our doors are open." He put his arms around me, then took a step back as soon as his belly touched mine.

Touching my little post-baby pouch, I made an exaggerated embarrassed face.

Brian shook his head, and we giggled. "All right. Go home, Mom."

After I do one more thing. I waited for Lorie outside.

She walked out of the company building and froze when she saw me standing by a parking meter, staring at her.

I reached for the diaper bag under the stroller, found her book behind the changing pad, and lifted it toward her.

She smiled at the sight of the pink and purple cover and approached me.

The tearstain was still there, the one from the tears I'd cried when I told God I didn't know how to make myself happy. Had Lorie figured out how to be happy? Had she snapped out of whatever had taken a hold of her?

She took her Bible and shook her head heavenward as her eyes filled with tears. "Thank you," she said, looking at me. "I thought you were still mad at me and were going to slap me or something—mommy hormones. You never know." She started laughing.

I shook my head and laughed too. She seemed to be in good spirits—especially for someone who was now sharing the top spot in the company.

Lorie bobbed her head in the direction of the RiverCenter. "I've got to go. It was nice seeing you." She hugged her book with both arms, looking like a schoolgirl and reminding me of the Lorie I'd first met—the one who was my friend.

"It was nice seeing you too." Pieces of that "all things together for good" verse I'd first read in Mallorca popped into my mind unannounced. *Romans...* Lorie waved and turned around.

"Cute baby," I heard her say.

"Thanks." Did all things work together for good? I watched her walk away. Her steps were quick and light, and soon a handsome blond kissed her and put his arm around her shoulders. In his hand, a violin case. It was *him*—the European guy from the symphony—the one she'd been dating before *Romeo and Juliet*. Good for her.

She rested her head on his shoulder and slowed down.

Maybe everything did work together for good.

On the ride home, I heard Massenet's "Méditation" from "Thaïs" on NPR, and with each lingering note, I realized I was happy, and with that realization, came fear.

Had I figured out how to make myself happy, at last?

Had God decided to help me even though I was not doing anything to warrant his favor? Or was I about to lose something? Or everything?

The thought made breathing difficult, and I swallowed hard.

But then I remembered something Brian had said when we were working on pirouettes the day after the last performance of *Romeo and Juliet*.

"Stay up!" he'd said. "Don't worry about the landing. You will land eventually. Gravity will take care of that. I promise you. Worry about staying up there in relevé! It's a beautiful place to be."

Chapter 25

In early spring, I'd finished landscaping sixteen homes and was looking for fresh ideas for five more, so I took Gabriel and Jäger to the Roosevelt Warm Springs Institute for Rehabilitation to look at the work of my favorite landscape artist— my husband. He'd been volunteering there for a little over a month.

At Callaway Gardens, his work was markedly different and reminded me of how he'd described the flower beds he'd planted with his mother in his childhood. There was harmony in the shapes, heights, and textures of the flowers, but colors clashed without the usual underlying unity, creating a dramatic effect that I liked. Some flower beds seemed like quiet riots while larger ones had a polite-scream quality to them.

"Let's see what he did here," I whispered, spotting the entrance to the institute.

The campus was much larger than I had expected and reminded me of a traditional college where Greek-inspired buildings meet bold modern ones without justification.

I drove past administration buildings, office buildings, clinics, dorms, and a chapel, looking for spring colors and flower beds that didn't seem to exist. The grass, trees, and green bushes were well distributed and taken care of, but that was all I could see: grass, trees, and green bushes—nothing that reflected Peter's love of color and flowering plants.

I kept driving, and I kept looking until I was so dizzy I had to stop.

Breathe. Where's his work?

Lifting my head and opening the windows, I saw two words on a wooden arrow that pointed to a road away from the buildings. "What's Camp Dream?" I asked Gabriel and Jäger. *Maybe that's where he's been planting.* My hand gripped the shift lever with determination and put the truck in drive again.

I followed a silent, winding road through tall pines, past one deer, a small cabin, and two rabbits. A reassuring second sign for the camp came to view.

"Aha." I arrived at a large lake and spotted several gorgeous flower beds right away. "Now we're talking. Here's his work."

But he hadn't done anything original. The patterns were the same he'd used at Callaway the previous spring: red tulips, yellow irises, purple hyacinth, and white asters. Pretty, but predictable, and in absolute harmony.

I drove around the lake and looked for more displays while enjoying the day's warmth. The reflection of delicate pines neatly spaced by the water's edge soothed my nerves. Rustic lodges and pavilions had similar flower beds, and the fishing dock had the same combination in containers of different heights. The canoe shed looked especially quaint with Peter's window boxes and hanging baskets. Near it, red and yellow paddleboats brightened the lakeshore, waiting for a swarm of summer campers that were sure to come.

But this was no ordinary camp. Every building, bridge, and trail were beautifully designed with smooth and wide access ramps to welcome all guests. Gabriel fussed in the back, reminding me that this could have been his summer camp if he'd had Huntington's disease.

A heaviness that wrapped around my chest like a boa constrictor hurt my heart and made breathing difficult. I imagined the struggles of the Camp Dream children and of their parents. Why had we been spared?

My lungs labored to fill up to capacity, and with the sick feeling came a deep desire to help. Was that why Peter volunteered here? Was it gratitude? And what could *I* do? Maybe this summer I should stop by and see what kind of work they do and what kind of help they need.

But it wasn't time for summer camp yet, and the place was deserted. The emptiness grew and became melancholy fast. "Let's go home, guys," I said, using the swimming pool parking lot to turn around.

Gabriel's fussing became stronger and louder before I could reach the road out of Camp Dream, though. I would never make it back to Pine Mountain without a feeding and a change. My eyes glanced at the clock. Eleven-twelve. "Well, let's stop."

We sat on a bench under a large magnolia tree, and I remembered the magnolia trees of the Warmer Damm Park in front of the Hessisches Staatstheater in Wiesbaden. *My old life.* Images of ballet classes, rehearsals, travels, and famous theaters danced before my eyes as Jäger chased pigeons and ducks, and as Gabriel nursed.

Would there always be a part of me that ached for that old ballet dream? Warm tears spilled from my eyes. "Come on, Jäger. Can you chase away old ballet ghosts?"

He came to me, wagging his tail. "Of course you can." A creamy pink magnolia petal fell on Gabriel's blanket, and a sweet and playful breeze blew it away. "See? Gone already."

I tossed a furry magnolia bud to get his attention away from my mood and back to doing fun dog things. But he found the bud and brought it back.

A burgundy Toyota Corolla parked next to my truck, and I used a baby wipe to pat my face dry before putting Jäger on the leash.

The driver, a woman about my age or maybe a little older, got out of the car and fixed her beautiful vintage sundress. The dress was a shade lighter than her honey-red hair, which was immediately disheveled by a gentle wind gust that also ruffled leaves and showered me with magnolia petals.

She walked to the lake with her eyes closed and her face tilted up to meet the sun.

The woman looked familiar. My mouth twisted as I tried to match her to people in houses where I'd planted, people at Callaway, ballet people in LaGrange … but I couldn't come up with anything.

She touched the water, as if drawing on the surface, and then looked over her shoulder, aware of me for the first time.

And from forty feet away, I recognized her smile.

For some reason, I'd imagined her younger. *How old was that picture I'd seen?*

She came our way, her steps unsure now. "Sorry, I didn't see you here until now. Hi."

"Hi." Jäger got up and waited for her to approach. "Shh," I told him firmly. He lay down with a snort, his tail tapping the green grass with force.

Repositioning Gabriel, I reached under the beige nursing cover and inserted my finger in the corner of his mouth to break his latch.

"You don't have to stop. I nursed all my babies." Her eyes studied Jäger.

"He's falling asleep anyway." I fixed my blouse before removing the cover. What was her name?

"He's so precious. How old is he?"

"Thanks. Seven months." Her eyes were on Jäger again. "He's not going anywhere. You can sit if you want."

Her chest rose and fell as she sat. "Sorry, I want to be a dog person, but I've had too many bad experiences."

"He won't hurt you, but I understand."

She brushed her thick hair with her fingers, away from her face and into a twist that came undone as soon as she let go. There was a hint of exhaustion in her eyes, but light freckles brightened her beautiful face. "Do you have family here?"

"I don't." *Will she freak out if I tell her that I know who she is?* "My husband volunteers here. He's the director of landscape operations at Callaway Gardens. He planted all the flowers you see around the camp."

"That's so nice. I love Callaway, and I love the flowers here—and there."

"Thanks." *I should tell her.*

"Do you guys live in Pine Mountain?"

"We do."

"We do too." She got a small bottle of water from her bag and drank half of it. "I'm sure we've seen each other around town before."

"Maybe." I chuckled, shaking my head.

"What is it?"

"You won't believe this, but I know you."

"You do? From church?" She cocked her head. "I'm usually good with faces, but I don't think I've seen you before. I just can't remember. Sorry."

"No, you don't know me. I know you from a picture. I met your mother-in-law at a church in Prague two years ago."

"I remember that trip. She was visiting some of our missionaries."

"She gave me a brochure." I dug in the diaper bag. "I still use it as a page marker for a little New Testament she also gave me." I pulled out the worn book and showed her the picture.

"You didn't have to lose your page," she said, seeing that I'd pulled the paper out of the Bible without opening it.

"I know where I was." *My grace is sufficient for thee: for my strength is made perfect in weakness.*

"We look so young." She held the paper with a grin. "It's an old tract."

"It's a good picture."

"Thanks."

"What did you call it?" I pointed to the brochure.

"A tract?"

I nodded. *That's right.*

"Here." She handed the old tract to me and pulled what looked like a newer one out of her bag. "In case you're still looking for a church home."

"Thanks. Maybe I'll check it out." *If I weren't religiously impaired or something, I would.* "I like the idea of going to church, but I never seem to do anything about it, despite my good intentions."

"Well, maybe this time." Her enthusiasm was endearing. "You already know me, and I bet you'll run into other people you know. We have several Callaway employees who are members."

"Maybe." I would probably never go.

"Did you go to church growing up?"

"Not much." This conversation wouldn't go anywhere new or productive. Would it? But she seemed nice. "I grew up Catholic and was really into it as a kid but kind of grew out of it."

"I was raised Catholic too."

"Really?" *Well, now I'm more interested.* "Why did you change?"

"It's a bit of a long story." She gave a lopsided grin, and her cheeks turned pink. "It's a love story."

A 'gone Baptist' love story? "You've got my full attention."

"Okay." She adjusted her position, eyes twinkling, and bit her lower lip. "I'd been dating a really nice young man—we'd been together since junior high. He was the only person I'd ever dated, and it was wonderful. But as we approached the end of high school, something changed."

She spoke fast and moved her hands with energy as she told me her story. Whatever the change was, it didn't seem to bother her anymore.

"He wanted to be a lawyer, like his dad, and had several college options open to him. I hadn't even applied to any colleges, and even though he'd never said it, I could tell that bothered him. During spring break, he decided he wanted to go to Notre Dame after graduation, so I considered moving to Indiana with him to be in the same area. He liked the idea but said he was hoping we could—"

She looked down, playing with her dress, and I had a pretty good idea where the story was going.

"He said he was hoping we could take our relationship to the next level by sleeping together to make sure we liked each other in that way before making moving decisions."

"What did you do?" And if she didn't want to go to college, what did she want to do?

"I said I needed time to think about it, but graduation came and went, and we still hadn't done it. A couple of weeks into the summer, his parents took him to Europe for a long vacation, and he expected me to make a decision about him before his return—'mature' or split up."

Talk about coming on strong. Did guys still do that? That seemed so wrong. And where was the love story she'd promised? "So what did you decide?"

"I loved him and could easily picture myself as a lawyer's wife in a pretty house and with children all around, so my mind couldn't entertain the possibility of losing him. I was ready to take our relationship to the next level, as he'd put it, as soon as he got back home."

Did she do it?

"But before he returned, I met Mark." She blushed again, and her freckles almost disappeared this time. "My husband…"

"Aww." My lips stretched, and I twisted on the bench, ready to hear more.

"People say Mr. Right won't come knocking on your door, right?" She giggled. "Well, mine did. It was his last year at home before Bible college, and he was door knocking with his dad."

"Door knocking?"

"Visiting people to talk about salvation through Jesus."

"Oh, right." I remembered all the people who'd knocked on Mom's door over the years. Did this woman do that? She looked too normal to be knocking on doors, talking about Jesus.

"My older brother was home from college for the summer. He'd been going to a Baptist church with his girlfriend in Chapel Hill, so when they came to spend some time with us, they went to a Baptist church and filled out a visitor's card. That's how Mark and his father ended up on my doorstep."

"And you fell madly in love with him as soon as you spotted him?"

"Kind of. It's fair to say he made an impression on me."

"How about your boyfriend? When did he get back?"

"Mark came to my house on a Saturday. I went to church with my brother that Sunday morning. Justin—my boyfriend—got back that Sunday night."

"Did you see Mark at church?"

"He spotted me arriving with my brother and invited me to go to teen church with him. We sat together." She blushed again. "Later, he told me he'd prayed all night that I would come."

"What did you do next?"

"Meeting Mark was enough to put the sleeping-with-Justin plans on the back burner—even if he did break up with me. But to my surprise, Justin seemed okay when I told him I wasn't ready."

"So he was bluffing?"

"I guess." Her brows drew together. "It was such a hard time for me because I was still with Justin, but Mark was in my thoughts all the time. There was something different about him, a manliness I can't explain. He can communicate a million words with the way he positions his body. He's sweet but assertive. He owns his territory. It's been almost twenty years, and I still don't understand it, but it's one of the things I love the most about him. Anyway … I'm sorry. I kind of got off topic."

"You said it was a love story." I winked. "So you're on topic."

She nodded. "It's definitely a love story with Mark, but that was also the beginning of my love story with the Lord. He sent Mark to my door to keep me from making a huge mistake—I would have regretted sleeping with Justin."

I thought of my old Prague story and knew what she meant.

"And then, when I was not sure which man I should be with, God showed me the way."

"How?" I picked up a magnolia petal that had landed on Gabriel.

"I was at the library studying water wells for a youth group service project.

The research was way more complicated than I'd expected, and soon I started thinking about Mark. But I felt bad because I was Justin's girlfriend, so I asked God to show me the way. Was it okay to switch boyfriends like that? What exactly was a Baptist? Was it something weird, like my parents had suggested?"

"And a little voice came from above?"

"The little voice had already come and had already told me what to do, but I was young, and I needed something more concrete. And as soon as I said 'show me the way'—within a minute—a volunteer who'd been helping me find more information on low-cost water wells came up with a professional magazine and said there was a brand-new trend called Baptist drilling."

"No."

"Yes." She laughed. "That was the early nineties, and people still use the Baptist water well technology I read about that day. Mark said he sent a thank-you note to the missionary who came up with it."

"Wow. That's good."

"But see, I could have said that was just a coincidence. I could have stayed in my comfort zone. But I didn't. That was the first time I stepped out in faith, and I was so blessed."

"If something like that ever happened to me, I would step out in faith, as you said."

"It already did. You got a tract for our Pine Mountain church while touring Prague, and then you met me here."

True. A lump formed in my throat. *That couldn't possibly be a coincidence.*

"Step out in faith."

"But I don't know how."

"Let me ask you this—if you were to die today, right now, are you one hundred percent sure that you would go to heaven?"

Here it comes. "I think so. Who can ever know for sure, right?"

"The Bible says you can know for sure ... I'm sorry, I never asked your name."

"Ana."

"I'm Jacqueline."

"Isn't your mother-in-law Jackie?"

"Yes, we are both Jacqueline, and my poor husband has yet to hear the end of it."

"I bet." She giggled, and her eyes shone bright—brighter than I'd ever seen anyone's eyes shine. There was definitely something special about this woman.

"Ana, you can know for sure. You do know God loves you and that you cannot save yourself, right?"

"I know the Romans Road. It's at the end of the green Bible." I pointed to the diaper bag.

"Then you know that Jesus already paid for your sins. All you need to do is accept it. Stop spinning wheels trying to pay a bill that's already been paid. When someone you trust offers you a beautiful gift, you should just take it. Say thank you and take it. Will you do that today, Ana?"

"Not today, but I'm working on it." That was the conversation I didn't want to have. I had too many unanswered questions. Best to get her talking about herself. "So why do you come here? Do *you* have family here?"

"My little girl has cerebral palsy."

"I'm sorry to hear that." I wasn't sure what that was, but I remembered noticing something about her posture in the old tract. *Ask her, she will understand.* "See what I mean, though? Why can't you live without suffering after all the years you've dedicated to God?" *And why did He give me a big dream without giving me enough talent? Shoo, ghost. Shoo.*

"God made many promises, but He never promised a struggle-free life. Quite the contrary. Jesus told His disciples that people had to turn from their selfish ways to follow Him. 'Take up your cross daily' is what He said."

"Then what's the point?"

"The point? Go home to heaven one day? Fix that anxious feeling we're born with and that no amount of drugs, alcohol, vacations, or fancy cars can ever fix? Adopt a definition of happiness that can bring fulfillment?"

"Seems like you have to give up a lot, and what you get in return is sort of abstract." *Might as well say it or she won't be able to help me.* "And cerebral palsy." *No, I shouldn't have said it.* "Sorry."

"I hear you."

Her gentle smile was genuine. I inhaled the creamy sweetness of the magnolias above us and resisted the urge to talk.

"You have to know that behind God's every no there is a bigger yes. You have to trust in His choices for your life, knowing that He sees the big picture and you don't." A sudden breeze played with her hair, and she brushed a strand away from her face. "And sometimes God just wants us to be willing to give up something. The moment we give it up, it comes right back to us, like Abraham and little Isaac."

What was the story of Abraham and Isaac?

"But listen, I can sit here and tell you these things all day long. Until you feel that tug at your heart, it will be just words. 'I decided to follow Christ because I've reached a logical conclusion,' said no man ever."

"Why can't religion be a logical decision? It should be."

"Because God didn't want it to be. It says so in the Bible. With human reasoning comes pride. God hates pride, so he set out to destroy the 'wisdom of the wise' and the 'understanding of the prudent' with the simple doctrine of the cross."

"He made it impossible for people to believe is what He did." I shook my head.

"People believe every day." Jacqueline shrugged. "New people come to faith every day."

"Weird people…" I raised my eyebrows. "Not you, of course."

She smiled.

"I still wish I could understand God."

"You can, by inviting Jesus into your life and becoming a student of the Bible. You'll learn fast that He's not the God we want Him to be or that we think He should be. He is who He is." Her bright eyes came alive, and her hands fluttered to the rhythm of her words. "His behavior is consistent, and His desires for us are clear. You will understand Him if you try."

"But to get to that point, I need to deal with hard questions like suffering and misery and poverty. Why does He allow it?" I shook my head. "It's too hard. It's impossible to understand." *Oh, how I want to have her faith.*

"Hard, yes. Impossible, no. Here's something that might help you. Do you remember why so many Jews rejected Jesus?"

"No." I didn't remember because I never really understood that either.

"They rejected Him because they'd expected the promised Messiah to be a conquering king, like David. They wanted a Jesus that would free them from Roman oppression, not die on a cross."

"Why didn't He defeat the Romans for them?"

"Because that was not His mission. He came 'to seek and to save that which was lost'—to offer people an eternal solution for their sin problem."

Where was she going with this?

"See that's the same reason why many people reject Jesus today. They still want a Jesus that will defeat the Romans—our modern-day Romans: poverty, violence, sickness, joblessness, cerebral palsy. And when it doesn't happen, they think He's not real or not good and give up on faith."

My heart tightened in my chest. That was me. I expected Him to defeat the Romans. I held Gabriel closer and breathed in his soft baby skin.

"Jesus hasn't changed and never will—that's a promise. He's still interested in eternal solutions for mankind's problems."

"But He cured cerebral palsy when He was on Earth."

"He might defeat a Roman or two on occasion—He suffers with our suffering, but when He died on the cross, there were more people who needed healing. He didn't delay shedding His blood to do more healing. Dying for us and providing us with an eternal solution to our problems was His mission."

I had to digest all that.

"Trust His love and His sacrifice today, Ana."

"Not yet, but I do appreciate all that you're saying. I'm getting it."

She nodded and pressed her lips together.

I picked up a magnolia leaf from the bench and let its softness touch my nose as I inhaled its delicate scent.

Jacqueline took a deep breath and closed her eyes. "Can I borrow your Bible?"

When I handed her the Bible, she opened it to 2 Corinthians, and for a moment I thought she would go to my chapter twelve. Instead, she went to chapter six.

"Good. It's underlined. I'd forgotten how neat these scavenger hunt New Testaments are."

"That's funny. That's what I call it too."

She shrugged with a grin before reading. "Behold, now is the accepted time; behold, now is the day of salvation." She kept the book on her lap, her finger marking the page. "Don't wait, Ana. This is the time. Once you die, it's too late, and none of us were promised tomorrow."

"Listen, I like you. There's something about you that I envy even. But my heart's not ready for all this."

Jacqueline shrugged with her eyes closed and a deep breath. "Okay." She got a pen out of her bag. "Do you mind if I write on the margin?" She pointed to the passage she'd read.

"Go ahead."

"I don't want to push you into believing. That's just not how it's done. But I want to make sure you can get a hold of me if you want to talk about it again one day soon." She wrote a local number in girly handwriting and moved the new tract from the front of the worn out New Testament to a page closer to the back. "Call me if you need anything, okay?"

I nodded, looking at what she'd marked. Hebrews.

"It's a good book," she said, getting up.

Jäger, who'd been napping, stood and stretched before looking at me. I lifted my finger, and he stayed.

"Keep reading, Ana, and let God speak to your heart—before it's too late. Don't fight this."

"You really think I would go to hell if I died today?"

"Jesus said He's the only way to heaven." She tightened her lips. "To believe there is a different way is to believe Jesus was wrong when He made that statement. And I think it's fair to say He knows the way to His hometown. Don't you think?"

"But I'm a good person. Certainly I wouldn't go to hell."

"The Bible says otherwise. If you don't want to believe that, you may as well find another book to carry around in your diaper bag."

That's heavy. That can't be right.

"You don't get to pick and choose which biblical truths suit you and which don't," she said. "He is who He is, remember? Not who you think He ought to be. The Bible says there's none good: all have sinned and come short of the glory of God. Mother Teresa, the Pope, me, my husband, yours, you—everybody. That's the truth."

Hell? Really?

"Can we pray together before I go?" She didn't wait for an answer. Her hands reached for mine, and I held them, noticing her fresh manicure.

"Dear gracious Father, please be with Ana and work on her heart as she searches for You. May she find You in time, so she can enjoy eternity with You, raise her baby for You, and be used for Your great works. We need more people for Your love to shine through, dear God. In the precious name of our Lord Jesus, we pray. Amen."

"Thank you for telling me all these things, and for praying with me."

"You're welcome." She squeezed my hands before letting go. "I'll see you later."

"See you later."

I got Gabriel in his car seat and helped Jäger to the passenger area. Was my watch right? Twelve forty? I'd better get home.

An older woman with short blonde hair and Dora scrubs parked two spaces from us and hopped out of her little car faster than I could get in the truck.

"Beautiful out here, isn't it?" she said, walking to the passenger door of her car.

"It is." I watched her remove her Crocs and reach in the car for a simple pair of tennis shoes. "It really is."

I was about to wish her a good day, but she spoke first.

"The young man who planted all the flowers is a patient here—early stages of Huntington's disease."

I leaned against the truck. *It can't be.*

"Ma'am, are you okay?"

My eyes riveted on the bench where I'd been talking to Jacqueline, the seat now dotted with magnolia petals.

Wearing one shoe, she hopped my way and helped me get in the truck. "Do you want me to call someone?"

I looked at the diaper bag. "No, thanks. I'll be okay." But would I?

Chapter 26

"Let's take Gabriel to Fantasy in Lights," Peter suggested when we finished decorating our house for Christmas. "We can take silly Santa pictures, drink hot cocoa, ride the trolley through the woods to see the lights…"

Did he realize we'd been to the Callaway Gardens light show twice since it'd opened for the season? I didn't think he did. Life with Huntington's was hard—going to a beautiful place over and over again wasn't, so I chose to ignore the repetition.

"Sure." My lips touched his cheek. "I'll have Mom and Dad meet us there. There's enough daylight left for us to enjoy some couple time at the park while they play with Gabriel. Good idea?"

"Great idea." He put his arms around me and rested his head on mine in a rare fidgeting-free moment.

In the seven months since my visit to Camp Dream, we'd learned to accept a reality we couldn't change. Early HD symptoms like fidgeting and restlessness had become a constant for him, enough that by Gabriel's first birthday in the fall, everyone could tell there was something going on with his health.

Watching his body struggle was upsetting and heartbreaking, but I got used to it. Watching his mind struggle was almost impossible for me to watch, and I would never, ever, get used to it. He'd been a brilliant landscape artist with works featured in some of the best professional magazines in the world, but those days were gone now.

The quality of his displays at Callaway had declined during the summer. The work itself was excellent but always resembled combinations he'd used before. There was nothing innovative about it—the creative spark was gone.

So in the fall, when he'd asked me if I would look down on him if he quit, I stopped short of doing a victory dance. He'd decided to step down while he was still ahead, and that's what I'd been praying for.

My relationship with God hadn't improved much during that time, but I'd learned to detect His hand in my life. My feelings toward Him often mirrored my feelings toward Mom—I knew the two of them were often right, God probably always—but my rebel heart struggled to acknowledge their wisdom sometimes.

I had to recognize, though, that it'd been God who'd put the desire to plant in my heart and that it'd been a brilliant move on His part. Planting wasn't like me and didn't seem to serve much of a purpose—until it did. When Peter quit the park, I'd just committed to landscaping twenty-three homes on my own. But all of a sudden, I wasn't planting on my own anymore—I had a partner.

We'd become a family business, going to work in my truck and bringing Gabriel and his playpen with us. We studied pond design and installation together, and soon we had water features in place in a dozen yards. In preparation for planting season, Peter taught me all he knew about gardening to keep pests away and to attract butterflies. He felt important, and I felt blessed. All things considered, we were having a lovely time, and regardless of Huntington's, both Peter and I still had pretty great lives.

Once we arrived at Callaway, Mom and Dad took Gabriel to the butterfly center while Peter and I went for a walk at the azalea bowl.

Some people didn't like azaleas because they flower beautifully for about a month but are otherwise uneventful-looking bushes. I liked them. They were hardy, much like I would have to be in the coming years. How hard would life get? And would there be flowering seasons for us? I wasn't sure.

I followed the reflection of the azalea bushes around the quiet lake, and I spotted another couple walking on the other side of the water. They were looking at us. Or maybe they were only looking at Peter, watching as he struggled to walk. They probably thought he was drunk. If only they knew.

"There it is." Peter spotted the sequoia from the main path.

I squeezed his hand. After only two years, our tree was already about twelve feet tall, almost twice Peter's height.

"By this time next year the roots won't reach down so much. They'll start branching out more. I read the lateral development of the roots is so strong that a very large sequoia can have an area of influence of four square acres."

I looked around trying to imagine the root systems beneath everything I saw, not sure how our sequoia would establish itself.

"Don't worry. Most of the root system is made up of tiny, threadlike feeders that spread out from the larger roots near the base."

"Oh." We walked through the bushes and got near our tree. Our hands touched the thickening bark before we sat on the ground by the trunk.

"Ana, do you really like planting?"

"I really do. Why?"

"This business is getting big, and it will only continue to grow. What are you going to do when I'm not able to work with you?"

"I don't want to think about it."

"You have to. I want you to."

"Peter, come on."

"Why aren't you participating in *The Nutcracker*?"

"Because I'm an ungrateful person. I can't enjoy what I have. All I do is mope over what I don't have. So I'm happy taking classes three times a week. That's all I'm going to do. No more parts. No more stage. No more setting myself up for failure."

"You had big dreams. Easy on yourself…"

I nodded, unable to speak. He always had such faith and confidence in me. Why couldn't I?

Peter put his arm around my shoulders. "We'll go full out next spring with the planting, but after that, you should dance more and plant less."

"No."

"Why?"

"Because it makes me feel like you are slipping away already when you talk like that. We're having fun with it. Let's just do it until we can't. Don't do this, Peter."

"You need to take care of yourself and think about what really makes you happy, Ana. You have a long journey ahead of you."

"Please stop talking like this. *We* have a long journey, and *we* will be just fine."

"Promise you will think about it. This is for me too—to have peace when I start feeling my body and my brain falling apart to the point I don't even understand what's going on around me. I'll need to know for sure that you and Gabriel are happy."

I nodded again.

"You'll marry again."

"No. You're not dying."

"I am."

"But not now. Please stop." *I can't live without you.*

He leaned his back against the tree and scanned the darkening skies above us.

We both watched the same red-tailed hawk in silence.

"I want to be that hawk." Peter looked less intense now. "Soaring on the thermals, hanging on updrafts. Not a care in the world."

"You wanna be a chicken hawk?"

"Yep. I wanna be a chicken hawk."

I stood up and reached for his hand. "Come on."

"Listen, I didn't mean to upset you, Ana, but it was important for me to say these things. I only have one more thing to ask, and I promise you—I promise you—I will never talk like this again."

"Here it comes. Shoot."

"Whenever I go, be it in five years or twenty, remember me strong."

"Too easy. You are strong."

"Bring Gabriel here and show him this tree. Watch it grow strong and think of me. Who knows? It could become the tallest tree in the world one day." He looked up at the growing crown. "I think I told you that its full name is Sequoia Sempervirens—it comes from Latin and means 'always alive'—evergreen. You'll find shade here always."

A lifetime welled up in his eyes—his lifetime—cut short, and I struggled to keep my lips steady as my eyes swam in tears too.

"I am not this disease, Ana. I don't want to ever be defined by HD. I am not HD. I am just Peter—a planter, a lover, a daddy. A strong man. I've made a good life for myself, and I've got all I ever wanted. Even if only for a moment."

I nodded and swallowed hard. I wanted to tell him we were going to get through it and that there would be a major scientific breakthrough in time to save his brain. But he already knew my feelings on this. I didn't have to say it. He knew it. He knew me.

"So you'll bring him here?"

"Of course."

Peace, instead of pain, shimmered in those blue eyes of his, but I wasn't quite there yet. We rocked in silence, dancing to the sound of whatever leaves were left, still blowing in the cold wind.

Could we still go to church together before he got too ill? I'd asked before but he'd said no. Maybe now? We'd never been to a mass, or whatever Baptists call what they do when they gather. "Why can't we go to church? What do you have against it?"

"You know how you feel about dancing? You should be happy, but you're not?"

"Yes."

"It's how I feel about God. In theory, I should be happy. I grew up in church. I know my Bible. I get it. But I don't feel it. Not anymore."

"So, you just don't believe anymore?"

"I believe. It's all real. God is real. Jesus is real. He is my Savior." Peter shook his head, and his thoughts seemed to drift somewhere else for a moment. "But religion doesn't work for me. I missed a turn somewhere, I guess. Too much hurt in my life."

"We should try just one time." Maybe I should tell him what Jacqueline had said about Jesus not defeating the Romans and being interested in eternal solutions instead, but he probably already knew that. His words echoed in my head: *I grew up in church. I know my Bible.*

"I'm not ready, Ana."

"But I need it, and I can't do this without you."

His chest rose and fell with a deep breath. "Tell you what, you think about planting less and dancing more, and I'll think about church."

"Oh, an ultimatum?"

"Call it what you will. I told you what's important to me, and you told me what's important to you. If we compromise a little, we can both get what we want." His eyebrows rose. "You also need to retire that little New Testament and get a real Bible—a complete King James Bible."

"I like my little Bible."

He shrugged, but I wasn't sure if he'd meant to or not. That's when I realized his body had been unusually relaxed by the sequoia. *Maybe this will be our special place to forget the disease.* I remembered the testimony I'd read when I was pregnant.

There is a beautiful garden there with a large pond and a fountain. We've always liked gardens... That's going to be our special time, a time to look away from the building, away from the disease, and into the life and love we can still share in these final years.

We still had many years. We had to.

"Let's go meet the others," Peter said. "It's getting dark."

We met up with my family and did what we'd planned to do. We took silly Santa pictures, drank hot cocoa, and rode the trolley through the woods to see the lights.

Gabriel looked at about two million of the eight million lights in the five-mile ride, but then the night and the rocking motion got the better of him. By the time we reached the Snowflake Valley display, he was asleep.

Mom turned back and handed Peter a blanket, and I used my free hand to help him spread it on our laps.

"If the light strings were all connected, they would stretch from here to Baltimore, Maryland," I heard the lady on the other side of Peter say.

"I'm sure glad they're not all connected," he said in my ear.

I put my finger on my lips and giggled.

Behind us, a cute little boy sang his way past the Swan Lake and Hummingbird Fountain exhibit. "Jingle bells, jingle bells, jingle all the way. Jingle bells, jingle bells, jingle all the way."

And as we traveled quietly from the last display to the parking lot, cloaked by the dark Georgia night, I wondered what a Christmas market in Germany really looked like. Claus had always said the one in Wiesbaden was beautiful and had promised we would hit a *Glühwein* stand every night of the holiday season to stay warm on the way home. I hadn't thought about him in a very long time. *Why now?*

But only God knows what if… And what a heartless thing to think. Shoo.

When the Jolly Trolley stopped, Mom put her arms around Gabriel, who was still asleep on my lap, and helped me down. Peter was having a hard time getting up from the seat and off the trolley, but Dad helped him.

I smiled at the memory of him leaping off the trolley and proposing on another cold night three years earlier, while keeping Gabriel warm in my arms.

So I would consider getting back on stage for him, and he would consider going to church for me. That seemed fair. It could be done. But I couldn't stop planting. My eyes filled up with hot tears. Images of us landscaping as a family filled my head. "I love you so much, Peter."

"I love you too." His hand rested on my shoulder as we walked to the truck.

Chapter 27

November 12, 2011

Novikova was finishing her last solo. *Don Quixote* was almost over. I checked my phone. Four fifteen. *Please, God.* My hands were shaking, the palms clammy. I exhaled.

And then I heard it. The doorbell. I pulled in a sharp breath.

No one ever came to our place unannounced. *No, God. No.* Maybe he's hurt. *Spare him.*

I opened the door and saw two police officers. The cold drizzle touched my face, and I heard the distant bark of our dog. But he was next to me. Had he barked? I saw one officer's mouth move, but I couldn't make out the words.

Memories of our wedding day and of our lives together flashed through my mind.

"I cannot lose him again," I whispered.

I woke up on the living room couch.

"Hi, ma'am," the older officer said. "I was trying to ask if we could come in and then you fainted. Are you okay?"

"I'm sorry." I saw the other officer now. "What happened?"

"Is Mr. Peter Engberg your husband?"

My head bobbed, my heart hurt. *No…*

"I'm so sorry, ma'am. He had an accident. He didn't—"

"Uh-uh." I stopped the officer before he could finish his sentence. If he didn't say the words, Peter could still walk through the doors.

But maybe he was just hurt and needed me. I had to get to him. "What happened?"

"The Silverado truck he was driving hit a large oak on State Route 18."

"Where is he?"

He shook his head. "He didn't make it, ma'am."

"Oh God." *Can this be true?* It was so hard to breathe. "Oh God. Oh God. What happened? Did he go to the hospital?" *Oh God.*

"He didn't suffer, ma'am. He died instantly."

Oh God. Help me...

"I'm so sorry."

Help me.

"Is there someone we can call?"

I nodded and was about to get up, but he stopped me.

"Let me help you. Do you need your phone?"

I nodded again, pointing to the counter. "And my purse," I said, my voice barely audible.

Looking through my New Testament, I found Second Corinthians 6:2. Next to it was Jacqueline's phone number, and I pointed to it.

The officer nodded and made the call while I turned to the end of the book.

Looking over the closing prayer, I realized I knew it—by heart.

"This is the time," I said when Jacqueline had arrived and was near enough to hear the strongest voice I could muster.

"What happened?" She reached for my hands.

"Can we pray first? I've been on a collision course with this moment for a while. I need to do it now. Please?"

"Of course." She nodded and closed her eyes. "Dear Lord—"

"No," I interrupted. Our eyes met. "Sorry. I mean, I'll pray. I want to get saved. I know what to do."

She smiled, squeezed both my hands, and bowed her head in silence.

I closed my eyes and started. "Dear Father, I know I am a sinner, lost and condemned for hell. But Christ Jesus the Lord died for my sins and rose again. And right now by faith, I receive Jesus Christ into my heart as my Savior, trusting in Him alone for the forgiveness of my sins and eternal life. Thank you for saving me; thank you for making me your child; thank you for giving me a home in heaven. Now help me live for you from this day forward. Amen."

"This is good." She put her arms around me. "Good decision."

"He said Jesus was his Savior. He said it. My husband. He..." I pressed my lips together. I wanted to count the books on the mantel, but I didn't. "My husband died today."

"I know, Ana... I am so sorry."

"I will see him again, right?"

"You will see him again. He is with the Lord now."

I nodded and took the tissue she was offering me. *He's with God... I'll see him again. My grace is sufficient, but how? Oh, God, help me.*

In the days following the crash, two questions bothered me above all others, and a nagging voice brought them up every time I felt something that resembled peace.

Did he do it on purpose? Dad was talking to Pine Mountain Police daily, hoping to get an answer, but it didn't look promising. I would, most likely, always have to live with that aching uncertainty—forever asking the second question that bothered me above all others: could I have done something different that rainy Thursday morning?

On Sunday, I went to Calvary Baptist Church. I'd declined offers for meals and childcare. But I wanted to get baptized and so, with a parent on each side, I heard Jacqueline's husband preach on the power of prayer before taking the plunge.

"Why are you trying to live life on your own strength, Christian?" He had asked the congregation. "Don't lose your place in Luke, but go with me to Philippians 2:4. Paul wrote in verse six, *'Be careful for nothing; but in everything, by prayer and supplication with thanksgiving let your requests be known unto God.'*"

Didn't He already know?

"He doesn't need to be told, but he will then know it from us. And when we do that and go to Him to ease our mind of a burden or to seek direction or help—with a thankful heart—look what happens in verse seven. *'And the peace of God, which passeth all understanding, shall keep your hearts and minds through Christ Jesus.'*"

Late that night, I knelt by Gabriel's bed.

Dear God, I'm a bit of a late bloomer. Always have been, I know. Thank you for not giving up on me. Help me find peace and direction. I can't do it by my own power. I don't know how I'm going to move ahead, but I now know that You know. And to me, that's good enough. Amen.

Monday morning, before the viewing, Jäger was prancing around the small box with the personal items the police found in and around the truck after the accident. I'd peeked inside the day before, but the sight of broken sunglasses and a broken Clint Black *Greatest Hits II* CD had been enough to keep me from going any further.

"You're a sniffer dog now?" I got the box from the living room floor and put it on the kitchen table. I still didn't want to go through it, but something compelled me to, and I heeded.

The smell of oil and gas and burned things was overwhelming, and after handling a few items, I noticed a dark residue on my fingertips. I dumped everything on the table and scrubbed my hands while eyeing a once-white shopping bag, the only thing that was unusual.

The contents—two books and a pair of delicate gardening gloves decorated with tree branches—were undamaged. I brought the gray and burgundy gloves to my nose and put the receipt aside. There was a hint of oil odor, but the smell of new leather was much stronger, its softness intact. I looked at the receipt. He'd bought it at the park on the day of the crash.

I knew what the books were and smiled. The first had a pink cover, soft and velvety, the name ANA ENGBERG engraved in gold on the lower right corner. The first page had a dedication. He'd used a pencil to fill in the blanks, and many erased attempts were still visible.

THE HOLY BIBLE. PRESENTED TO MY WIFE, ANA. FROM YOUR HUSBAND, PETER. ON CHRISTMAS OF TWO THOUSAND AND ELEVEN, AS WE BEGIN A NEW WALK.

Printed at the bottom of the page was 1 Peter 2:2.

AS NEWBORN BABES, DESIRE THE SINCERE MILK OF THE WORD, THAT YE MAY GROW THEREBY.

The other book was another Bible, with a simple black cover and the name "Peter Engberg" on the lower right corner, also in gold. The dedication page was blank.

I reached for a pen and wrote a note to our son.

PRESENTED TO GABRIEL ENGBERG. FROM YOUR PARENTS, PETER AND ANA ENGBERG. ON CHRISTMAS OF TWO THOUSAND AND ELEVEN, AS WE BEGIN A NEW WALK.

"It was an accident," I whispered, clutching my Bible. "It was an accident." I closed my eyes and took a deep, cleansing breath. *Thank you, God.*

Sitting by the large living room window, I rested my eyes on the calm lake, and when my heart was ready, I opened my new Bible to Paul's letter to the

Philippians and read to prepare for the viewing.

The next day, Peter was laid to rest in a garden cemetery on the outskirts of town. There, elegant landscaping complemented the gentle Georgia hills and winter flower beds held the promise of spring. The clear waters of a rocky creek moved idly past an arched stone bridge, visited dozens of gravesites, and then arrived at a pond where wood ducks were wintering and forming pairs. Could they have come from Stow Lake? Peter had said it wasn't likely, but I still thought it was possible.

Back-road birds. Because not all birds stick to a pattern—doesn't make them lesser birds.

One month later I was at the azalea bowl, walking to the sequoia.

My parents had Gabriel, and we were going to meet at night to visit the Christmas display. *National Geographic* had just named the top ten places in the world to see holiday lights. Alongside famous destinations in Denmark, Austria, Belgium, and other countries was Callaway Gardens' Fantasy in Lights in Pine Mountain, Georgia. The park was busier than ever, and we'd purchased our tickets online, a week in advance, to guarantee a spot on the Jolly Trolley.

I saw our sequoia's green crown as soon as I got to the main trail around the lake. It had grown eight feet that year, a faster growth rate than the first two years, and I'd been wondering if that had something to do with the roots spreading out.

Peter would know...

My hand left the warmth of my quilted down coat, and I reached through the cold, gray air for where his hand should have been.

I took the now-manicured path to the base of the tree and saw the wrought iron bench the park had installed along with a plaque. *In loving memory of Peter Engberg—a planter, a lover, a daddy.*

I touched the cold metal plate and traced his name.

Remember me strong...

The cold wind was blowing harder than usual at the azalea bowl. A red-tailed hawk screamed a hoarse "kee-eeeee-arr." Scanning the late-afternoon silver clouds, I found it soaring high above Falls Creek Lake.

I missed him so much. And I would always miss him. So much...

Dance more and plant less, he'd said. I only got involved in this year's Nutcracker *because of him. I'll dance it for him. And for the girls. But then what? I want to plant this spring. I want to plant up a storm. Plant less?*

I shook my head and walked back to the main trail. *Too soon to think. One day at a time. That's how we'll do this.*

Tomorrow, I think. Today, I remember.

I remembered the first day I'd met Peter. The chapel, the organist playing Vivaldi's "The Four Seasons," and the little girl with the white sandals that showed her cute little toes, her dress flowing as she ran. I remembered the warmth and the sweet scents of that beautiful spring day. Turning the corner, my eyes looked for the bridge where we'd first seen each other.

There it was, but in my mind, it wasn't winter anymore.

It was spring and the peak of azalea season—Callaway Gardens in its spring splendor. The smells of the earth and of the woods invaded my nose without effort, and I didn't have to remember the warmth of brighter seasons. I *was* warm, and thousands of azaleas commanded my attention with their bright whites and deep reds, hot pinks and brilliant purples. And Peter was there, on the bridge.

He turned to me with his usual boyish grin. *Baby...*

He wore my favorite black button-up shirt, and he had his old Gibson guitar by his side.

I reached out for the metal rail to steady myself once more. He was handsome and strong, and he was waiting for me. I wanted to walk to him, but he shook his head and donned his guitar.

The sound was clean, the instrument perfectly tuned. He performed "Honey Bee" with boot heels marking the strong beats, strumming and singing with abandon—singing about two people who were absolutely different, but who completed each other in the most simple and wonderful ways.

"Beautiful," I said when he finished. "You're beautiful."

He grinned and looked down, his cheeks flushed.

"I will see you on the other side." I kissed my fingertips and lifted them in his direction in one last "see you soon."

Chapter 28

Isat on my front porch after the Easter service at Calvary Baptist Church and watched Gabriel play on his new jungle gym. From four hanging baskets, small petals of white trailing geraniums fell to the ground in a delicate drizzle. My spiral wind chime, a Christmas gift from Mom, played the opening notes of "Sweet Hour of Prayer" to the slow rhythm of the rose-perfumed air that always graced the ranch on warm days.

It was nice to slow down. I had been planting so much for so many people that even my new gloves looked tired. But I had finished every job, and I told everyone that I wouldn't be landscaping anymore.

Jacqueline was teaching me about surrendering old dreams and finding God's purpose for my life. Dance was part of that purpose, or He wouldn't have given me the gift, but I also knew that the fruit of my old approach to dancing had come short of His glory.

I wasn't dancing to feel justified anymore—I had all the justification I needed from Christ, and the freedom that came from not craving an audience's approval was absolutely exhilarating. A freeing, huge step forward.

I was dancing to discover the purpose and the joy that I knew were there, pleading to be found—at last—after all those years. So I said yes to projects and ideas I wanted to reject and considered carefully the value of the ones I ached to embrace. I made sure that every effort was fresh and took me someplace new.

The first batch of changes had come immediately after the Christmas break. I'd started taking a ballet class every morning, and on Tuesday and Thursday evenings, I taught and rehearsed the LaGrange Youth Ballet, part of the school.

Mrs. B. had invited me to stage *Paquita* for the company and to dance the lead role, and I was seriously considering it.

I'd also been teaching Jacqueline's little girl, and her joy inspired me to develop a ballet program for Camp Dream. I would volunteer there twice a week in the summer.

"Ma! Car!" I heard a car in the distance as Gabriel ran to the porch. "Car!" He looked at me and pointed to the woods that hid the driveway.

"Yes, baby, a car." I held his little hand and listened to the muted hum of a familiar engine.

He jumped down a step when he saw the Thunderbird. "Car!"

Claus parked next to the truck and removed the square Ray-Ban sunglasses that suited his ballet superstar status. He had the top down and was listening to Johann Sebastian Bach's "Air."

The corners of his eyes crinkled as his lips stretched, and he looked beautiful with a shorter haircut, navy blue shirt, and my favorite white cashmere sweater over his shoulders.

Gabriel hid behind me.

The corners of his mouth tilted up as he walked to me with a dozen sunflowers in a beautiful round bouquet. "Hi," he said, coming up the steps.

"Hi." I took the bouquet and noticed my old neck scarf was tied to the handle. As I freed the aquamarine chiffon, Gabriel came halfway out of hiding to look at the flowers.

Claus got down to his level. "You must be Gabriel. I've got something for you." He reached into his shirt pocket and pulled out a little Ostheimer knight.

Gabriel smiled and took his new toy to the jungle gym.

"He looks just like Peter."

"Doesn't he?" I put the scarf around my neck. "He's a good boy."

"I got him a whole castle set." He pointed to the knight that was now going down the small green slide. "It's at your mom's. I'm staying there."

"You are?"

He nodded. "I have that picture of you and Barysh, too, and a few more things I thought you would be missing."

"Is that why you came? To bring back my stuff?"

He shook his head and pulled a piece of paper out of his pocket.

I recognized the yellow paper from the old legal pad Peter used to keep on the kitchen table. Unfolding the note, I traced the words with my fingertips. The first part was an old note. He'd used a pen and the handwriting was intact. He later added a paragraph below his name, in pencil. He'd had to erase and rewrite most words. Remembering his mighty hands, I felt a lump rise in my throat.

CLAUS,

I'M NOT SURE IF I WILL EVER MAIL THIS LETTER. I CERTAINLY HAVE NO DESIRE TO WRITE IT. BUT I HAVE TO WRITE IT WHILE I CAN.

I HAVE HUNTINGTON'S DISEASE. YOU CAN LOOK UP THE DETAILS IF YOU WISH, BUT THE BOTTOM LINE IS, I AM GOING TO DIE A SLOW DEATH, AND THIS IS GOING TO BE HARD ON ANA.

SHE IS ABOUT TO GIVE BIRTH TO OUR BABY BOY. GABRIEL DIDN'T INHERIT THE DISEASE. WE HAD HIM CHECKED EARLY IN THE PREGNANCY.

WHEN I DIE, I WANT YOU TO TAKE CARE OF THEM. I WANT HER TO HAVE A FUTURE, AND I WANT GABRIEL TO HAVE A FATHER PRESENT IN HIS LIFE. I KNOW YOU ARE THEIR BEST CHANCE.

ONCE YOU GET THIS LETTER, KEEP IN TOUCH WITH ANA'S MOM TO KNOW HOW I'M DOING.

PETER

P.S. SHE LIKES WAGNER'S "BRIDAL CHORUS."

I AM GOING TO FIND MY FAITH AND PRAY FOR A CURE, BUT IF A CURE AND A DECENT LIFE ARE OUTSIDE GOD'S WILL, I WILL PRAY THAT YOU ARE ABLE TO CONTINUE WHAT I'VE STARTED.

"I'm so sorry, Ana."

I felt his arm around my shoulders as hot tears burned my eyes. Gabriel came our way, and Claus picked him up, spinning him around to what sounded like German nursery rhymes. I walked to the edge of the porch to the music of Gabriel's giggles.

Peter knew my tendency to be stingy with myself. I was scared to dream again, to an extent. I wasn't sure his plans for me would work. I had stopped planting. I was dancing more. But I wished he was still with us. I missed him. What did Peter mean by "continue what I started"? The family?

"Guess when I got his letter?" Claus approached me with slow steps.

Over his shoulder, I saw Gabriel sliding with the knight again. "When?" My voice came out hoarse.

"When I started going to that American church in Wiesbaden."

"Calvary Baptist Church?"

He nodded.

"When was that?"

"About a year and a half ago."

That last visit to Fantasy in Lights. "How did you end up at that church?"

"The guy who fixed your car invited me."

"Must have been a killer pitch."

He shook his head. "It was pretty awkward, actually." He looked down. "There'd been enough coincidences, though. I had to go check it out."

"Was that old tract still on your corkboard, where I'd put it?"

"Yeah." He chuckled. "It was."

"That's funny."

"Going there made me feel close to you, somehow, so I became a member and attended regularly. It's been good."

"Calvary's been good for me too."

He looked puzzled.

"Remember the lady from the Catholic church in Prague?"

"The one who gave you the little green Bible?"

"Her son is my pastor here."

"Really?"

My head bobbed. "He's good. His wife's become a dear friend. She's helping me with my walk."

"That's an amazing story. You had to leave Georgia, move to Germany, and travel to Prague to learn about a church back in Georgia where you'd one day grow. Hmm." His royal blue eyes gleamed.

Oh, I'd missed those eyes.

He reached for the letter, folded it, and put it back in his pocket. "I realize now that if you try to make things happen your own way, somewhere down the line, there will be trouble." He caressed my hands. "I'm sorry, Ana. I really am."

"I know."

"I finally let go of my dreams of a life with you. It was hard, but I did it. And then God brought me here, and I have a chance to be with you—on His terms." Claus kissed my fingertips. "Now I know we can be happy."

"It's hard to let go…"

"I hope I can help."

"You already have."

I knew I was blushing, but I didn't care. *Is he blushing too?*

He looked away with a smile. "I see you're growing your own sunflowers now." He'd noticed the small patch just beyond the porch.

"Trying." I shrugged, looking at the twelve plants that were growing strong for early spring. "Your seeds. Remember?"

He cradled my hand and closed his eyes. We embraced and rocked to the slow sounds of the wind chime. I put my cheek on his shoulder and felt the softness of the white cashmere.

Dear Heavenly Father, thank you for putting Claus back in my arms. Now here it comes. This morning I didn't feel ready, but now I am. I'm sorry for being angry and for thinking your gift was insufficient. Obviously, being a prima ballerina or dancing at the Met is not your will for my life. I'd already let go with my mind, and now I'm letting go with my heart. I'm letting go of my old dreams and making room for You to plant Yours. Guide my steps, Father. In Jesus' precious name I pray. Amen.

A wind gust made the wind chime play forte.

"Sweet Hour of Prayer?" Claus whispered.

I nodded. *I love you, Lord.*

Chapter 29

Claus and I were celebrating our second wedding anniversary at home while Gabriel and Emma, our baby girl, spent the weekend with my parents. We would pick them up Sunday before church.

We finished our Saturday rehearsals early and spent the rest of that first day of summer on the lake. Claus cooked a German barbecue on a Mosel-made swinging grill I'd found online, and I cooked my favorite white asparagus with melted butter, roasted potatoes, and a side of fragrant homegrown strawberries.

I was cleaning the kitchen and listening to the iPod shuffle Claus had loaded with ninety-nine beautiful songs. He'd attached the iPod, along with a note, to a gorgeous bouquet of red roses and white ballerina freesias.

> Loaded. Because people like you should never have to stop to do mundane things like putting songs on an iPod. You keep on moving, darling girl, and I will always keep on watching you. Happy anniversary.

He'd wanted to take me to New York to celebrate. The American Ballet Theatre was dancing *Le Corsaire* at the Met, and one of the ABT soloists was a friend, so he knew he could get me on stage after the performance.

But I'd been busy with *Les Sylphides* rehearsals in LaGrange, and some quiet time at home was a much better treat. I'd become a studio owner soon after dancing *Paquita* with Claus, when Mrs. B. died, leaving the school and the company to me.

Claus was busy too. He was dancing *Les Sylphides* with me in two weeks, and he was dancing *Swan Lake* in Atlanta. He was also choreographing there, and some of his work was being featured in the repertoire of major companies in the U.S. and in Europe.

In October we would dance something new he was choreographing for us, but we wouldn't start rehearsing it until after our summer program at Camp Dream. I had a feeling the new ballet would have to wait even longer, though. I was eleven days late.

"There, the kitchen is clean," I whispered, scanning the area. I leaned against the counter for one more breath of the sweet citrus scent of the delicate freesias and the warm roses.

Gabriel's castle set was on the kitchen table, but he'd left it neat. He loved to put on elaborate plays for Emma, who always watched from the comfort of her highchair while eating quartered grapes of every color and size. He'd left the prince and the princess side by side on the steps of the tower. I moved the toy knight and his horse from the cannon position to the castle gate, put my iPod down, and turned off the kitchen lights.

The first notes of Prokofiev's balcony scene drifted toward me from the living room stereo system.

I'd reread *Romeo and Juliet* while staging it for the company. The star-crossed lovers did kiss during the masquerade ball, but I was surprised to learn there was no kiss in Shakespeare's balcony scene. That moment was simply a well-liked choice in both theater and ballet—one people had come to expect.

How had I missed that the first time I'd read it? *A choice.* Six years ago I'd made a bad one on Juliet's balcony. A wave of guilt hurt my heart—the old boa constrictor squeezed me tight. *Their sins and their iniquities will I remember no more.* My lungs filled up to capacity against the sensation.

Claus saw me walk into the living room and reached for my hand. "Dance with me, Ana."

My lips stretched, and my heart beat loud and strong. I reached back, and his arms enveloped me in his tender embrace. We slow danced in the peace of the darkened house, lit only by the full moon above the lake and the sequoias.

A scent of violet surprised me—it was the perfume he'd used in Prague, and I was immediately transported to the *Natal.* His lips touched mine, and mine parted against them. Prokofiev's lyrical music filled the night. He'd once said, "There are still so many beautiful things to be said in C major." How so very true.

"*Ich liebe dich,*" Claus whispered in my ear.

"*Ich dich auch.*" I felt his heartbeat against mine and closed my eyes. *Happy anniversary.*

Epilogue

NEW YORK GAVE THE RHINE-MAIN BALLET AN ENTHUSIASTIC WELCOME AS THE COMPANY CELEBRATED THE ART OF GERMAN DANCER CLAUS VOGEL GERT IN TWELVE WORKS, SIX CLASSICS THAT MADE HIM FAMOUS AND SIX PIECES THAT HE CHOREOGRAPHED.

MR. GERT, WHO IS A PRINCIPAL IN THE ATLANTA BALLET, WAS CONSISTENT AT ALL TIMES, AND HIS STAMINA IS IMPRESSIVE FOR A DANCER WHO'S BEEN A PROFESSIONAL FOR TWENTY YEARS. HIS *THEME AND VARIATIONS* WAS IMPECCABLE, AND IN THE PAS DE DEUX FOR LES CORSAIRE, HE FINISHED PIROUETTES IN BALANCE, JUMPED HIGH, AND LANDED EFFORTLESSLY.

AS A CHOREOGRAPHER, HE IS KNOWN FOR FOCUSING ON ARTISTIC AND LYRICAL QUALITIES, WITH MANY OF HIS WORKS PROMINENTLY FEATURED IN THE REPERTOIRE OF MAJOR BALLET COMPANIES IN THE WORLD.

THE MUCH-ANTICIPATED PREMIERE OF *PRAHA*, A CELEBRATION OF LOVE SET TO THE LARGO MOVEMENT OF DVOŘÁK'S "NEW WORLD SYMPHONY," WAS FLAWLESS, FLUID, AND WELL WORTH THE EIGHT-YEAR WAIT. THE PIECE WAS THE FIRST MR. GERT EVER CREATED, AND WATCHING HIM DANCE IT WITH HIS WIFE, ANA, THE BALLERINA HE CALLS "HIS CONSTANT SOURCE OF INSPIRATION," WAS A SPECIAL DELIGHT.

THEY ALSO DANCED A FANTASTIC *ROMEO AND JULIET* BALCONY SCENE PAS DE DEUX THAT LEFT ME WANTING TO SEE THEM IN THE FULL-LENGTH BALLET. THE JOY THEY SHARE IS PALPABLE AND CHARMING, AND THE AUDIENCE REACTED WITH SHOUTS OF "BRAVO" NORMALLY RESERVED FOR MORE ACROBATIC PERFORMANCES.

"SWEET HOUR OF PRAYER," SET TO A GORGEOUS INSTRUMENTAL VERSION OF THE TRADITIONAL HYMN, CLOSED THE EVENING. THE PIECE REMINDED ME OF SUNDAY MORNING CHURCH WITH MY PARENTS IN RURAL WEST VIRGINIA—A TIME WHEN THE SOUL FELT MORE COMPLETE AND AT HOME. THAT WAS MY MOTHER'S FAVORITE HYMN, AND I COULD ALMOST HEAR HER SINGING. WHEN MR. GERT PUT HIS ARM AROUND HIS WIFE, AND THE TWO BOWED DOWN, I PRAYED TOO.

After New York, they perform this program with the Rhine-Main Ballet at Le Palais Garnier in Paris, the London Coliseum, and the Czech National Theatre in Prague. They will finish the European tour with two performances in Wiesbaden before returning home to Georgia, where the couple teaches children with disabilities and where Mrs. Gert owns a studio, complete with a youth ballet company.

—THE END—

Author Note

I didn't grow up in a Christian home, but for most of my life I believed there had to be some kind of god out there and that being a good person was important. But in 2012, tired and lonely, I decided the notion of a loving god was absurd. There was no loving god, if there was a god at all.

Self-gratification became the chief end of my existence, and I looked behind every door for happiness and satisfaction. I didn't find anything worth keeping though, and at the end of every new pursuit, I was still tired and lonely—and this time surrounded by a darkness and a hopelessness that was brand new and incredibly scary.

Then Jesus passed by, and where I saw the end, He saw the beginning. He fought for me, lifted me out of what had quickly become a murky and joyless existence, and brought me into His perfect light. I was born again in January of 2013, during the writing of this novel. For more on that, check out "A Season to Dance: the Book that Wrote Me."

I share that with you here to tell you that if you don't know Jesus as your personal Savior, He's fighting for you right now—or you wouldn't be reading this book. He's fighting for you just like He fought for me and for Ana. He's passing by. "Behold, now is the accepted time; behold, now is the day of salvation," (2 Corinthians 6:2).

Jesus was in such agony as the day of His crucifixion approached that He sweat blood. He knew His death would be brutal and dreaded it, but He endured it anyway. He suffered because He didn't want you to. That's His gift to you. Will you take it?

If you believe that Jesus died for your sins and that God raised Him from the dead—victor over sin and death, say so in prayer like Ana did and like millions of people around the world have been doing for almost 2,000 years now. Ask him into your life and into your heart. "For whosoever shall call upon the name of the Lord shall be saved," (Romans 10:13).

"Dear Father, I know I am a sinner, lost and condemned for hell. But Christ Jesus the Lord died for my sins and rose again. And right now by faith, I receive Jesus Christ into my heart as my Savior, trusting in Him alone for the forgiveness of my sins and eternal life. Thank you for saving me; thank you for making me your child; thank you for giving me a home in heaven. Now help me live for you from this day forward. Amen."

I've been praying for you, the readers of this novel, for years and will continue to do so.

If you've been blessed by this book, please consider writing a review on Amazon and/or Goodreads to help other people find it. The reviews I write are often one sentence long—two on occasion. The length doesn't matter, the number of opinions does.

Thank you so much for spending time with my words. I would love to hear from you!

Web - www.patriciabeal.com
Facebook - www.facebook.com/patricia.beal.author
Twitter - www.twitter.com/bealpat
Pinterest - www.pinterest.com/patriciasbeal
Goodreads - www.goodreads.com/bealpat

Reading Group Guide

Please enjoy this reading guide as if you are sitting down with Patricia Beal. She has specifically crafted this discussion guide in such a way as to fully share her heart and delve deeply into the many layers of this story with you, treasured reader.

1. Early in the story, a young man named Josh rescues Ana from the top of the theater's marquee and places her safely on the ground. That's the story's first salvation. The Hebrew meaning of *Joshua* is "Jehovah is my salvation." Joshua is also the original Hebrew form of the Greek name Jesus.

   What were the other small rescues before Ana's conversion? How was God's hand visible in the lives of Peter, Claus, Ana, Lorie, and others early in the story?

2. Ana said that Peter was her rock, that as a young woman with Claus she'd felt like "the worthiest person on the planet because of his love." She also said dancing at the Met was an attainable goal—her "holy grail." She tries to fill the God-shaped hole of her heart with Peter and Claus, with ballet and the Met, but ultimately realizes that a relationship with God is the only way to live a fulfilling life. If she had been a better dancer or if there'd been less ups and downs in her romantic life, could she have found enough happiness to not notice God's pursuit of her?

   Was there a time in your life in which you tried to fill the God-shaped hole of the heart with misguided romantic and professional pursuits?

3. Two men with very different personalities are significant to Ana's journey. Ana said that with Claus she felt like she had to always be doing something to feel good about herself and that with Peter she was more relaxed and happy to "just be."

   Who did you like best—Peter or Claus? Why?

4. Every person Ana meets on her journey to Jesus has a first name that starts with "J"—Jill, Josh, Ms. Jiménez, John, Jakob, Jack, Judah, Dr. Joel, Jackie, Frau Jutta Jöllenbeck, Jovana, Jacqueline—and Ana was Juliet.

   That happened to me when I was journeying to Jesus. It's as if He were jumping up and down, waving, and saying, "Me! I'm still the answer."

   Has something like that ever happened to you?

5. Luci's name is a different story. It's short for Lucifer, because he used her to put destructive ideas in Ana's head—ideas that resulted in Ana and Claus sleeping together before they were married. Ana went from being content with being in separate rooms, to taking the initiative to sleep together when in Prague—a decision that she regretted in the morning on the bridge.

   What was going through her mind on that bridge? What troubles was she able to recognize? What things did you come to realize first that Ana didn't yet understand?

6. After the bridge scene we have the rainy day at the Prague church. Ana arrives by cab under dark skies, unsure of everything and somewhat fearful. She leaves with a map (a Bible!) and a timid sun trying to shine through the thinning clouds, and she begins to walk in the direction of the river.

   How is this a turning point for Ana in the story?

7. What is the role of purity—or lack thereof—in the novel? Early on when Ana and Claus first talk, she asks him if things would have been different had they not slept together in their youth. What do you think? Would he have ended up in Germany with Hanna either way as he tells her?

8. Ana's relationship with Peter provides pivotal changes in *A Season to Dance*. Their relationship, already challenged by Ana's relationship with Claus, is challenged once again by his diagnosis with Huntington's disease.

   Where does Peter fit into God's plan? Was Peter and Ana's relationship a blessing in the end even though there was pain at first? How was he blessed in life? How about his death? Are you as convinced as Ana that his death was accidental?

9. How about Claus and his journey? He makes big mistakes, sets Ana up, and lies about it. Does he learn important lessons and mature? How so?

10. Ana is incredibly close with her dog, Barysh, much as many of us are with our pets. I wrote Barysh with a bleeding heart, as I was in the process of losing my very first dog in the same manner—a female boxer named Kyllian. She too had been left behind when her first family went to Germany, so when my husband and I went to Germany, we took her.

    In real life, after a one-year struggle in which she lost thirty pounds of muscle, I had to ask the vet to put her down four months before my husband came back from a deployment. No amount of wishing for a natural death made it happen. In my novel, I gave Barysh the death I wish Kyllian had had. For Barysh death came "gentle and comforting, like a warm moonlit night bringing quiet peace."

    How do you feel about Barysh's journey, his trip to Germany, and burial by the Rhine? Did Barysh enrich Ana's journey and the novel? How so?

11. Ana has a loving relationship with her parents, but situations often become contentious with her mother. Early in the story she says she hates when her mom is right and there are some tense conversations between the two.

    Have you ever experienced something similar? When Ana discovers Claus had indeed lied, she thinks her mom will say "I told you so," but she doesn't. Do you think she wanted to say it but chose not to? Did that conversation change their relationship? How so?

12. Ana didn't have many close friends for most of the story, and the two she had, Lorie in her youth and Luci in Germany, ended up having a negative impact on her life. How do you feel about Ana's friendships? How about your own? Have you ever had a friend lead you into trouble or flat out betray you?

13. What did you think about Lorie's journey? She often speaks truth amid irrational statements and actions, and in the end she seems to make peace with her mistakes—with her boyfriend and with God. Why was she so mad at God? What do you think happened to her?

14. What character did you identify with the most? How did you like the preacher's wife, Jacqueline? How about her mother-in-law, Jackie?

Did you feel that the Camp Dream scene was full of light because of Jacqueline's passion and faith? If not, how would you describe it? Should we be more like her? Are we light to the world?

15. Did you enjoy spending time in Ana's ballet world? What about the ballet world surprised you the most? How about her desire to be better than she was as a dancer and her desire to dance at the Met? Did you think she was going to make it? Why or why not? How did you feel about how and when it happened?

16. Symbols are significant in *A Season to Dance*. Ana's light-blue cherry-printed scarf symbolizes her relationship with Claus. Claus has it every time he doesn't have her, so should he have been concerned when she leaves it draped around Barysh's photo in Germany during the trip to Georgia?

17. Ana's sunflower seeds are a symbol of growth. They'd matured but it was "too early to harvest" when they fly to the US, but in the end the seeds had been planted, and the sunflowers are growing well. How else did flowers and planting reflect the action in the story?

18. Ana's whole story is hidden in a seemingly meaningless paragraph:

A car alarm went off. A woman helped a man cross the street. A little girl ran ahead of her father. "Don't you let go of my hand," he said, crouching down to her level when he caught up with her—stubborn little fingers still squirming under his massive hand. The alarm stopped. The little girl let her father hold her hand.

The idea behind the above paragraph is to show Ana's ending journey in *A Season to Dance*—from returning to a relationship with Peter, to his death, to her struggle and eventual relationship with God.

When Ana looks back at her life and her struggles, will she see that every erratic step had a purpose and brought her closer to where she needed to be? Or will she wish she'd done things differently?

19. The story opens with children, but Ana doesn't want to teach. She is solely focused on her dreams of dancing professionally and on Peter. The story ends with children—she teaches children with disabilities with Claus and owns a studio "complete with a youth ballet company." What changed, and what was redeemed?

A Season to Dance: the Book that Wrote Me

When I wrote the first line of my first novel in January of 2011, I wanted to get published because I was desperate to feel important.

I finished writing *A Season to Dance* that fall and hired coach Gloria Kempton via Writer's Digest to look at the whole thing and tell me if it was any good. She saw potential in the story of a small-town professional ballerina with big dreams, but explained I needed a clearer quest, more telling details, better scene structure, and better balance between sequels and dramatic scenes. I joined Gloria's critique group and spent a year rewriting.

During that year, my husband got orders to move the family from Fort Benning, Georgia, to Germany, and he deployed for the sixth time soon after we settled on a lovely mountaintop in Idar-Oberstein.

When I finished rewriting, Gloria said the novel looked good and had everything a novel was supposed to have. But… "Something's still missing. I don't know what it is. We've covered it all."

So of course I did what any writer desperate for validation would do. I told my coach that surely nothing was missing and that it was time to query. I hired a service to blast queries everywhere for me. I know… Shame on me… But God used that.

God's Plan—Phase One

One query ended up with Mrs. Joyce Hart, of Hartline Literary. The novel wasn't Christian—I wasn't a Christian. She shouldn't have received my query. But she did. She sent me a note saying she liked the storyline but that in Christian novels the protagonist couldn't live with her love interest without being married. She was very kind and said that if she was missing the point and if the novel was indeed Christian, that I should resubmit explaining the living together piece.

When I read it, I laughed and rolled my eyes. I started typing a condescending reply. Something about Christian fairy-tale brains and me living in the real world, but I decided not to send it.

Days passed. A week passed. A month passed. And all I did was collect rejections. I became bitter. Bitterly sad at first. Then bitterly discouraged. And then bitterly ugly. I'd never been ugly before. Not like that.

See, up to that point, I'd believed that there was some kind of "god" and that somewhere, somehow, being good was right and that it paid off. But with the disappointments of the publishing journey those beliefs became a joke to me. I stood in the middle of my empty German kitchen—husband deployed, kids at school, my first dog had just died. And I looked at that inbox full of rejections and stated to whomever or whatever was out there: "God is dead."

Mercy. Surely I said that to the "god" of my imagination, and not to the real God—God as He reveals Himself in the Bible. But I know that He was in that kitchen with me. And phase two of His plan was about to start.

Luke 22:31–32: "And the Lord said, Simon, Simon, behold, Satan hath desired to have you, that he may sift you as wheat: But I have prayed for thee, that thy faith fail not: and when thou art converted, strengthen thy brethren."

God's Plan—Phase Two

As I lost all restraint and became the worst version of myself, God removed me from my green German mountaintop.

After less than eighteen months in Germany, we were sent back to America, to the Chihuahuan Desert in West Texas. To a place called Fort Bliss—a place from which you can see a Mexican mountain with the words: "Cd. Juárez. La Biblia es la verdad. Leela." That translates to "City of Juárez. The Bible is the truth. Read it." Gotta love it. God is good.

During the first six months back in America, I went to two secular writers' conferences and met more rejection. My lack of restraint and my selfishness didn't really make me happy. I wanted to go to therapy. I wanted a job. I still dreamed of that book deal that had to be just around the corner. I wanted, I wanted…

But nothing happened, and it didn't matter how hard I tried to get help, get happy, and find any kind of relief for the pain I felt. Nothing. Happened. I'd never seen so many closed doors—slammed-shut doors—ever in my life. Even the shrink kept double booking, closing early, and somehow canceling on me. It was ridiculous.

The One Open Door

When God planted our family in the desert, He planted us two blocks from a friend from the Fort Benning years. A friend whose claim to fame was church shopping whenever the Army moved her family. I asked her to take me to church on the first Wednesday of January of 2013.

I fell in His arms. Surrendered, defeated, and dependent. Or what God likes to call—ready. I was born again two weeks later and was baptized on Super Bowl Sunday that February.

Gloria's "Something Missing"

I had tickets to go to New York for the Writer's Digest conference that spring, but sometime in March, it dawned on me: "You silly goose of a girl. You wrote a salvation story without the salvation piece." My first coach, Gloria Kempton, had been right all along. There was something missing!

A Season to Dance isn't just the story of a small-town professional ballerina who dreams of dancing at the Met in New York and the two men who love her. It's also the story of a girl desperately trying to fill the God-shaped hole in her heart with often misguided career and romantic pursuits.

I deleted Mrs. Hart's email that week. Yes, it was still in my inbox. Job well done, Mrs. Hart.

Now, I had work to do. I spent 2013 and the first half of 2014 rewriting the novel. Five ladies from my Sunday school read chapter after chapter as I produced them and cheered me on through that gruesome process. I couldn't have done it without their support. God is good.

Jeff Gerke edited my novel in the summer of 2014 and had me read Robert McGee's *The Search for Significance: Seeing Your True Worth Through God's Eyes*. God is good.

I went to my first Christian writers conference, the ACFW 2014 in St. Louis. Two weeks later, Les Stobbe offered to represent me. God is good.

While in St. Louis for the conference, I also met Marisa Deshaies, who in early 2016 became the managing editor of Bling! Romance and decided to publish *A Season to Dance*. God is good.

My family got saved too. My husband in July of 2013. Our son in December of 2013. My mom in the fall of 2014. And our little girl just this past summer, the summer of 2015. God is amazingly good.

("*A Season to Dance*: The Book That Wrote Me" first appeared in the International Christian Fiction Writers Blog.)

About the Author

Patricia Beal is from Brazil and immigrated to America in 1992. She fell in love with the English language while washing dishes at McDonald's, and she learned enough to pass the Test of English as a Foreign Language (TOEFL). She put herself through college working at a BP gas station, and she graduated magna cum laude from the University of Cincinnati in 1998 with a B.A. in English Literature. She was the news editor of the university newspaper for two years.

After an internship at the Pentagon, she worked as a public affairs officer for the U.S. Army for seven years. She was a spokesperson for five general officers, providing statements for television, radio, and print.

Patricia was in Guantanamo Bay, Cuba, when the first Operation Enduring Freedom detainees arrived, and the stories she filed during the early days of the detention operation there gained national attention. Writing from Iraq in the first year of Operation Iraqi Freedom, she focused on feature stories for Army newspapers, and a feature on a day in the life of "Bad Luck Squad" won her a Keith L. Ware award in print journalism.

She fell in love with a handsome airborne infantryman during a stint at Fort Bragg, married him, and quit her special operations speechwriting job to have his babies.

Soon came the desire to have book babies too. Gloria Kempton and Writer's Digest author Jeff Gerke have been great coaches and mentors. Patricia is an American Christian Fiction Writers member, a 2015 Genesis semi-finalist, and a 2015 First Impressions finalist. She became a Christian as an adult and writes about searching for God with compassion, humor, and understanding.

She has danced ballet since her childhood and has performed with pre-professional companies in South America, Europe, and the United States. Her dance experience brings great flavor and authenticity to her debut novel, *A Season to Dance*. She's been stationed in Germany twice, and that experience, too, brings great flavor and authenticity to the story.

In addition to becoming a successful author, Patricia aspires to become an advocate for autism awareness. She and her son have Asperger's syndrome, an autism spectrum disorder.

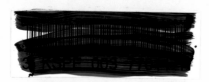

Made in the USA
Lexington, KY
12 April 2018